Introducing the First Book in the Sideways Series...

Sideways

D. R. Swan

This book is a work of fiction.
Any resemblance to persons, places or incidents are either
the product of the author's imagination or are used fictitiously, and any
resemblance to actual persons, living or dead,
locales or events are completely
coincidental.

It's fiction. Have fun!

Sideways
By D.R. Swan

Book cover image by
Evan

(RW096 ver 2)

Dedication

This book is dedicated to any parent who lives with a special needs child
and has had the patience to receive the gift.
The gift is the knowledge that you can never give these kids more than they
give you. May God bless you all.

Acknowledgments

My name is D. R. Swan and I wrote this novel with aspects of stories that I love to read myself. I am a fan of science fiction, historical fiction, and romance, and my main characters, throughout the book, mention some of the stories and authors that I have enjoyed. I am also the parent of a wonderful, special needs child and have included much of our daily lives as part of the story. I want to thank Donna, Fred, Mark, and my mom, who suffered through the rough drafts that I handed them, to get an idea of how they liked the story, and whose input and opinions were invaluable. I want to thank Blair and Donna W. who made me look at my writing more critically. They helped bring my attention to some of the things that I overlooked but shouldn't have. Anything else that I missed was my fault, not theirs. Finally, I want to give special thanks to my other wonderful son, Evan for his help, support, and encouragement, and without him, I might not have finished. This novel was a great deal of fun to write. I hope you enjoy it. Thank you.

Prologue

In the spacious bathroom, the air crackled and the smell of ozone filled the room. What was happening? She stepped, dripping from the shower, then further to get a better look at what appeared to be multi-colored lights dancing along a vertical line, suspended in the air. They lit the space not five feet in front of her. The air split then and she froze as sound rushed into her ears, but it wasn't the sound of wind. It sounded like the voices of a million souls crying out at once. A shadow emerged from the rent in the air, approaching her. Suddenly, she was chilled, frozen where she stood and it seemed that she could feel each cell in her body detach, one from another.

Confusion...

Hopelessness...

Darkness...

Oblivion...

1

"Mary, could you turn the TV down?" Stephen shouted crankily.

"Sor-ry," Mary replied, shaking her head. She knew how irritable Stephen got when there were no ideas coming. As she reached for the remote, the power in the house went out, and everything became dark and silent. For the past few weeks, the earth had been bombarded by solar storms, and the power kept going off as the electric utility had some trouble with the effects.

"You don't have to worry about the sound now," Mary commented sarcastically, gazing at Stephen in the other room, his face lit by his computer screen, now on battery power.

"What the hell?" Stephen said aloud, as he rustled for the small flashlight that he usually kept in his desk. "Have you seen the flashlight?"

"No," Mary replied.

She stood and walked to the kitchen to find something to light the room for Stephen. Finding a flashlight, she walked back towards Stephen's study and the power and lights in the house flickered back on.

Stephen Fremont had always been a very successful writer, publishing at least thirty-five popular novels all in the science fiction and horror genre and making buckets of money. Now, though, he had hit the wall. Nothing was coming to him, no story, no words, no ideas, nothing. He just sat at his laptop and stared. His new publisher, Backstreet Publishing, was pushing him to finish and publish a book that he hadn't been able to begin.

He could feel the pressure and stress making his chest tight and his mind go even more blank. He flashed back to when he wrote for the fun of it, always wanting to sell the books of course, but having real fun imagining and writing the stories that he saw in his mind. If I were smart, he thought, I would have only written in that spirit. I should have never sold out for the fat payday with a three-book deal.

Mary walked in. "Hey, Stephen," she said, throwing her arms around him. "Let's go out to dinner and you can relax a little. You've been working too hard on this project."

"No, not tonight," he said shortly, not looking at her.

"Hmmm," Mary said, extracting herself from him and walking from the room. She had been around this block with him before, but this time it seemed worse than normal.

As she left, Stephen felt his irritation ebb and guilt set in, knowing how he had acted. He knew that she had been through this with him, but... I'm really not accomplishing anything, he thought. He guiltily got up and walked after her.

He walked from his study and into the TV room. Mary wasn't there. He walked into the kitchen and could see Mary reaching for her keys, and startled, turned to face him.

"Where are you going?" he asked.

"I'm hungry and don't feel like cooking," she said shortly.

"Oh... Okay," Stephen said with a puzzled look.

"You can take care of your own dinner, tonight. See you later," she said and walked from the kitchen into the garage.

Stephen stood there dazed as the kitchen door closed. He could hear the rumble and rattle of the automatic garage door opener. Mary had always been very supportive. She could, from time to time, get irritated about the time he put in on a novel, but this seemed different from normal.

Maybe it's because I've been different from normal, he thought, disappointed by his attitude. "I'll make it up to her," he thought aloud and walked back to his study.

He sat staring off into space, thinking about his book and watching ideas float, imagining different scenarios. Nothing felt like a book and from his years of experience, he had developed very good instincts. He could feel his eyes grow heavy and decided to see what was in the kitchen to eat.

Walking by the living room, the TV was off, no lights were on and the room was silent. It felt so empty. It wasn't undecorated, no, it was full of furniture and décor. It even had a few nice pieces of art.

It was just missing Mary. He stopped, shook his head and then started to the kitchen.

As he began to make a sandwich, an inkling of an idea flashed through his mind. It wasn't a complete idea, just one word.

"Dimensions?"

He stopped, frozen, holding the knife.

"All these solar storms."

He looked at the two pieces of bread lying open on the plate and waiting for the ham... and the mayo... and the mustard...

"Where did this idea come from, and what was the idea?" he wondered aloud about this odd vision that played in front of his eyes and then disappeared.

"I've got to stop talking to myself."

He shook his head, then cursed the loss of the idea which arrived in a flash, then was gone. He stood frozen, trying to recall the images.

His mind wandered to a science program he recently watched about multiple dimensions. In it, the scientist speculated that we may live in some multilayered reality. He said that it's in the math. In another program, it seemed the Nazis had a device called the *Bell* that just disappeared. The rumor was that they had figured out a way to leave this dimension, and cross over into another. His new idea was different, though.

As he concentrated, he began to conjure images of the people who had previously jumped into his mind. There was a child and...

"I need to finish this sandwich."

After making it, he walked from the kitchen and sat down in a chair in the barely lit living room. He took a bite and slowly chewed, staring forward into the dark silence, and rolling around this idea in his mind and the characters that he saw. He finished the sandwich and sat back in the chair. His eyes grew heavy and he drifted...

He woke startled, hearing the back-door close and seeing a silhouette.

"Stephen?"

"Mary, you're back. I'm sorry."

"I know, Stephen. What's wrong with you?"

He sighed, "I can't seem to start the next book. I've told the publisher it's almost finished. I had started the book and was about halfway through it, then scrapped it. It just wasn't going anywhere. Since, I haven't even put one word down that's worth a damn."

"You will. This has happened before," Mary said, hugging him.

"I know, but this seems worse. Honestly, I didn't feel anything until I was making a sandwich, and then something entered my mind. It's percolating now. I think it's something."

"I'm sorry you're having such trouble. I really didn't know. You should have told me."

"I know. Let's go to bed," Stephen said.

They both changed and slipped into bed. Stephen laid flat staring at the ceiling. Mary slid over and put her hand on his stomach.

"Do you feel better?" she asked, laying her head on his shoulder.

"I think so," he said, rolling her onto her back and cupping her breast.

"I can see that," she said, smiling.

The next morning, Stephen woke around nine. He had been dreaming all night, a vivid dream of two people and a child. The dream was so vivid that it filled his mind and began to blend with his daydream from the night before, the one that started to inspire the characters for the problem book. He slid from the bed, went to his computer, and started to type an outline for a story that to this point had eluded him. He became excited as ideas flooded into his mind's vision and he began talking to himself, "This is what I've been waiting for. It may not be my best work, but it feels good."

The story ballooned into his mind and flowed like no other story before. He could see the people, the places, the scenario, the feel of the book and the fear of the main character, a partial movie playing in his mind, almost in front of his eyes. He typed frantically, both recalling his dream, and seeing these new visions. He saw the book moving, scenes flipping forward and backward like time was distorted. The scenes hovered like smoke from a fire, twisting, disappearing and then only to emerge again.

Mary could hear him banging on the keys and she peeked into the study and said, "Damn, Stephen."

"I know. I'm on a roll," he said, smiling but not taking his eyes off the screen.

Mary walked from the room, recognizing the manic state of Stephen's concentration, hoping it would continue, and give him the book, and the peace of mind that he needed.

Stephen stopped, losing the story. "I have part of it, but the rest is gone in some mind mist," he thought aloud. What just happened? I need to write what I have:

Sideways

Part 1

Chapter 1

Jonathan Bartoli drove up a slightly winding road...

Stephen looked at the page and then finished typing the first chapter easily…

Chapter 2

I woke up startled from a reoccurring dream...

"No, that's not quite right," Stephen thought aloud...

Night, I hate the night because I dream...
I woke, startled by a dream that constantly reoccurs...

"That's it," Stephen said and the rest of the chapter wrote itself.

Flowing from his mind were the main characters, Dennis Olsen, his special needs five-year-old son, Bryan, the grandparents, Liz and George, and the girl whose name he hadn't conjured, also the setting for some of the story. All of it pouring out easily.

Stephen began to laugh. The pleasure of enjoying what he had written filled him. He continued through the next chapters, and what he had written felt like a final draft, not the first draft that it was. As he wrote, he was struck by the sheer volume of ideas that passed his mind. It was a far cry from the stumbling that had occurred just a few days before. He needed to type faster.

He finished the first four chapters easily, got stuck for a bit, but then the next two chapters flowed. "It's like fine wine, needing to happen in its own time," he said aloud. This story was starting to take shape.

Mary could hear Stephen talking to himself, and she smiled, hoping that this inspiration would continue.

Stephen stopped typing, picked up the phone and called his publisher, telling her that he was going in a different direction with the story, and asking her for a little more time. He assured her that it would be worth the wait.

She agreed, understanding writers and their quirks. The fact of the matter was, that she had just landed Stephen Fremont from another publisher and wanted this to be a successful partnership. She could afford him some leeway.

Stephen continued hammering on his keyboard and had the first six chapters finished. "This book is almost writing itself," he thought aloud. As he typed at this fevered pitch, the ideas started to slow and the visions became murky. He paused a little confused and decided to read what he had written to this point.

2

Cliff Evans woke confused to hear a sound that reminded him of his cell phone alarm. Disoriented, he opened one eye looking for the time on the alarm clock by his bed. "Damn," he said seeing the clock blinking 12:00. "Must have lost power again." He had gotten in the habit of setting two alarms lately because the power had become so unreliable.

He sat up, rubbed his face, slid from bed and rummaged around for the cell phone that he had set away, so he wouldn't turn it off and go back to sleep. It was 11:05 PM, and time to get up.

Cliff lived alone in a small apartment, and since his bitter divorce, all he seemed to do is work and sleep. He turned on the TV and went to shower and dress for another fun-filled night of slinging frozen food at the local Safeway.

"It's lucky I have an audiobook by Stephen Fremont to get me by," he thought aloud.

He was twenty-nine and already greying. He peeked in the mirror, and catching his prematurely aging image, watched his shoulders involuntarily droop. Reaching for his belt, he needed to expand it another notch. "I'm falling apart," he said in despair to no one. "I need to stay away from this mirror."

After a quick bite to eat, he drove the short distance from his apartment towards work. On the way, a daydream flashed in front of his eyes and as he drove, his path dissolved before him. It was so distracting that he had to pull over, his tires sliding in the dirt.

He saw an odd sight in his mind. A girl was in danger. She was beautiful and stepping out of the shower when she saw something, something that she didn't understand. The air around her seemed to part, and she froze as the sight filled her with fear, but there was something more, a shadow approached her. Was it from the odd hole in the air? She stood transfixed with her mouth slightly parted and her eyes glazed, dripping and paralyzed.

The vision abruptly ended. Cliff rubbed his face and started back out towards work. A little shaken by the images that appeared, he wondered what it was that he had seen. It almost seemed real, like a vision or premonition, but he had never had anything like that happen to him before. Writing it off to an overactive imagination, and some lack of sleep, both things not uncommon for him, he thought it peculiar. It wasn't one of his normal daydreams, but what was it?

Cliff had always wanted to be a writer. From time to time, he would drift into his imagination and roll ideas for a novel around in his head. His real dream was to write. In the last year, he had begun and then given up writing at least three novels. With his imagination in overdrive, now, from this strange vision, he felt like he could maybe use it as an inspiration for a story. It seemed to be a more intense form of imagination than he had ever experienced before with the images seeming nearly real and he saw the story complete in a flash. Lost in thought, he pulled into the store parking lot, got out and walked to the door.

As he entered the store, the spell of the vision faded and he could see Rich, the night crew foreman, smiling and heading his way.

"Hey, Cliff, I've got some good news and some bad news."

"What? I haven't even punched in yet," Cliff said.

Rich smiled that, you're not going to like this smile.

"What!?"

"Go clock in, then come and see me," Rich said, walking to the doors and locking them.

Cliff walked to the time clock and scanned his time card. He looked over at the store coffee pot, half full of very old coffee. Grocery clerks can drink the worst coffee and like it. It's an acquired taste. He filled his commuter mug and walked back looking for Rich.

"All right. Let's hear it," Cliff said.

"Cliff, you get the pleasure of helping us spot our load before you start yours. We were all in the check stand after the lights went out, and until the store closed, so we're way behind. The boss told me he will get you some help in the morning and you won't have to check."

"Crap, Rich, I don't ever get out of the check stand in the morning. You know that. I don't care what he said. Can't you guys deal with your own stuff? I got a monster load tonight... So, what's the good news?"

Rich patiently let Cliff finish his rant and then said, "Oh, the good news is that you helping us spot our load is good news for us."

"Gee thanks," Cliff said, shaking his head.

"Just help us spot our load, and then you can get on yours. By the way, half of your load is in the meat box."

Cliff asked, "So, how many pallets do I have tonight?"

"Nine I think. Five in the frozen box and four in the meat box."

"How many pallets do you guys have?" Cliff asked, his irritation growing.

"Ten or eleven," Rich said.

"You got four guys and I'm alone and I need to help you?"

"That's life in the big city," Rich said, walking away.

Cliff shook his head and walked into the back room to get a tow motor (a hand driven forklift), to drive out the night crew's pallets. Spotting the load means placing each item on the floor in front of the shelf space where the product belongs. For a big store, it can take close to two hours of all-out hard work before even one case can be put on the shelf.

Cliff put on his headphones and started working on the night crew's pallets, listening to the audiobook that he got from the library. It was well written, and he disappeared into the story while he went through the mundane task of spotting the product.

"Hey, Cliff, what you listening to?" Greg, a young worker in his early twenties asked.

"What?" Cliff asked back, lowering his headphones.

"What- are- you- listening- to?" Greg asked again, this time repeating the words slowly as if Cliff had a hearing problem.

"Oh, I got this audiobook by Stephen Fremont. It's an older one, but I haven't read it yet, and it's really good."

"Oh, I thought you had some music going."

"No, I started listening to audiobooks when I thought this job was going to make me jump out a window."

"You mean like tonight?"

"Yeah. Hey, if you guys finish early, maybe you could help me?" Cliff said back sarcastically.

Greg laughed, "Only in your dreams."

Cliff shook his head and went back to work.

A little over an hour later, they had finished spotting the grocery pallets, and Cliff was freed to start his own work. It was going to be impossible to work his load correctly, so he needed to improvise. He knew that a nine-pallet load of frozen food was huge and some of the items belong to other departments, so first, he walked his department looking for holes and low spots. Yesterday was scorching, and the ice cream section was wiped out.

I need to hit the lowest spots first, and then I need to get that stuff out of the meat box, he thought planning the night. Cliff walked into the back room, opened the meat box door, to find one of his pallets strewn all over the floor.

"SHIT!" Cliff yelled, unable to contain himself.

Rich walked by, looked at Cliff and grinned. "Oh, I forgot to tell you, one of your pallets fell over."

"Thanks, butt head," Cliff said, walking by Rich and looking for a dolly.

Rich couldn't contain his laughter.

"I need to find another job," Cliff said.

"You're on the lotto retirement plan, just like the rest of us," Rich said, continuing to chuckle.

"Yeah man," Cliff said, now laughing also.

Greg walked by overhearing. "Hey, Cliff, you're always listening to books, why don't you write one?"

"It's funny you mention that. I've had this idea floating around in my head, and I almost feel compelled to start it."

"Oh, you write a book?" Rich said sarcastically. "I was thinking about doing some brain surgery. I think I should give it a shot."

"Well, do us all a favor and start on yourself," Cliff said, and he and Greg laughed.

Rich shook his head, laughed a bit sheepishly, and then walked off.

Cliff started picking up the cases that fell on the floor and noticed that they mostly belonged to the meat department. He separated those to one side and dollied his items out to fill the shelves. Without too much time wasted, he quickly got to the trashed ice cream section.

Lunchtime rolled around and everyone sat outside and ate, leaning against the building, and enjoying the cool damp air. It was 3:00 AM and the morning bakery, produce, and deli crews were arriving to get their departments ready for the day.

"So, Cliff, what's your book going to be about?" Greg asked half-jokingly.

"It's going to be about how everyone who works nights at this store are really condemned to hell by God, but they just don't know it," Cliff said, too tired to explain the book's real plot. He could feel his eyes droop. Resting his head against the building, he began to drift off.

"Have you ever written a book before?" Rich asked interrupting Cliff's nap.

Cliff opened his eyes. "I've started three but haven't finished any of them. It's harder than it sounds and it sounds pretty hard."

"Come on. Give us a preview," Greg said.

"Okay. I had a kind of vision that... It's like this... There are these people... I'm too tired and can't think straight, let me rest for a minute," Cliff said, closing his eyes, exhausted.

"Great book, Cliff," Rich said and laughed.

Cliff didn't hear him though, instantly falling asleep, which is not uncommon for people working nights. He jerked, only nodding for five minutes. "Damn. I'm beat," Cliff said, waking, not feeling rested and barely able to open his eyes.

"Let's get back to work gentlemen, and you too, Greg," Rich said.

They all scraped themselves up and headed to the time clock. Cliff reheated the five-hour old coffee and drank it with a grimace.

Two more hours passed and it was time for the last break. "Let's take ten, children," Rich said over the loudspeaker, calling his crew for a ten-minute break.

Greg and Cliff walked together to meet the rest of the night crew at the front of the store.

"I was really interested in what you were thinking about writing," Greg said as they walked.

"I know this is going to sound kind of weird, but I saw this book idea in my head. It flashed in front of my eyes while I was driving to work. I don't even understand where the idea came from. It was weird. I've been rolling it around in my mind all night, and I think I'm going to go home and put an outline on my computer. I'll tell you more about it the next time we work together."

Cliff's shift ended, so he punched out and started the short drive towards his small apartment. About halfway there, he nodded off at the wheel. The speed bumps woke him, and he stared at a pole coming up fast. Instant terror shot through him as he veered back right, and adrenaline rushed through his body. He felt nauseous and drove the rest of the way home a little shaken.

Happily, he pulled into his parking place, amazed by how long it seemed to take to get the few blocks home. He walked in the door to his apartment and noticed the detritus. I'll get to it later, he thought, and he turned on the TV and then switched on his computer to check email. He grabbed an apple and sat on the couch staring at the screen. The adrenaline still rushed through him, and he knew it was going to be impossible to sleep. His mind flashed back to the strange vision, and the possible book idea that filled his thoughts all night. He glanced at the clock, it was 9:00 am, and by this time, he was usually sleeping.

He got up from the couch, threw the apple core into the garbage and then walked over to his computer and pulled up emails. There were too many papers lying on his desk and it bothered him, old bills and mail he needed to open. He sat there and began replaying the vision, letting his mind drift, and seeing the images in his head, the characters, the setting, and the odd circumstances that surrounded the people involved in the vivid daydream. He pulled up his word processor, created a folder, and started an outline of the story.

The outline was very rough. He knew he had never finished writing a book before and he felt in over his head. "I can't write a book. I can barely keep myself alive. How am I going to write a book?" he said aloud and in despair to no one.

Cliff stopped the outline, not finished, and sighed, "What am I thinking?"

He pushed himself back from the computer and walked into the bathroom, then looked in the mirror. He didn't like what he saw. Dark circles colored the space under his hazel eyes, and his face, pasty white, looked like the vampire that he had become. I have the life of a vampire without the girls falling all over me, he thought, not to mention that cheeseburgers were definitely favored over blood.

His mind drifted back to the book. I saw a man with a child and some tragedy happened. He's lost his wife and needs to raise the child alone. There's a girl. She's very attractive and in great shape... They meet... Something strange happens... That shower thing.

"What am I doing? I can't do this," he said aloud, overwhelmed by the images jumping around in his head. Now, I don't even really remember... There's a house, and it's not his, or is it? And creatures from somewhere, the word "Sideways" strong in his mind. Cliff started just typing words, ideas, and impressions hoping that the strange inspiration for the book would return.

He finally started to get tired, and he could hear the TV droning on in the background. The anchorman was discussing last night's large sun storms, which had some effect on the earth's electronics, and probably the reason for the local power outages.

He moved back to the couch and thought, I'm on vacation next week and maybe I'll be able to think at least one coherent thought with some real rest. His eyes grew heavy, and he slid off to sleep.

When he awoke, the story nagged at him, and he felt compelled to try this writing thing again. He walked back to his computer and sat clearing his mind. The images flowed back and he could see the characters. The house appeared as if by magic and an older man...

Sideways

Part 1

Chapter 1...

After a few sentences, Cliff stopped, stuck by his lack of detail. He could no longer see the story, and frustrated, he plopped onto the floor, put his legs up on his computer chair, and stared at the ceiling. Before he knew it, he was drifting off. Somewhere between wake and sleep, he began to see the visions return. He rose and sat back down in his chair holding onto the mental pictures.

That's it, Cliff thought and started to type as fast as his one finger would let him. Four hours flew by and he had written six rough chapters on the computer. He pushed back from the desk and couldn't believe what he had accomplished. "How did I do this?" he thought aloud and started to reread his work. Except for some misspellings and poor sentences, his work was far better than he had ever imagined possible. He made a few corrections and then tried to type more of the story, but nothing was there. He pushed back away from the computer and quit, hoping to have this odd inspiration return.

Sitting on the couch, he stared over at his computer screen. It seemed to beckon him, so, he got up to reread what he had written to this point...

3

Sideways

Part 1

Sideways Chapter 1

Jonathan Bartoli drove up the slightly winding road to his secluded home in the hills, outside Sacramento, California. In between songs on the radio, a reporter announced highlights for the news coming up on the hour. "Major solar storm expected to hit earth. Communications and the power grid may be affected. More on the hour," he finished.

"Not this again," Jonathan said with dread.

Several weeks ago, the earth was hit by a similar sun storm. It didn't affect the grid, but it did something, something Jonathan couldn't explain, and right in his own house. He pulled a small compass from his pocket as he drove into his driveway. Looking at it, the dial gyrated back and forth between north and east. The last time this had happened, the dial was going crazy, arching from north to south, sometimes making a full rotation.

He reached into the back seat for the two bags of groceries laying there. Stepping out of his car, he looked warily at the windows trying to see anything unusual. He shrugged and started for the door.

Lately, he hadn't been feeling well and thought he should make an appointment to go see the doctor. A little breathless, he fit the key into the lock, opened the door and stared at his dining room wall, scorched as if someone had held a torch to it, and the lamp, which hung from the ceiling over the table, gone.

The room smelled like burnt wiring, but there wasn't any smoke. He looked back at the compass and saw that the needle was arching much further than before. A sound like static electricity made him look up and seemed to emanate from the scorched wall. As the crackling grew, the wall seemed to ripple like heat waves rising over a blazing highway. Colors began to swirl in his eyes, and blackness began to fill his vision from the edges with pain traveling down his arm. Clutching his chest, he sank to his knees.

4

Sideways Chapter 2

Night... I hate the night because I dream...

I woke, startled by a dream that constantly reoccurs. In it, I had forgotten to pick up my wife at the mall. Remembering, I rushed to get her, but the more I tried, the more things happened to stop me. By the time I got there, she was gone.

I lost my wife three years ago in a car accident, after a particularly rough argument in which I lost my temper and she flew out of the house in a rage. The dream is obviously about the guilt that won't let me be.

I must have been loud. My little boy Bryan was standing in my doorway holding his Pooh Bear.

He walked in and asked, "Papa, okay?"

"Yes, baby. I just had a bad dream."

My son is a five-year-old, special needs child, suffering from a genetic deletion syndrome. He is short for his age with light brown hair. His words are very hard to understand, not being able to pronounce all the consonants, so he uses sign and speech to communicate.

"You wa Pooh?" he asked, holding out the bear.

"No thanks, honey boy, but I will tuck you and Pooh back in bed. Do you need to use the bathroom?"

"No, Papa."

"We need to get a good night sleep. You have swim lessons tomorrow."

Bryan's eyes lit up at that. Swimming lessons are big fun.

I took him back to bed and tucked him in. "Sweet dream magic," I told him, putting my hand on his head and giving him a kiss.

I crawled back into bed. It was 2:20 and sleep escaped me. As I lay there, I thought about the dreams that reoccurred constantly. The one that always comes to mind is also the most disturbing. In it, I'm searching for my late wife. I get some lead as to where she is, and I desperately go looking for her. I never find her of course, but the strange thing about these dreams is that after my search, when I go back home, I don't arrive in the conventional fashion. I drift back into my room, through solid walls, as a disembodied spirit. Each time, I'm shocked to see myself sleeping, separated from my body, and I always wake, gasping for breath, startled as if my soul is rejoining it. I feel that my soul wanders the night, looking for my lost wife. I hate my dreams; they're always so twisted.

I woke this time to the sound of my alarm. 6:30 am... Beep, beep, beep...

"Damn, it can't be morning already."

I briefly remembered the night, and then scraped myself out of bed, and into the shower, letting the hot water run over me to help me wake. I turned my body allowing the water to hit me on each side, my mind defogging, and I involuntarily drifted mentally into the future when I would be old. I try not to get too far out there; it seems so bleak. What's going to happen with Bryan? Who's going to love and take care of him? At least when my wife was alive if one of us died, we had the other to take care of him. Now that she's gone, though, it's like losing one kidney with no long-term backup. So, I drifted farther out into the future and worried about how he would live, and would people be mean to him because they couldn't understand him, conjuring images in my mind of abuse. For now, I guess I would need to take it one day at a time, but I shook my head in despair.

I turned off the water and stood there naked and dripping, with my head against the tile, locked in the thought. I shook myself free as I began to get cold, and toweled off, now looking more to the immediate future when I would have a cup of coffee in my hand. That was something I could handle at least. Time to get Bryan ready for his day.

Bryan has school. It's Friday and I'm off work, not that I've been working much lately. After dressing, I walked into his tiny room, decorated with Pooh Bear sheets and comforter, and not much else.

"Okay, itty bit, it's your turn."

Bryan signed, "Five more minutes."

I chuckled, "All right but Pooh Bear is hungry. I will get him his honey pot for breakfast."

I headed to the kitchen to make coffee, breakfast and pack Bryan's lunch for school, and then back to my son's room.

"It's your time now, buddy boy," I said.

"Five more minutes," Bry signed again.

"How about one more minute?" I offered.

"Ah um," Bry responded, meaning yes.

This is a morning ritual.

Finally, he was up and eating. Once done, I finished dressing him and then wrapped up his teeth brushing, and hair combing.

"Let's go, Bryan, school time," I said, picking him and his backpack up and walking out the door.

We live about ten minutes from Bryan's school and we pulled up right on time. His school is like most schools these days, paint looking a bit shabby, lawns in need of trimming, but the teachers that I've encountered in special education have been great.

"Let's go see Miss Kathy, buddy boy."

I got him from his car seat, picked him up and lowered him to the ground. I took his hand and we slowly walked to his class with Bryan taking four steps to each one of mine.

"Hi, Miss Kathy," I said, walking into the classroom.

"Good morning, guys," she replied.

Miss Kathy is a wonderful person, very helpful to me, but most of all very kind.

Bryan walked off not looking back. He loves school.

"Hey, dude, how about a kiss goodbye?"

Bryan turned and headed back to me, and I got down on one knee. He threw his arms around my neck.

"Have a great day, sweetie boy, and be safe in everything you do." As he started off, I signed I love you to him and he signed it back.

"Miss Kathy, don't put Bryan on the bus today. I will pick him up. He has swimming lessons."

"Oh. Okay, see you then," she replied.

I take Bryan to school in the morning, but he usually rides the bus home in the afternoon. I'm always a little apprehensive when I leave him and as I walked to the car, I hoped he would be okay.

My health club is about eight miles from the school. Today, I'm in the mood for a good sweat. I decided to first drive to my favorite, local coffee shop, which is on the way. The owner, Lenny, I don't think that's his real name, is an immigrant from Vietnam and one of the nicest people you could ever want to meet.

As I walked in, I could see the regulars sitting at their usual tables. A local artist was there with some of his paintings on the walls, and the smell of coffee and pastry filled the air.

"Good morning, Mr. Den," Lenny called as he looked up to find me third in line.

"Hi, Lenny," I said, knowing that when I got to the counter, my usual would be waiting. As expected, when I reached there, Lenny handed me my non-fat mocha, no whip. "Thanks, Lenny," I said dropping a tip into the jar.

I walked out sipping and headed to my health club. After the short drive, I pulled into the parking lot and saw my friend Jason's car. Jason and I solve the world's problems each time we work out together. It's always easier to solve other people's problems than it is to solve your own.

I stepped from the car and noticed that, though it was only 9:00, the day was starting to get hot. I opened the front door to the club and walked towards the check-in desk on the left. On the right, there was a sitting area, access to the pool, and most importantly, the coffee pot. The familiar odor of coffee and chlorine permeated the air, and people sat reading the newspaper and magazines. I glanced forward and could see my friend, Jason, pushing some weight. As I approached the front desk, a new person, who didn't know me, turned and smiled.

"Dennis Olsen," I said.

"Got ya. What are you doing today?" she asked.

"Weights, then some racquetball."

"Thanks," she said.

I walked through the two glass doors into the weight room. "Let's get big," I said to Jason who turned to see me.

"I'm already getting big," he said, rubbing his stomach.

Jason, I call him Jay, is a six-foot-two-inch, strongly built, African American with kind eyes. He thinks I look like Tom Hanks. Although Jason's in good shape, he could, *maybe*, lose a bit in the middle.

"You may need to use those new "plate push away" exercises," I chided.

"Yeah man. Hey, did you hear Adrianne quit today to go away to school? There's a new girl at the desk," Jason said.

"No, I didn't hear. That's too bad, I liked her. She was nice... Oh, swimming lessons! She was Bryan's teacher. I wonder if lessons are canceled today. I'd better check before I go."

The chatter was muted in the weight room for the rest of our workout. Jason was on the Tom Hanks thing this morning and wanted to know when I was going to make another movie. He said Sleepless in Seattle made him cry. He thinks he's funny, haha.

We went about, doing our work, and on my last set, I was spent. I saw the club's personal trainer, Willie, walk by.

"Hey, Willie, why do they make these weights so heavy?"

He smiled and said, "I don't know. I'll check with the manufacturer."

Willie walked out and I turned to Jason. "Well, Jay, that's it for me. I'm going to pound some walls. Catch you later."

"Take care, Dennis. See you tomorrow."

I grabbed my sweatshirt, walked from the weight room, and approached the desk, getting the attention of the new girl, who turned and walked to me.

She smiled and I said, "Hi, I hear Adrianne quit. My son has swimming lessons today. Are they going to be canceled?"

The new girl listened, looked down at a schedule and said, "Yeah, she quit, and no, the new teacher's name is Shannon."

"Thanks, my son Bryan has the 3:00 lesson today. I'm glad they're not canceled."

She smiled and I turned from the desk and walked down the dim hallway to the racquetball courts. I didn't hear any balls hitting the walls, so I didn't think I was going to get a game. As I turned the corner, I saw one of the guys I sometimes play with sitting outside the courts, waiting.

"If it isn't Bob O'Shea, by the grace of God," I said in a terrible Irish accent.

Bob is a freak of nature. He's eighty-nine years old with all his hair and it's not all gray. He's a little overweight but can still play a pretty good game of racquetball.

"Where's Sammy?" I asked but before Bob could answer I said, "Getting his beauty sleep?" Bob smiled and then I said, "He'll have to sleep 'till November."

"Hey, I heard that," Sam said as he entered from around the corner.

We all laughed a bit.

"Let's play," I said.

The three of us entered the court to play some cutthroat, a three-man game where the two players play against the server. Each person takes turns serving, and the first player to get to fifteen, wins. Bob could only play two games before he tired, and then Sammy and I played a couple of games of singles. Bob watched and recovered as Sam and I finished, walking from the court.

"That's it for me," I said. "I have to get groceries, and then I need to pick up Bryan. Catch you later."

I live in a small mother-in-law, slash, pool house, behind my in-laws on their property. Bryan and I moved in there shortly after the death of my wife, their only daughter. They also help with Bry, and keep an eye on me, too, in a loving way of course.

My in-law's house is a very nice Tudor style, with the small house I'm in, a pool and at least two acres of land. I can drive behind the property to park, and I usually do, so I don't bother them.

Both of my in-laws are retired. George was in finance and his wife Liz, a nurse. In their late sixties, both are in great shape, lean, fit and much sharper than I am.

I pulled into the small parking place behind the fence and could see George with his shirt off cleaning the pool.

"Man, I hope I look like you when I'm your age," I called. "You could do magazine covers!"

George waved me off, always self-deprecating.

His wife, Liz, came out of the house with something in her hand and waved me over.

"Hi, Liz," I said, giving her a small hug.

"This came for you today in the mail."

"Hmmm. It's from a law firm," I said apprehensively. "Well, let's see what's in here."

I opened the letter and unfolded the page inside. "It says that there is going to be a reading of my uncle's will and that I'm mentioned in it. I can't believe he would leave me anything. He hated me. Maybe he will leave me some old shoes saying, 'Try to fill these, PEASANT'."

We all laughed a bit sheepishly.

My uncle Jonathan, died of a heart attack a while back with no wife or kids. I did go to the funeral.

"Hmmm?" I said again, this time totally puzzled.

Jonathan Bartoli was my mom's brother and moved close to us when I was a teenager. I must admit, though, that I was a shitty teenager. All I cared about was sports and cheerleaders, then work maybe, (I had a job at the time at a local grocery store where I stayed for five years, first bagging, then checking, and then other jobs in the store). Everything else, school, family, etc. came a distant last in my self-absorbed teen life. I barely noticed my uncle at all.

After thanking my in-laws, I headed back to the car to get the groceries which were starting to get warm. Opening the side door to my house, I walked into the kitchen, strewn with unwashed dishes. There were pajamas on the floor of the living room where I changed Bryan and a general disorder in the area. We left in a hurry this morning.

I put the groceries away, did some straightening and wandered over to the television, turning it on. I threw a load of wash in the machine, and then parked myself on the couch to watch the business news, and doze for a bit...

I woke startled, opening my eyes wide, knowing in a confused way that I had forgotten something. I looked at the clock. 1:30. Damn, I need to get to Bryan's school by 2:00. I rushed around trying to clear my head, packing our swimming suits and towels, and then I was out the door and on my way.

I pulled up to the school just as the bell rang, pushed open the car door and saw Miss Kathy, the aides, Bryan, and his class walking from the classroom. Bryan had a very happy look on his face. I smiled thinking that God must sometimes send his angels to earth as these special children to show us how to live. I think it's debatable which of us is the real "special needs people." Although the world will never know it, the innocence and purity of these special people are so beautiful that the rest of humanity should barely be able to even look upon them, but they are often viewed with laughter or disgust. The fact of the matter is, that we, who consider ourselves "normal," probably don't deserve to share the same planet as these precious souls.

"Hi, Miss Kathy. Did you have a good day?" I asked.

Bryan ran up and hugged my leg.

I went down on one knee hugging him back. "Hi there, sweetie boy."

"Bryan had a great day," Miss Kathy remarked. "You know, Bryan is really great with anything with buttons. Today, he kind of fixed our computer!"

"You're a star," I said to Bryan, picking him up.

He beamed back at me as if to say, I know.

"Thanks, Miss Kathy. I'll see ya."

"Oh, Dennis, don't forget our I.E.P. Meeting next Thursday."

"Okay, I'll be there," I said turning to the car.

I.E.P. meetings are the norm for anyone with a special needs child. It stands for Individual Education Plan but should stand for Incredible Endless Pain, because the majority of the time is spent talking about what's wrong with your child. It's very painful. The meetings are important, though, because they help map out the child's year in school. It's attended by all the professionals that work with your child, the teachers, therapists, and administrators. These meetings can be grueling.

"All right, Bryan, let's go get wet," I said reminding him that it was time to swim.

"Ahhh," he said, not able to pronounce the "y" in yeah.

5

Sideways Chapter 3

As I pulled into the club's parking lot and turned off the car, I could feel the heat. "Great day for a swim, buddy boy," I said to Bryan, looking back over my shoulder at him in the back seat.

Bryan agreed saying, "Ah ha."

I grew up in the Sacramento area and you would think, by now, that I would be used to the heat, but the older I get, the harder it is to take.

"Let's go."

We left the car and I took Bryan's hand. I could feel the sun bear down on my shoulders and could smell the asphalt in the parking lot melting.

We entered the health club through the double doors. It's not a new club, in fact, it's much older than I am. We approached the front desk and the manager was there.

"Hi there, Bryan," he said. Bryan is very popular. "Swimming today?" he inquired and Bryan smiled and nodded.

"I hear you lost Adrianne," I said half questioningly.

"Yeah, she's going away to school. Does Bryan have a lesson today?"

"Yes, with Shannon."

"Oh. You'll like her. She's great."

"Thanks. Let's go, buddy boy," I said, directing him towards the locker room.

"Have fun," the manager said, walking away.

We walked into the locker room to change. It smelled musty like always, and I brought Bryan to a bench in the corner. I put him in his suit and then changed into mine. As I passed by the mirror, I caught my reflection and took a bit of inventory of my own. Hmmm, looking a bit squishy in the mid-section, I thought. I just shook my head and walked away with Bry for the showers.

We quickly showered off and then headed down three steps and into the pool area. This pool is completely indoors which is great because you can swim here all year, rain or shine. It's hard for Bryan to get much exercise because of all of his physical problems, so this is a big help.

We were about twenty minutes early and Shannon wasn't here yet, so we went into the pool for some play. I told Bryan that all the Sesame Street characters had jumped into our pool and we had to get them out! I said silly things making the voices of the different characters, and Bryan giggled as we swam around pretending to put them into a magic bag that he carried on his back.

Bry signed, "We need to call Jim Henson to come and take them back to Sesame Street."

"That's a pretty good Big Bird," I heard from behind me.

"Oh, hi. I didn't see you there," I said a little embarrassed. "Ah, you must be Shannon?"

"Yes. Hi, and this is Bryan?"

Shannon had walked dripping from the locker room and I must admit that I was a little taken aback. She was very pretty with short, light brown hair and dancing green eyes, but in her swimsuit, well... The wet, navy blue, one-piece suit looked painted on. She looked to be in her early twenties, I thought, so she had that going for her, but she looked extremely fit from top to bottom. I could see most everything through this thin, wet suit including a pretty impressive six-pack. I need to be careful here, I think I'm staring.

"Are you ready to get started?" Shannon said looking at Bryan. "Come on, young man, let's see what you got."

Shannon walked down the stairs into the pool, and I walked up the stairs, having some trouble taking my eyes from her. I was going to swim some laps and then sit in the hot tub for a few minutes, but now I think I'll watch the lesson. I grabbed my towel and Shannon took charge of Bryan right away, assessing his abilities. I smiled thinking that Bryan loved her already. I could tell. He was beaming.

The lesson went well with Bryan and Shannon working good together, and the half hour flew by.

"That's it, Bryan. You are all done," Shannon announced.

Bryan and Shannon walked out of the water. I could see her next lesson arrive, an adorable four-year-old girl with brown hair and big brown eyes. She strode towards the pool and I watched her enter the water with grace, strong and sinewy with the promise of an athlete to come. I smiled at her mom, while my mind wandered to Bryan and his problems.

Lost in the thought, I heard Shannon say something that I didn't understand.

"Excuse me. I'm sorry, what was that?" I asked, missing the beginning.

"Bryan really did well today. He has some skills," Shannon repeated.

"Yeah, thanks, I think he's more at home in the water than on dry land."

Then Shannon asked a little shyly, "You were having Monday, Wednesday, and Friday lessons with Adrianne. Do you want to continue with me?"

"Yes, of course, you were great with him."

She smiled, "See you Monday. Bye, Bryan."

She walked back into the water, and we headed to the showers to get some of the chlorine off our bodies. I thought about the healthy young girl now with Shannon for lessons. It's never easy to be a parent, even when the child seems perfect. There are so many worries, and I couldn't love Bryan any more than I do, but I felt a tiny bit of what might be jealousy. A little ashamed, I led us to the showers and then wrapped towels around our wet swimsuits to blot them dry. Still feeling guilty about the jealousy, I gave Bryan a big hug and told him what a great job he did in his lesson. I really could never imagine life without him. We put on our shirts and walked through the lobby to our car.

I opened the car door and it was scorching hot inside. I carefully put Bryan in his car seat, making sure that he didn't touch anything metal, rolled the windows down, and started off to our house.

The club isn't far from home, maybe fifteen minutes, so I put a Silly Song CD in the player for Bryan. I don't mind these CDs but Bryan likes to hear the same ones over and over. Today, I wasn't in the mood for "Old McDonald's Farm," so I listened to an audiobook that I got from the library with earphones. Bryan bounced to the tunes, and I slipped into the fun world that my author had created.

People piss me off the way they drive. They are rude and downright dangerous. When I have a book in my ear, it doesn't even matter to me. I drive and enjoy the story. If I commuted, I would be living on these audiobooks.

"We're home," I announced to Bryan. "Let's go see what we can rustle up for dinner."

I climbed from the car, walked around to Bryan's door, pulled him out and then got our bag from the trunk. We went into the house, and thankfully the air conditioning had the place just below eighty degrees. Downright chilly after being out in the sweltering Sacramento heat.

I set Bryan down in front of the TV, switching it on. "Let's find something you like," I said, turning the channels. Bryan wasn't happy with anything, so I put a DVD into the player.

With Bryan settled, my mind wandered to my life. My wife, being the only adult in the room, usually, planned for the chance that she would die by leaving us a life insurance policy. I have invested the money to produce enough for us to live, but the market is so up and down, some days, I lose as much in the value of the stocks as I make in three months of dividends. Luckily, I have no debt and live rent-free. For now, we're okay... For now.

My mind wandered back to my crazy Uncle Jonathan and the will. What's he up to? Well, I won't find out until next Tuesday when it's read. I think I'll give my mom a call, see how she is, and see what in the world is up with this will.

Bryan and I were still damp, so I changed him out of his suit, and put him in some shorts. I went to the washing machine, took off my suit, threw our towels and the suits in, and started the wash. I walked back into my room, put something on, and then walked back into the front room where Bryan was smiling, watching Cookie Monster eat the Moon. I picked up the phone.

"Hey, Mama," I said, getting her answering machine because she never picks up the phone. "Are you there?"

"Hi, honey," she said answering.

"Hey, Mom, you will never believe this, Uncle Jonny put me in his will. Have you heard from your sisters to see who else is in it?"

"Yes, each cousin, my two sisters and I have also been mentioned," she replied.

"I know he was closer to my cousins than me, so, I can't, for the life of me, figure out why I'm in this will. In fact, I'm not sure it would be an exaggeration to say that if I were on fire, he wouldn't cross the street to pee on me."

"Dennis!" Mom exclaimed.

She hates it when I talk like that.

"I'm sure in his last days he tried to consider all the people who were in his family, and I was close to him, you know."

"Yeah, but I can't help but think that there may be some arsenic in the cupcake," I responded. "So... do you think I should go?" I asked.

"Of course, I'm sure there will be some kind words for everyone," my Mom added. She always sees the best in everyone.

"Okay, Mom. So, how are you doing?"

We finished our call with the usual, how are all my relatives, their kids, sports events, and the other wonderful things about being a family. I always feel better after talking to her.

Okay, well, I guess I'll go to the will reading for my kind words. It will be nice to see some of the people there that I haven't seen for a while, but I can't help but feel a little like Custer. "Sure, come on into the Little Big Horn party; don't mind the Indians, they're just here for the dancing... Hmmm."

I started dinner for Bryan and me, spaghetti and salad. We ate, then he played on a laptop computer that I keep loaded with some programs for him. The night passed and I tucked him in bed. I read a Doctor Seuss book, *Fox in*

Sox. "I can't say such blibber blubber, my tongue is not made of rubber," I read, enjoying the clever book myself.

With the story finished, we said our prayers. I gave him sweet dream magic and pretended his two stuffed puppies were wrestling in bed, and I told Bry to pat them to make them sleepy. He laughed and then smiled at the two stuffed animals, patting them as I left the room. My day was full but not hard. I found myself tired, though, and my mind drifted back to... Shannon?

6

Sideways Chapter 4

Saturday: I woke late and turned to see Bryan lying next to me with one of his stuffed puppies. I sort of remembered him coming in last night. I slid from bed and headed to the coffee pot. We had no major plans for the day, shopping, gas and to the park for some big-time swinging. Our weekends are very laid back, and I must admit that I like day-in and day-out life, when there are few demands.

At 9:30, I peeked back in on Bryan who was starting to stir, got him up and fed.

We took care of the rest of our morning chores and duties. "Come on Bry, let's handsome you up," I said, bringing him into the bathroom to brush his teeth and comb his hair.

We finished and I grabbed my keys, money, and phone and we walked out the door. We passed by George, who was busy gardening.

"Morning, George," I called.

"Good morning, guys. Hey, Dennis, we're having a barbeque tomorrow evening. Want to come?"

"That sounds great. What should I bring?"

"Some wine might be good."

"I'm headed to the store right now. I'll pick some up. See you later."

We went to the park, had lunch, and then to the local Safeway where I got gas and groceries. Our running around finished, we headed back home.

Pulling up to our place, I could see George and Liz by the pool in their swimsuits.

Liz watched us walk up and asked, "Want to come for a swim, Bryan?"

He glanced at me for affirmation.

"I don't know," I said teasingly.

He looked at me as if to say, "I know you're kidding me," and I smiled.

"Let me get him in his swimsuit and sun screened up. Come on, Bry, let's get you ready."

I carried him into the house. Bryan likes a certain swimsuit, so I put it and some sunscreen on him. Then, I put on my suit, grabbed a book and brought Bryan out to the pool.

Liz was sitting in a lounge and George was in the water. He walked out to meet us giving Bryan a silly look.

Bryan giggled knowing that Ampa was going to play.

"Hi, guys. Great day for a swim," I said, but the reality of the Sacramento area is that most days are a great day for a swim. As I said before, it's hot here.

Liz smiled and George picked up Bryan and jumped into the shallow end, making him shriek with laughter. George made sure he barely got wet.

Suddenly, I missed my wife. Liz looked at me with a smile, watching the pool play, then I saw it melt as she instinctively knew what just entered my mind. Our eyes touched briefly, and I had to look away. George was oblivious and continued to splash with Bryan, setting him on different floating toys.

We both turned our attention back to the pool and George said, "Hey, Bryan, show me what you're learning in swimming lessons."

Bryan slid off a floating alligator and swam underwater all the way to the side. He popped up with a look of sheer pride on his face.

Liz looked back at me.

"She should be here, you know," I said, glancing back at Liz, and thinking about all the times when Lauren and I brought Bryan to their pool.

With a sympathetic look, she said, "You know it doesn't work that way, Dennis, but for what it's worth to you, I'm glad you're here."

I looked back at her and half smiled.

"Thanks," I said, torn by the memory and helped by her comment.

I pulled off my tee shirt and jumped into the pool making a huge splash. Bryan rolled with laughter. He loves big splashes. I swam a bit, cooling off, but not interfering with George and Bryan's play. George was having a great time. He loves Bryan as much as I do.

George said, "Liz you better get in the pool, I think you're melting."

She said she didn't want to but relented.

The pool was cool and refreshing. As she walked in, I walked out to read a bit more. My mind flashed back to when Lauren, my late wife, and I would visit George and Liz. Bryan was very young, and Lauren would get in the pool and walk him around getting him wet. I see her, beautiful in her swimsuit with her long brown hair, and Bryan so small in her arms. It seemed like yesterday, though it had been more than three years. I grabbed a lounge chair, drug it into the shade, and sat and read, but my mind continued to flash back to Lauren.

We stayed there for another half hour, then said goodbye and walked to the house. It was early for dinner, so I got out Bryan's computer. I'm always amazed at how well he manipulates it. Bryan enjoyed clicking on his favorite parts, then it seemed to lock up.

"Augh," Bry said in frustration.

"You know what to do," I said.

He shut it down, then restarted it.

"You're a marvel," I said and he smiled at his cleverness.

Bryan and I ate dinner, watched some of his favorite tapes and CDs and I finished my book. Bedtime arrived and I tucked him in with a bedtime story.

I got myself ready for bed and slipped in. My mind wandered to the will. I really don't want anything from this guy. In fact, I'm sure I will feel guilty if he gives me anything. It's just weird. I hadn't seen him in years. I drifted off with these thoughts repeating over and over in my brain...

The next morning, I woke, and Bryan had slept through the night. I did my usual zombie imitation of dragging myself from the bed, checking to make sure he was okay, and going straight for the coffee pot.

Every morning since Bryan had been born, I would wake up fearing that he had died in the night. At his birth, the doctors had put that fear in me and I could never shake it. I probably never would. I remember when he was very young, waking startled and walking into his room with dread expecting to find that we had lost him. I still do that to this day.

I shook off the thought, and with the coffee brewing, headed to the shower before he woke. I finished, got my coffee, and sat on the couch, staring into space, lost in thought. I could hear Bryan start to stir, and I went to his room to see if he was awake yet. He was blinking and coming to.

"Hey there, buddy boy. Are you ready to get up?" I asked softly.

"Five more minutes," he said.

"That's what weekends are for," I said and walked out.

I sat back on the couch and wondered who Liz and George had coming to the barbeque. They have a large network of friends.

I turned on the TV and couldn't find anything interesting, and then heard Bryan say, "Papa." I got up and walked into his room.

"Good morning, my sweet," I said.

Bryan smiled and signed that Pooh Bear had a bad dream last night.

"Oh, I'm sorry. Was it about ephelumps and woosels?" I asked.

"Ahh," he said.

"Well, you just tell him that a bad dream is just silly thoughts in his head. It's not real."

Bryan gave Pooh a hug.

"Come on and get up," I said.

After breakfast, we went for a walk by the river and then took a trip to the library. I love the library and so does Bryan. I found an audiobook by James Lee Burke and Bryan found a Kids Songs videotape.

We got some lunch and headed home. I carried the audiobook and the videotape inside and we sat together on the couch, him watching the vid, and me watching, but not paying attention to his tape, and listening to my book.

The time passed and it was getting close to the barbeque. My mind wandered back to the will and what I needed to do tomorrow. I heard George and Liz talking outside.

"George, can you help me with this table?" Liz asked.

"Be right there," George replied.

I got up and opened the door. "Can I help you guys set up?"

"No, I think we're finished," Liz said.

"Okay, see you in a bit," I said and went back inside. "Let's get you ready for the party, Bryan."

Bryan signed, "Birthday?"

"No, baby, a just for fun party," I explained.

"Oh," he said clearly.

7

Cliff headed back to work after a night off. When you work nights, having a night off isn't like having a day off, you mostly sleep and try to help your body survive the next few nights' work. On the drive, he thought about his book, *"Sideways,"* and was happy about how the writing was going.

Walking in the door, he saw Rich, who turned to him. "Cliffy, Cliffy, Cliffy. What's up?"

Cliff smiled warily.

"I've got some good news and bad news for you tonight."

"Aw, come on Rich, not again."

"Just kidding. You get to work your own stuff."

"Gee thanks. Are you sure you don't need me to wipe your ass for ya?"

"Not tonight. That's why they pay me the extra ten cents an hour because I can make those executive decisions," Rich said laughing. "But if the need arises, I'll let you know."

Cliff laughed and walked to the time clock. He had filled his coffee cup at home but glanced at the store pot, anyway. It was empty, and he was glad that he had brought his own. He scanned his time card and got out his headphones and strung the cord under his shirt and behind his back so it wouldn't get in his way while he worked. He was about one-third of the way through Fremont's book, and he was anxious to get it started.

He walked to the backroom and tried to open the frozen food box door. It was frozen solid and he had to strain to open it. He looked at the temperature gauge near the door. "Ten degrees below zero! Damn, I'm not ready for this," he said, shuddering and knowing that he wasn't warmed up enough to face that kind of cold, coat or not. I'm pulling this stuff out fast, he thought.

He listened to the book and with the earphones keeping his ears warm, quickly pulled out two pallets, spotted them and filled the shelves. He listened to a couple of chapters, and then pulled out two more pallets.

Rich called over the loudspeaker, "Okay, boys and girls, break time."

Cliff started walking to the front and ran into Greg.

"Hey, Cliff, did you finish writing your book?"

"Yep, all done. Actually, I wrote around twenty pages and then the ideas stopped. It was kind of weird because they came so easy. It was like the TV went off."

Greg looked at Cliff puzzled and then said, "That does seem strange. Do you know what comes next?"

"Yeah, sort of, but it's foggy. I'm hoping for another streak of inspiration. I feel it will come, but it's not like I'm in some big hurry. No one's going to read it anyway."

"I'll read it," Greg said smirking.

"Yeah, and I won't hear the end of it," Cliff said laughing.

With break time finished, Cliff got back to work. He walked back to his walk-in box. As he opened the door, he pictured a barbeque. It jumped into his head and he stood still with the fans roaring and his hair blowing. He could see his characters, Dennis, Bryan, Liz, and George. Hmmm, the visions were back. He pulled off the headphones and watched the scenes appear in his mind. Now, if I could just get this down before I forget it.

He replaced the headphones and paid more attention to Fremont's writing style, and the structure of the writing. He loved the way Fremont wrote and he got discouraged. I don't have a chance to finish this, it's just too hard, he despaired.

Cliff went back to work with the time flying. He looked at the clock and his shift was nearly finished. Being stuck in the check stand for the last hour, he wasn't able to finish his load. Oh well, there's always tomorrow, he thought.

His check stand replacement walked up and let him out. As he walked to the time clock, the store manager stopped him.

"Did you finish your load?" he asked.

"No. There are two dollies loaded that could go up, but I don't think you will run out of anything today. I'll finish tonight. I didn't face though." Facing meant pulling all the product forward so that the department looked full. He doubted that anyone would face the frozen foods for him. It was just too brutal on the hands.

"Thanks, Cliff," the manager said, walking into his office and closing the door.

Out of sight out of mind, Cliff thought as he walked to the time clock. He punched out, walked from the store, climbed into his car and drove out.

As he pulled up to his apartment's parking place, the story started again in his mind. He froze, watching the visions. They seemed so real. He got out of his car, ran up the stairs and turned on the computer. Delighted, he grabbed an apple, and pulled up the folder, "*Sideways*," and got to work.

For the next four hours, he typed nonstop. He looked at his half-eaten apple, now brown from neglect and pushed back from the keyboard then collapsed into bed, not even changing.

8

Sideways Chapter 5

It was about 4:30 and George and Liz's guests started to arrive. They were expecting around fourteen people. I glanced out the window and could see George scurrying around the barbeque, getting ready to cook.

I called out the door, "Hey George, do you need some help?" I would rather work than mingle.

"No thanks. It's all under control," George said as he bounced from job to job.

I had charged Bryan's laptop to keep him busy until we ate, tucking it into a bag, and setting it by the door. Now that it was time for the party, I wished I had an excuse to skip it. Well, no getting out of it. I just hope I can quietly slip away after dinner.

I glanced out the window again, and the backyard looked beautiful, shaded now by large trees that sat on the west side. It looked like Disneyland, with flowers everywhere and not a leaf out of place.

There were a couple of George and Liz's old friends here already, Joyce, a nurse from the hospital where Liz used to work, and a couple of other friends from the same hospital. Next, I saw a couple of George's other friends pull up and get out of their car, smiling and waving.

A large black BMW pulled in then and a couple in their late sixties stepped out, followed by their daughter, an attractive lady in her late thirties. I think she's a lawyer. I could see another lady step out of the back car door. I didn't recognize her. She seemed dressed a little too nice for a backyard barbeque, wearing a black skirt, white long sleeves and high heels. She looked uncomfortable.

"Well, enough spying from the window. Let's go," I said, picking up Bryan and his laptop and stepping out.

I walked towards George and saw Liz carrying a large flat platter out of her back door. It looked heavy and she seemed to be struggling. I set Bryan down and walked swiftly to her.

"Let me help you with that," I said reaching for it.

"Thanks, Dennis," Liz said.

I could see that she was relieved to give me the platter. It was filled with hors-d'oeuvres. I placed it on a large foldout table that George had set up away from the barbeque.

I walked back to Bryan, who was standing by himself.

"Come on buddy, let's set up your computer over here."

I led him to a corner table that was kid-sized, just for him, and got out the machine, and then sat in one of the small kid-sized chairs with Bryan, trying to be invisible. I was hoping to not mingle much, being no fan of small talk and socializing. It's not that I'm antisocial, it's just that I don't have a lot to say.

Liz waved me over to where she was standing. She and George were talking to the couple from the black BMW.

"Dennis, I would like you to meet John and Natalie, and their daughter, Maureen."

I shook each of their hands and said, "Hi."

Then Maureen said, "And this is my friend, Monica."

"Hi, Monica," I said shaking her hand.

Monica took my hand and looked into my eyes and said, "Hi," giving me an uncomfortable feeling, and holding my hand for a beat too long.

I released her hand and said, "It's very nice to meet you guys. I need to catch up with my son. I'll talk to you later."

As I walked away, I could hear Maureen and Monica laughing at some inside joke.

I walked back to Bryan and could see that he was impatient and wanted me to watch him click on a Living Book. I glanced up and saw Maureen and Monica being served a drink. Monica looked my way from across the yard and slightly raised her glass. I smiled and turned my attention back to Bryan. Did she seem a bit attracted to me? No.

Seven or eight more friends of George and Liz's arrived. There was a guy who looked like a stockbroker, and he was all over Monica. I thought he looked a lot more like her type than I did, and then I realized, much to my chagrin, that I found her attractive. This caught me off guard, and I quickly tried to repress the feelings. Liz brought a couple more of their friends over to meet Bryan and me, thankfully, distracting my attention away from Monica.

Most of the people here were mingling and laughing, having been friends and acquaintances for years. I walked over to get some chips and dip for Bryan, his favorite food.

As I scooped up some dip, Monica walked up behind me and said, "That will make you fat."

I smiled, "Well, it's not really for me. It's for my son. He loves chips and dip." I turned to face her and she gave me a visual once-over.

"You do look pretty fit," she said.

"Ah, thanks," I said with a little growing discomfort. "You look fit yourself, Monica. Do you work out?"

"Noooo," she said laughing out the "oooo". "I just control everything I eat."

"Oh," I said shortly.

"So, I guess you do work out, Dennis?" she said a little sarcastically, emphasizing my name.

"Well, yes, I enjoy exercise. I like the way it makes me feel."

"It's important to feel good," she said subtly suggestive.

"Ah, yeah. I need to take these to Bryan. I can see him getting antsy."

"I want to meet your son."

I thought I was getting away, but obviously, Monica had no interest in rejoining her friends right now. She followed me over to the table in the corner.

"This is my son, Bryan."

"Hi, Bryan," she said.

Bryan looked up for a split second, and then looked back to his computer, and then looked back at Monica again, and shook her hand.

"Oh, a little gentleman, I see," she observed.

Bryan went back to clicking on his *Living Book*.

"Here's your chips and dip," I said, putting the plate down by his keyboard.

He began crunching and Monica said, "I'm really glad to get away from that guy over there."

"The stockbroker looking guy?"

"Yes, but he's really an orthodontist. He keeps talking about things he wants to do with my mouth," she laughed.

"Oh," I said, a little speechless. Monica seemed to have two meanings in everything that she said.

"So, Dennis, do you get out much?"

"No, not much, I'm pretty busy."

"Oh, doing what?"

"Well, I have a child who needs constant attention."

"So, you never date?" she said, not quite believing me.

"No, I haven't had a date since I lost my wife."

"Poor boy," she said and I think she was trying to be understanding, but it came out condescendingly.

"Not really, I'm pretty happy," I responded, but not quite convincingly.

"You look ecstatic," she said, glancing away as if she was suddenly bored to death. "I think I need another drink," she stated, walking away, and I got the distinct feeling that she was finished with me.

"Food's ready," George announced.

I waited for everyone to get their food, and then I walked up and got some burgers, fruit, and chips for Bryan and myself.

Liz walked over with her plate. "I saw you talking to Monica," she said, both making a statement and asking a question at the same time.

"Ah, yeah," I said, trying to say nothing.

"She's a very successful lawyer at Maureen's firm."

"I'm not surprised."

"Oh," Liz said very perceptively getting my point. "It seems all the single guys and half the married guys are trying to get her attention," Liz observed.

"Not all the single guys," I said.

"No, not all of them," she said understanding. "Dennis, you know if you decided to start dating again, it would be okay with us," Liz said with a look of concern on her face.

I looked directly into her eyes, taken aback by the unexpected comment.

"Thanks," I said shortly, at a loss for words, and not really wanting to go there.

"I don't think it's healthy to be alone," Liz added.

"I know," I said shortly, trying to extract myself from this conversation.

"Okay, Dennis."

Liz walked off getting back to her guests, and I went back to Bryan and his *Living Book*. I had for the most part been able to avoid the mingling. Monica looked my way from across the yard and extracted herself from three guys who suddenly looked a bit disappointed.

She strolled over to me and said, "I was wondering if you might be free for dinner tomorrow night?"

"Ah... well... I... I'm not sure," I stuttered, not expecting the question or the directness. "I need to have someone watch Bryan for me and--"

"Well, I was just talking to Liz, and she said she could watch him and that you need a night out," she said interrupting.

I love Liz. She is as wonderful a person as you could ever want to meet, but right now, my thoughts are not so charitable. "I'm not sure," I said, not knowing what to say.

"Oh, come on, Dennis, you might even enjoy yourself," she added, chiding me. "I'll tell you what, meet me at this restaurant," she handed me a card, "at seven o'clock," she said not taking no for an answer.

"Why do I get the feeling that you always get everything you want?"

"Because I do," she said, smiling and walking away.

"Huh," I said, looking for the number of the truck that just hit me. I am unfortunately attracted to her. So was Sampson to Delilah. Huh.

I picked up Bryan and his computer and walked towards Liz and George.

"We're heading out," I said, looking mostly at Liz.

"So, are you going?" Liz asked, having a little trouble making eye contact.

"I guess so," I replied without enthusiasm.

"Bring Bryan over about six o'clock," she said, already knowing the plans.

"Okay," I mumbled.

I couldn't wait to leave. I turned and walked to the small house. I know Liz's heart is in the right place, but I'm so far from this lady's type that we might as well be from different planets.

I carried Bryan inside and turned on the TV. Jim Cramer, a business station guy with his own stock show, came on, pounding the table about a stock I wish I owned. He was pushing buttons that made funny noises and Bryan was laughing hysterically. He loves Cramer. Then I remembered that it was Sunday and Cramer wasn't on?

"Did you record this show?" I asked Bryan, astonished.

"Ahh," Bryan said like, who do you think did it?

"Damn! You're amazing!" I said, remembering what his teacher said, 'Anything with buttons'. Damn!

We watched the rest of the program together.

"Bath time, sweetie boy," I said, scooping him up.

We finished and then I laid him down in bed and made a stuffed cat dance as I sang MC Hammer's, Hammer Time, although I changed the words to Kitty Time.

Bryan laughed hard, and I thought that I might have made a mistake by winding him up too much to sleep.

"Okay, precious boy, sweet dream magic," I said, patting his head. "Good night." I kissed him and headed off to bed.

Lying there, I thought, what an uncomfortable night... What did I get myself into? Tomorrow night won't be fun. Damn...

The alarm started its harping. I glanced up through one slitted eye. Yep, 6:30. I threw back the covers, rolled to the edge of the bed and flopped out. I couldn't sleep after agreeing to meet Monica for dinner. I must be crazy. What was I thinking? What was she thinking? Maybe this is pro bono, and Liz asked her to ask me out. That's a silly thought. I don't think Monica does anything that she doesn't want to do.

I wandered into Bryan's room to check on him and then straight for the coffee pot. I started it and then turned on the business station to see if I was losing any money this morning. The market was flat and that's fine with me. I showered and wrapped up the rest of the me needs, and with a good dose of coffee starting to take some effect, I walked into Bryan's room.

"Hey there, buddy boy, it's gettin' up time."

"Five more minutes," I heard Bryan say muffled, with his head deep in his pillow, and a five-hand pointing at me.

"Yeah, I know. Back in five," I said, walking from the room and into the kitchen to start breakfast and pack his lunch for school.

I headed back to his room. "Okay youngin', the time is now."

We finished all our duties, walked out the door into a beautiful morning and drove to school. I dropped Bryan off telling his teacher that I would pick him up, then I drove the short distance to my health club. As I pulled into the parking lot, I saw Jason's car.

I checked in at the desk and then glanced into the weight room. Jason was on the bench press. As I entered the room, I asked Jason if he needed a spot, which means making sure that the weight is safe by standing close to catch it if he couldn't lift it.

"I need a new shoulder," he responded.

"Well, if you weren't trying to bench the whole gym, you wouldn't be having a problem," I said.

Jason laughed, "I can't even bench your weight." Jason outweighs me by thirty pounds.

We began our workout, but I was quiet.

Jason noticing asked, "What's up with you today, Dennis?"

"Well, I have a date tonight," I said looking away.

Jason stopped his workout and stared at me disbelieving with his mouth slightly open. "Must be a blind date."

I glanced back. "Are you saying the date's blind or the girl's blind?"

"YES," Jason laughed.

Len walked in with a white towel wrapped around his neck. "How's the market doing today, Denny?" he asked.

"The market's flat, but everything I own is in the red," I said.

"That's why I don't own stocks anymore. They make me crazy."

Len is a former government worker in the state department, and in his mid-seventies. He's very fit and is a walking testimony to exercise, not to mention great genetics.

"Hey Len, guess who's got a date tonight," Jason announced.

Len looked at me, raised his eyebrows and said, "Must be a blind date."

"All right. Don't you guys have some exercise to do?" I laughed, trying to change the subject.

Jason wasn't finished though. "I think Denny boy here is about to get back on the bike."

"I think you mean on the horse," I said.

"Close enough," Jay said. "You know, Den, at least half the women in this gym have been signaling you for a long time."

"Signaling me?"

"Dude, I'm not sure why you haven't noticed, but it's been pretty obvious to me," Jason informed me.

"Honestly, Jason, when a lady flirts with me, I really don't know how to act. I just feel uncomfortable."

Len laughed, "Yeah, I get that all the time."

"I bet you do, you hound dog," I said.

I glanced out of the weight room and looked at my nearly empty coffee cup.

"I'm going to refill my coffee," I said. There is always coffee brewing in the lobby. I walked out of the weight room and to the coffee pot. Donna was behind the desk, she looked up.

"Time for some sports drink," I said.

"Sports drink, huh?" she said.

"Yep?"

I walked back into the weight room.

Len looked up and said, "Did you save me any coffee?"

"There's still half a pot out there," I said.

"Good, see ya later," Len said walking away.

After Len left, Jason said, "Have fun tonight. Don't do anything I wouldn't do."

"The funny thing about this date is that the woman I'm meeting for dinner truly isn't my type, and I'm not hers. I'm really not looking forward to this, at all."

"You'll be fine," Jason said trying to help.

"I guess," I replied, not confident.

We got to our workout.

Once finished, I walked from the weight room and Jason followed me to the coffee pot. "Have fun on your date tonight," he said, pouring himself a cup. Donna looked up. Shannon had just walked in from the pool and turned to me also. I looked at them both, my face reddening.

"Ah, yeah," I said, then looking down, turned and stepped out the door.

I walked to my car and couldn't believe that I didn't crack the windows. When I opened the door, I was hit with blistering heat.

I drove home sweating with my car never cooling, then pulled into the back of my small house, and walked inside. I sat down and dozed and the next thing I knew, my alarm was beeping. I glanced at the clock to see that it was 1:15. got up from the couch, reheated some cold coffee left in the pot from this morning, washed my face, drank the coffee, and walked out.

I drove the short distance to Bryan's school to pick him up for swim lessons with my mood darkening. My mind started to wander to my date tonight. I could feel myself sweat and it wasn't from the temperature. I really wasn't happy that I said yes. I could have said no and I wouldn't be stressing right now... I know I'm nervous because I haven't dated for a long time, but I also know that Monica isn't right for me.

I pulled into my son's school, walked to the classroom door, and could hear Miss Kathy lining up the kids. She opened the door, and the kids and aides filed out, following the teacher. As they left the room, Bryan saw me, his eyes lighting, and he spread his arms to greet me.

"Hi there, sweetie boy," I said, picking him up. "Hi, Miss Kathy. Did you have a good day?"

"We had a great day, see you tomorrow," she said, as she walked the rest of the kids to the buses.

"Come on, Bryan, let's go get wet." Bryan smiled now remembering that it was swimming lessons day.

We drove to the club and as I parked I could see Shannon's small gray SUV. We checked in, walked to the locker room, changed, showered and walked to the pool.

As we entered the area, I could see Shannon swimming laps. She moved like a seal in the water. She had a very smooth, easy stroke, but swam with a lot of speed. Bryan and I walked over to the stairs and stepped into the pool. I saw a friend, Big Jim, swimming. He waved and said hi to Bryan. Bryan loves Jim, and he waved and smiled back.

Shannon saw us and swam over. "Hi, guys," she said. "I'll be back in a minute."

I watched her walk out of the pool dripping. Jim was talking, but my attention was diverted to Shannon. As she left the pool, I couldn't help but be distracted by the way she looked in her suit, all wet and clingy. This is a building attraction that I haven't experienced in a long time.

Jim continued to speak... "What?" I said.

He looked at me and smiled wryly.

"Sorry about that," I said.

Jim continued to smile like a cat with a bird in his mouth and said, "I asked if Bryan has a lesson today."

"Oh, yeah, at 3:00."

"Shannon seems like a good swimming teacher."

"Bryan really likes her," I commented flatly.

"Maybe not just Bryan," Jim replied, again with the returning wry grin.

"Ah... Well...," I said dumbly with a shrug.

Jim and I continued to chat when Shannon interrupted.

"Can we start a bit early," she asked.

"Sure," I said, a bit tongue-tied. Shannon walked into the pool, and Jim moved to the other side to grab a lap lane.

"So, you have a date tonight?" Shannon asked.

"Ah... Well...," I said, again, with an eerie echo.

Shannon smiled, "I hope you have fun."

"Thanks, but I haven't dated for a long time. It feels strange. Do you date much?" I asked, trying to change the direction away from me.

"Some. Come on, Bryan lets swim," Shannon said, leaving me, moving to Bryan and taking his hand.

I walked from the pool, wrapped my towel around me and sat on the side in a plastic lounge chair. The lesson flew by. Shannon and Bryan walked out of the pool and she patted his head and said, "He did great. See you on Wednesday." I smiled, nodded, and watched Shannon walk into the women's locker room.

Bryan and I packed up our towels and walked into the men's locker room to shower some of the chlorine off. We left the showers, toweled off and headed to the car.

As we drove home, I started stressing about the date, again. I needed to feed Bryan, shower again, find something nice to wear, and then run Bryan over to Liz and George's. I must be really nervous because my mind had gone completely blank. I'm not even forming one coherent thought.

Arriving home, I showered, fed Bry, did some chores, and then got dressed. I checked the clock. 5:45. "Time to take you to Amma's, Bry." I got his computer, picked him up, and walked across the flagstones to their back door, knocked and Liz answered.

"Hi, Den. Don't you look nice," she said grinning.

"Thanks, Liz. I won't be late."

"See you tonight. Have a good time," Liz said.

I smiled a little grimly, and walked away, sweating, then stopped and walked back forgetting to give Bryan a hug. I could feel the stress. Damn.

I got in my car and drove the roughly twenty-five minutes into Old Sacramento, feeling the perspiration, and I shook my head.

As I pulled up to the restaurant, I couldn't help but hope she wouldn't show. I'm not sure I understand why she wanted to have dinner with me. I'm no great catch. I'm not great looking. I don't have any money. I really don't get it, and it makes me even more nervous. I'm not even sure that I think Monica is very nice. I'm not saying that she is middle school or high school mean, just mean for the fun of it, but she seems to take some delight in making people uncomfortable. I'm also not a great debater, so I hope the evening isn't full of me ducking verbal assaults.

I decided to park down the street. I could have parked closer but seem to feel a bit embarrassed that I'm driving a Civic. Well, this isn't starting very well. I'm already on the defensive. "Wow, Den, you-are-pitiful," I thought aloud. So, what are the positives? She is very attractive and I can't help being attracted to her. That isn't any reason to say yes to an invitation, though. So, why? Hmmm... Loneliness... Boredom... Ego? Augh... I shook my head.

I started off to the restaurant and could see a small, two-seat, silver BMW pull into the valet parking. Monica stepped out dressed very businesslike in a gray skirt and jacket. She took the valet ticket without looking around and entered the front of the restaurant. She floated as she walked, and exuded confidence. I thought, what am I doing here?

I picked up the pace and got to the door only seconds behind her. As I walked in, she was looking at her watch.

"Hi, Monica."

She looked up. "Hi, Dennis."

"Would you like a drink?" I offered.

She nodded. We checked in with the hostess and went into the crowded bar, found an open table in the corner and sat across from each other. The cocktail waitress came over and asked for our order.

"I'll have the Clos Duval Cabernet," Monica said.

"I'll have the same," I said.

"Well, you showed up," Monica said, looking at me and half smiling.

"Yeah, I don't tend to back out when I've made a commitment."

"So, you're reliable, and a jock, too."

"Yes, in that order," I said smiling.

"I haven't seen it yet, but I have a feeling you can be charming when you want to be."

I glanced up and smiled. The waitress brought the wine. I paid, and at the same time, our name was called to go into the restaurant.

We followed the hostess to a nice table, carrying our wine glasses. Although the restaurant was upscale, the tables were set close and were full. I helped Monica into her seat and then sat across from her. The hostess handed us the menus and walked off.

"Do you have dinner here often?" I asked.

"Yes, it's one of my favorite restaurants."

"It has a nice menu. What looks good to you?" I asked.

"I'm not sure. How about you?"

"I think I'm going to get the filet with Béarnaise sauce. I love Béarnaise sauce."

"I think I'll have the salmon," Monica said.

"I have really tried to make a good Béarnaise sauce," I said. "I can never quite get it to be as good as what you get in a restaurant."

"So, you cook?" Monica said amazed.

"Yes, I just hate to clean up," I said smiling.

Monica looked back down at her menu, not smiling. I could feel my discomfort starting to rise.

"So, you don't cook?" I asked.

"Noooo," she said laughing out the "oooo," just like at the party.

"Oh," I said quietly.

The waitress took our order. I asked Monica if she would like another glass of wine.

"I certainly would," she said a little too enthusiastically.

I was hoping that the wine might loosen up Monica a bit, or at least make her happier, but I can see by the look in her eyes that she's probably not a happy drunk.

As I gazed at my half full glass, I was instantly transported back to my childhood, when my father would drink too much. I recognized Monica's look because of him and learned to fear it. He would get started early in the night, and soon his left eye would sag. Bad news, everything after that became an argument. It didn't matter what was being discussed, the volume increased, and the spirit of the discussion became mean with only one right answer, his. I remember my mom even agreeing with him to try to calm him down, but he would still argue. So, as a result, I would naturally become quiet when I saw that look. The fact of the matter was, that as the sun sank, my childhood home became a battleground.

I think I'm going to need to be careful what I say. Not that it would matter if Monica wants to cross swords.

"Have you known Maureen long?" I asked, hoping to make the conversation a little bland.

"A couple of years from work. We hit it off," Monica said, but she isn't one to want bland conversation. "So, Dennis, you really haven't dated for three years?" she inquired.

"I cook, work out, I'm reliable and truthful," I responded.

"Yes, but you don't like to clean up," she said with a tone that sounded derogatory.

"Nobody's perfect," I said and she looked directly into my eyes.

"You haven't dated because you haven't had any takers, or because you haven't been interested?" she cross-examined.

"I wasn't interested, to be honest with you. It has taken me a long time to get over the loss of my wife."

"I'm curious, Dennis, was it one of those fairytale marriages you hear about?" she asked in an edgy tone, and obviously not believing in such a thing.

"No, Monica. It was day-in and day-out hard," I said with some force, warning her that she was approaching a line.

She looked at me, rubbing her chin, her left eye sagging a bit, and not phased in the least.

"So, how long ago did you decide to date?"

"I'm not sure I consciously did. I have found myself attracted to women recently, when that just wasn't even remotely happening before."

Thankfully, the dinners arrived. The waitress brought the food and asked if we wanted anything else.

Monica said, "I'll have another glass of wine."

Oh, boy, I think this is going to get interesting. I'm still sipping my first glass, and I could feel Monica getting more aggressive.

"This steak is wonderful," I said. "The Béarnaise is perfect. How is your salmon? It looks great."

"It is very good," she said pleasantly with no qualifiers. We ate quietly for a time.

"I'm surprised you asked me to dinner, Monica, I'm not really sure why," I stated curiously.

"It was a whim," she said. "Honestly, Dennis, I think you're a pretty man, but I must admit, I didn't think you were very interesting," she added. "Why would you come?"

"Well, I must admit, I was in the mood for an adult evening, you know, no Big Bird. It has been a while," I said, and we sat with the conversation stalling.

"So, what do you find interesting?" I asked, breaking the silence.

"Well, someone who is educated, well-traveled, and filthy rich, but I am also intrigued by a man who moves my more basic side. That's where you come in. I find you somewhat, *moving*," she said, slowing the words, and making eye contact.

My face flushed and I quietly said, "Oh."

"You're blushing!" she said laughing. "So, Dennis, you haven't taken any women to your bed since you've been alone?" she asked, a little loud.

"Ahhh...I've really enjoyed the dinner, are you going to want dessert?" I asked desperately trying to change the subject.

Monica switched from aggressive to flirtatious. "Oh, Dennis, I hope so," she said, looking directly into my eyes again and continuing to enunciate my name.

"Monica," I said and sounded like I was whining, "I don't want you to get the wrong idea. This is kind of an experiment for me. I'm not sure we are both after the same ending here."

Monica's attitude took on a more edgy tone if that was possible. "You may want to be careful."

"You know what, counselor, I think I have a pretty good idea about what I'm looking for."

Monica folded her hands on the table and looked at me inquisitively. "Why don't you tell me what interests you, Dennis."

"Honestly, I'm really looking for someone who likes me."

"You know, you never answered my question about bringing anyone to your bed." she cross-examined.

"No, I haven't," I said, looking around self-consciously as if I was going to be overheard. Like anyone cared.

"You must be a little... frustrated," she said with a half-smile and enjoying watching me squirm.

"Depression is not a great aphrodisiac," I said.

The waitress walked over and asked if we would like coffee or dessert. Monica looked at me condescendingly and said, "Nothing for me, thanks."

"Could you bring the check please?" I asked.

The waitress nodded and brought the check while we waited in another uncomfortable silence. I could feel the date going bad from the beginning, but there wasn't anything that I could do to stop it.

I paid and then we got up from the table. We walked out of the restaurant and Monica handed the young man the tag for her car. As he ran off, she turned to me.

"You know, Dennis, you're a bit more damaged than I thought you were."

"Yeah, I'm sure, but I'm getting better."

Her car pulled up and the guy held open her door. Then a curious thing happened. She softly kissed my cheek and laid her hand on the kiss, lingering there. She smiled warmly and said, "Take care of yourself, Dennis. I think you're a really nice guy."

I smiled and watched as she walked around to the driver's side of the car.

She tipped the guy and said, "We could have had a lot of fun tonight, you know."

The valet tried not to look at me but couldn't help himself.

I smiled again, "See you later, Monica."

She looked over her shoulder at me, climbed into her car and drove off. I glanced at the valet who was looking at me, his eyes wide, and his mouth slightly open.

I shrugged and smiled and turned to the street. As I walked to my car, I thought, what a weird date. Then I laughed, "Man, that was bizarre." I sprang into my seat, happy that was over, and glad to be alone. I'm not sure, but I don't think I'll be up for another date for a long time. I drove home relieved.

I pulled up to my house, got out of the car and walked to Liz and George's back door and knocked.

George answered, "I'm not going to ask how the date went since it's only 9:00."

"It was okay, George," I said, not in the mood to convince him.

"Come in," he said.

"Hi, Liz," I said and looked at Bryan. "There's my boy."

He ambled over to me.

I picked him up and gave him a big hug. "Thanks for watching Bryan."

Both Liz and George gave me the sorry eyed look.

"It's really okay. The date wasn't that bad," I lied.

George and Liz looked at each other, communicating silently, the way couples do who have been together for a long time.

"Good night," I said, and walked out the door carrying Bry.

After the door closed, I hugged Bryan again. "I missed you, tonight," I said. "Let's get to bed, buddy boy." I slung him over my shoulders and he rode to our house giggling as I bounced.

George and Liz had already bathed him and put on his PJs. I brushed his teeth and carried him to his room. I laid down next to him and found one of his favorite stories, "*One Bear, Two Bears*". As I read the story, I purposely would make mistakes and change the words. He would giggle and catch me because he knew the book so well, and I would use my silliest voices and do anything just to hear his laugh. We finished the book, and I tucked him in with prayers and sweet dream magic. I turned out his light and got ready for bed.

I slipped in between my sheets, laid there staring at the ceiling and reflecting on my date, but my mind wandered to Shannon. I thought about her smile and her easy way, and I thought that anyone who was with her was lucky.

An hour later I still couldn't sleep so I put the DVD of the first Star Wars movie in the player. I don't know why, but if I can't sleep, I put that movie on and I go right out. Maybe it's the Force. Maybe I could get George Lucas to license it to Bristol-Myers as a sleep aid... Weird.

I dozed, but my sleep was restless, and I woke to find that I had kicked off the covers and was cold. I picked the covers off the floor, went to the bathroom, checked on Bryan, and tried to get back to sleep. I put the DVD back on and finally drifted back off.

9

Sideways Chapter 6

BEEP, BEEP, BEEP... I reached up to hit the snooze alarm, missed and slapped the clock to the floor.

"Okay, I'm up," I said to no one.

No gym today. I need to drop Bryan off at school and go to the will reading. I looked at the ceiling and dozed back off. The alarm sounded again, startling me, it now on the floor. Two more weeks of school, then summer and then no alarms for a bit.

Clearing the cobwebs of sleep from my brain, I reached down and picked up the insistent clock, turning it off. I dragged my sorry ass from bed, realizing that I was no longer a morning person, and the thought troubled me. I stretched and shuffled to Bryan's room to check on him. He was snoozing.

I left his room and headed straight for the coffee pot, yawned, stretched, and started the brewing. With coherence returning, I thought about the date with Monica, but the thought was brief and I shrugged not concerned.

I switched on the business station, could smell the coffee, and walked back to Bryan's room to start him waking up.

"Okay, buddy boy, time to get this day started," I said, leaning down and kissing his head. "Ah oh. Dude, you got a fever."

Bryan barely moved, and I placed my hand on his forehead. "No school today, honey boy," I said, kissing him again.

I pulled the blanket down and left the sheet on him, and he turned to his side and fell back asleep.

Back to the couch. I sat and looked at the television, the market was down seventy points. No will reading today. I didn't want to go anyway. They can mail me my huge inheritance and nice words. I felt that cloud of depression, and I stared into space.

At 7:00, I called Bryan's school, got a machine, and reported that Bry wouldn't be there today because of his fever. I started to worry. I hoped he was okay. He was fine yesterday. Kids get sick so fast. I got up and checked on him, and he was sleeping peacefully.

I was supposed to go to the will reading at 9:00. I'll call mom at 8:00 and let her know that I won't be there. I showered, ate breakfast, and had more coffee. I couldn't even imagine what might be in the will. I don't think he had very much. He lived alone, outside of town. I don't know.

Finishing, I picked up the phone and dialed Mom. "Hey, Mom, are you there?" I said to her machine, hoping that she hadn't left yet.

"Hi, Dennis," she said like she was expecting my call.

"Hi, Mom. I can't go to the reading today. Bryan has a fever and I may need to run him to the doctor."

"Okay," she said a little suspicious.

"Maybe they can mail Jonathan's bottle cap collection to me," I said, giving her a bad time.

"I thought I was getting that," she said, giving it right back.

"Ha."

"Okay, Dennis. I'll get you as much information as I can."

"Talk to you later, Mom. Love ya."

I spent some time on chores, not wanting to be too loud, and wake Bryan, who had been sleeping soundly. By now, it was about 10:15, and I walked in to check on him. He was stirring a bit.

"Hey there, my sweetie good boy. How ya doing?"

He barely opened his eyes and I could see the fever in them. I felt his forehead and it was very hot, so I took his temperature, 102.

He got up on his elbows and signed, "Get up."

"Are you hungry?"

"Ahh," he said, meaning yeah.

"Okey-doke," I said, hoping he could keep breakfast down. I had Pedialyte just in case. I always worried though, when he got a fever because he had seizures when he was very young and a high fever could bring them on.

I brought him into the front room and sat him on the couch. He did well with breakfast, and we sat together watching Sesame Street. Bert and Ernie were counting sheep in bed, and he managed to smile but was lethargic, though thankfully, didn't seem to be in any real discomfort.

The phone rang and I got up to answer it. "Hello."

"Dennis, Hi," my mom said, sounding funny.

"Hey, Mom. Have you finished already?"

"Yes, Dennis. Do you mind if I come over?"

"Well, Bryan's pretty sick but, sure."

About twenty minutes later, Mom pulled in front of the house and knocked at Liz and George's front door. They exchanged pleasantries, and then Liz walked her through the back gate, and towards the small pool house. I watched them walking together. There was something funny about the way they were talking, and I could see Liz shaking her head.

They stepped to my door, and I opened it as they knocked. "Hi, ladies," I said, unlocking the screen.

Liz said, right away, "I hear Bryan is sick."

Bryan hearing his name bounced off the couch and waddled to the door. I opened the screen to let them in and Bryan gave them both big hugs.

"In about four days, you'll both have fevers," I said smiling.

My mom still holding Bryan said, "It was worth it," and snuggled his neck.

"I'm going to go," Liz said, after feeling Bryan's head, and figuring that he wasn't too sick. "Bye, Kate," she said, stepping out.

"Bye, Liz. It was good to see you," Mom said.

I waved goodbye to Liz and had Mom sit down.

"Do you want coffee?"

"No thanks," she said and I could tell that she wanted to get on with it.

"Did you bring my bottle cap collection?" I asked.

She looked at the floor, smiled with a smile that said, you may want to hold off on the sarcasm.

"What?" I said.

"Dennis, your uncle was worth a little more than anyone knew. His estate and assets came in around four million dollars.

"WOOH," I said, blown away.

"Most of the cash, stocks, collections, and other possessions went to other relatives."

"Okaaay," I said, drawing out the "aaay."

"Jonathan left you this letter," she said, handing me a sealed envelope, "and his house, land, and fifty thousand dollars to make any necessary repairs."

I just looked at her speechless with my mouth agape. "I don't know what to say."

"I'm not surprised the cat has your tongue," she said.

I just stared.

"I'm not sure you will be able to get into Jonathan's house until late August, though," she said.

"Why, do they need to sweep it for mines first?" I asked.

I got the familiar, you've been a naughty boy look from her. One I know well.

"Come on, Dennis. First of all, the things that need to be divided among the relatives have to be sorted. When that's finished, you will be contacted by my sister, who is the executor."

"Okay, Mom, thanks," I said losing the humor.

"I got to go," she said. "Give me a hug, Bryan."

Bryan jumped from the couch and gave her a hug.

"You get better," she said, reaching for his forehead. "I'll be in touch to let you know if there is any more information."

I stood and she looked at Jonathan's letter in my hand.

"Oh, yeah. Let's see what's in here," I said, first holding the letter up, sliding my thumb under the flap and then ripping the envelope open. I could see that it wasn't very long.

Dear Dennis,

There are some truly, strange things that have happened to me at this house, lately. I can't offer an explanation. Bring a compass with you when there are sun storms. This is when things seem to happen. I'm sorry to put this on you. I can't offer any other help.

Jonathan Bartoli

"Damn! Do you think Jonathan had flipped?" I asked seriously.

"I talked to him a few weeks before his death, and he seemed fine. He didn't say anything about the house," she offered.

"Well, what do you make of this?" I asked, waving the letter.

"I don't know, Dennis. Maybe he had a small stroke or had dementia coming on. When you get it, you can have hallucinations. I just don't know, but I don't think the house is haunted."

"Well, this is just weird. I told you there was arsenic in the cupcake."

"Whatever happened to Jonathan, I'm sure has a reasonable explanation," she said.

"Yeah, I'm sure you're right," I said, thinking more rationally.

She stood up and I walked over and gave her a hug. "Thanks, Mom. When do you think they will start carting stuff out of there?"

"Well, as I understand it, everything will be done in stages. The belongings need to be sorted, and the financial portion also needs to be done. I'll get back to you when Francis calls me."

"I don't feel right about this," I admitted, now thinking about Jonathan's generosity.

"I know, Dennis, but he wanted to give you, and everyone else, what he gave them. No one was holding a gun to his head. I think you can take it at face value."

"Thanks, Mom," I said again, unable to say anything else.

"Dennis, relax. It was nice of your uncle to think of you and everyone else. He could have just left it to charity, and that would have been fine also. It was his to give, and he gave it freely. Just be thankful and let the guilt go."

I smiled at her perspective.

"Thanks," I said again.

"I will be in touch. Take care of that precious grandson of mine."

"You know I always do."

"I have always been proud of you, Dennis, but that's why I'm most proud."

"Love you, Mom."

"Love you, too. I'll be in touch," she said smiling. She gave me and Bryan another hug and walked out the door.

I closed it behind her and sat back down on the couch next to Bryan. I really didn't know what to think, and I sat in a state of shock. On the one hand, there was this generous gift, and on the other, there was the bizarre letter. If I had to guess, I would think that the will was done a long time ago and he added the letter at some later date. It seemed that way, but I couldn't be sure... Hmmm?

"Hey, Bryan, how are you feeling, good boy?" He looked up at me with fever in his eyes and I felt his forehead. "Where did you get this bug?" I asked rhetorically.

He said nothing.

I called the school telling them that he would be off on Wednesday also, and then I called the club to have them let Shannon know that we would miss his swimming lessons. I must admit, though, that I was a little sorry that I didn't get to spend that time with her, myself. Sigh... "Ha, silly schoolboy," I thought aloud.

10

Sideways Chapter 7

Thursday morning, the alarm was rude as usual and I looked up at it through slitted eyes. I pulled my bones from bed and checked on Bryan, feeling his forehead. No fever. He's back. Great. I went straight to the coffee pot and turned on the business channel and all was in order. The market was down again. Well, at least that was predictable, just not predictable enough.

I showered and started to get Bryan's lunch ready for school and then I walked into his room to give him a shake.

"Guess what time it is?" I asked.

Bryan barely moved.

"That's right. It's getting up time, buddy boy," I said with enthusiasm.

"Five more minutes," he signed predictably.

"I know, but all your school friends have missed you the last two days," I said, trying to get his brain working.

He looked up and smiled.

"I'll be back in five minutes."

"Ahh," Bry said, meaning yeah.

I went back to the kitchen to finish his lunch, and start his breakfast, then walked back to his room and he was sitting up looking at a stuffed friend.

"Time to handsome you up, sweet boy," I said, sitting on the edge of the bed.

He smiled and I gathered him up, took him into the bathroom, dressed him and then carried him to his breakfast. While he was eating, I got myself ready for the gym and then brushed his teeth and we were out the door.

As I drove up to the school, I could see Miss Kathy leaving the buses and walking to her room. We caught up. "Hi, Miss Kathy," I said.

"Hi, guys. Bryan, how are you feeling?" she asked.

Bryan signed, "Good."

"I'm glad to hear it," she said and looked at me. "Dennis, we have our I.E.P. meeting today."

"I'll be there. 2:15, right?"

"Yes, see you there," she said.

"Put Bryan on the bus, his grandparents will meet it," I said.

Having a special needs child, you are constantly working on the logistics. It must be perfect every time. You can't make any mistakes.

I left the school and decided to hit the coffee shop on the way to work out. I parked and as I left my car, saw Shannon and a guy walk in before me. Maybe she does have a boyfriend?

I walked in the door and stood in line a couple of people behind them. Shannon turned around and saw me.

"Hi," I said and smiled.

Shannon's guy turned around but didn't give me much notice.

"Hey, Den. How is Bryan?"

"He's much better. We will be ready for swimming lessons on Friday."

"I'm sorry, Dennis. I need to cancel our lesson on Friday. I promised to help set up for the club party that night."

"Oh, that's right. I forgot. Bryan would be mad if we missed that. He loves Big Jim and his band."

"Is there anyone Bryan doesn't love?"

"Well, no, not really," I said truthfully.

"I don't think there is anyone who doesn't love him, either."

"Shannon, what do you want?" Shannon's guy asked a bit impatiently, reaching the counter.

"So, you're coming to the party?" she asked temporarily ignoring him.

"Oh yeah. We'll be there," I said.

"Good. Talk to you later," she said, turning back to order.

They went and sat down, and I got to the counter, "Hi, Lenny. How are you?"

"Busy. Good to see you, Mr. Den," he said and handed me my usual.

I put a tip in the jar. "Thanks, see ya," I said.

I turned and walked to the door with my coffee. Shannon and her guy were sitting at a small table by the front window. I smiled as I walked by and Shannon smiled back. Her boyfriend was busy looking at his smartphone.

As I drove to the club, I wondered if Shannon was giving lessons today. I doubted it. She looked busy. I arrived and walked through the front door and saw Donna at the front desk.

"Hi, Dennis. What are you doing today?"

"Weights and then some racquetball," I said.

She nodded, logging it in, and I walked from the desk into the weight room.

As I entered, I could hear Jason and Len arguing politics. "Morning, guys," I said.

Jason looked at me and nodded and I thought he was going back to his discussion with Len.

"Hey, date man. Let's hear the details."

"I thought you would have forgotten about that by now," I said.

"Did she bring her white cane?" Len asked.

Jason laughed too enthusiastically.

"That wasn't that funny. There isn't much to say," I replied.

"Struck out big time, huh," Jason said with too much glee.

"Yes, now can we just drop it?"

"Kicked to the curb," Jason said, making a statement, not asking a question.

"Yeah, well," I said, allowing them both some satisfaction.

"No details for us?" Jason pressed.

"Picture an evening being cross-examined by an overzealous prosecutor," I offered, hoping to shut him up.

"Ouch, the only thing that I could think of that would be worse is an overzealous proctologist," Jay said.

"Same thing," I said. "We did at the end of the night, agree mutually, that we weren't quite right for each other. Okay, let's pay some dues so we can be strong for our declining years. No offense, Len."

"Who's declining?" Len snapped back and no argument there, the guy's a rock.

We each worked out using different weights.

"Hey, Len, have the Republicans figured out how to fleece the rest of the middle class yet?" Jason asked, continuing their discussion.

"No, we're still working on the old and the poor, but we'll get there," he teased back.

We all laughed. Len is a middle of the road Republican, but the best part of them, not wanting people to get something for nothing. Jason and I are both moderate Democrats, but find ourselves agreeing with moderate Republicans more than with far-left Dems. You might say that we're Republicrats, or maybe more appropriately, Demopublicans. I have a great deal of trouble with far-right Republicans and far left Democrats. Neither lives in the real world.

Len finished and said goodbye.

Jason was also about to leave when he said, "Well, Den, there is always Shannon."

I looked up not expecting the topic to swing back to my love life.

"I just saw her in the coffee shop with a guy. I think she's taken."

"I do think she has a thing for you," Jay said and then added, "No accounting for taste."

I laughed and said, "To tell you the truth, Jay, I have a bit of a thing for her, too."

"Do I sense a "but" in there?" he asked, walking to the locker to get his sweatshirt.

"I don't know. Maybe I think I'm a little too old for her."

"How old are you?" he asked.

"Thirty-one."

"I think she's twenty-three or twenty-four. I'm not sure. Do you think that's too young for you?"

"Maybe," I said truthfully.

"Personally, I think it depends on the people. I don't think the total years is that bad, but some people are very old at thirty-one, and some people are very young at twenty-three. In this case, I don't think either is true, but it's your call. See ya, Den," he finished and walked from the room.

I got my bag and walked down the hallway thinking about what he said. As I turned the corner to the courts, I hadn't reached any conclusions. I guess I'll just wait and see what happens with Shannon. If we both end up single and free at the same time, and Jason is right about her having a thing for me, well, who knows.

There was no one playing in the courts, so I practiced on my own. After an hour, I finished, walked from the courts and passed the desk. I looked around to see if Shannon had come in. I didn't see her. I walked into the parking lot, heading for my car, and glanced for hers, but it wasn't there.

I drove home and my mind turned to Bryan's I.E.P. meeting at the school. Pulling into the parking place behind my home, I could see Liz by the pool.

I got out of the car, waved and said, "Hi."

"Hi, Dennis."

I walked over and she was pulling some weeds and grass that had sprouted between the flagstones, which surround the pool.

I said, "I wanted to remind you to meet Bryan's bus today. I have that meeting at his school."

"I remember," she said.

"Thanks, Liz. I hope you know how much I appreciate you guys."

"Dennis, it's our pleasure. You know that." She stood.

"Just the same, I don't think I could make it without you."

Liz walked up to me and gave me a hug. She held me there and then pulled back and smiled.

"You okay, Dennis?"

"I'm fine," I said but she could see the depression. "I need to get cleaned up. Thanks again."

As I walked away, I could feel her watching me. I know her and George worry about me.

I stepped in the door and then walked to the bathroom to start the shower. I glanced at the clock, 12:05. I should have a bit of time to rest before the meeting.

Finishing my shower, I put on some gym shorts, grabbed a sandwich, turned on the TV, and then sat down on the couch and ate. My eyes grew heavy, so I set the alarm in case I dozed off. The business station droned on...

My late wife and I were suddenly supposed to be at work at the same place. She had gone in before me and I was supposed to be there later. I was at our old house, and I kept getting visitors. Each time I would get rid of someone, another person would knock on the door. Finally, I could leave, and it was getting late, so I needed to hurry. On the way, my car broke down, and now I was really late. I decided to run the rest of the way, (which made perfect sense in this dream), but it was too far to run. I finally arrived, panting, and sweating, and it was time to close the business. My wife was boiling mad at me, the expletives were flying, and I was trying to explain when...

BEEP, BEEP, BEEP. Augh. I opened my eyes in disbelief that this was a dream. It seemed so real. My mind was fogged by my sleep and I looked at the clock. 1:30. Got to go. How could I have such a long, detailed dream in such a short period of time? The dream left me more depressed. I can't think about it now. No time. I brushed my teeth, changed, and headed to Bryan's school.

The drive barely woke me, and I arrived at the school feeling groggy. I walked into the classroom and said hello to all the people arrayed around the table. I sat and the meeting began and I wished I had a cup of coffee.

Each professional took turns talking about Bryan and all his deficits and problems. They gave goals and short-term solutions. At least they placed Bryan back with Miss Kathy next year. The meeting left me even more depressed and overwhelmed.

I said goodbye to everyone and as I was walking to the car, I remembered the dream. It left me feeling the same way. Maybe the dream represented this meeting in my subconscious. Maybe I should just never go to sleep again. I hate my dreams, they're always so haunting.

I drove home lost in thought. It was 4:40. I parked and saw Bryan, George, and Liz in the pool laughing. I waved and walked up.

"How was the meeting, Dennis?" Liz asked.

"Fine," I replied shortly. "Hey, Bry. Are you having fun in the pool?"

"Ahhh," he said enthusiastically.

"Dennis, I'm going to burn some burgers out here, would you like to eat with us?" George asked as he pushed Bryan on the floating alligator.

"Thanks, George, that would be good," I said with a half-smile.

"Good. You need to go put on your swimming suit, though, you are not appropriately dressed."

"You guys are great. Thanks, I'll go change."

I entered my house, shuffled in the door, feeling exhausted and went to the phone to check for messages. I walked to the bedroom and sat on the end of the bed for a minute trying to collect myself. Then I flopped back, lying down, and staring at the ceiling. I thought about the meeting, but mostly I thought about the dream. I sometimes feel haunted by my wife, Lauren, but it isn't her. It's my own fear and loneliness without her. I never have good dreams about her, but sometimes I even like the bad ones because I miss her, and for those moments, she's at least, with me. In my heart, I know Bryan would have been better off if I was the one who had died. "Well, that's not the way it is," I said to no one and thought, I'm all he's got, so get your head out of your ass. I forced myself up.

I put on a swimsuit, tee shirt and a smile and walked back outside. Liz greeted me with a glass of wine, and I sat by the pool watching George and Bryan finishing their game on the blowup alligator.

"I need to start the burgers," George said.

Bryan signed for me to get in the pool and then signed whale by moving a "w" up his arm meaning that he wanted a big splash. He shivered with glee as I cannonballed into the pool making a huge splash. As I came back from underwater, I looked at Liz, soaked from head to toe with her arms extended, and water dripping from her nose.

"Liz, I'm sorry," I said, shocked by her dousing.

She half-smiled but was also a bit annoyed.

George laughed and patted her butt and said, "You'll dry."

Liz loosened up a bit more, and I said that I was sorry again.

Bryan and I pretended that all his Beanie Babies had gotten into the pool and were being very bad by not getting out. So, we gathered them up with magic words and made them go back to his room. Bryan giggled and Liz, now mostly dry, laughed. George had some great smells coming from the barbeque.

George worked the grill and we sat at the table drying off. Liz asked again how the meeting went and I said it was fine, with not much expansion. I just didn't want to talk about it.

"Well, I'm glad to hear it was at least fine," she said.

I smiled at her and she smiled back wryly.

By now it was 6:00, and although the sun was lower and blocked by the trees, it was still at least ninety degrees and no breeze.

"Let's eat," George said.

Liz added to the burgers some oven fries and fruit salad. I was on my second glass of wine and had let most of the day go away.

"Thanks for dinner," I said finishing. "Tomorrow night, we are going to a party at the health club. Our friend, Big Jim, and his band are playing."

Bryan's eyes lit up now remembering the party.

"That sounds like fun," Liz said, looking at Bry.

"Ahhh," he responded back excitedly.

The mess was mostly paper plates, and Bryan and I helped clean a bit.

"Thanks again for dinner. That was an unexpected pleasure," I said.

George and Liz smiled at me, but they both had a good idea how I was feeling from the meeting. Bryan and I said goodbye and headed to our house.

We watched TV and did our standard nighttime procedures, but I was in a rare dark mood, even having trouble joking with Bryan.

I put him to bed. "What shall we read tonight, sweet boy?" I asked.

Bryan picked a book called *Very Worried Walrus*.

"Appropriate. Okey doky," I said.

I finished reading and we said prayers. I gave him the usual sweet dream magic, patted his head, and kissed him goodnight. I think I'm the one who was going to need the sweet dream magic.

Though exhausted, I laid in bed thinking. My mind wouldn't be quiet. I glanced at the clock, it was 11:45. I turned from the TV and faced the wall, finally getting drowsy...

I was in a deep well, and I could smell the stagnant water and mold filled walls. Looking up, the top was far above, and the sun was sinking. I could almost climb out because there were places for me to get small handholds, and small footholds, but because the walls were slick with water and mold, each time I reached halfway out, I slipped and fell back down into waist deep water. I knew that Bryan was alone and that he needed me, so I kept trying only to fall again and again. The rank water covered me sometimes filling my mouth, and causing me to wretch...

I jerked, sitting up suddenly. Crap, another bad dream! I listened for Bryan, thinking I must have been loud, but there was no sound. I looked over at the clock and it was 3:52. I got up, checked on Bryan and he was sleeping. I went to the bathroom and then headed back to bed to hopefully grab another couple of hours. I laid, looking at the ceiling with the dream foremost in my mind. When I dozed back off, I ended up back in the well...

BEEP... BEEP... BEEP... Thankfully the alarm woke me from my dream hell.

I got up and made the slow walk to the coffee pot. I got myself ready for the day with my mind wandering to the awful night's sleep. I stopped at Bryan's door. This is a real, Thank God, it's Friday with the will, the I.E.P.

meeting, oh, and the date, who could forget about the date, I thought, smiling, though it seemed longer ago than Monday. What a week.

I continued to Bryan, and he was sound asleep. I hated to wake him, but it was time to get ready.

"Hey there, sweetie boy," I said, smoothing the hair from his eyes. He got annoyed and gave me the five more minutes' line, cuddling three stuffed kitties.

"Okay, I'll take these two kitties to have some breakfast. This one needs a bit more sleep. Be back in five," I said.

Bryan smiled and hugged the stuffed animal.

I know it seems silly and mundane, but I love my mornings with Bryan. I wondered how I could be so happy, and yet, so lonely at the same time. Hiding in the very back of my mind was a disturbing thought that had begun to surface. It's that even if I find someone who I like, Bryan and I come as a set, and I think that may be a deal breaker. Even the most understanding person might not be willing to enter into a relationship with a special needs child involved. It's pretty restrictive. Oh well, I can't do anything about that. I will just take it one day at a time. I must admit, though, that this is the first time that the thought had weaseled its way to the surface of my consciousness, though it had been lurking. The thing is, that I wouldn't trade Bryan for all of Bill Gates' money, but I would give my right arm for him to be okay. My thoughts became random and I wondered if I even deserved to be happy because I felt responsible for my wife's death. Grim depression set in, and I felt like sitting and brooding, but I needed to get Bryan ready, and I needed to get on with it.

I finished fixing breakfast and Bryan's school lunch, then walked back to get him. He was sawing logs.

"Dude, you need to get up," I said, a little exasperated.

"Five more minutes," he said and signed.

"We have already been around that block. Time to wake up."

"Ah hum," he said sleepily.

"We are going to be late, and your kitty is going to be late for kitty school."

Bryan smiled and hugged his stuffed kitty again.

I finally got him up. We may be a couple of minutes late. He ate and I dressed him and we were out the door.

When we arrived at the school, all the buses were gone and the kids were inside. We walked to his class and I opened the door. The class was already doing circle time, the first thing they do each morning.

"Hi, Miss Kathy. Sorry, we're late. I needed a crowbar to get Bryan from bed this morning."

"That's okay, Dennis. Morning, Bryan, come join us," she said and he waddled over. "Oh, do you have swimming lessons today?"

"No. Put him on the bus. Thanks," I said, turning for the door.

"Okay, Dennis," she said.

I drove from the school towards the health club, deciding to stop for coffee. Walking in the door, I had a sudden craving for an apple fritter. I walked to the counter and saw Lenny. "Man, do you pipe doughnut smells in here. I could gain five pounds just smelling it."

"Mister Den, you need to allow yourself an occasional self-indulgence."

"You are funny, but you are the Devil."

"Do you want your usual, today?"

"Yes, thanks, Lenny."

I got my nonfat mocha, dropped a tip in the jar and drove to the club. As I entered the parking lot, I involuntarily looked to see Shannon's SUV. It wasn't there.

I walked through the door and Sara was at the desk.

"Hi, Sara," I said.

"Hi, Dennis. Are you and Bryan coming to the party tonight?" she asked.

"Yes. Are you coming?"

"No, I can't make it."

"Oh, too bad. I think it will be fun."

"You guys have a good time," she said.

"Thanks."

"Racquetball and weights?" she asked.

"Am I that predictable?"

"Everyone is," she laughed.

I walked into an empty weight room and looked through the glass wall into the gym. People were decorating for the party, hanging streamers and setting up tables.

I got to my workout routine and then walked down the hallway to the courts. There was someone who I didn't know practicing there, and I could tell he was very good by the way he was hitting the ball. I asked him to play and we went hard for an hour and a half.

Leaving the courts, I stopped by the drinking fountain and walked down the hall sweating profusely. As I turned the corner to the desk, I saw Sara. She took one look at me and said, "Your face is purple."

"Purple?"

"I hope you can make the party tonight," she said teasingly and making me embarrassed.

"I'll be there. Bryan will make me go," I said laughing.

I walked out the door and drove home. A little rest, some water and I'll be as good as new. I entered my house and got a big glass of water, then set the alarm and sat on the couch to recover. Soon Bryan's bus arrived and I jumped up to meet it. Bryan side stepped down the steep stairs with the driver's help. He saw me and waddled over and I waved at the driver. I picked him up and gave him a hug.

"I'm so happy to see you. Did you have a good day in school, today?"

"Ahhh," he said smiling. He's such a happy boy.

We relaxed, I showered and got ready for the party. "It's time to go see Big Jim's band," I said, gathering him up.

We drove to the club arriving around 7:00. There was a line of about a dozen people waiting to get in, and we walked to the end standing with two people that we sometimes swim with. They were an older couple and the lady was carrying a plate full of cookies. I could hear Big Jim's band playing an old Beatles song.

We reached the front of the line, and I could see friends and acquaintances mingling. Off to the right, I saw Shannon and her boyfriend. She saw us, smiled, and left her guy, walking over. We were becoming friends quickly. Some people you are just drawn to and friendship comes easy.

"Hi, Dennis. Hi, Bryan," she said, roughing up his hair.

Bryan smiled and said, "i," not being able to pronounce the h in hi.

"There's lots of food here. I'll see you inside," she said, walking back to her guy.

We went from the desk to the gym where tables and chairs were set up. Bryan and I sat to the left of the band. There were people dancing to an old Motown tune in a space left open in the middle. I saw Shannon enter the gym with her man and stand against the back wall. They were both leaning against the wall with their hands trapped behind them between the wall and their bodies, not touching, and I couldn't help but notice the negative body language.

Jim's band continued with Motown, and around fifteen couples got up and started dancing to "Soul Man" by Sam and Dave. I picked up Bryan and danced around holding him. Shannon saw us, walked over leaving her guy again, and asked to take Bryan. She danced with him and I danced next to them.

"How come your guy isn't dancing?" I asked loud enough for her to hear me over the band.

"He tells me he doesn't dance," she said with a look and a shrug.

"Never end up with a guy who doesn't dance," I teased.

Shannon laughed, "Not a chance."

The song ended and Shannon asked, "Bryan, will you dance with me again?"

"Ahh," he said, loving to be the center of attention. She handed him back to me.

"See you in a bit," she said, turning and walking back to her guy. I'm not sure, but I don't think the future is bright for that relationship.

The band took a break and Jim walked over to say hello.

"The band sounds great, Jim," I said.

"Thanks. I'm going to get some food," he said.

"That sounds good. We'll go with you."

We headed out of the gym and walked into the room where the food was set up. Because the band had stopped playing, the line was long and we walked to the end. This wasn't a catered party. It was all potluck with members bringing the food and the club providing the drinks. I glanced over and saw Shannon and her guy sitting on the stairs that led to the pool, looking sort of miserable. He seemed angry, and she was just waving him off. From a distance, it was hard to say, but it seemed that they had reached an impasse. They sat quietly together for a time, talking little. He looked at his smartphone and she stared off. I could see Shannon lean over and whisper something to him. He got up and I thought he was coming to the food line but he walked by and out the door. I looked back at Shannon but she didn't look upset. I thought she looked relieved. She looked my way and smiled. I smiled back, and then she stood up and walked to the back of the food line.

Jim, Bryan, and I finished getting our food and headed back to our table. A couple of minutes later, Shannon walked over and asked if the open chair next to Bryan was taken.

"No. Sit down," I said.

"Thanks."

Jim had finished and said, "Well, time to get this party started back up." He walked back to the corner of the gym where the band was set up. Slowly the rest of the band followed.

I looked over at Shannon who was picking at her food. "Trouble in paradise?" I asked.

"He doesn't dance," she said and we both laughed. "I'm going to get a glass of wine, Den. Do you want one?"

"You could talk me into that," I said, reaching into my pocket for some money.

"This one's on me," she said and she rose and walked over to a small table where the club was charging a buck for a glass. She walked back with two small glasses of red.

"Thanks," I said.

She smelled it, "Ah, a fine boxed vintage," she joked but wasn't happy. There was a note of sadness in her speech and in her eyes.

"I hope you're okay?" I said.

"I'll be fine," she said and Jim's band broke back into Motown. Shannon picked up Bryan and said, "Come on, Bryan. I need a date for the night." She danced with him for the next two songs as I sat there smiling.

Shannon danced back to the table before the second song was finished. She set Bryan in his seat and bowed to him, "Thank you, kind sir, for the dance." She walked over and sat next to me. She smiled and took a healthy sip of her wine. "So, Dennis, I never heard anything about your date," she said, gazing out of the gym doors.

"I... Ah... Well... I haven't dated for a long time. This lady asked me out, but I think she was more interested in me in a way that I wasn't expecting."

Shannon looked sideways at me, and then her eyebrows rose getting my meaning.

"A hookup?" she said, maybe a little too surprised.

I looked away and shrugged, "I guess. Only if she found me interesting enough, which I don't think she did. That doesn't interest me anyway. What she wasn't offering, and she made it clear, was friendship."

"She was going to kick you to the curb afterword, huh."

"Unceremoniously," I said.

She shook her head, drained the last drop of her wine, put the glass down a little harder than I thought she meant to and grabbed my hand while scooping up Bryan. She dragged us to the dance floor and we danced until we were all tired. I held Bryan sometimes and she danced crazily around us. Then she would hold Bryan and I would dance crazily around them. It was a great time and a lot of laughs. Shannon danced with such joy that it was infectious.

We both had another small glass of wine and then the band finished playing, saying goodnight.

Shannon said, "Well, time to work on the clean-up detail. I told them I would help. Thanks for the diversion, Den. It was fun." She turned her attention to Bryan, "And thank you, for gracing me with your presence."

With a slight bow to Bryan, a look, and a smile back to me, she walked off.

"Time to go, buddy boy," I said.

He signed, "Funny girl, swim teacher, dance with me."

I smiled a little sadly and said, "Yeah, funny girl."

We walked to the car saying our goodbyes to some of my friends and acquaintances. I put Bryan in his car seat and walked to the other side of the car and got in. Bryan wanted one of his favorite CDs. I put it in the player and drove from the club. My mind was clearly on Shannon and as I drove, I mentally replayed the evening.

"We're home," I said. I picked Bry up and carried him in the back door.

I got Bryan in the bath, washed him up and while I dried him he signed and said, "Fun time with swim teacher."

"Yep, great time."

"More dance?" he signed.

"Not for a while, sweetie boy."

"Augh," Bryan said in his most exasperated voice.

"Let's get to bed."

I tucked him in, then I finished getting ready for bed and turned in.

11

Sideways Chapter 8

Saturday was laid back and with another sweltering 90-degree night, we decided to go out for a nighttime swim. We finished our evening together with a story, prayers, and sweet dream magic. As I slipped into bed, my mind wandered to Shannon. I find that, in general, I'm content with my life. I love Bryan more than I thought I could ever love anyone, but I'm becoming lonely. I find this thought disconcerting and feel a little guilty. My mind wandered to Monica, not that lonely, she scares me, and I laughed.

I could feel myself start to drift off, and I began to dream something disturbing. I woke startled and then drifted deeper...

Shannon was getting married and had invited me to her wedding. I didn't understand the place that she had chosen for the wedding because it seemed to be a series of platforms that floated in midair attached by stairs. I finally found the reception and the room looked like the inside of a cathedral, with domed ceilings, but the only thing inside this expansive room was a bar serving cocktails.

I could see Shannon and she looked beautiful in a long flowing white dress, tastefully low cut in the front with long sleeves. She walked up to me and said, "Hi, I'm glad you could come, but you're too late."

"I know," I said, knowing that she wasn't talking about missing the ceremony. She was saying that I could have prevented the wedding, and she would have left with me. I felt such sadness, that I needed to look away. When I turned back, she was walking towards a man that I didn't recognize. She stopped, glancing once over her shoulder with a look of pure sorrow in her eyes, and then turned and continued walking away...

Startled, I jerked and looked at the clock. 3:34, realizing that I had been dreaming. I hate my dreams but this one had a definite message from my subconscious. I'm starting to think of Shannon a great deal. Am I going to be too late?

After tossing and turning, I finally went back to sleep and woke with the dream haunting me. I crawled out of bed and to the coffee pot, then got Bry up and ready for the day.

12

Sideways Chapter 9

I felt summer flying by. As I've gotten older, time seems to pass more quickly. Bryan had already been in summer school for two weeks with four remaining.

On our last session of swimming lessons, Shannon seemed quiet and I sensed some distance from her. I thought we were getting closer, but I could feel her pull back.

The next day, Friday, I dropped Bryan at summer school and drove to the gym. Shannon's car was there and I was happy that I would see her. I wondered how she would act towards me because of the way she seemed yesterday. I have to admit, though, that I'm a bit sensitive... A bit? Well, maybe a bit more than a bit.

I walked into the club and saw Shannon working out in the weight room. She saw me and smiled.

"Hi, Dennis. I'm glad to see you. I need to cancel swimming lessons for the next two weeks. I'm going to visit my grandmother in Arizona with my mom."

"Okay. Have a good time. Are we going to pick it up when you get back?" I asked.

"I think so. I'm kind of getting a bad time from the management for leaving because I haven't worked here very long. I think they will keep my job."

"Oh... Well, I hope you come back," I said, disturbed by the prospect of her leaving for good.

"I should be back by the third week of July and we can start back lessons then."

I nodded and walked from the room to play racquetball with a friend who was expecting me. Shannon headed to the pool for a swim.

We both finished at the same time and ran into each other, by the door on the way out.

"It was really a ghost town in here today," I said.

"Yeah, it's dead. Everyone must be on vacation," she said.

I glanced up at the clock. "I got to go. Bryan gets out early today. When do you work again?" I asked.

"Today is my last day until I get back."

I saw her holding a book. What are you reading?" I asked.

"*The Taking*," she said holding it up.

"That was a fun book, but very eerie," I said.

"You aren't kidding. I just got to the part where it's raining and all the coyotes come to the house. Eerrrrie," she said drawing it out.

"Oh, yeah, I remember that part. Well, I guess I'll see you when you get back."

"Yeah, Den. I'll see you."

I walked out the door miserable. It felt like there was something left unsaid. I watched her get in her SUV and I started in her direction, but then stopped, turning back towards my car. I didn't know what to say. Honestly, I was afraid of being rejected by her, and I was starting to think that this building attraction and fantasy wasn't something that I wanted to risk. I slipped into my own head and wondered why I would rather have the fantasy than try for something real. Maybe it's because it might just be my fantasy, and not shared by her. We have had some nice flirtatious moments, but Shannon is so kind that she may only like me as a friend. It's been so long since I've thought about anyone other than my wife, that I don't know if I could read the signs if someone liked me or not. I wasn't sure, so I just drove home miserable.

Arriving home, I got a call from a friend who had some work for me at a store in a half-empty strip mall that needed a facelift. He said I could work while Bryan was in summer school, and that it would be perfect for him. I agreed, jumping at the chance, and starting next Monday.

I walked from the phone and sat on the couch with a glass of water, staring out the window, and waiting for Bryan's bus.

13

Sideways Chapter 10

The next week dragged by. I worked while Bryan was in school and we
swam at the club when he got home, but the pool now seemed empty. I missed
Shannon. Maybe I should have asked her out before she left. At least if she
said no, I wouldn't be dragging my butt around, feeling that we had something
between us. It felt like we did or at least it felt like something was sprouting.
Maybe I was wrong. I just don't know.

Time, which had been flying by now seemed to drag. By the end of the
third week of Shannon's visit to her grandmother, I was starting to wonder if
she was going to return. She was a week overdue and a sweltering July was
coming to an end.

I stayed an extra week to help finish up the job at the strip mall. These last
three weeks of work had been grueling, not helped by the oppressive heat. I
must admit that I almost forgot what it was like to work on a job, and how hard
the work could be, but also that I really like building, and the pleasure of
seeing what you've worked on come together.

Now, finished with the job and summer school winding down, Bryan and I
would have almost three weeks to play before school began again.

Standing in the kitchen, I glanced over at Bryan to see him pounding away
on his computer, and he looked up at me.

I said, "You are the sweetest boy that there could ever be. Do you know that?"

He looked back down at the computer screen and continued with the *Living Book*.

I smiled and started dinner.

As I cooked, my mind wandered. With the strip mall job wrapped up, the pace of my life could move back to normal. I hadn't been exercising and I needed to get back in shape. I'm feeling a bit squishy.

Shannon continued to cross my mind and each time I had taken Bryan to swim at the club, I had looked for her, but she still hadn't returned. Maybe she wouldn't. The thought of her not returning darkened my mood, and my old friend depression tried to reemerge.

I finished cooking dinner, ate with Bryan watching some TV, and then got him ready for bed.

I tucked him in with kisses good night and sweet dream magic and headed off to bed hoping for a good night's sleep.

Tomorrow, I would head back to the gym for the first time in a while. I hoped to sleep quickly, but my dreams had been so horrible and frustrating lately, they robbed me of it.

I laid there for two hours worrying about going to sleep, which always seemed to make it worse. I kept looking at the clock and then finally dozed...

My alarm sounded at 6:30. I got myself ready, Bryan off to summer school and then drove to the gym. As I pulled into the lot, I saw Jason's car and Len's motorcycle.

I walked in the door to the club and saw Donna, tall and stately with graying hair pulled back into a ponytail, working at the check-in desk.

"Hi, Donna," I said.

"Good morning, Dennis. Weights and racquetball today?"

"That sounds like a plan," I said. "Hey, Donna, has anyone heard from Shannon?" I asked.

"I haven't heard anything," she said.

"Thanks. I was just wondering."

I walked into the weight room and a couple of guys were pushing some serious weight. At the end of their set, they would let the weights drop and hit the floor with a boom. Len was talking to Jason and when the weights hit, he jumped like a cat in the dog pound.

"I'm back," I announced to Jay and Len.

"Hey, Den, where you been? We were about to put your face on a milk carton," Jason said and the weights hit the floor, again, making Len wince.

"I was working on a short-term job but it's finished now."

"Time to pay some dues, Den," Jason said.

"Yeah, I wouldn't want to be me tomorrow when the soreness sets in."

"I hate to tell you this, but you are you," Len said.

"Oh, too bad," I said, shaking my head.

The two guys finished and put their 95-pound dumb bells back on the rack and walked out.

"I thought I was going to get a headache," Len said, happy that they left.

"So, Den, what happened to Shannon? Did you chase her off?" Jason said with his typical sarcasm.

"I don't know. I haven't heard. She told me that she was going to Arizona and that the management of the club wasn't happy with her for going. She thought they would keep her job, but she wasn't sure about that either," I said.

"You kind of look like a sad puppy," Jason said smirking.

"To be honest with you, Jay, I am. I thought we almost had something going. If she comes back, I think I'm going to work a little harder at trying to get her attention."

"I think that would be a good idea," Jason agreed.

Len finished his workout, "That's it for me. See you tomorrow."

"Take it easy, Len," I said as he walked from the room.

Jason and I finished also, and he said that he was getting together with his son today. He beamed when he talked about his son and I was happy for him.

Jason left and I walked down the dim hallway to racquetball. There was no telltale sound coming from the courts, so I guessed that I would be solo today. I spent forty-five minutes practicing my shots and listening to music on my iPod.

I walked from the courts, past the front desk, and said goodbye to Donna. It was about 11:00 and as I opened the door, I was hit in the face with Sacramento's unrelenting heat.

"Damn, this is even hot for Sacramento," I thought aloud, starting to think about the coast which was always about twenty degrees cooler.

California is a very special place. You can drive a couple of hours in one direction and get snow, a couple of hours in another direction and be on a beautiful beach. There are primeval forests with huge, towering redwoods or the wine country of the Napa Valley lined with acres of grape vines. California is a very rich and beautiful place, but right now it's too hot.

I drove home. Walking in the door, I turned on the air conditioning, wanting it to be cool when we got home from Bryan's appointments. I turned on the TV and set the alarm to wake me just before it was time for Bryan's bus to arrive.

I seemed to always be sleepy these days. I think its depression again. It seems to have a cycle. When I'm in the cycle, it's hard to see out, but as I emerged from it, I can see it for what it was. Right now, I'm deep in the middle.

I dozed and then my alarm went off. I woke, feeling refreshed for a change. I went into the bathroom and washed my face. Fifteen minutes later, Bryan's bus arrived. Because he gets out a little early during summer school, we have a little time before we need to leave for his therapies in Sacramento. I got him a snack and then we got ready to go.

Once finished with his appointments, we ate dinner on the road and after arriving back home, put on swimsuits for a nighttime swim.

Liz and George saw us in the pool and they joined in.

I see them occasionally slip into the pool at night and I picture them young and in love. It's not hard to see. They swim and then cuddle. It's beautiful, their affection is so evident. I wondered if Lauren would have lived if we would have been the same. It didn't seem so, but... I let the thought go.

Liz asked about our day and I filled them in a bit, but we mostly just lounged in the pool with the sun going down and the temperature still hovering close to eighty-five.

"This feels great," I said, sitting on the steps and up to my neck in water.

"It really does," Liz replied.

"I'm glad your trip went well," George said.

"Yep. We got some stuff done today, huh, Bry," I said, turning to Bryan who was on the floating alligator.

"Ahhh," he said enthusiastically, having fun with his nighttime swim.

I smiled. No matter how depressed I felt, when I saw him having fun, it lifted my mood.

We stayed in the pool for about an hour and then said goodbye. I brought Bryan in, showered him and tucked him into bed. I slid into my sheets and went right to sleep.

I woke early, around 5:00 am. I was wide awake for this time of the morning and I thought I should get up. I turned on the TV in my room and saw that the stock futures were way down. I listened to the account of why, and worriedly thought about my money, then turned away from the TV.

I started to get drowsy and thought that I would probably fall back asleep just before my alarm went off at 6:30...

Beep... Beep... Damn, I was right about that at least. I felt groggy and wished I would have just gotten up. I looked up at the market. It was down 105 points. Damn.

I got up and peeked in on my beautiful boy. When he sleeps, he looks like an angel. I know every parent feels that way but it's one of the feelings you never experience if you haven't had kids. I walked to the coffee pot, fired it up and then turned on the TV for more financial abuse. I showered and headed back to Bryan's room. We dressed and then headed off to school.

Pulling up, I could see Miss Kathy, the aides and the rest of the kids starting for the classroom after meeting the bus. Bryan wanted to catch up and he left me.

"You better give me a hug," I said.

He walked back and hugged me, then he stepped back and signed, "I love you."

I nearly teared up. It just struck me deep. I signed it back to him and turned to my car, hiding the sudden emotion.

Driving to the gym, I started planning things that we could do in our open three weeks. There are so many fun day trip ideas in northern California, that we'll stay busy, but I think, sleeping in will be the first plan.

I went through the motions, weights, racquetball with Sammy and Bob, and no Shannon. I finished and walked to my car. I felt like I was in a daze. I knew the problem. It was Shannon's absence. I missed my chance with her, a fact that I was going to need to accept. I was stuck in this mental loop and each thought seemed to come back to her.

When I arrived home, my mood had darkened further and all I wanted was silence. The phone rang and I didn't pick it up. The caller didn't leave a message. A telemarketer I guessed. I think I'm going to avoid the club for a couple of weeks. Instead of it being beneficial, I think it's just making me more depressed.

I found myself actually feeling angry. Angry about my life and some of the turns it had taken. I know that rationally the anger emotion probably doesn't fit, but there it was. What really am I angry about? Well, losing my wife for one, missing an opportunity with Shannon for another. Maybe I'm angry because no one fits into my circumstance. I calmed and thought of my wonderful boy, who I was determined, would not suffer for the way I was feeling. This may be a remove your head from your backside moment.

I think people need to be happy themselves. If they expect someone else to supply the happiness or to make them feel fulfilled it will probably never happen. I do think, though, that severe disappointment can tip an already fragile person into a deeper depression, so I'm disappointed that I couldn't get closer to Shannon, and I feel tipped.

If it's one thing that I've learned from life, though, it's that once you've hit a very low point, there is nowhere to go but up, and I know that the turn will happen. I do think it will take a while, though.

I rested then drove to get Bryan. Miss Kathy led her class out of the room, and Bryan saw me and smiled that wonderful smile. He's always so happy to see me.

"Hi there, Bryan, my sweet boy," I said, picking him up and giving him a hug. "Hi, Miss Kathy," I then said, turning my attention to her.

"Hi, Dennis," she said and looked at me somehow knowing that I needed that hug.

"Thanks for the great summer school and we will see you in about three weeks or so," I said.

"You guys enjoy your time off," she said.

"See you," I said, turning for my car.

I put Bryan in the car seat and got in. "Well, buddy boy, it's you and me for three weeks. I have lots of fun stuff planned." I drove home and walked into the house, happy for the AC.

The next three weeks, Bryan and I enjoyed some of the California sites with day trips. Time was drifting and Shannon hadn't returned.

Three days of vacation remained. A dense fog had settled over the Sacramento valley and had cooled down the sweltering summer weather.

I thought that it may not be so easy to get Bryan back into the school routine. I'm sure he will be tired for the first few days, and I'm not sure I would slide right back into it either with my nights having gotten progressively later and so had my mornings.

Tomorrow we were going to meet with a new speech therapist in Sacramento, and I think we'll eat dinner out for a little fun after the appointment. That usually lightens Bryan's mood from the stress of being talked about for an hour.

The next day, we met Debbie MacDonald, the therapist, and she had suggestions. We spent an hour talking about Bryan's strengths and weaknesses. Debbie let Bryan play on one of her computers that had simple games on it, and it distracted him enough so we could talk. I liked Debbie but by the time we were finished, I ended up in depression land again. It's very predictable. I go to another professional, spend an hour talking about Bryan's pluses and minuses and then want to drink.... heavily. Now, I was going to need to bring Bryan to the city every Tuesday for speech therapy, a serious commitment.

14

Part 2

Sideways Chapter 11

As the next morning heated, and the brief day of fog cleared. The reprieve from the heat was over. By the time it was closing in on the afternoon, mid-nineties was not out of the question.

A small moving van wound up the road to the late Jonathan Bartoli's house.

"I think that's the place," said John, an overweight man in his early thirties. His stomach pushed up against the van's steering wheel and sweat beaded on his forehead.

"Hey man, you got the list?" Miguel inquired.

John reached into his top left pocket and pulled out a piece of paper.

"Right here," he said handing it to Miguel.

"Good, it looks quick and I'm off after. Let's get this done," Miguel said, with his mind on an evening with his wife and two kids. It was his youngest boy's birthday, and all the relatives were coming to the house for a party.

The truck slowly approached the driveway. It was narrow with a gap in between the rock fence, only wide enough to let two cars pass. They parked and the two men climbed out of the cab and stared at the front door.

"I'll open the back of the truck," John said. "Why don't you knock on the front door."

"It doesn't look like anyone's home," Miguel said and took two steps towards the front door. He stopped in midstride, hearing a car pull in and crunch on the dirt and flagstone driveway.

A small Ford Focus pulled up behind the moving van preventing John from pulling down the ramp. He straightened, wiped the sweat that had gathered on his brow and waited for the lady to step out of the car. She was a petite woman in her late sixties with an energetic step and a look of all business.

As she approached, she smiled broadly, "Hi. I'll let you in. Do you have the list of things to take?"

"Yes Ma'am," Miguel said respectfully.

"Great, there isn't much left in the house, and the things you are to take are all separated in the front room," she noted.

"No problem," John replied, straining to keep his shirt tucked in.

She opened the door and let in the movers. The air was stale and the room dim. She directed them to a pile of boxes and several pieces of furniture pushed to one side of the front room.

"I need to go. Can you lock up for me?" she asked.

"Yes, Ma'am," Miguel said.

"Thanks. There's some coke or water in the refrigerator if you want."

"Thank you, Ma'am," Miguel said.

She smiled, turned, walked out the door to her car, backed out, then drove off.

"Well, let's get to it," John said.

They both grabbed sealed boxes and began to cart them outside. John pulled down the ramp and they stacked the boxes by the truck to see what they had and how to pack it. They worked fast and then each took a Coke from the refrigerator. After an hour and a half, they had finished.

Standing by the truck, Miguel asked, "Is that it?"

"I think so. Let's go back in the house and take a look to make sure we didn't miss anything."

They walked inside and John pulled out the list. "That looks like all of it," he said.

"I don't see nothing else. Let's go," Miguel said.

"I need to use the head," John said and turned to the short hall that led to the bathroom.

As John turned the corner, Miguel heard a slight crackling that sounded like electricity sparking and coming from the direction of the fireplace.

"Hey man, did you hear that?" he said thinking that John could still hear him. There was no reply from John, so he turned and stepped warily towards the sound. In the stone of the fireplace, he saw a faint rippling of color, like looking through clear water blown by a slight breeze. He glanced over at the dining room and could see the burnt mark that jetted up the wall and onto the ceiling. He looked back at the fireplace.

"What the fu-?" he said stopping in mid-word. The rippling intensified and then abruptly stopped. Miguel rubbed his eyes thinking it may have been a trick of the light. This had only taken seconds and John hadn't returned. Then a barely visible vertical line appeared in the air close to the fireplace. It was pale blue and so faint that you could miss it if you weren't looking closely. The line seemed to open and pinpricks of color sprang from the edges as it folded back. Miguel stood frozen. The air appeared to part and then a black formless shape emerged from the opening towards the top by the ceiling. Miguel paled, crossed himself and whispered, "Ay Dios Mio."

The shadow began to move across the ceiling towards Miguel. Grainy translucent tendrils seemed to reach for him. He felt pressure push him back away from the dark shape, and electricity touch his face, tingling it. Then suddenly, like a door closing, it pulled back and disappeared. As it left, Miguel felt pulled towards it and he almost lost his balance. Waves appeared to ripple across the stone of the fireplace and then were gone, becoming still.

"Damn," he said in a low whisper and he walked quickly out the door.

John turned the corner seeing Miguel's back as he exited hastily out of the house. "Hey, dude, where's the fire?" he said still trying to get his shirt tucked back in. He picked up his pace trying to catch Miguel. "Miguel! Miguel! What's up with you?"

Miguel stopped and turned slowly towards John. He had a look of shock on his face. He didn't say a word and then he turned and walked away from John. John grabbed his sleeve and tried to pull him around.

Miguel shook him off. "Let me go, John," he said and he turned on John with first anger and then fear in his eyes.

"Miguel?"

"Let's go," Miguel said and he walked to the other side of the truck. Before he climbed in, he glanced warily at the house and then climbed into the cab, closing the door.

John shook his head and then walked to the back, sliding up the ramp, and closing the roll-door and locking it. He climbed into the driver's side of the van and turned the key in the ignition. As they pulled out, Miguel looked back towards the house and real fear lit his face. He seemed to shudder.

"Miguel, what's wrong with you, man?"

"Just drive," Miguel said.

"Dude, come on."

"Shhhhit," Miguel said softly, with a sigh and his eyes fixed on his shoes.

"What?" John said again.

The truck got down the road and put some distance between themselves and the house.

"I saw something in that house. I don't know what it was, but I didn't want to wait for it to come back," Miguel said quietly.

John began to nervously laugh, "Come on dude, you pullin' my chain?"

"No!" Miguel said shortly.

"Okay. Okay," John said.

"Look, I can't explain this to you. I can't even explain it to myself, but you wouldn't catch me dead in that house. If we're called back, I'm calling in sick."

"So, what did you see?"

"I was in the front room when I heard a noise coming from around the fireplace and then there was this dark thing that... I don't know... came out," Miguel said, trying to explain, but knowing that he wasn't making sense.

"A noise and a dark thing?" John said with a nervous grin, not getting the picture of the scene.

Miguel shook his head and didn't speak as his anger rose.

John could feel that anger. "A noise and a dark thing. Man, I'd of shit myself. I almost did anyway," he finished stupidly, trying to be funny.

"Man, just drive," Miguel said, turning to the window.

John continued to drive and couldn't get another word out of Miguel.

15

Sideways Chapter 12

Looking out the window, I saw George and Liz in the pool. Bryan was watching Sesame Street. "Hey, Bryan, want to go swimming?" I asked, interrupting Big Bird.

Bryan looked up, "Ahh," he said, meaning yeah.

I opened the door and called to Bryan's grandparents, "Mind if we join you?"

"Come on in," George called back, loving any chance to be with Bryan.

"We'll be right there. I need to put some sunscreen on Bry."

I slipped into my suit, first and then turned to Bryan.

"Let's get you ready, buddy boy."

I picked him up and carried him to his room grabbing his favorite suit. Then, I got him ready and carried him to the pool.

"There's my good boy," George said, watching us walk up.

I set Bryan on the pool step to get him used to the water.

"Here comes the whale," I said, jumping into the deep end.

Bryan shrieked with laughter.

I resurfaced, walked towards Bry and said, "Splash," throwing water towards him. As I got closer, I could hear the faint ring of my phone inside the house.

"Can you watch Bry while I get the phone?" I asked, not wanting to impose.

"Sure," Liz said.

I walked out of the pool dripping, grabbed my towel and jogged to the house. As I reached the door, I could hear a woman leaving a message on the machine.... "a call," was all I heard. I hurried to the phone. Too late. I played back the message.

"Hi, Dennis. It's Fran. Give me a call."

Fran is my mom's sister and executor of Jonathan's will. She didn't leave her phone number, so I got out my address book, found it and dialed.

"Hello," she said.

"Hi, Fran. I just missed your call."

"Hi, Dennis. I have news for you. The money Jonathan left you is going to be deposited into your account. I also have the keys to the house, so you can pick them up at your leisure."

"Thanks, Fran. Is everything else all wrapped up?"

"Yes, your keys are my last official act and I can't tell you how happy I am that it's over. It was a lot more work than I thought it would be. By the way, how is Bryan doing? I haven't seen him for a while."

"He's doing great. I will bring him with me when I pick up the keys. Should I come by tomorrow?"

"Perfect. What time might you come?"

"I'm thinking around 2:30. I'll pick him up from school and drive over from there."

"Sounds good. See you then."

"Thanks, Fran, see you," I said, feeling some shock. This had never felt real to me and I walked back out the door to the pool. Liz saw me and could tell that something was different.

"Dennis?" she said, a little alarmed.

"That was Francis, my mom's sister. She said I could pick up the keys to my uncle's house."

"That's a pretty serious asset and some prime land," George said.

"Yeah, I know," I said, feeling dazed.

"I wonder what the assessed value of it is?" George said.

"I'm not sure," I said.

"I think your uncle liked you more than you thought," Liz speculated.

"I'm not sure about that either, but it seems so. I wish I had a chance to talk to him again, though. This inheritance has left me with a lot of questions."

Bryan jumped into the water splashing George.

"Hey, you rascal," George said reaching for Bryan only to see him swim underwater back to the stairs.

"You're a fish," Liz said laughing.

Bryan smiled and splashed George again.

"You come here. I'll get you," George said, pretending to miss Bry, and falling into the water.

Bryan thought that he made George miss, and shrieked with delight.

"I'm happy for you, Dennis," Liz said, watching the pool fun.

"I'm weirded out," I said. "I really don't get it."

We turned our attention back to the pool. I watched Liz, watch George and Bryan, and could see such love in her eyes for them. I suddenly felt lonely even though I was surrounded by people who I loved and who loved me. Again, I returned to the persistent thought that something was missing in my life, but it wasn't the kind of thing that could be filled by just anyone. Of course, my mind drifted back in its predictable direction, and I knew who my thoughts revolved around. I wondered what happened to Shannon. My mind drifted into a darkness that moved like a fog to cover the sun and brought that chill of depression. I heard Bryan laugh, and it broke the dark spell that had just enveloped me. I shook free of my head and came back. I put on a smile and watched George and Bryan play. Liz watched me but didn't say anything. She seemed to have a sixth sense about what was going on in my mind.

We said our goodbyes and I slung Bryan over my shoulder, potato sack style. I carried him into the house and plopped him in front of the TV, while I started planning everything for his first day of school. "Time to get back into the routine," I thought aloud.

We enjoyed dinner and some TV together. I laid out his clothes, bathed him, put him in his pajamas and carried him to bed. The PJ's had animals on them and I told Bryan that the animals were making too much noise. He giggled as I poked each animal telling them to be quiet while tickling him a bit and making him squirm. Then I said the magic words to keep all those silly animals quiet. We said prayers and I tucked his blankets around him.

"Night, night, my sweet boy. I love you, you know."

Bryan smiled and then lifted his blanket shushing the animals on his PJs, wanting to keep the game going.

"You need a good night's sleep. You have school tomorrow," I said, tucking him back in and kissing his head. Bryan knows full well that school starts tomorrow, of course, because I've been talking about it all day. I saw him relax, hug Pooh, and I kissed him again and went to bed.

16

Sideways Chapter 13

My alarm rang. I didn't sleep well fearing that I would oversleep for Bryan's first day of school. Silly.

I thought about Fran's call, hopped from bed and to the coffee pot. I jumped into the shower, shaved and got ready for my day. I briefly thought about Shannon, gone, M.I.A. and I'd come to the conclusion that I'd never see her again.

I could feel the dark cloud of depression drift over me, dimming the light, and it felt like I had missed my last chance to be with someone. It felt final.

I wasn't going to dwell on that, not today. I needed to get Bryan up, and I wanted him to have a happy day. I walked into his room and he was already awake.

"Good morning sweetie boy. You're awake."

"Ahh," he said.

"Are you ready for your first day of school? Miss Kathy is going to be very happy to see you."

"Ahh. Tim too," he signed and said.

"And Tim too," I repeated. Tim's one of his aides. "Do you need five more minutes?" I asked because I wasn't ready to get him up yet.

"No," he clearly said.

"Okey-doke. You go to the bathroom and I'll get your breakfast started."

"Pooh?" Bry said, holding up his bear.

"Okay. I'll take Pooh and get him his breakfast while you're in the bathroom."

I carried Pooh in and set him where Bryan would eat, then I walked to the kitchen and poured some coffee. Bryan ambled in and I heard the TV change to PBS. Elmo's high-pitched voice rang out "Elmo's World." I brought out his breakfast and went back to the kitchen to finish packing his lunch.

Bryan started giggling as the Count counted batty bats. I peeked in to see if he had finished eating, but he sat holding a piece of toast, mesmerized by the Count. I finished his lunch and looked back in on him.

"Are you all done with breakfast?" I asked.

"Ahh," he said.

"Good. Let's handsome you up, then."

I picked him up and took him to the bathroom to brush his teeth, comb his hair, and dress him for school. He decided to pick today to fight me, and struggled, trying desperately to stop me from brushing his teeth.

"Bryan, sometimes it isn't fun to be beautiful, I know, but you must endure it and it takes work."

He didn't have any idea what I was talking about, so he continued to thrash.

"There. All done. You are beautiful," I said, finally finishing with him.

He looked in the mirror, turned his head slightly to the side as if inspecting my job and smiled with approval.

I just laughed. "Okay, buddy boy, we're out of here."

We drove the short distance to his school on a beautiful late summer morning. It was warm and the shadows of the trees were starting to lengthen as fall approached. The traffic was heavy with all the parents taking their kids to school for the first day. I saw a car pull out of a good parking place and I pulled in. I got Bry from the car, set him on the sidewalk, took his hand and led him to the classroom. The door was open, and I could see Miss Kathy smiling at another parent. She is a very special teacher. I wished that Bryan could have her for the rest of his time in school.

"Hey, Miss Kathy," I said.

"Hi, Dennis. Hi, Bryan. Welcome to the first day of school," she said enthusiastically.

"We are glad to be here. How was the rest of your summer?" I asked.

"It was fun, but I'm glad to be back to school with my kids," she said. It sounded like a cliché, but she meant it.

"The kids are happy to be back with you, too, I'm sure," I said and I meant it.

Bryan had wandered away from me, already, and over to see what Mr. Tim, the aide was up to. I said hi to Tim and asked Bryan for a good-bye hug. He waddled back to me and I got down on one knee.

"Have a great day at school. I'll see you when you get home." I signed I love you to him and he signed it back.

I stood up saying goodbye to Miss Kathy and the aides and started from the room.

Miss Kathy called, "Do you have swimming lessons today?"

"No," I said a little dejectedly. "Put him on the bus."

She nodded.

I walked to the car thinking. I had dressed for the gym, but I wasn't sure that I wanted to go. I started the car and still didn't know where I was driving to, but I ended up heading to the health club. Maybe I would ask the club manager about Shannon.

I pulled into the parking lot and saw Jay's car. I parked, hopped out, and walked in the front door. As I looked at the coffee pot, I stopped frozen, with my mouth agape. Before I could think, a word escaped my lips and it was a lot louder than I expected.

"Shannon?!" I blurted out.

She had stepped out from the manager's office behind the desk and she looked up startled.

Two older ladies stopped what they were doing and stared my way.

Oops, I thought, feeling stupid.

Shannon smiled broadly at me and said warmly, "Hi, Dennis."

"When did you get back?"

"I got back yesterday," she responded, and I saw a shadow cross her face.

"Oh. Is everything alright?"

"Well, my grandmother passed away when I was in Arizona. That's why I was gone so long."

"Oh, I'm sorry to hear that. It's hard to lose someone close."

"Yeah, it was unexpected," she said and I could see her fight back the emotion.

"No offense, but you do look a little tired," I said.

"Charmer."

"Sorry about that."

"It's okay. I'm sure you're right," she said. "Got to go, I have an early lesson, today."

"Oh… Okay," I said.

"Have a good workout," she said, turning and I felt dismissed.

I walked into the weight room thinking, that didn't go very well. I was so happy to see her, and the best I could do was tell her how tired she looked? Damn... That's smooooth, Dennis...

Jason and Len were standing by the drinking fountain arguing politics as usual.

I said, "Good morning. Have you guys solved the world's problems yet, or are you still working on the United States'?"

They both looked my way and nodded hello but went back to arguing.

"Okay, I'm going to get some exercise while you two exercise your vocal cords."

They both looked back at me but went right back to the argument.

I laughed.

We worked out separately for an hour, and then I saw Shannon walk from the pool area. She was dressed and walked to the coffee pot. I could see that she was carrying a book.

"Excuse me, guys," I said.

Len and Jason restarted the unwinnable debate.

I walked towards the coffee.

"Are you enjoying that book?" I asked.

Shannon looked up and smiled. "Yeah. It's a lot of fun and I'm almost finished."

"You do read a lot," I commented remembering how many books she seemed to go through, and also subtly saying, remember me, we were becoming close.

"I do. I usually get through each pretty fast, but it depends on the book. Short books I can read in a couple of days. I get started and I can't stop. It's like an obsession."

I nodded. "Are you done with work for the day?"

"Yeah, but I need a better cup of coffee," she said, glancing down into her cup with an unsatisfied look on her face. "I think I'll run down to that coffee shop around the corner."

"I was just thinking that a mocha sounded good. Would you like some company?" I asked with the feeling that I was going for broke and hoping that I wasn't bothering her.

She nodded but I couldn't tell if she was happy or not that I was joining her. I quickly picked up the conversation.

"Have you found any new authors lately?" I asked as we walked out the door.

"No, but I'm always on the look-out for someone."

"Let's take my car," I suggested.

Shannon nodded and we walked to my Civic. I opened her door and closed her in and then I got in my side. Driving to the shop, she was quiet.

I asked, "Are we going to start swimming lessons again pretty soon? I don't want to rush you. I was just wondering."

"Yeah, Den, let's do Wednesday."

"That sounds great. I'll tell Bryan. He'll be happy."

We pulled into the parking lot and got out of the car. As we walked in the door, the smell of the coffee shop flooded my nose making me want pastry. There was no line and we walked up to the counter.

"Hi, Lenny. How are you?" I asked.

"Fine, Mister Den. What can I get you?"

"Shannon, what looks good to you?" I asked.

"I'll have a medium coffee," she said.

"Room for cream?"

"No thanks."

"Do you want something to eat, Shannon? I'm buying," I asked.

"Not today, thanks."

"I'll have a nonfat mocha, Lenny," I said.

We stood in silence for a minute, waiting, and then took our coffees to a small table in the corner. The table had newspaper spread out on it, so I carried it back to the rack, and then sat down across from her.

"It sounds like Arizona was a pretty tough trip," I said, hoping that she would open up to me.

"Yeah. Grandma wasn't doing very well, but I sure didn't expect her to pass away."

"I lost my father about five years ago, and it hurt much deeper than I could ever have imagined," I said. "So, were you and your grandma close?"

Shannon nodded staring into her coffee, "She sort of raised me. My father hiked when I was six. Mom and I moved in with Grandma. We lived there until I was almost finished with high school."

"Do you ever see your dad?"

"No, he left not looking back. I think it's better when someone like him just leaves. He would have been nothing but trouble."

I left that subject not wanting to pry. "Your Grandma sounds like she was pretty special," I said.

Shannon teared up and embarrassed, apologized. She contained it, blotted an eye with a napkin and finished.

"We really had fun together. My mom worked and Grandma was always there when I got home from school. We would play and laugh. Those were great days."

"You were lucky, being a single parent myself, I'm constantly reminded of how much I need Bryan's grandparents. They sound a lot like your grandma."

We sat quietly for a minute or two and I broke the silence. "You told me you like Stephen King?" I said, wanting to lighten the mood with Stephen King? Ha. "I just read *"Dreamcatcher"* and really liked it. Did you ever read it?"

"I did read it, and maybe ten more of his books," Shannon replied.

"I know they made a movie of *"Dreamcatcher,"* so I want to see it," I said.

"I'm usually disappointed by movies made from the books I like," Shannon said.

"Me too, but there are exceptions. I loved both the book and the movie, *"The Green Mile."* That was a great story. I think I liked the movies made from the *"Lord of the Rings"* trilogy better than I like the books."

"I loved the *"Lord of the Rings"* movies, but I didn't read the books. That was high adventure," she said.

"Yeah, great stories. I also listen to audiobooks. I'm usually listening to one book and reading another," I said.

"I have never tried audiobooks."

"Well, they're great if you have a project. I disappear into the book while I work. When I've finished, I have spent the time getting something done and enjoying a book. It's great."

"That does sound like fun," she said.

"I seem to like most popular fiction," I said. "I don't think I'm all that discerning. As long as I can believe that the main characters are real, then the story seems real, and I'm along for the ride."

Shannon smiled and agreed, then said, "I like romance, especially if it has a supernatural twist, but, like you, if I get into the characters, I generally enjoy the book. I don't ever put a book down and not pick it back up, although, sometimes I wish I had."

"That's probably why we like the same authors. I have a definite bias towards romance. It makes the characters seem more real. Sci-fi and supernatural, when they are blended with romance, are my favorites," I finished.

Shannon smiled and nodded.

We finished our coffees, and got up from the table, tossing our trash, and headed to my car. Driving back, we rode quietly until I parked.

"Shannon, I'm really glad you're back. I wasn't sure I would ever see you again."

She smiled and said, "Thanks for the coffee, Den. Maybe we can do it again."

"I would like that."

We got out of the car and I walked into the club. Shannon drove off, and I went back into the weight room. It was nice to see Shannon, but the conversation was a bit strained. It felt like getting to know her again.

Len was gone but Jason was still working out.

"Hey, lover boy," Jason said, never missing an opportunity to give me a bad time.

"Jay," I said shortly.

"You disappeared," he said.

"Like magic," I said, walking back to the weight rack.

"Well, Dennis, stick a fork in me, I'm done," he said, grabbing his sweatshirt.

"So soon?"

"I was working out, remember, not chasing Shannon."

"Got me," I admitted.

"It's nice to see the world is back in order," he said. "I'll catch you later."

"You take it easy, Jason."

"You have good taste," he said walking from the weight room.

I watched him leave and stop by the front desk. He chatted with Sara, the new girl, for a couple of minutes, then left.

Time to run, I thought, finishing my last sets. I walked back to the racquetball courts. Sammy was warming up. I peeked into the court and said, "Are you ready to lose some of that table weight?"

"Yeah. Let's play," he said and we played for about an hour. Walking off the court, I told him about the house that old Uncle Jonny left me.

"I would love to see it," he said.

"I'm going out there today after I get the keys. It will be interesting. Maybe you could run out there with me, sometime."

"Sounds good," Sam said. "You and your uncle must have been close."

"Not really, Sam. I'm frankly mystified and that's only part of it."

"Well, let me know how the place is. See you later," he said.

"See you tomorrow," I said.

Sam walked out and I followed after drinking some water from the drinking fountain. Walking by the desk I saw Sara staring off into space.

"See ya," I said.

She smiled and I walked out the door, and to my oven of a car. I had forgotten to crack the windows. Driving home, I felt like I won the lottery. I really never expected to see Shannon again. It's too bad about her grandma. My mind bounced like a pinball from subject to subject as I thought about the house and the keys that I was going to pick up, today at Fran's. I'll have some time to rest and shower before I need to pick up Bryan.

17

Sideways Chapter 14

I arrived at Bryan's school ten minutes early and sat in the car waiting for the bell to ring. As I sat, sweat began to roll down my forehead. The car was hot.

I was about to get out when a short spot came on the radio called StarDate. It's usually interesting because it has astronomical news like comets coming close to earth, meteor showers and other things that happen in the sky of interest. Today's show was about a huge explosion on the sun, a coronal mass ejection. It seemed that the sun had been misbehaving lately, throwing plumes of particles towards the earth. As I listened, I thought about Jonathan's warning.

The bell rang as the program ended, and I could see Bryan and his class walk out of the room. He had a happy look on his face and I knew he had a good day. After a quick chat with his teacher, I picked him up and walked to the car.

"Let's get this car cooled off, buddy boy," I said as I put him in his seat. I cranked up the AC, rolled down the windows, backed up, and drove out of the bustling parking lot.

We drove the short distance to Fran's house. She lived alone after losing her husband a few years back in a modest house, very neat, with a small lawn and flowers around a covered porch.

"Let's go see Aunt Francis," I said lifting Bryan from his seat. He was sweating and so was I. The car had never cooled. We knocked on the door and Fran answered.

"Hi, Dennis," she said. "Come in."

I smiled. "Hi, Aunt Francis," I said, having always called her that. I hugged her and so did Bryan.

"How are you, Bryan?"

Bryan signed, "Fine," by putting a five hand on his chest.

Fran looked at me for the interpretation.

"That means fine," I said smiling.

"Well, I'm happy to hear it," she said. "Can I get you something to drink? I have iced tea or soda."

"Iced tea sounds good to me. It's an oven out there. Bryan can have a small amount of soda."

"I'm happy to see you. It's been a while," Francis said, bringing in our drinks.

"Thanks," I said, taking mine. "It has been a while. I know my mom has probably told you how I feel about this inheritance," I said changing the subject. "I'm frankly shocked."

"I know you didn't know Jonathan that well, but he was really a good guy. I don't know all his reasoning but he was always very decisive about the things he wanted to do. He gave you exactly what he wanted to, and I'm not one to question him."

"What do you think about the letter?" I asked, hoping for some insight.

"That's a different story. I'm really stumped. I've spent some time in the house and I haven't noticed anything weird."

"I thought I would go out there today to have a quick look around," I said. "Do you think Jonathan may have been having some mental problems?"

"I don't know. I saw him a couple of months before his death and he seemed fine. I could find out when he gave the lawyer the letter if you want me to, but I'm not sure that it would help."

"No, I was just wondering. Maybe something happened to his mind, like a stroke or something," I said.

"I don't know. There is one odd thing in the house, though. There is a strange burnt mark on the wall, and it stretches up to the ceiling. The dining room light is missing also. No clue about what happened there."

"Okay. I'll check it out."

"Here are your keys. Give me a call if you have any questions and let me know if anything out of the ordinary happens. I've been alive a long time and I've never seen anything supernatural. I'm sure there's an explanation for whatever Jonny was talking about."

"My mom said the same thing," I said.

We finished our refreshments and walked out thanking Fran.

She smiled, "See you, Dennis, and congratulations. It's some beautiful land and a pretty nice house, too."

I smiled and waved as I carried Bryan to the car, and we were off to see the house.

I drove the twenty-five minutes from Fran's house towards Jonathan's. As we exited the freeway, we wound up a tree filled, winding road that was just wide enough to let two cars pass. It reminded me of driving to a lake in the country, rural and quiet. The trees that lined the road were tall and filled the hillside that climbed to the left.

As we approached the house, I could see that a rock fence lined the property, separating it from the road. There was a break in the fence, and I slowly drove through it and onto a narrow flagstone driveway that led to the house. The driveway branched off leading to the garage and also to the front door. The space between the rock fence and the front of the house was only about fifteen feet, and most of the ground there was also flagstone with dirt outlining the stones. It looked like he meant to plant something there but never got around to it.

The house itself was modest with light brown exterior paint covering stucco and dark brown trim. To the left of the house, there was a tree covered hill that was at least three times the height of the house and I could also see the tops of trees in the rear over the roof, and to the other side.

"Pretty nice house, huh, buddy boy," I said, as I pulled up and parked. I'm not sure of the dimensions of the land, but the house is all by itself, and I couldn't see another neighbor. As I got out of the car, all I could hear were birds.

I lifted Bryan from his seat, setting him down to walk with me. I approached the house warily because of the letter but didn't feel anything sinister. We stepped up the two steps that led to the front door and stood under a small covered porch. There were a couple of flower boxes under the window with dead plants from neglect.

I fit the key into the lock and opened the door slowly, still a little spooked from the letter that old Uncle Jonny left me. I peeked first to the right and then to the left. In front of me, straight ahead, there was a very large stone fireplace, the kind you would see in a lodge. It seemed too big for the front room, but it was still pretty cool. To the right, there was most of the front room, and a hallway that I'm sure led to the three bedrooms. As I stuck my head further in, the house was hot, and I could smell an acrid odor like burnt wiring. With all the windows and shades closed, the house was dim and musty. I glanced back to the left and saw the dining room and kitchen. Over the dining room table, I could see a prominent burnt mark that stretched from halfway up the wall, almost to the small hole in the ceiling, where the light had been. I wanted to open the place up, and let in some air, but didn't plan to stay long.

"Let's have a look around, Bryan," I said, leading him in by the hand.

We walked right and into the hallway. As we entered, the bathroom was to the right, and to the left was a bedroom with a large bookcase on the right wall.

It was strangely ajar, leaving a gap between it and the wall. There was also a twin bed, with no bedding under a window. The mattress looked new. Down the short hall, there were two more bedrooms, one of which had a similar bookcase.

As I walked into the bedroom with the bed, I took a closer look at the bookcase. When I put a hand on it, the case gave way and moved from the wall startling me. It seemed to be on a hinge. I swung it out and saw some kind of small, private room.

"What the hell?" I said.

"Aah," Bryan said, surprising me and making me laugh because he had no idea why he agreed.

The small, hidden room was about five or six feet by ten feet and between the two bedrooms. He must have used the closets and knocked down the wall between. There was a small fold-down table with a large bundle of wires coming from a hole in the same wall. I thought this must be a panic room.

Wild! Uncle Jonny may have been a bit paranoid.

I could see how the bookcase would bolt from the inside and there was also a bolt on the other wall that led to a bookcase in the other bedroom. Jonathan could probably hold out here for a while if he needed to and had some means to communicate out. I looked more closely at the wires and I could see a phone line, a cable television line, and what looked like camera wires. There were some shelving and a door that led under the house. I hoped that it didn't lead to a dungeon. I opened the door and looked to find that it just led to the dirt crawl space underneath. That's good. I was afraid I might find some skeletons down there.

I glanced at Bryan who was getting bored. "Let's go check out the kitchen," I said, leading him by the hand, back out and into the front room. We walked up to the burnt mark in the dining room. "I think I may need to get an electrician out here."

We went into the kitchen and I looked at the appliances. They appeared to be fairly new, and then we walked into the garage from a door that was on the wall between the dining room and the kitchen. It was a one car garage and looked nearly empty with the exception of some paint cans, a nice ladder and a smattering of other things, including a short length of rope. There wasn't a washer or dryer there, though, and if I moved in, I would need to get those.

"Let's go, Babe," I said, and we walked back into the house, locking the garage door and then into the front room. I stood and gazed around, imagining the living room with furniture, and then I took Bryan's hand and we walked outside locking the front door.

I wanted to have a look at the back, so we walked around the house to the right. When we got there, I was amazed. There was a large flagstone patio with a barbeque, shaded by a majestic oak tree. Weeds were starting to push through the flags and I could tell that it wouldn't be long before the yard was completely overgrown. The rest of the property was untouched and natural. On the left, there was the hill, but directly behind the house, the land looked flat, and it backed up to a forest with a stream running through and emptying into a pond on the right side of the house. "Man, this is just beautiful. It's a dream come true. If it's haunted, I'm fightin' the ghosts for it," I thought aloud laughing to myself. "I guess I'm going to need a compass... Nah," I laughed again.

Bryan was looking at me blankly trying to make sense of my disjointed sentences.

"Alright, dude, we're out of here," I said, picking him up.

He was by now sick of being drug around. We walked around the house and to the car. I buckled him in and we were soon driving down the winding road towards the highway.

With a Kid's Songs CD playing, we happily got on the highway and headed to our home.

As I pulled in, I could see George by the pool, spatula in hand.

"Hi, George," I said, putting Bryan on the ground next to me.

"Dennis, where you been?"

"Bryan and I just ran out to Uncle Jonny's house."

George stopped what he was doing and looked up.

"Oh," he said softly. "How was it out there?"

"It was beautiful, George. I think the property is just beautiful. The only thing wrong, that I could see, was a burnt mark on the dining room wall. Everything else looks perfect."

Liz walked out hearing part of the conversation. George gave her a funny look that I caught but didn't understand.

"Hi, Dennis, hi, Bryan. You went to the house?" she asked.

"Yeah. Bryan and I went to Fran's and picked up the keys, and then we took a drive to see the place."

"Well?" she asked.

"Well, it's just the house of my dreams. That's the only way I can describe it," I said and I could see a shadow cross Liz's face.

"I'm happy for you, Dennis," she said but there was something hiding in her eyes. She did her best to try to conceal it, but it was there.

"What's wrong, Liz?" I asked, not quite understanding.

Liz looked at George and then back at me. I saw the same look from George that I saw earlier.

"Nothing, Dennis. I'm happy for you."

Then it made sense. Understanding dawned on me and I said, "Oh... Um... I really didn't think..." I stopped. "Moving, I mean."

Liz tried to hide her feelings.

"You don't want me to move?"

"Dennis, this isn't fair to you, but no," Liz said.

"Liz, I love you guys and I don't really want to move. I guess I didn't put the two things together yet. As usual, you are both way ahead of me. I couldn't be happier here. I wasn't planning to move out there anytime soon, but it really is a pretty piece of land."

Liz and George looked somewhat relieved, but not convinced.

George said, "We are behind you, whatever you decide."

"Thank you. I know that I may not be able to make you feel much better, but I really don't have any plans to leave here anytime soon."

"I picked up four New York steaks," George said. "I was hoping you would make some of your Béarnaise sauce and we could all clog an artery together, tonight."

"I don't know how you could ever think that I could leave your cooking, George," I said smiling.

Liz laughed, "I'll get the wine."

Bryan and I went into the house and I made the sauce.

We came back out with a bowl full of pure arterial sclerosis. "I've got the vein clogger," I said, walking towards the barbeque.

"I've got the liver killer," Liz said, holding up a Cab. "But, it's full of antioxidants and while our livers and hearts die we won't get cancer," she added.

I smiled now understanding that we had all become a family. We sat, enjoying the meal, drinking the wine and talking about the property without any unspoken fears plaguing us.

Bryan and I said good night, after helping clean up. I thanked them for the great dinner and we left to get ready for bed. We walked into our home and turned on the TV. Bryan wanted a little computer time and I caught a rerun of my current favorite sitcom, The Big Bang Theory. At 8:00, I got Bryan's clothes ready for school...

18

Cliff Evans stopped writing with Dennis and Bryan getting ready for bed. Something had happened. Interference seemed to jumble the story and his mind. He couldn't even recall some of the story that he had already written. He recognized that this was different from when he had lost the story before. This was a disruption. Chaos. Like a tornado in a trailer park, leaving nothing but destruction in its wake.

I need to stand up, he thought. His mind was disoriented and he felt dizzy. He walked from the computer and didn't understand why, when the story had been coming so easy, now it was nowhere to be found.

He sat on the couch and stared, disconcerted, and began wondering about the very nature of this inspiration. Where did this come from? He thought back to the night when he was driving to work and the visions flooded his mind, then glanced at the clock. It was 8:30 pm. He grabbed the remote and turned on the TV. A news story was just ending explaining how a star exploded in our galaxy which should be visible to the south for most people, and how we may from time to time, have some trouble with our electronics.

In the past, there had been supernovae visible from earth. Cliff peeked outside to see if he could catch a glimpse of it, but his field of vision from the window was small and he couldn't see anything, so he dressed for work, and then lay on the couch to grab a nap before his grueling night. He set his cell phone alarm for 10:30 and drifted.

The alarm woke him, and he dragged himself into the bathroom and shaved, brushed his teeth and left. Tonight, he had to go in an hour early to cover the 11:00 to 12:00 check stand, and he thought about the work that he needed to finish from the night before. Walking from his apartment, he turned the corner and looked into the clear night sky to see a small, odd smudge low on the horizon. That may be the supernova that the news was talking about, he thought to himself.

He arrived at work and as he walked in, could see the night crew spotting their load. He waved at Greg, working in the first aisle. Cliff clocked in, then walked to his check stand. It was slow and they didn't need him up front. There was only a smattering of customers in the store, so he walked his department to see how it had held up.

At 11:15, all the lights went out throwing the store into complete darkness. The emergency lights came on in the back aisle and in the front lobby, barely lighting the store. It was too dark to shop, so most of the customers were ushered to the check stands with what they had in their carts. Some employees helped other customers find items to finish their lists and by 11:45 the last customer had left the store.

Cliff walked into the backroom looking for a tow motor to drive out his back stock. Unfortunately, no one had plugged in the motors and the batteries were dead, so he had to use an un-motorized hand-jack to drag out his pallets.

He pulled a pallet by isle one and saw Greg holding a flashlight looking for a tag to a new item. Greg looked up and saw Cliff.

"I wish I wore my miner's hat," Greg said, holding the package and trying to find its place on the shelf.

"They really need to equip us with those," Cliff laughed.

"Especially lately. It seems like the power is always going off," Greg said.

"I'm sure it will give the utilities a reason to hike our rates."

"Yeah man. So, Cliffy, what's up with the book?"

"Well, it was going pretty good until today. I was working on it and finished about a hundred pages and-"

"A hundred pages!" Greg interrupted, shocked. "I didn't think you even had a hundred words in your vocabulary."

"Funny, dumb ass. I didn't say it was rocket science. Anyway, all of a sudden, I lost everything. I could barely remember the direction of the story. I needed to stop, and I'm not sure if even one more word will come out of me. I think I'm going to give up."

"That's pretty weird Cliff. So, what's the story about?"

"It's about a guy raising a special needs child. He's raising the kid alone because his wife died in a car accident. He falls for this girl whose teaching his son to swim. It's kind of them getting together, kind of him raising the kid alone, but it's also about this weird house that his uncle left him after he died. Strange things happen in the house and in my mind, there are these shadows of something that is going to happen, but I haven't quite figured everything out yet, at least not completely. I mean I saw something in my imagination but I don't fully understand it. The girl has an encounter with something while she's getting out of the shower in the strange house, and I almost want to warn my characters not to go there."

Greg stopped his work and looked at Cliff with the blank stare of someone who had just glimpsed madness.

"What?" Cliff said.

"Did you fall on your head?" Greg asked.

"No... Or I don't remember falling on it," Cliff said laughing. "Honestly, Greg, since this whole book idea started, my brain doesn't seem to be working quite right. I have the story then I forget parts and then remember them again or have what I think are new ideas that I've written before. Sometimes the ideas seem like imagination, but other times they seem like visions. It's so odd."

Rich, overhearing said, "I don't remember saying it was break time."

"Got to strap back on my miner's hat, Cliff."

"See ya," Cliff said and got to work.

By 5:30 am, the lights still hadn't come back on. The pallets were being pulled from the floor, and the cleaning crew started to sweep and mop the floors. Some of the night crew were writing orders for the next night, and the rest were pulling baskets full of cardboard to the back to be baled. With no power, the baler didn't work, and the cardboard was stacking up. The backroom receiving clerk was upset with the mess. If the power didn't come back on, they couldn't open the store until it was restored.

At 5:50 the power came back on. It blinked, and the sound of freezers starting back up could be heard. The power failed again for a couple of minutes and then came back on. At 6:00 the store was opened and an inordinate number of customers streamed in. Cliff was facing the items that he didn't fill and was surprised to see a crowd around him. Usually, at this time of the morning, there weren't more than six or seven people in the entire store. But this morning, there were quite a few people in each aisle and the front was already calling for back up checkers.

Greg walked by. "What's up with all these people? Did a bus stop here?"

"I don't know but I better get ready to jump in the check stand," Cliff said.

"See you tonight," Greg said as he headed to the time clock.

Cliff could overhear people talking about the supernova with some worry, and gazing into their baskets, he could see unusual items, flashlights, batteries, water, and food that doesn't spoil easily. My stuff spoils, so maybe my shelves won't be wiped out, he thought knowing full well that he didn't order for a panic.

This did have that kind of feel, like a panic. There was this paranoia radiating from these early customers and he wondered how well placed it might be. While they were probably overreacting, the fact of the matter was, that if the power went out for extended periods of time, it would cause a great deal of problems.

Throughout the rest of the morning, people continued to shop much heavier than normal and in greater numbers. It felt like holiday volume, but the holiday wasn't a celebration. He finished his shift in the check stand, not able to get out to work his department.

On the drive home, he wondered about his book. There was disappointment creeping into his mind. He didn't want to give up. Hopefully, the story would return.

He got home, skipped breakfast and pulled off his clothes, laying down in bed and sleeping for ten straight hours, completely exhausted.

19

Stephen Fremont continued to type frantically with the story flowing like a river on steroids. Suddenly he felt an overwhelming need to sleep. The story scrambled in his mind and became incomprehensible. He stopped and looked at the screen to see what he had written and his eyes blurred, giving him double vision. His eyelids drooped, and he laid his head down by his keyboard.

He woke an hour later with his page full of random letters, and his temple sporting a dent from lying on his mouse. He raised his hand and rubbed at the dent in his skin.

"Man, I've never fallen asleep at the keyboard before."

He erased the random letters that he had inadvertently put on the page, and then he tried to pick up the story where it had left off. He thought back to when he had become so tired and could see the pictures of his story playing in his head and then suddenly exploding like a water balloon, gone.

He pushed back from his computer and walked into the family room, close to his study.

"Hi, Stephen. You look tired."

"I just took a little nap," he said.

Mary gave him a quizzical look and went back to watching a news report about a supernova that just appeared in the sky. Again, the news reporter stressed that the power grid and electronics might be affected. Stephen watched the report with Mary and remembered that when he had the original idea for the story, the earth was going through severe solar storms.

"I need to go. I have an idea," he said, walking quickly from the room.

Mary stared at him and watched him leave, thinking that he was acting odd, again.

Stephen's reality blended with the *"Sideways"* book. He saw his characters struggling with the effects of the supernova, and its possible effect on Jonathan's house. Sun storms already seemed to be behind the phenomena. He paused... It doesn't just fit, he thought, it belongs.

He sat down at his computer again and tried to picture the events taking place. As he began writing, the pace was lumbering and the ideas murky. He stood up and walked to the window and for the first time in his life, saw an aurora, pale in the sky, undulating mildly with shades of blue and green. The pictures of the story in his mind were unclear. He sat back down at the computer, and when he would type, he would quickly delete what he had just written. He could see the picture of Dennis and Bryan in his mind and some reaction to the supernova, but he couldn't seem to build the story. He would write and delete and start again only to delete again. Frustrated, he got up and went to bed.

As he slept, he dreamed, but the dreams didn't make sense. They were always about Dennis and Bryan and the supernova, but like most dreams, they were mostly nonsense. This continued for three days and three nights. At night, nonsense and frustrating dreams and during the day, write-delete, write-delete.

On the third day, he sat staring at his computer screen. "This is grinding," he thought aloud. Since the supernova, his mind seemed to be as disrupted as the electrical grid, and not just his writing, but also his thought processes. He began to suspect that it had something to do with the supernova, but how? It just didn't make sense.

Baffled, he pushed back from the computer and walked into the kitchen where Mary was cleaning up after lunch.

She smiled. "Hi, Stephen," she said, watching him aimlessly enter the room. "Do you need something?"

"No," he trailed off. "Mary, have you noticed feeling different since the supernova happened?"

"No, I feel fine. Why?"

"Hmmm... Well, this may be a coincidence, but I haven't been able to get much down on my book since it happened. I write a page and then delete it. I'm not happy with the way anything is coming out. I've lost the insight that I had. I just can't see the book anymore. I don't get it... This whole book has been... different."

"Stephen, I have never seen you so... what's the word I'm looking for... obsessed maybe, with anything before. Maybe you're just tired or a little burnt out."

"You may be right, but..." Stephen said, trailing off, slipping into his mind.

"Have you written anything in the last three days?" she asked interrupting his thoughts.

"Yes, but I haven't been satisfied with what I've written, and I've rewritten it numerous times. I seem to be in a fog, it clears but then fogs back up and the images just fade."

"I think you need to relax. Come and take a walk with me. You haven't left the room for a couple of days."

"Good idea," he said, even though he wanted to say no.

"Okay, let's go."

They walked together on a dirt road by their house, under the trees and Stephen took Mary's hand. She looked at him knowing how much he loved her. He looked back smiling and then forward lost in thought, considering the very odd nature of the images that he was receiving for this story. Something was bothering him around this book, but he couldn't put his finger on the problem.

Finishing their walk, Stephen and Mary returned home. Stephen had a moment of clarity about the story. "I think I'm going to try to write a bit," he said.

Mary smiled and hoped for the best, understanding that there was something different about the inspiration for this story.

Stephen sat at his computer and the story slowly began to appear...

20

Sideways Chapter 14 continued

… "It's bath time, sweetie boy," I warned, to give Bryan a head start at stopping his computer game. I cleaned the tub and ran the water adding bubbles and some floating toys for fun. As the bath filled, I could hear a special news report break into the TV program that I was watching.

I walked into the front room to hear the announcer, "You may have seen something unusual in the night sky. No, it's not a UFO," he joked. "A supernova has appeared in the southern sky and its appearance means that the earth is being bombarded by particles from the star. Even though the star is part of our Milky Way Galaxy, scientists say we have nothing to fear. Our magnetic field is protecting us from harm. You may also have noticed that a faint aurora is also showing up to the south, where the star is now visible."

A new voice came on and said, "We are now returning you to your regularly scheduled programming."

With Bryan on the computer, I stepped outside and looked south. I could see the aurora tracing the night sky from a point near a small white smudge low on the horizon. The smudge was brighter than any star, but not as bright as the moon.

I walked back in with one last look at the northern lights now showing from the south. They undulated mildly with blue and green being the main colors and the sight was so unusual that I couldn't help but enjoy the view.

As I entered the room I sang, "Sack of potatoes, sack of potatoes, you are my sack of potatoes," and I picked Bry up and slung him over my shoulders continuing to sing.

He giggled and I delivered him to the bathroom.

"Time to take care of business, buddy boy," I said, hauling him in front of the sink. I brushed his teeth and then plopped him into the bubble bath. "Oops, I forgot your jammies. Be back in a flash," I said, walking from the bathroom, leaving the door open.

The news broke back in with another special report explaining about the electrical grid and electronics, and also reporting that there were some power failures going on probably related to the supernova, and the large sun storms we were experiencing. I grabbed the PJs and went back to wash up Bryan, not able to hear the full story.

I washed and dried him and then got him in his PJs. "It's bedtime, sweetie boy," I said, carrying him to his room. We read a story and I gave him sweet dream magic and a kiss good night.

I left him with his stuffed animal friends and locked up, turning off all the lights in the front of the house. I went into the bathroom and the lights dimmed way down. It was eerie because I had never seen the lights go so dim without going out.

"What the hell?" I said, walking out of the bathroom.

Bryan could tell that something wasn't right about the lights, and I guess my response to it. He followed me into my room and the lights dimmed again.

"Lights Papa?" he signed and said with some dismay.

"It's okay, sweetie boy. Don't be afraid," I said, trying to reassure him.

"No like," he signed and said.

"Do you want to come in bed with me?"

"Aah," meaning yes. "Pooh, too."

"Okay. Go get Pooh."

"Kitty, too," he said.

"Okay, but that's all," I said, not wanting to share the bed with too many stuffed animals.

"Ah huh."

I made sure that I had my flashlight near me and that it worked.

Bryan ran into his room and came back with his friends.

I turned on the TV and there was another special report, but this time it was national news, not local. I caught the report in the middle, and all I heard was that the supernova combined with the solar storms were causing some challenging problems for the electric utilities and the cell phone carriers. They said that we may experience problems for the next few weeks to months including interference and disruptions. The newscaster left with the promise that he would keep us informed.

"Well thanks, that makes me feel better. If the TV works," I thought aloud, sarcastically. I looked over at Bryan who was now sound asleep, then turned off the light and the TV, keeping him in bed with me for the night. I always feel better when he's there anyway.

I woke to the sun peeking through the gap in my blinds. I'll have to fix that someday, I thought, again. I turned to see the time, and noticed that my alarm clock was blinking 12:00, and glanced over at Bryan who was still snoozing. I got up and walked to the coffee pot and noticed that every clock was flashing. I started the coffee and turned on my cell phone to check the time. My cell read 11:00 pm, and it didn't work. The disruption must have been worse than the scientists thought. I walked over to the TV and turned it on, nothing but snow and then a blue screen.

"Damn," I said aloud. I thought I might check outside to see if George or Liz were up. They weren't, so I picked up the phone to see if I had a dial tone. "Good. At least something's working," I said.

I called Liz.

"Hello," George answered.

"Hey, George, did I miss something last night?"

"Yeah, Den. There have been some real disruptions from space. A lot of things aren't working."

"Is it from the supernova?" I asked.

"Yep. That and there are some severe solar storms, also. It kind of looks like the perfect cosmic storm."

"Is your TV working?" I asked.

"No, it just went out."

"Okay, George, I'll talk to you in a bit. Oh, by the way, do you know what time it is?"

"It's 7:10."

"Thanks. See you later."

"Bye," he said.

I tried my cell phone again to see if it would work. Still no service. The lights were working, so I was sure Bryan's school would be in. I needed to hustle, though, because it was late.

I know from time to time, the earth has had visible supernova, but the earth has never been so dependent on electronics before. I started to worry that there could be catastrophic problems like nuclear power plants losing cooling, or the power grid going off for long periods of time. I wondered how prepared we were for some of the things expected, and unexpected that could happen with no electricity being piped into population dense areas. I remembered the problems associated with hurricane Katrina. I thought about the food and water supply, and then my imagination took over conjuring up images of the collapse of society. "Down boy," I said to no one, trying to reign in the runaway freight train of imagination that had just left the station. Just the same, I think the next time I go to the store, I'm going to stock up on water, and nonperishable food. I think I can do that without feeling too silly.

I walked into my room where Bryan slept last night, and I could see him waking. "Let's go, sweetie boy. Time to get ready for school."

21

For the past two days, Cliff had been unable to write. He would sit at the computer and stare, his thoughts completely disorganized, and his thought processes would not re-boot. He stumbled through one night at work and another off.

Tonight, back at work, he was reaching the end of his shift, and nothing had improved. Work that came so easily, now was difficult because he felt so distracted. With only twenty-five minutes left, he hadn't finished. He rushed around trying to pull his department together, faking some displays and just leaving others. "What's wrong with me?" he thought aloud. His mind was muddled. Forget about writing his stalled book, he couldn't even finish an easy night's work.

This was more than distracted. It was something else, but what? Cliff had no idea. This had never happened to him before, this lack of the ability to concentrate. He tried to shake off the sense that he might be losing control of his mind and he felt some fear at the thought.

Without talking to any of his coworkers, Cliff slinked to the time clock and punched out. He walked straight out of the store and to his car. All he wanted to do was go home and go to bed. Maybe I'm just exhausted, he thought. I may not have been getting the sleep that I usually do.

He pulled out of the parking lot and drove two blocks when a flash of insight struck him. As it did, his mind cleared and the visions of the book returned. It was like switching on a light. He had a sudden explosion of creativity. That was the only way to describe it. "Where did this come from?" he wondered aloud. The book was back... Back? But where did it go?

He drove the rest of the way home wide-eyed. His mind was alive with scenes from the book. He pulled into his parking space, jumped from his car, and ran up the stairs to his apartment. He opened the door, breathless, and went directly to his computer, turning it on. As he waited for it to start, he began jotting down notes, afraid he was going to forget the story unfolding before his eyes.

"Damn, nothing and then this?" he said to no one, feeling overwhelmed. The supernova had moved from reality to a place in the story. Cliff typed frantically trying to keep up.

He typed for an hour, and one character called the supernova, *"A Biblical moment."* Cliff smiled, satisfied with his new progress, but the night was wearing on him and his eyes drooped. He got up and laid on the couch to grab a nap. He planned to not sleep long, so he could continue the story that was back and in full swing. He looked at the computer, still on, and almost got back up to type, but changed his mind and drifted off. He woke two hours later and felt refreshed, then briefly glanced at what he had just written, and started back at the story...

22

Sideways Chapter 14 Continued

After dropping Bryan off at school, I drove to the health club. Entering the front door, Donna was checking people in at the desk and I walked up.

"Hi, Donna," I said. "Did you guys lose power last night?"

"Yes. I heard that most of the Western United States went out for some of the night."

"Man, it's hard to believe that something so far away could cause such disruptions here," I said.

"Yeah. It seems better now," she said.

"Well, get me started before the lights go back out, and I have an excuse to not exercise."

Donna smiled, "Are you going to the usual places?"

"Yes, I'm the typical creature of habit."

"Okay, weights and racquetball it is," she said.

"Thanks."

I walked into the weight room and saw Jason already into his sets.

"Hey, Jay," I said.

"Den, what's up besides fearful signs in the sun, the moon, and the stars?" he said, quoting the Bible.

"It did seem like a Biblical moment," I admitted.

"Did you lose power last night?" he asked.

"Yep. Donna said that she heard that most of the Western U.S. went out for a time."

"Man, that's some serious stuff," Jay said.

Len walked in overhearing. "It's a Democratic conspiracy to tax us more and give more power to the government," he said deadpan.

Jason and I both laughed. "Did you lose power, too," Jay asked Len.

"Yep."

"No more lagging around, time to get started," I said, walking to the bench press.

"Yeah, you haven't been here much," Jay said, looking out the glass doors to the front desk.

I followed his eyes and saw Shannon walk behind the desk and say something to Donna.

"Be right back," I said, strolling towards the door.

"Take your time," Jason said smiling.

I walked through the glass doors and to the desk where Shannon and Donna were talking about the supernova.

"Hi, Shannon," I said, turning to the coffee pot.

"Hey, Den," Shannon said with a smile, walking from behind the desk.

"How long until school starts again?" I asked.

"Mid-September, I'll start back. Next week, I get my schedule."

"Sounds like it's almost time to get back to it," I said, making small talk.

"Yeah, but I have a little more play time," she said with an interesting smile.

"Speaking about getting back to it, I'd better get back to my workout," I said.

Shannon nodded and turned to the pool area and I strolled back into the weight room.

As I entered, Len and Jason were discussing the supernova, and I joined in offering my unscientific speculations about any lingering effects. We talked about how dependent we all were on electricity and if the power were to go off for extended periods of time, how the world could descend into chaos.

We continued the cheery discussion throughout our workout. I wrapped up my weights and saw Sammy check-in.

"Racquetball time," I said. "See you guys later."

"Take it slow, Den," Jason said and Len waved.

I walked out. "Hey, Sammy, I was just heading back to the courts."

"Great," he said. "So, how was the house?"

Shannon had just finished the lesson and stood by the door to the pool. She said, "What house?"

"Dennis' eccentric uncle left him a house on some prime real estate."

"That sounds pretty nice, congratulations, Dennis."

"Thanks," I said shortly, not being comfortable with the gift. "Let's play some racquetball."

"I need to change. I'll be right there," Sam said.

I turned and walked down the hallway and could hear the sound of racquetballs hitting the walls. As I entered the court area, I could see Bob and Ken warming up. They waved me in.

"Hi, guys. Let's play. I just saw Sammy. He'll be here in a minute."

We played cutthroat for fifteen minutes and then Sammy walked in. We divided into teams, and the four of us played doubles for a little over an hour. Finishing, we left the court dripping.

"That was a good run," Sam said.

Bob and Ken said goodbye and walked around the corner.

I turned to Sam. "I'm going to run out to the house right now, do you feel like a ride. I can only stay there for a couple of minutes, but I would like you to see it, and then I can run a couple of things by you."

"Sure, I have a little time. Besides, if I go home, I'll have to work in my attic and it's too hot up there."

We walked past the desk. The manager was there, and we waved on the way out.

"I'm parked over there," I said. "I need to be home by 1:30 to pick up Bryan for his speech therapy in Sacramento."

"That sounds good," Sam replied.

We got in the car and drove roughly twenty minutes to Jonathan's house.

As I pulled into the narrow driveway, Sam said, "What a nice piece of property."

"Yeah, I can hardly believe it myself."

I drove slowly up to the end of the driveway. We got out of the car and I showed Sam around. After hearing my plans, he offered some good suggestions.

As I pulled out of the driveway and onto the narrow road to leave, I told him about Jonathan's strange letter.

"What kind of strange?" he asked.

"He wasn't specific. I've been here a couple of times and I haven't noticed anything too weird."

"Well, he sure left you some beautiful land."

"Yeah, it's really nice," I said.

We chit chatted about the house on the way back. As I drove into the club's parking lot, I thanked Sam for his suggestions and he headed to his car. I just had time to get home, shower and make it to Bryan's school by 2:00, then to Sacramento by 3:00.

23

Sideways Chapter 15

I ran out to Johnathan's house for another look around, spent a half-hour there and then drove to the club.

Walking in the door, I saw Donna at the front desk.

I checked in, then turned to the weight room. Jason was opening a locker and taking out a maroon sweatshirt.

"Was it something I said?"

"Gotta run, Den. See you tomorrow."

"Take care, Jay. I'm not staying long today. I'll see you then."

Jason walked out, and I finished a basic workout, and then left for home. The afternoon was warming into a beautiful day, and I thought it might stay under ninety degrees for a change.

I pulled into the back of my small house and could see George gardening as usual.

"Hi, George," I said, waving and closing the car door.

"Den, how's the house?"

"Fine. The burnt mark is a bit of mystery though but I'm not worried about it. I noticed that there are a lot of mouse droppings in the house, though."

George nodded.

"I have a couple of things to do before I pick up Bryan for swimming lessons. I'll see you later."

"Bye, Den," George said with a wave, and he plowed back into his gardening.

I walked into the house, got our swimsuits and towels packed, grabbed a bite to eat, and sat thinking about Bryan's swimming lesson. I was looking forward to seeing Shannon with these odd butterflies appearing in my stomach.

There was no question that my feelings for her were growing, and I hoped I was reading her right, thinking that she felt the same.

I drove to get Bryan, and we walked into the gym, changed, and showered. As we walked out to the pool, I looked for Shannon. I had seen her car, but she wasn't in the pool yet, so Bryan and I played a game in the pool while we waited.

Out of the corner of my eye, I saw Shannon walk out of the girl's locker room. As I looked up, she smiled, and I indulged myself in a moment of pure shallow pleasure at the way she looked in her suit, with her wet hair slicked back.

"Hi," I said, as I watched her walk towards the pool.

She said, "Hi," and stepped down into the pool smiling at Bryan.

"Hi, Bryan. I've missed you," she said.

"I," Bry said back meaning hi. "Me oo," he finished clearly.

Shannon smiled warmly at him. I walked out of the pool and enjoyed the lesson. For the first time since Shannon had disappeared on the Arizona trip, all seemed right. The lesson came to an end, and Bryan and Shannon walked out of the pool, dripping.

"That was great, Bryan," I said, walking over to them.

"It was good work," Shannon said.

Bryan beamed, turned to her, and gave her a hug. I smiled.

"I guess he missed you," I said.

"Well, I missed you both," Shannon said and being close, briefly hugged me also. I looked at her, and we had a moment, locked in each other's gaze. She looked down and then smiled.

"Do you work tomorrow?" I asked.

"No, and I have to cancel for Friday. I promised my mom I would help her."

"Oh, okay. I'll see you Monday, then," I said.

"That sounds good," she said. "Bye Bry."

She turned and walked to the locker room. I wondered if she knew that she was starting to drive me crazy. Probably not, but she clearly was.

Bryan and I drove the short distance to our house. I took care of some chores and dinner. At about 7:30 Bran was watching TV and the lights went out. The house was instantly thrown into complete darkness.

"Papa!"

"It's okay. I'll get you some light."

Our electricity, for the first time in my life, had become unreliable. The supernova and the sunspots had, together, caused a lot of trouble for the electric utility, and on top of that, we were in the middle of a heat wave. Today was the first day in two weeks where the mercury didn't top one hundred.

I picked Bry up, and got some flashlights, then sat him at his computer which had battery power and put a stand-up flashlight by him that worked like a tiny lamp.

"There you go baby boy. Have fun on your computer. Everything's fine."

Bryan turned his attention to a game. His keyboard was lit by the light, and I carried another light and got his clothes ready for school tomorrow.

Bath time arrived, and I brought him in for a short shower by flashlight, and then in the middle of drying him off the lights came back on.

"There we go, sweetie boy, we have lights."

"Aah," he said, happy to see the power restored. "Seep wa Papa," he said and signed emphatically.

I could see his concern. "Sure," I said, and I brought him, Tigger and Pooh to my room. I made Tigger bounce up and down crazily and I scolded Tigger telling him to behave, and saying it was time to settle down to sleep.

"But bouncing is what Tigger's do best," I made Tigger say with my best impression.

I laid Bryan down and put Tigger on one side of him and Pooh on the other. We said our prayers and I gave the three of them sweet dream magic. Bryan cuddled his two friends and I could see him relax and get comfy.

I slipped into bed which was not quite as roomy as usual, now that I was sharing it with Bryan and his cartoon friends, and I stared up at the ceiling and thought about my dreams. I hoped that I wouldn't wake Bryan tonight. Lately, I'd been having the worst dreams. Maybe tonight I would just sleep. I could feel some fear from the nightmares, and even though I was exhausted, I fought sleep. My eyelids grew heavy and I drifted...

I brought Bryan to a concert at the Arco Arena to see a band that I enjoyed. The place was packed and we were down on an open floor area where there wasn't any seating. The crowd was rowdy and everyone was close. Two girls walked over seductively and began flirting with me. They were dancing side by side, dressed provocatively, and I was enjoying the scenery and the attention. They began dancing with each other, loosely embraced, and beckon me to join them. The moment was very sexually charged, with this obvious invitation for a threesome, and it reminded me of a beer commercial. The girls were sweating, and their clothes were stuck to their bodies, revealing most of what lay underneath.

I looked around for Bryan, but couldn't see him, having drifted from where we were. The girls beckoned me again, but I panicked leaving them, and I frantically looked everywhere for Bry, finally finding him, sitting alone and crying. I thought that someone had hurt him, and I ran to reach him, but my shame for losing track of him was like an anchor around my neck, pulling me and causing my legs to fail. Bryan continued to weep so sorrowfully that I thought my heart would break. I finally reached him and...

I woke up startled, fear and sorrow boiling to the surface of my consciousness. I opened my eyes wide and realized that it was just a dream. Bryan was sitting up looking down at me, staring crankily into my face.

"Papa, too loud!" he said and signed, exasperated.

"I'm sorry, baby. I had a bad dream. Go back to sleep," I said, giving him a hug and happy that it was only a dream.

I dread sleep, I thought, as my mind left the dream and returned to reality. I had gotten in the habit of trying to interpret my dreams to try to figure out what they mean and, hopefully, to take their power away. If I waited until morning, the dream would fade and the meaning would be lost. I considered that I put Bryan at risk for my own fun by wanting to see the band. That probably wasn't the best place for a five-year-old, special needs child. I needed to consider that in the dream, I also lost track of him, distracted by the two sultry girls. I wondered what they represented. I don't think it was sex, even though it's been a long time since I've had the pleasure of someone to share my bed.

Hmmm... They were my idea of beautiful... So, what in my real life might be so alluring that I might neglect Bryan, or be tempted to? Shannon, maybe? The house? I don't think so. Maybe I'm feeling selfish for wanting to be with someone romantically. I got the feeling that I was being warned. Maybe my dreams, lately, have been trying to bring my fears to the surface, using my own symbols... I hate my symbols.

Arriving at no clear conclusions about the meaning this time, I tried to go back to sleep. I looked over at Bryan, who was snoozing, and I stared back at the ceiling and drifted...

My alarm sounded at 6:30 on the dot. Time for the morning routine. I stiffly slid from the bed, not rested, and to the coffee pot.

24

Sideways Chapter 16

I dropped Bryan off at school and drove to the gym. No Jay or Len today, so I did a quick weight workout and headed to the courts. Sam was there and warming up. He hadn't seen me, so I knocked on the window, and he waved me in.

"I can't play long today," I said. "I need to run out to Jonathan's house."

Sam nodded.

"Let's play," I said and we played until 11:00. We walked off the courts sweating and I told Sam I'd be back tomorrow.

"See you tomorrow," he said.

I walked down the hall, passed the desk and out. It was only a couple of minutes past 11:00 and a hundred-degree heat enveloped me as I stepped into the sun.

"Damn, how can it already be this hot, this early?" I said to no one.

I got in the car, rolled down the windows and drove to my house. Pulling into the parking place I could see George swimming laps and I waved. He saw me, smiled, waved, and then continued with his exercise.

As I entered the side door, I glanced at the clock. It was a bit after 11:20. The next thing I saw was the mess that I had left this morning. I grabbed some dishes and rinsed them, made a quick sandwich, and then ate while I picked up some clothes that I had left in the front room.

I called Bryan's school and asked Miss Kathy to please not put him on the bus because I would be picking him up. I sat down and finished the sandwich then turned my attention to the TV and planned to rest a bit. The business anchor was sounding like a broken record, stating again how tax breaks for the very wealthy were the best way to jump-start the economy, and her guests couldn't agree more.

I clicked off the TV. Since the financial meltdown, my tax rate had gone so low, that these kinds of discussions no longer applied to me.

I pulled a box out and packed some provisions like toilet paper and paper towels, some snacks and waters, then I laid on the couch to grab a short nap…

I dozed and woke at 1:30. jumped up and washed my face to help me wake, grabbed some old coffee, then drove the short distance to the school. It was almost 2:00, and there was a lot of traffic pulling into the parking lot. I got lucky as a car pulled out from a close spot and I pulled in.

I saw Bryan's classroom door open and the kids and teacher started to the buses. The wheelchair kids came out first, pushed by the aides, followed close behind by Miss Kathy and the rest of the kids. I walked up.

"Hi," I said to everyone.

"Hi, Dennis," Miss Kathy said, walking Bryan over to me.

"Papa," Bryan said, hugging my leg, not expecting to see me. He signed, "Swimming?"

"No, baby. Today we are going to see a house."

"Oh," Bry said sufficed, but not really understanding.

"How was the day?" I asked Miss Kathy.

"It was a great day. Bryan has blossomed this year. He's pointing and questioning, and you can see the wheels turning. Are you seeing that at home, also?" she asked.

"Yeah. I can tell that I'm going to need to get better at sign language," I said.

We attend a basic sign class on Thursday nights back at the school, given to the parents of mostly deaf students, but anyone is free to go. The kids go to one class where they mostly play and watch movies, and the adults go to a class that's more structured.

"Thanks, Miss Kathy. See you later."

She waved and went back to help get the wheelchairs onto the buses.

I picked up Bryan, and gave him a hug and a kiss, and carried him to the car. I left all the windows down, but it was still hot.

I got on the road to Uncle Jonny's house, blasting the AC with it barely cooling the car. We turned onto the winding road and followed it to the flagstone driveway. As I drove in, I wondered again about Jonathan's strange letter, and I stared at the approaching house trying to see something sinister.

I slowly parked, crunching on the rocks caught between the flags, and stopped, pausing for a moment, trying to shake an odd sense of discomfort. It's just in my mind, I thought, but still felt disconcerted.

"We're here, sweetie boy," I said to Bryan.

I got Bryan from the car seat and set him down to walk with me, then grabbed the box I had packed which contained some provisions, his laptop, and a snack.

As we were approaching the house a cat stepped out of the bushes and walked up to the house like he owned the place. He was a calico with fur beautifully marked with rich orange, black, and white colors that looked to have been poured from paint cans and allowed to dry in interesting patterns. He looked too healthy to be a stray.

The cat rubbed on our legs as we approached the door, and I fumbled for the key. I unlocked the door and the three of us entered into the musty, burnt smell that permeates the house.

We stepped inside and I closed the door behind us. Jonathan's house had nearly nothing in it, except a twin bed in the first bedroom, and a dinette set in the small dining area by the kitchen where the wall was burnt. The cat, who joined us as we entered, ruffled his whiskers which gave him the look of someone sucking on a lemon.

"It does smell pretty bad in here," I agreed.

He looked up at me and then stepped further into the room, peering above himself like something was going to fall on his head.

Bryan watched the cat and I asked him, "Would you like some chips and a drink?"

He signed yes with a smile and I brought him over to the fireplace and sat him down on the floor. I got a plate from the kitchen and set his laptop up on the short fireplace stone ledge. I also set his plate next to the computer, poured the chips onto it, and then placed his drink box next to that.

Bryan turned on the computer and the display didn't light. "Papa," he said loudly.

"What's up, baby?" I asked.

"No work!" Bryan signed in frustration. I reached over and plugged it into the wall. It must need to be charged. The display came up right away.

"I need to do a few things," I said. "Eat your snack and play for a bit. We aren't going to stay here long today."

The cat had drawn on some courage and was about halfway to the hall. I followed the cat, carrying some toilet paper for the bathroom and looked down at him.

"Well, what do you think of the new place?" I asked rhetorically.

"YEOWWRRRRR!" the cat said, growling out the last part. I wasn't sure if he was growling at me or if he didn't like the house.

"Does that mean you're not happy?" I asked.

He started to slowly walk further into the short hallway and I continued into the bathroom.

Bryan began playing on his computer. I followed the cat into the first bedroom where I saw him slip under the bed and felt my ears pop. I had that strange sensation that the room tilted, as before, but the feeling quickly passed, and I walked out of the bedroom.

"Papa!" Bryan yelled as I turned the corner.

"What's wrong, baby?" I asked.

"Computer problem," Bryan signed.

I noticed again that the pressure in the room seemed to change. I looked over at Bryan's computer, and a Word folder was opened with random letters, numbers, and symbols:

fhgihfvhngfuiH[GBVFU[[[Bgoi[[cnsdgy-
Rh[qwd]QERI99T74JSDHUHF8TRT4Nf
hvytprtvpgntryuqopppbup48uw0jg[02lnwrha'k
]q\qjjjjjjjj101$%&&Bgfh9845owhh;t[
jfhruty89pP^O&*uhpg45-=325jynajfagwbeww
1gltng`npyuj569thlt[t\h.;tjun28ty85u8

"What the hell?" I said.

The cat walked back into the living room and began hissing at the computer with his back arched, and the hair standing straight up on it. The hair was standing up on the back of my neck, also. Bryan started laughing at the cat, distracted from the computer.

"I think we're done here. Let's get, Bry."

I picked up Bryan and unplugged the computer feeling that the plug was exceptionally hot. "Huh," I said now wondering if there might be a more serious electrical problem in the house.

I started for the door, and the cat quickly followed. He didn't look distressed, but he seemed to glance at me and then warily back at the fireplace.

I stepped out the front door. The cat scurried behind me and disappeared back into the bushes.

I buckled Bryan into his car seat and glanced back at the house. It left me with the strangest sense that we weren't alone there. It was odd. I didn't look in all the rooms. It was probably imagination, but I don't know. It was something. The place does seem a little strange, but Jonathan's note might just be playing with my mind. There was that odd feeling like vertigo, again, the same as last time I was here. Hmmm... The house left me with an uneasy feeling that I just couldn't put my finger on. Something's different here.

I drove home thinking about the house, but as I drove further, I began to worry that there may be something wrong with Bryan's computer. It wasn't acting the way Bryan is accustomed to it acting, and he's very good with it. I'll check the plug when I get home and have him use it a bit to make sure it's okay.

The next morning, I told Miss Kathy that I would pick up Bryan. I skipped the gym, ran some errands, and decided to pick up a few things for the house. I didn't know how much time I would spend there, but I want a decent TV, and some other basic things for comfort.

Since Bryan doesn't have swimming lessons after school today, he and I can run the new supplies out to the house. Besides the TV, I'll bring my own laptop, which I'll leave, food, toiletries, towels, and some kitchen utensils. I briefly thought, again, about yesterday's weirdness, but I wasn't going to worry too much about it.

By 1:45 I had the car packed and I started for Bryan's school. Got him and we drove the twenty minutes to Jonathan's house. As we approached the door, the cat reappeared and walked in behind us.

Bryan giggled at the cat who seemed right at home. I wondered if it might have been Jonathan's cat or maybe a stray that he fed.

"Hello, cat," I said. I tried to pet him, but he wasn't having any of that.

He looked at me with disdain and turned for the back bedroom. I shrugged and set Bryan up at the dining room table with his laptop, plugging it into the wall and he began clicking the icon for one of his favorite games. It has balloons that pop when you read the correct word, and then click on it with the mouse.

He giggled as it started, and I began running out to the car to bring in the supplies. After several trips, back and forth, I was carrying in my new flat screen TV, and I heard a faint crackling sound that startled Bryan. I glanced over and the sound stopped, but Bryan seemed frustrated and was banging the mouse on the table.

"That's not going to help," I said setting the TV by the fireplace.

"Papa!" Bryan said wanting my help.

"Okay. What's up?"

"Someone in my computer," Bryan said and signed emphatically, which I interpreted to mean that there was something wrong with the computer.

"Well, restart it, baby. You know what to do."

"NO. NO. NO," he signed frustrated.

I didn't want to stop what I was doing, so I thought he could figure it out, and I made another run to the car.

When I returned, Bryan said, "Ouch," and he took his hand off the keyboard, but then he began laughing hysterically. At first, my attention went to his finger because I thought he may have gotten a shock, but then I looked at him laughing.

"What's so funny?" I asked.

"Funny, funny," he signed, putting two fingers on his nose and pulling them forward.

I turned from him and looked at the computer. It was randomly making many balloons rise from the bottom of the screen, and there were different numbers and letters in each. I stared. I had seen this program many times and had never seen it do this before.

"What the heck is this?" I said confused.

Bryan stopped laughing but was content to watch the screen, obviously amused.

The balloons were rising and popping on their own, but then they picked up speed rising more rapidly until it was impossible to read, they then became a blur of color. The balloons then slowed and rose in columns, at first unorganized, but then forming a recognizable order, and they were repeating. I wasn't sure, but this reminded me of a computer code that I remembered from junior college when I took a programming class. It looked familiar, but I really couldn't remember much about the course. It was something about the numbers and letters in the balloons.

Because the code kept repeating I decided to write down the balloon sequence...

```
45 6E 74 65 72 20 73 6f 6d 65 20 74 65
78 74 20 68 65 72 65 20 74 6f 20 62 65
20 63 6f 6e 76 65 72 74 65 64 20 74 6f
20 68 65 78 61 64 65 63 69 6d 61 6c d a
77 68 6f 20 61 72 65 20 79 6f 75
```

"This does not make sense," I said staring at the screen. "Bryan, your computer is wigging out."

"Aah," he said, no longer as entertained by the computer's odd behavior.

The balloons were now slowly rising up in their repeating order. I grabbed a pen and paper and jotted down the number sequence to see if it was some kind of error code, telling me of some malfunction. What kind of error code or self-diagnostic used balloons? I laughed at the thought. The balloons continued to rise.

"Funny people," Bryan said and signed again.

I thought the comment odd and I looked at him. "I think we're all done here," I said, now wanting to leave with another uneasy feeling. I reached down to pull the plug from the wall and got a mild shock. I pulled back and the plug fell to the ground. The computer went to battery power, and the balloon code instantly disappeared with the usual interface of the game returning to normal. I considered the shock wondering if something was wrong with the wiring. "Huh," I said. I looked closer at the electrical socket and noticed a faint darkening at the point where the plug was inserted. I picked it up and it was still a bit warm. I think I may need to give an electrician call.

As I straightened, I looked over my shoulder to see the cat was back. He had walked into the living room from the hallway and seemed agitated. He was hissing quietly, turning circles, stopping and peering in the direction of the computer. I picked up Bryan and the computer and walked to the door. When I opened it, the cat scooted outside.

I thought, weird cat, but I was getting a sense of what Uncle Jonathan was talking about. There definitely is a strange vibe in the house, and the odd, nearly unexplainable things that have happened there which separately could be written off, but together? I don't know. Maybe something.

I put Bryan in his car seat, and as I drove out, the time and distance increased, and I started to doubt the oddness of the place and just thought it might be the oddness of me.

25

Stephen had just returned to his computer for the tenth time today. He had glimpses of the story, and he would sit and write, but it would stop and he would come up short, sometimes not even completing the sentence. The images were now lumbering along, like a train leaving a station, the wheels grinding on the track and the steam barely able to push the train forward. He had spent the last hour pacing his study, impatient for the story that seemed to want to be told. He typed a few words, and then stopped, again, knowing that he couldn't rush this odd process. Quite suddenly, he had a flash of insight.

"Oh man, here it comes," he said aloud, as images flooded his mind and began to pick up speed. He began to type, but now not able to keep up, and the story seemed to roll like an avalanche picking up speed and taking everything in its path. Now Stephen wasn't just typing, he was smashing the keys as the story roared into his mind and making him lose all track of time.

For the next two days, Stephen typed at a fevered pitch, and Mary had been worriedly observing him. He hadn't come to bed, and she didn't think he slept at all. She wasn't sure if he even took a bathroom break. He typed as he ate and he shut out everything around him. She began to wonder if he was on something. It wouldn't have been the first time, but to be honest, he didn't seem high, he seemed possessed.

On the second day, Mary decided to run to the grocery store for dinner and she peeked in on him. "Stephen," she called quietly as he frantically typed. "Stephen," she called again, this time a little louder, but he still didn't seem to hear her. "Stephen," she called even louder still amazed at his focus. "HEY!" she said this time getting some response.

"Huh. What?" he replied, but not stopping and not turning towards her.

"Stephen. I'm going to the store; do you want anything?" she said louder and making him turn to her.

"Oh, umm," he said, confused and not sure of what she asked.

"Wow is all I can say. I've been trying to get your attention for a couple of minutes and haven't been able to break through."

"Really?"

"Yes."

"Damn. I can't explain this but the visions of this story are coming at me fast and furious and if I don't keep up I'm afraid it'll go right by. I keep getting this strange Doppler Effect.

"Are you nearing the end?"

"I'm reaching an important point where the story changes."

"I know it usually takes you more days to finish your rough drafts of a story, but I'm not sure it takes you more hours. You've been going at this one pretty hard."

"The weird thing about this story is that when I get into this writing frenzy, I lose track of everything."

"You're telling me," Mary said.

"Sorry, Mary. I'll be back soon from this strange trip."

"I'm going to the store. Do you need something? I mean without caffeine."

Stephen laughed, "No thanks."

Mary shook her head and walked from the room. Stephen smiled to himself, knowing that he could never find anyone better to share his life.

As she left, Stephen drifted back into his mind's eye wondering if he would have trouble picking up the images, again. He concentrated and saw that Dennis and Shannon were becoming very close. Dennis was explaining to her about the loss of his wife. He finished the next two chapters and then began a chapter where he had first seen Dennis and Shannon. It was roughly the setting where they were when his mind was first flooded with the images of the story. They were together in the new house. Disturbed, he typed frantically as the events unfolded before his eyes.

"That's bizarre," he said aloud as he finished the next two chapters.

26

Cliff's work week ended with a heavy load, and him needing to write a note to Dan, his replacement, explaining the important details for maintaining the frozen food department for the next week while Cliff was on vacation. Cliff was jazzed. He had a week off and the ideas for his novel were returning. The writing had slowed, but in the last day, the odd visions seemed to reassert themselves into his conscious mind, imposing their presence. It was difficult to concentrate on anything else. The story seemed to take on its own life.

Arriving home, Cliff started up the computer and sat impatiently waiting for it to boot. Although he had worked all night and didn't sleep well the day before, he wanted to get down some of the story that had haunted him as he worked on his frozen load. He had begun seeing the same images that had nearly forced him off the road the first night and had made him decide to try to write this novel.

The computer flashed to his desktop and he opened the file labeled *"Sideways."* A list of all the chapters appeared and he clicked on the one that he had begun before work, last night. Chapter 16. He began to reread what he had already written, conjuring up the images of the story. Dennis had dropped Bryan off at school and then raced to the club hoping to see Shannon. Her car was there, but she wasn't in the pool... He began to type.

At first, he saw the images and typed what he saw, but then a strange thing happened. As he would type with increasing speed, the images would appear after the words appeared on the page. It was an odd reversal. His fingers flew on the keys, typing faster than he had ever typed before, and the story moved in pictures and sound in his mind, clearly in view.

Cliff paused, "I wonder if this is what real writers experience?" he said aloud. "This doesn't make any sense to me." He shook his head. Despite feeling this way, Cliff was having the time of his life with the book and the process, and he had an inner glow at the progress that he had made. Oddly, it almost seemed like there was a proofreader between the images and his fingers on the keyboard.

"Huh…"

As he continued, he couldn't wait to see what would end up on the page. The images jumped back out ahead of his writing and he glanced at the clock. It was noon and he had been at this for over three hours. He couldn't believe it. It seemed like he had just sat down. This break in concentration forced the story further in time and suddenly Dennis and Shannon were at Dennis' Uncle's house. This is weird, he thought perplexed by the images that flooded his consciousness. He stopped and opened a folder called *Notes* and typed these future events into the folder.

Cliff wondered where these ideas were coming from. He knew that he had an active imagination, but something was different here. Maybe it's the very nature of creativity. It does seem to come from somewhere else. Ideas spring to life out of nowhere. He thought of Einstein, and how he thought of things that no one else had ever thought of before. "Well, I'm no Einstein," he laughed to himself, but the principle may be the same.

He started back on his notes and the pace picked up. The girl, Shannon, and then her fear from what had happened next. He typed frantically... "Damn!"

27

Sideways Chapter 17

With Bryan in school for the second week, our routine was fully in place. It was difficult for him to get used to his full day, and he would come home tired. I was making daily pilgrimages out to Jonathan's house before Bry would get home, so I wouldn't need to drag him out there. I must admit, though, that I didn't really want to bring him there. Nothing else even remotely odd happened, but the place gave me an uneasy feeling and, well, I felt better going alone. I've kind of adopted the stray cat. I feed him and have brought a litter box. Bryan gets a kick out of him, but, though he comes inside, he's still untouchable.

On Thursday, I took Bryan to school and drove to the club. As I entered the parking lot, I saw Shannon's car, but she wasn't in the pool. I checked in, hit the weight room, and then played some racquetball.

I finished my workout, dripping sweat and dehydrated, and as I passed by the desk, Shannon was starting for the door. I quickly caught up.

"All done for the day?" I asked, hoping to engage her in a little small talk.

"Yep. That's it for me. I only had a couple of lessons."

"So, do you have some big plans for the rest of your day?"

"No, not unless you consider laundry and a new book big plans."

"Well, knowing you, a new book might be big plans."

"It'll do in a pinch," she said smiling.

"I was thinking about grabbing a coffee. Are you interested? I'm buying," I offered.

"Sure, why not," she said.

We walked into the bright sunny day.

"It's going to be hot," I said.

Shannon nodded, and I directed her to my car. I opened the passenger side door and waited as she slid in. After closing her door, I walked around to the driver's side and climbed in. I drove the short distance towards the local coffee shop around the corner, owned by my friend Lenny. Shannon was quiet and seemed preoccupied.

"So, how's your day going?" I asked.

"Okay, I guess," she said shortly.

"Hey, sometimes okay's a keeper. It beats terrible or horrible," I joked.

She smiled but was subdued.

We arrived at the shop and left the car, walking into the place. "I love the smell of this coffee shop," I said. "It smells like coffee and pastry." There was no line so we walked right up to the counter. "Hi, Lenny," I said.

"Hi, Mister Den," Lenny said in his usual friendly manner.

"What do you want, Shannon?" I asked.

"I'll have a double espresso," she said.

Lenny nodded and looked at me.

"I'll have a nonfat mocha," I said.

We stepped back from the counter and waited as Lenny whipped up the drinks.

"Double espresso? That's pretty strong," I said.

"Yeah, I like the rush," she said half-jokingly.

Lenny handed us our coffees, and we walked to a corner table. The shop was slow by this time with the morning rush over, and most of the tables were empty. Shannon seemed quiet, and for the first time knowing her, I felt that I was going to need to carry the conversation, a talent I don't possess. To this point, she had always been easy to talk to.

"Shannon, is something bothering you?" I asked, hoping it wasn't me.

She smiled pleasantly and said, "I am a bit distracted today, but it's not all that important, I guess. I've been trying to get my classes for next semester. Some of them are already full, and some have been canceled, so everyone like me is scrambling to fill their schedule. I'm not a great scrambler. As it is right now, I'm two classes short, and school starts in mid-September."

"It's been a while since I've been in school, so what do you do?"

"I'll have to sit in and hope someone drops the class," she said.

"That sounds pretty iffy," I responded.

"Yep, that's the way it goes," she said. "My professor has offered me a kind of internship on an archeological dig, also, but I would miss a year of school.

That wasn't in my plans, but I would get paid a little, and the experience would be great. If I can't get my classes, I might consider that. I don't know."

I felt my heart sink a bit at the prospect of her leaving again. "But you're a history major?" I said.

"Yeah, I would be documenting it, not digging. The guy who's running the dig is a good friend of my professor's. They have come across some huge new discovery and it's a big secret. I think they are looking for bodies they can kidnap, and pay almost nothing to get the work started," Shannon said, smiling and she seemed to loosen a bit.

"So, where is this at?" I asked.

"I'm not sure. I don't think they want anyone to know. He said Wyoming, or Montana or someplace like that but he was purposely vague. I wasn't really even considering it until I couldn't get my classes. He also gave me the impression that we would be living rough, some dorm-like-place in the middle of nowhere, with no TV and no privacy. He did say, that at least the boys and the girls would have separate facilities," Shannon finished.

"Yeah, nothing like showering with the boys," I said jokingly.

Shannon laughed but gave me an interesting look. It was subtly shy and innocent, but suggestive at the same time, and I thought that I really liked that look.

"Bryan's a great little guy," she said changing the subject.

"Yeah, he's more than special. He gives me so much."

"You're doing a good job with him. You seem like a good dad," she said.

"Thanks, but I feel very inadequate for the job," I said, looking at my coffee.

"You seem to be doing pretty well," she said, wanting to compliment me.

"Thanks," I said, again looking down.

"I don't think you're comfortable with compliments," she observed.

I looked back up. "It's just that when you have a special needs child, you never feel like you have done enough. Never," I said, and we sat quietly for a minute.

Shannon broke the silence. "So, what's your story, Den?"

I looked up and our eyes met. "I'm not sure what you're asking?" I said apprehensively.

"Well, I know you lost your wife, and I'm curious," she said directly.

"It's a long story, Shannon."

"Do you mean it's a long story, Shannon, and it's not your business, or it's a long story Shannon, and are you sure you have or want to devote the time to hear it?"

"The second one," I said truthfully.

"Okay?" she said and looked at me expectantly.

"But not here. Maybe we could go for a walk down by the river?"

"I think I would like that," she said.

We finished our coffee, and I waved at Lenny, and then walked out the door, throwing our cups into the trash.

We got on the freeway and drove out to a small tree-filled park by the American river. It took about fifteen minutes to get there and we didn't talk much along the way. I'm not sure what she was thinking, but I was trying to decide just how much to tell her.

I parked, and we walked down a gravel path with our feet crunching. It was almost completely in the shade with huge trees spreading their branches high overhead and the faint smell of the river in the air. I could see some empty picnic tables, and we walked in that direction.

Shannon is a very direct person, and sometimes that can be sort of disconcerting, but she's also very kind, and by her nature, sympathetic. She broke the silence looking ahead and not at me.

"Your wife died in a car accident," she said and it wasn't a question.

I looked at her, my eyes widening, surprised that she knew that.

She looked at me and smiled. "Jason told me."

I smiled and said, "Asking about me, huh?"

"Yeah, Den."

"That's the story, but not the story behind the story, and that's where it gets long."

Shannon looked at her arm where a watch would be if she wore one. "Well, you're on the clock," she said.

I laughed, "Okay. Here goes. It isn't easy to raise a special needs child. Not many marriages survive it. As it is, over fifty percent end in divorce anyway, but more like eighty-four percent end when there's a special needs child involved. When the child is born, you hear from all the doctors the absolute worst-case scenarios about how your child will end up, and it's bleak. You're confused and afraid, and don't know what to do. Then you go through all the tests and diagnoses, and this takes place over some months. It seems like you're always waiting for the results of the last test or you're scheduling the next one. Each time you get to hear the latest speculation about what may be wrong with your child, and some new one about his future. While this is going on, you're trying to work and live and keep the house up and... Well... It's very stressful, but most of all its very destructive to the relationship. What you're left with in the beginning is deep depression, but the real thing that destroys is the grief that you experience. When a child dies it's devastating, but grief has a cycle, and at some point, you move on. When you have a special needs child, though, the grief cycle never occurs. You just live in the grief. My wife and I were living deep in the grief."

"But I don't understand the grief. What died?" Shannon asked.

"The dream," I said looking down. "The dream of what you thought your child would be, and it's..." I stopped, tears coming to my eyes. Shannon put a hand on my shoulder and we walked quietly until I was ready to continue.

"Sorry about that," I said and decided to move the story along. "I had lost my job again because the housing market collapsed. My wife was working hard to support us as a nurse, like her mom. I was doing most of the doctor's appointments and therapies for Bryan, but money was becoming tight because we had always been used to two incomes. So, the night I lost her, we were having a terrible fight about money, and how worthless I had become. I told her what a monstrous bitch she had become. Neither of us really meant it, at least not completely. The last words I ever heard from her was, 'You're impossible.' And I guess I was. She grabbed her keys and drove off... I got the call about an hour later. I rushed to the hospital, but she never woke up. I know that if I had tried to reason with her, she wouldn't have left, but I wanted to fight. I wanted to hurt her the way she had devastated me. It wasn't pretty. I go through my life, one day at a time, carrying all this never-ending guilt and sometimes it paralyzes me. I feel like I can't move forward as if I'm stuck in cement, and then there's this beautiful child, stuck in the middle, who needs me so much."

I looked up at Shannon to see if she was running for the road, but she was just looking at me with sympathy in her eyes.

"You want to know the worst thing?"

"What, Den?"

"Well," I said hesitating. "The truth, at that moment... when she left, I was hoping she wouldn't come back. I wouldn't wish her harm, but..." I trailed off. "And then she didn't come back," I said in anguish, almost a whisper, gazing down. I felt all the emotion from the past well up inside. Taking a deep breath, I looked up, and out through the trees, and then back at Shannon. "And that's a lot of baggage," I finished.

"Yeah, Den, that's a lot of baggage," she said with a small shake of her head. "So, how are you doing now? It sounds like it's been about three years."

"Better. I've learned something very important. If you hang in there with these special needs kids, you get something that you didn't expect. The more you give them, the more you get. When I lost my wife, I promised my child that I would give myself away to him, and love him no matter what, and then I got the gift."

"The gift?" she asked.

"Yeah, the gift that you can never give these kids more than they can give you."

Shannon smiled and said, "I think I understand."

"I need to go. I have to be home for Bryan's bus. I'll drive you back to your car."

We walked back to my car silently, lost in our own thoughts. I have the sinking feeling that dumping all this on her was a mistake. We climbed into the car and started out.

Shannon interrupted the silence and said, "I think some people are their circumstances, they cause them, but I think from hearing your story, you are more victim than the cause. I hope you can reach that conclusion someday, Dennis, but I'm not sure you will. You are more a victim of the law of unintended consequences."

"Ah, my favorite law. You know about that one," I said respectfully.

"Yeah, I think it can make you live far more conservatively," she said.

"You got it," I smiled.

We drove the rest of the distance to the club in companionable silence. I pulled into the lot and parked near her car.

"I had a good time with you, Den," she said.

"So did I," I said, hoping that I hadn't completely scared her off.

"Maybe we can do it again?" she suggested with a nice smile.

"I would really enjoy that," I said smiling back. "I hope you enjoy your new book today," I added.

"Sometimes when I read a book that I love, it's hard to start the next one, but I just kind of fought through the last one, so I'm anxious to start this one," she said, and after a pause, she turned to me with some sadness in her eyes. "So, Dennis, do you think you and your wife would have stayed together if she had lived?"

"I don't think I would have left her, but I honestly think she could have done better than me, at least for herself. We weren't a match made in heaven, but no, I don't think she would have left me either. We had our troubles, and that was a dark time, but she had a way of keeping a balance. The funny thing is that now, I think she would like me better. I've really grown up. Hell, I like me better."

She opened her door to get out. "Bye, Den, see you around."

"Swimming lessons tomorrow?" I said.

"Hey yeah. See you there," she responded and smiled, lifting the mood in this way she has.

I watched her leave my car and get into hers. I couldn't help but wonder if I'd given her too much information. It's no picnic living with a special needs child, and I'm starting to hope that she'll want to spend more time with us. Better she knows all those things up front that might change her mind. I drove home lost in thought, and full of hope.

28

Sideways Chapter 18

The next day was typical, school for Bryan and a workout for me. Shannon's car wasn't in the lot. I checked in and got to my exercise.

Finishing, I headed home and bustled around the house doing chores, then ate, and packed towels and swimsuits for Bryan's lesson. I picked him up from school, drove to the gym, and automatically looked for Shannon's SUV. As I entered the parking lot, I saw it parked under the only tree that threw shade.

We changed, showered and walked into the pool area. Shannon was in the pool swimming laps.

"Man, Bryan, look at her go," I said, impressed by the speed and strength with which she swam.

"Aahhh," Bryan said surprising me, and I laughed. She finished and swam to us.

"Hi," she said with that smile.

"So, are you going to try out for the Olympics?" I teased.

"No, but I felt like a good workout."

"You were tearing up the pool. Did you swim on a team?"

"In my early teens. I quit just before my junior year in high school."

"I don't think you should have quit," I said and meant it.

She smiled. "Okay, Bryan, your turn," she said, walking up the stairs to meet him.

"Shannon, I really enjoyed our coffee yesterday," I said.

She guided Bryan into the pool, turned to me, smiled, and said, "Me too, Den. I think we should do it, again." She looked into my eyes a long time, and I looked back, not breaking eye contact. "Time to swim," she said to Bryan. Then she looked back at me, not turning away, as they walked all the way into the water.

For the next half hour, my mind wandered, and I couldn't say that I remembered much about the lesson. All I could think about was that smile.

"That's it, Bryan. You were a star again, as usual," she said as she walked Bryan from the pool.

"Thanks, Shannon," I said, and she smiled.

A young girl and her mom arrived for the next lesson, and as they walked through the door, Shannon said, "Dennis, let me see your hand."

I looked at her perplexed. "What?" I said. "Are you going to read my palm?"

"No, but your near future may be affected," she said as she picked up a pen from a small table by the pool. She pulled my hand towards her and began writing on it. I looked down and saw a phone number.

"I know I'm not very bright, but is this yours?" I asked teasing.

"No. It's the number of the local police in case you are robbed on your way home."

"Oh, well, that's very useful information," I said.

"Call me, Den," she said, looking directly into my eyes. I could see that sparkle and I smiled.

The mom walked her daughter into the pool area, and she got her ready for her lesson.

Shannon turned from me and then turned back. "Oh, and don't wash your hand before you write it down, I only give it once," she said and I laughed.

Bryan and I left the club and walked to the car. Driving home, Bryan listened to one of his favorite CDs, and I couldn't see the road because Shannon's face kept getting in the way. I pulled into our driveway and could see George and Liz starting the barbeque. They looked up and waved.

"Hi, guys," I said, stepping from the car.

"Hi," George said.

I walked around the car and got Bryan from his seat.

"Coming from swimming lessons?" Liz asked.

"Yep. It was great," I said with a glint in my eye.

Liz gave me a funny look, far too perceptive.

"Oh? So, Dennis, it sounds like you really enjoyed this lesson, more than normal," Liz said with a wry smile.

George looked up at the comment, first at Liz and then at me. Liz's eyes fixed directly on me.

George said, "Why don't I throw a couple more pieces of chicken on the barbeque, and you guys can eat with us."

"That sounds good," I said. "Let me check my messages, and change, and then we'll be right back."

I turned, carrying Bryan and walked into the house. I directed Bry to the bathroom, while I picked out some clothes for him. He then ambled into his room, and I put him in some dry shorts and a tee shirt. Then I walked back to the phone and checked for messages, grabbed a pen and paper, and jotted down Shannon's number.

I glanced out of the window and saw George cooking on the grill, and Liz coming out of her house with something on two plates.

"Okay, sweetie boy, let's go eat," I said, picking him and his computer up, and walking out the door.

George and Liz were talking way too quietly, and as we walked up, they stopped.

"Okay, what are you speculating about?" I asked but having a good idea of the answer.

"Dennis, you look different," Liz said.

"Yeah, you look happy," George said.

"So, what's up?" Liz asked.

"Well," I said pausing. "I've met someone... Someone I like, and who I think likes me."

"Oh," Liz said not too surprised. "Who is she?"

"I bet she isn't a lawyer," George laughed.

"No lawyers for me," I said, smiling and knew he was talking about Monica. "Her name is Shannon and she gives swimming lessons at the pool. She's in college and graduating this year."

Bryan made an agitated noise.

"Sorry, buddy, I didn't set up your computer." I looked back at George and Liz, who were both smiling at me oddly.

"What?" I said a little defensively.

"So, what is she like, and when can we meet her?" Liz asked.

"She's very nice and kind, and I don't know when you'll meet her... Maybe pretty soon, I think."

"Dinner is going to be ready in about fifteen minutes, Liz. Do you need to bring anything else out?" George asked.

"I think I'll get some wine to go with the chicken," she said.

"That sounds good," he said.

Liz walked into the house, while I set up Bryan's computer. He loves his new *Living Book, "Harry and the Haunted House."* Bryan giggled at the program as he clicked on a picture of a smiling guy, who screamed, and then went back to normal. He continued clicking around on everything on the screen.

Liz had returned with a nice bottle of white wine, and she poured a glass for me, a rather tall one, and one for her and George. We sat there quietly sipping, while George finished the chicken.

"All done. Let's eat," George said.

Liz handed me two plates and I got food for Bryan and myself.

"This chicken's great," I said to George.

"Ahh hum," Bryan agreed but was enjoying the chips more.

Liz and George were polite and didn't pry too much, allowing me to leak out information about Shannon. They asked a few brief questions to which I gave brief answers. I explained how we met, and about her teaching Bryan swimming lessons after Adrianna left to go away to school. Mostly I talked about her personality, and what a quality person that I thought she was. In general, though, their questions were brief, and I was able to exchange enough info. Honestly, I was more worried about their feelings, telling them about Shannon. I know they still have some very bad days thinking about their daughter, as do I. It's odd, and I don't feel like I'm being unfaithful to Lauren, but I kind of feel like I'm being unfaithful to them. I think it may be more important to respect their feelings than it is for me to find someone to be with, but I had to admit, that I really liked Shannon, a lot.

We finished dinner, and I said thanks. They said that they hoped things would work out with Shannon and that they looked forward to meeting her, and I knew that they meant it. Bryan and I walked into our small house.

I put Bryan down in front of the TV, and also set up his computer so that he would have a choice of what he wanted to do. I walked into the kitchen and glanced over at the phone where Shannon's number sat out in plain view. I stepped towards the phone, paused, and then walked over and got a drink of water. I turned back to the phone and looked again at her number. Hmmm... I wonder if she gave me her number or a dry cleaner in Hong Kong. I took a deep breath and decided to call.

"Hello," she answered.

"Hi, I just thought I would test drive this phone number," I said.

"What? You didn't think I was going to give you my real number?"

"Well, let's just say I was hopefully optimistic."

"I'm glad you didn't wash it off, I didn't want to break a hard and fast rule, not to give it twice."

"I wrote it down as soon as I walked in my house. I didn't want to give you an excuse to change your mind about giving it to me. I was thinking that maybe tomorrow we could get together."

"I don't know, Den. I'm a very busy person, you know, with people to see, places to go, things to do, you know, very busy."

"If I call tomorrow, and dutifully grovel, might you consider squeezing me in for a small portion of your day?"

"Well, since you put it that way, maybe."

"I'll call you tomorrow around ten," I said.

"Okay. Talk to you then," she said, hanging up.

Bryan and I hung out watching some of his favorite DVDs, and then we got ready for bed. I tucked him in with the most sweet dream magic that I could give him, and I slipped into bed, mentally replaying the day. My mind drifted to Shannon, and I had this wonderful fantasy of a rainy day, and the two of us by a fire with our noses stuck in books, sipping wine, and having fun discussing them.

I could feel sleep approach, and I turned to lay on my side, happy, and drifted...

29

Sideways Chapter 19

I woke late. Again, the night was full of disturbing dreams. I drug myself to the coffee pot, started it up, and stood there in my underwear, staring and unblinking. The coffee began to brew, and I thought that I might bring Shannon and Bryan to Uncle Jonny's house for a picnic and a hike. As the smell of the coffee began to reach me, I started to plan the food that I would pack. I looked at the clock and it was already nine, and I could feel that the day was going to be hot with no morning chill in the house.

From the corner of my eye, I saw someone pass by the window. There was a knock on the door. I grabbed some sweats lying on the couch and pulled them on. I was sure it was Liz, replaying the brief image, and I walked over and opened it.

"Good morning, Dennis. You look like you just got up," Liz said and the coffee beeped as it finished it's brewing.

"Hey, Liz. What's up?" I said a little embarrassed, knowing how bad I looked, shirtless in my sweats, and my hair tangled. Bryan ran to the door to see his grandma. I didn't even know he was awake, but Bryan has grandparent's radar, and if they're around he knows it, even from a dead sleep.

"Amma!" he exclaimed, reaching to hug her.

She picked him up. "George and I were wondering if we could take young Master Bryan for a fun day, today?"

"Oh, I don't know," I said, teasing Bryan.

He looked at me as if to say, "What? Why not?"

I smiled at Bryan. "Well, I guess so," I said, continuing to tease. "What's the plan?" I asked Liz.

"We were thinking about going to the State Fair, then out to dinner," she said setting Bryan down.

"Boy, does that sound like fun. Since you have Bryan, I'm thinking about running out to Jonathan's house."

"Alone?" Liz asked, looking at me with a sideways glance.

"Well, I was thinking about maybe asking Shannon to go."

"Oh. That sounds like a good idea, Dennis," Liz said. "Maybe we can meet her soon."

"Yep," I responded shortly, wanting to change the subject.

Liz smiled wryly and didn't press me.

"I'll get Bryan ready, and have him there in twenty minutes. Thanks, Liz, you guys are great."

She smiled at me knowingly, and said, "See you in twenty minutes."

I closed the door and turned to Bryan. "All right, let's dress you and brush your teeth, and you're going to need some sunscreen."

I walked into the kitchen and looked at Shannon's phone number lying by the phone. I decided to get Bryan ready before I called, so I fed him breakfast, then brought him into the bathroom and took care of our morning duties. I laid out some cool clothes for him. Bryan wanted to go right now, but it was still a little early, so I set up his computer to entertain him.

Shannon's number caught my attention again, and I decided to call. I could feel little butterflies in my stomach. Silly schoolboy, I thought as I dialed.

"Hello," she said.

"Hi, Shannon," I said.

"Dennis, what a surprise," she said, teasing me.

"So, is there any chance you are free today?" I asked.

"You said you were going to dutifully grovel," she said.

"Oh, that's right," I paused. "Shannon, this unworthy man would like to know if you would accompany him for a small portion of your day, even though he knows he is not deserving of the honor," I said, laying it on thick.

"That's not bad. You grovel well," she said.

"So?"

"Hmm... Well, let me check my very full calendar," she said pausing, and her voice became stern. "Oh, darn, I'm so sorry, had you called just five minutes earlier I could have squeezed you in. I had a small opening between 12:00 and 12:10, but now I'm far too busy," she finished.

"That's just my bad luck," I said in my most pitiful voice. "I can be there in about two hours?"

Shannon relented, "Okay, I'll squeeze you in. See you in two hours."

I wrapped up a couple of things in the house and decided to shower before I brought Bry to Liz and George. I jumped in, leaving the door open so I could hear Bryan, and thinking about what I would pack for lunch. I could hear him laughing at a program on his computer, and for just a moment, I thought about how happy I was. It was an odd thought, and it felt unusual for me, considering the road that my life had taken. As I dried off, I thought I would pack turkey sandwiches with fruit, chips, and cookies. What if she doesn't like turkey, I thought? Maybe I should pack peanut butter and jelly also. Hmmm...

I was already a few minutes later than twenty minutes, so I quickly finished drying, put on some sweats and a tee shirt, gathered up Bryan and his computer, and walked across the flagstones towards George and Liz's back door. I had Bryan knock, and George answered.

"There's my big boy," he said smiling.

Bryan reached for George, and he picked him up.

"Hi, Dennis. I hear you're going to Jonathan's weird house today," he said.

"Yeah. I'm going to take a ride over there. I have a little maintenance to do."

Liz came to the door, and said in her most understanding voice, "Dennis, I hope you know that we're happy you might start dating again."

I looked up and made long eye contact with her. "I know, Liz," I said, but the fact of the matter was that I really didn't know what to say. I know that they want me to be happy, but it still surprised me again. It can't be easy, wanting your late daughter's husband to see other women. They know the whole story about Lauren and myself, with no editing. I've tried to be completely honest with them. I fully understand my loss, but I'm not sure that I could ever fully understand their pain. It makes them even more remarkable.

"I should be home by seven," I said.

"We were hoping to have Bryan spend the night, tonight if that's okay?" Liz asked.

"Oh. Sure. Do you need some PJ's?" I asked.

"No. We have some here that will do just fine," George responded, smiling again at Bryan.

"Okay, good. See you in the morning then. You better give me a big hug, and a kiss goodbye," I said to Bryan. George handed him to me and I hugged him. "Be good for Amma and Ampa." I set him down and signed I love you to him, and he signed it back, and then he waddled back to George.

I waved. "See you in the morning," I said, turning and striding back to my small house.

I finished packing the lunches and looked at the clock. All of a sudden, I was in a big hurry, and I felt like I couldn't get to Shannon's place fast enough.

What a schoolboy I am. I changed and checked my look in the mirror. "Hmmm, so, now, every detail matters?" I asked myself aloud.

I turned back to my closet and changed from a Tommy Bahamas shirt to a sportier Nike in navy blue. I looked back in the mirror and shrugged.

I grabbed the lunches and walked out the door with a bounce in my step. Striding to my car, I noticed how dirty it was. I should have washed it, and as I opened the door, I could see a patina of dust coating the dashboard. I glanced into the back seat and could see three sweatshirts there. I grabbed them and wiped down the dash making it look like the person who owned the car at least cared a bit. I popped the trunk, took everything that looked like clutter and walked behind the car. As I opened the trunk, I became more embarrassed.

"What a pig," I said aloud.

I threw the sweatshirts, and a couple of other things into the trunk which was full of more neglected items, like my racquetball bag, empty water bottles, and various tools that I hadn't used for two weeks. I sighed. If I keep up all this involuntary introspection, I'll never make it to Shannon's. I decided to put a lid on it, climbed back into the car and drove out.

I could see Liz, George and Bryan walk out of the back door. I honked the horn, and caught Bryan's eye, and blew him kisses. He did his best to blow them back. I couldn't imagine how I could ever be happier than I was at that moment.

Shannon's apartment was about twenty minutes from my place in a complex largely inhabited by college students. I pulled into her lot, surprised by how little activity there was. I couldn't even see one person walking around. There was a parking place next to Shannon's car, and I pulled in. It was tight. I parked and then squeezed out of the car door.

She lived on the second floor at the top of an austere cement staircase. I started up the stairs and for some reason, felt tired. I think my attraction to her is a little draining. I could see her number and the nerves began. I knocked, Shannon opened the door, and suddenly everything was all right.

She was dressed in tan shorts and a green tee shirt, with shoes that looked like they could stand up to a good hike, and I instantly remembered why I was so attracted to her. She was wearing no makeup, and her natural beauty and lean, athletic body was the picture of what always got my attention.

"You're seven minutes late," she teased.

"I'm sorry, but I couldn't get past the guard at the gate."

"I'm not surprised, I told him to keep the riff-raff out."

"I bribed him with a few bucks. I think you are going to need to pay him better."

"Come in," she said, grabbing my shirt sleeve and pulling me in the door.

As I entered, I could see that she was orderly, but not fussy. Like most students, her furnishings were Spartan. She had a large bookcase stuffed with books of all kinds. There were history books of course, but there were also rows of fiction stacked every which way. It seemed to me that she wanted to be able to see all the titles that she had ever read.

The place looked like a one bedroom with a kitchen and a small dining area. The living room had a couch, one side table with a lamp, her desk, a laptop, a TV on a roll around cart, and a coffee table with a Stephen King book, *"Bag of Bones"* sitting on it, and a book marker at least three-quarters of the way through.

"Are you enjoying this?" I asked, pointing to the book on the table.

"Yeah, it's good. Have you read it?"

"Yeah. I liked it a lot," I said.

"Okay, Dennis, where are we going?"

"I thought we might have a picnic at the house that my uncle left me. It has some beautiful land, and I thought we might hike, and explore a bit."

"That sounds great," she said.

"My uncle also left me a letter that I haven't told anyone about, except for my in-laws of course. It's kind of an obscure warning that there's something wrong out there."

"Wrong?"

"Well, you have to understand, Uncle Jonny may not have been quite right," I said.

"Are you saying that the place is haunted?" Shannon said with a gleam in her eye. "OOOOHHH," she finished, wriggling her fingers at me.

I smiled. "I'm not sure why. He was vague, but he suggested that I bring a compass out there when we're having sun spots and walk the property. We've been having them, and there is also the supernova. I think we may have a chance to see what he means."

"What does the supernova have to do with it?" she asked.

"I'm no physicist," I said, qualifying my answer, "but I think we are being bombarded by particles from the sunspots and from the supernova. I know you've seen the aurora in the sky. It's from the supernova and its particles striking our magnetic field."

"Okay, this sounds like an adventure," Shannon said, now into the mystery.

Her television was tuned to the History channel, and there was a guy with wild hair talking about ancient aliens. He was explaining how some artifacts found in Egypt pointed to us being visited by creatures in spaceships.

"Let me grab a sweatshirt and we can go," she said.

"What's this?" I asked about the program.

"It's a TV show that tries to convince you that we've been visited, raped, seduced, and probed by aliens since we crawled out of the sea."

"Huh… If Big Bird isn't on the show, I probably haven't seen it," I said and Shannon smiled. "I would like to stop at a store and buy a compass," I said as we walked towards the door. Shannon reached over and turned off the TV.

"I have one, Den. I'll grab it," she said, turning back towards her desk. She plucked up a small compass and held it out to me.

"Oh, thanks," I said a little surprised.

She read my expression and said, "I'm full of surprises." She gave me an interesting smile, full of possibilities, and I had to admit that I loved it.

She shut the door and made sure it was locked, and then we walked down the stairs and to my car.

From Shannon's place, Uncle Jonny's house was maybe a half of an hour away. I opened her door and she squeezed in, and then I got in my side awkwardly, plopping into the driver's seat.

"I know you're a fiction reader, but I have this audiobook I would love you to hear. It's called *"Outlander,"* by Dianna Gabaldon. The writing is wonderful and it's an interesting story with unexpected twists. The reader, Davina Porter, is the greatest reader of all time. It takes place mostly in Scotland two hundred years ago."

"Sounds good to me," she said.

We got on the freeway and Davina Porter made magic as she altered her voice for Scottish ladies, English men, young girls, and the rest of the characters in the book and we disappeared into great writing and equally great reading. We both were involved in the story, but I thought that the drive was starting to lack conversation, so I asked, "Do you like the reader?"

"Yeah, I'm enjoying this very much."

"I think she's brilliant," I said.

We continued to listen and soon we reached the exit to Jonathan's house.

"Here's our exit," I said, pulling from the highway and onto the winding road. In the last turn, we could see the rock fence, and I turned in and drove on the flagstone driveway up towards Jonathan's front door. The driveway was narrow, but there was a turnaround just past the house, so I turned the car around, and pointed it out of the fence opening, parking partially in the dirt. I'm not sure why I wanted to park this way. It may be because the house gave me an uneasy feeling, and I wanted a quick getaway.

I stepped out of the car and walked to open Shannon's door, but she had already jumped out. I joined her by her door.

"That really is a great book and reader," she remarked.

"Yeah, I like it a lot. There are a few more in the series. I thought you might enjoy it."

"Thanks, Den. Let's listen to more when we leave."

Pausing, I looked at the front of the house. "Well, do you feel anything strange?" I asked.

"Yessss," she said, sounding like she had entered a trance. "I'm hungry!"

I smiled, held up a bag, and said, "Lunch is served."

As we approached the house, Shannon said, "You know, this is a pretty cool house. Are you sure your uncle didn't like you?"

"Honestly, I never really gave him the time of day, I'm a little ashamed to admit. It was like he was invisible."

"Maybe he thought you were expendable," she said with a wry grin.

I laughed, but shook my head and said, "I just don't know. He didn't say much in the will, and the letter that he gave me was even shorter. Maybe he was getting dementia. It can bring on hallucinations."

"Or maybe he was tipping the bottle too much?" she offered.

"Beats me. Let's walk around to the back first. I want you to see the forest and the land. It's beautiful."

I led Shannon around the garage to the left, and into the backyard. It was overgrown with tall weeds poking up through the flagstone patio. Shannon stopped as she saw the forest, stream, and pond.

"Man, Den, this is really something," she said.

"I know, I can hardly believe it myself."

We spent some time talking about the property and admiring the setting.

"Let's take a short walk to the stream," I suggested. Shannon nodded, and we walked about a hundred yards to the edge of the forest, where the stream wound from and continued to the pond. The trees were so dense here that they blocked the sun, making it look dark.

"Maybe it's the forest that's haunted," Shannon said. "It almost looks primeval."

The stream looked to be about four or five feet deep, and six to eight feet wide. It was flowing and had more water than I expected.

"This would be a great place to hike," she said.

"Maybe after lunch, we could hike up the stream. I've been wondering what it's like further out."

Shannon's eyes brightened. "That would be fun," she said, and I could see that she was excited for an adventure.

"Let's go eat," I said.

We walked back towards the house. It was the first time that I looked at it from this direction. I imagined my ideas about the changes that I would like to make, and I shared them with her as we walked back towards a stone barbeque that was shaded by a hundred-year-old oak tree.

"I like your ideas, but I think you would need to be careful that you didn't lose the beauty that lies behind the house," she said, as we walked back around, and toward the front door.

"Honestly," I confessed, "I think I may have had a change of heart about moving out here."

"Really, why?"

"I'm happy where I am, and George and Liz don't want me to move. They're involved with Bryan and I could see it in their eyes that they were heartbroken at the thought of him moving, and he's so young, I think he would feel some loss from moving away from them. He's already had to endure a big loss."

Shannon nodded.

"I don't know. I still haven't decided."

We made it to the front door and I said, "Let's go inside." I unlocked the door, and we walked in. The cat, who I hadn't thought of a name for yet, greeted us at the front door.

"Awh, a cat," Shannon said and leaned down to pet him.

"Pet him at your own risk," I warned. "He's a wicked beast."

Shannon pulled her hand back and said, "What's his name?"

"He's a stray that just appeared one day, so we're just getting to know each other. I haven't named him. Any ideas?"

"Not off hand."

"Come on, I'll show you the rest of the house."

"Here's the kitchen. This door leads to the garage," I said pointing. "You can see my dining area, with wall art," I motioned towards the burnt wall.

"Wall art?" she said questioningly, looking at the large mark that started at the missing light over the table and ended halfway down the wall. "It screams of man's inhumanity towards man," she joked. "So, what's up with it?"

"Don't know. I was thinking about having an electrician look at it."

I turned from the dining area, and we walked through the living room, and past the cat. "There are three small bedrooms and a bathroom, with a nice walk in shower, with heads that spray you all over at once," I said, ushering her in.

"Nice bathroom," she commented.

"Yeah, I call the shower, the car wash."

"Hmmm, it kind of looks like fun," she said.

"It'll give you a wax on the way out," I said, smiling flirtatiously.

"I could use a wax," she said back smiling.

"You have to see this," I said turning from the bathroom and leading her into the first bedroom. "Check this out," I said, swinging out the bookcase and exposing the small odd room that hid behind it.

"What the heck?" she said.

"I think it's a panic room."

"Wow, that's kind of creepy," Shannon shuddered.

"I guess unless someone was trying to get you."

"I think your old Uncle Jonny was maybe a couple of cards short of a full deck," she commented.

"I can't help but agree. Let's have lunch, I've spared no expense."

"Oh, five star?" she asked.

"Nothing but the best turkey or peanut butter and jelly sandwiches," I responded.

"My favorites."

We walked back into the living room, and Shannon stopped by the fireplace. "That's nice," she said pointing.

"Yeah, it may be my favorite thing in the house," I said. "It looks like something that would be in a lodge in the mountains."

"I think my favorite thing is the shower," she said, "but the wall art is nice too."

"Great, I've saved us a table just under it. It's the best seat in the house."

"Ah, it's the only seat in the house."

"Best, only, same thing," I said. "Jonathan left the table and chairs, a bunch of kitchen utensils and a twin bed here for me, along with a smattering of other things in the garage. I brought the TV, food, some toiletries, a radio, and a laptop."

We walked to the table, and as we passed the cat he reached out to scratch me. "Hey! You missed me, cat," I said, ushering Shannon to the table.

We sat down and I open the lunch bag. Shannon looked at my opened laptop on the table, while I pulled out three sandwiches, two turkey and one peanut butter and jelly, some chips, chocolate chip cookies, and two peeled mandarins.

"Three sandwiches?" Shannon commented. "Are you hungry?"

"I'm just a growing boy," I said. "Actually, I wasn't sure what you would like, so I made turkey and P.B. and J."

"Thoughtful," she said smiling. "I'll have half a turkey and half a P.B. and J."

"I have water or soda in the fridge."

"Water please," she said.

I handed the water to her and divided up the already cut sandwiches. I had water myself and sat down eating quietly with her for a couple of minutes.

I asked, "What do you think of Patches for the cat's name?"

"Not bad. He does kind of look patched together."

I nodded.

"I'm getting antsy to explore with the compass," she said.

"Do you have it with you, or did you leave it in the car?"

"It's in my pocket," she said sliding it out, not looking at it, and handing it to me.

I took it and set it on the table.

"Shannon?" I said.

She could hear that I had an odd tone in my voice, and she glanced my way, wondering what was up. I pointed at the compass. The needle was slowly moving back and forth between north and east. It seemed to quiver, stop and then arc again.

"Okaayyy, that has my attention," she said, somewhat creeped out. "Has anything strange happened here, Den?"

"There have been a couple of oddities. Bryan's computer wigged out one day. I had a couple of strange sensations like vertigo, but everything could have been written off to something else... I don't know," I finished.

"Is this the computer that acted strange?"

"No, I brought my laptop here, so I wouldn't have to keep carting Bryan's."

"Oh," she said. We both continued to eat and watch the compass needle do its odd dance. "The sandwiches are good, Den," Shannon said taking her eyes from the compass.

"Thanks," I said and just then my eyes widened.

Shannon looked up, and then around.

"Did you feel that?" she asked quietly.

"It felt like a tremor," I said.

These happen in California, but they're not that common around us. The tremor with the compass together felt eerie. I looked back at the compass, and the needle seemed to arc further past east.

"Ah oh. Here we go," I said.

Shannon's eyes grew large as a full-blown earthquake rolled the house, building in strength until we both held onto the table.

"Damn," I said, as I heard things falling. I watched the kitchen light swing on the ceiling and the cat jump in the air. The shaking seemed to settle under the house, and then roll away in the direction of the forest. It didn't seem like it was going to stop. Finally, the ground settled down and we looked at each other.

"I'm no expert, but that felt pretty strong," I said.

"I hope crazy Uncle Jonny didn't scrimp on the building materials," Shannon said, glancing up at the ceiling. We both got up, not finishing our lunches.

"I want to have a look at the fireplace," I said. "They usually don't fare too well in an earthquake. They tend to crack and fall."

We walked over and I took a good look. There was a minor aftershock, but the stonework looked perfect.

I shrugged. "Let's go outside and check the chimney. I hope it's still standing."

We headed out the front door, but I could only see the top, so we walked around the house to the back to get a better look. "It looks fine," I said.

There was another strong aftershock.

"Man, it's rockin' and rollin' up here today," I said checking the stucco on the house for cracks. I glanced over at Shannon who looked distracted. "What's up?" I asked.

"I'm not sure, Den. Follow me," she said, walking away from me towards the hill that rose to the left of the house. "Is that smoke?"

"Where?" I asked.

"Over there, by that cleft. Do you see it?" she asked.

"Kind of, why?

"Well, it looks like a cave," she said, continuing to walk, and not taking her eyes off the spot in case it would disappear.

"I've been around that hill, and I never saw a cave," I said.

"I thought I saw smoke, but I think it was dust coming from it," she said as we reached the hill.

We needed to climb around ten feet to reach the cleft. It was rocky and there wasn't a footpath, so we wound our way around some huge boulders. As we made it to the entrance, it did look like a cave. There were loose rocks strewn around the front and we carefully stepped over them to peer inside. It was difficult to see with dust clouding the air and the lack of light.

"The quake must have uncovered this," Shannon said excitedly. "Come on." She stepped over the stone filled ground.

"Wait, Shannon. What if we have another shaker?" Shannon wasn't listening to me, though, and she stepped out of sight.

"Hey, Den, you need to come in here."

I was already stepping into the entrance, and I waited for a second for my eyes to adjust. I could see a small light about ten paces in front of me. Shannon was squatting, holding her cell phone in front of her at arm's length, down into what looked like a hole.

"I'm glad you didn't fall in," I said.

"I turned my cell phone flashlight on when I entered," she informed me.

"Oh, good idea."

"Turn yours on," she said.

"I don't have one."

"Oh. Check this out."

I carefully walked up beside her and crouched.

"Do you have any flashlights?" she asked.

"Yeah, back at the house. Do you think it's safe?" I asked, looking over my head.

"I think so. It didn't fall from the last two shakes. I can't quite make out the bottom. This doesn't look that deep, but I think there's a tunnel down there."

"Really?" I said. I squinted into the hole.

"Go get the flashlights. I'll wait for you."

"Okay, but you need to wait for me outside the cave," I insisted.

We had another aftershock that shook some dust loose, but no rocks fell. It looked like most of the loose rocks were from the entrance that suddenly opened with the first quake. The cave went back maybe twenty feet with the hole ten feet in, and there were no loose rocks in the back. Shannon still agreed to wait outside, and I hustled to the house and brought back two flashlights.

Shannon was standing outside the cave when I jogged back up the slope.

"Let's go have a look," I said, resigned, handing her one of the lights. We reentered the cleft. It was narrow and only one could enter at a time. We turned on the flashlights, illuminating the interior. It was craggy, with no smooth walls, and dust filled the air making the light beams stand out. We kept the flashlights pointed down, so we wouldn't step into the hole.

We carefully approached the opening into the abyss. It was no more than eight feet in diameter, and we both peered over the opening looking down and letting the beams travel to the bottom. Shannon was right. There was a tunnel set partially into the floor, and also the wall. It was pointed in the direction of the house and seemed to slope in a downward direction. The bottom was littered with stones that probably fell in the initial shake.

"Shannon, look at those marks on the floor of the cave, by the opening of the tunnel," I said.

We both pointed our flashlights in that direction. They looked like crop circles, round with lines passing through them. There were also circles by circles.

"It looks like something that would be on that show with the guy with crazy hair," I said and she moved closer to me to get a better look.

"We need to go down there," she said excitedly then added, "Those glyphs are old, maybe ancient."

I could see the historian emerging from her.

"I'm not sure it's safe," I said.

"Do you have a ladder or some rope?" she asked.

"I was afraid you were going to ask me that," I replied apprehensively.

Shannon looked at me and smiled. "Come on, you big baby," she chided.

"Let's go see what we can find," I relented.

We walked out of the cave and into the bright afternoon sun. The shadows were lengthening, and I couldn't believe how fast the day was flying by as I enjoyed Shannon's company. The earth wasn't behaving though, with swarms of aftershocks. They were mild but still disturbing.

"Maybe we should come back tomorrow," I said with some concern.

"You said you wanted to explore a bit," she said, mimicking me.

"Yeah, around the grounds, not under them."

We continued to the garage, opening the large door. I went into the kitchen, through the garage, and grabbed a couple bottles of water, and handed one to Shannon. We sat on the step that led inside, next to each other, close, and it felt good. We looked at the eight-foot ladder, laying on the ground, and finished our water. Our shoulders were touching, and my attention was leaving the cave and traveling to my exploding attraction to Shannon.

"Let's go, Den. I want to check out those glyphs," she said, breaking that interesting moment.

"Okay."

I grabbed a rope, and hefted the ladder, and carried them out of the garage. Shannon followed, and I pulled down the garage door. As we walked to the hill, I handed Shannon the rope, and I carried the ladder up to the cleft. Shannon walked in first with the flashlight on and pointing at the hole.

"Are you sure you want to go down there?" I asked, hoping she had a change of heart.

"Hell yes," she said forcefully.

"Okay, let's be stupid and go down there," I said.

"Big baby."

I knew I was being coerced into this adventure. I didn't mind exploring, it's just that the earth would, from time to time, give a rumble and I didn't want the roof to cave in. I slid the ladder into the hole and it rested on the bottom. The top of it was a foot below the ground, so I figured the hole was about nine feet deep. I shook my head and stepped onto the top of the ladder and then stepped down each rung until I reached the bottom.

"Okay, Shannon, come on down." I saw one foot followed by another, and then two very fit legs worked their way down. I held the ladder, and Shannon bounced down the rest of the way, and as she hit the floor of the hole, she turned to me with a sparkle in her eyes.

"All right," she said.

The ground under our feet was moist, and a trickle of water wound its way towards the tunnel. She peered at the glyphs and shook her head.

"Interesting," she commented.

"Do they look familiar?" I asked.

"Well, kind of. Let's walk into the tunnel."

"I don't know," I said apprehensively.

We turned our flashlight into the blackness of the opening.

"You know, Den, at some point this tunnel may be full of water, stopping us anyway."

"You might be right," I said. "Let's go in a little way and see. I want to go slow, though. I'm not sure what shape this underground network might be in. If it seems unstable in any way, we are out of here. It looks like it leads under the house."

It appeared to slope downward, and we had to lower ourselves a bit into the opening. The top was about six-and-a-half-feet overhead, and the width was no more than four feet, but the darkness made it feel smaller. I carried the rope, and we started forward with me in the lead. The slope wasn't steep, but the trickle of water made it a little slippery with it pooling in patches here and there. As we continued, the temperature dropped, and we came to a bend and then a fork in the tunnel. The water bent left, leaving the right direction dry.

"What now?" I asked.

"Let's go right, first. We won't follow it too far, and if it branches off again, we'll turn back. I don't want to get lost," she said, making sense.

"Okay, that sounds like a plan," I said agreeing. "I hope there isn't a maze down here."

We started through the right branch of the tunnel, keeping our flashlights forward. It was so dark that the flashlights barely illuminated the space around us. It seemed like the light was being swallowed by the tunnel, and I was becoming claustrophobic. After about twenty-five or thirty yards, we felt a small aftershock. Some pebbles fell, but nothing major. The humid air around us smelled stale with the dust drifting into our light.

We reached the bend, and Shannon came up beside me to get a better look. We both flashed our lights far forward, and Shannon took a small step in front of me. I stopped her, reaching for her stomach, and pulled her back. Her front foot slipped, but she stayed upright, and I turned my flashlight down. She gasped to see a pit just two feet in front of us.

"Shit!" I exclaimed.

"Did you see that coming?" she asked, flashing her light into the hole.

"No... I don't know why I stopped you," I said wiping my forehead, and trying to control my adrenaline.

"Man, that would have been nasty," she said.

"Yep," I said, taking a very deep breath.

We stepped back a bit further and peered into the pit, flashing our light down to the bottom.

"I bet it's at least twelve feet deep," I said.

The pit filled the path and the only way to continue was to jump it. Shannon shined her light towards the end of the tunnel, and it seemed to continue for another thirty or forty feet. We couldn't tell, but there might be another bend at the end. I continued to shine my light into the pit, looking at the bottom. It had a small amount of water that seemed to slowly flow and something white and green shined wet just underneath.

"What is that?" I asked, looking over the ledge. Shannon shined her light with mine into the water.

"I don't know," she said.

"Huh," I said, moving my light to get a better look.

"It looks like bones, Dennis," she said, shining her light to the left, and what appeared to be a rib stuck out of the mud.

"Damn, Shannon, I think you're right. That looks like the top of a skull, I'm almost sure."

"Human remains?" she said questioningly, "Do you think this is a crime scene?"

"I don't know, maybe. I'm probably going to need to tell the authorities," I said.

"Let's go back and see what's in the other direction," she said.

I nodded and we turned back in the direction that we came from. As we approached the fork, I could see how people could get lost underground. It's very disorienting. To the left was the way out, and to the right was the other tunnel. We turned to the right splashing in a shallow puddle. The water trickled in this direction and I wondered if we might find it full. We both kept our flashlights on the ground fearing that we might run into another pit.

As we proceeded, I asked, "Hey, Shannon, do you think that was a trap of some kind?"

"Well, if it was, it was an effective one for the poor guy at the bottom if those were bones."

"No kidding, I have bad dreams about things like that," I said.

We reached what we thought was the end, but there was a bend that turned sharply to the left. As we raised our flashlights, we both stopped dead in our tracks.

"What the hell?" I said staring.

"Man," Shannon said.

In large holes, maybe three feet in diameter, cut into both sides of this portion of the tunnel were bones, neatly stacked, completely filling the space of each hole. Some kind of spider had filled each gap between each bone with web. We walked slowly gawking left and right. The bones looked human and appeared to be sorted.

"These look ancient," she said.

"What is this? The passageway to hell," I said, staring and shining my light into each hole. "Am I mistaken or do they seem to be separated by bone type?"

"That's what I thought, also," she said. "Where're the heads?"

I gazed back over the holes and shrugged. "Do you think this is some kind of burial chamber?"

"Could be, but it might also be the remnants of some kind of ritual or rite," she said.

"The tunnel seems to end up there. Let's go to the end, and then hike out of here," I said.

"Good idea. This place is giving me the creeps. I have a feeling that the guy in the pit probably died around the same time that these guys did," Shannon speculated. "The pit might have recently filled with water."

I started forward and Shannon followed. "So why separate the bones?" I asked feeling some fear crawl up my spine.

"I don't know, Dennis."

I said, "It looks like the tunnel bends to the left. I thought it was going to end, but now I think it may go further."

We started forward again following the bone corridor.

"Who or what do you think did this?" I asked.

"My guess is that it was probably some kind of shaman. Maybe this is how some ancient tribe buried their dead, or it may have been some form of sacrifice. It's hard to say," she said as we reached the end.

Near the very back of the tunnel, there was a slight bend to the right and then a black spot that looked like a narrow opening. I stepped forward and shined my light into this pitch-black space. As my light breached the darkness,

I could see depth. I took another step, looked down and saw a drop, and then stretched out my arm pushing the flashlight forward into this darkness.

"Hey, Shannon, you need to see this."

She slid close to me because the opening wasn't very large, and she added her light to mine.

"Wooh," Shannon said wide-eyed.

"Ho-ly crap," I said, amazed at the sight before me.

Through the opening, we could see a very large circular room. It looked to be about thirty feet across, and the ceiling seemed about twelve feet tall. In this chamber was a stone circle.

"I need to get a better look," Shannon said squeezing further towards the room. "Well, now we know what happened to all the heads," she said as she shined her light at some holes in the walls that surrounded the stone circle. Stacked neatly like apples in a store, were human skulls. They filled each hole that we could see, and the same spiders that did their work in the bone hallway had filled every space with webs.

The stone circle looked like a mini Stonehenge, without capstones. There were thirteen stones, each nearly as tall as the roof. They seemed to be cut similarly, rectangular, and flat to the middle of the circle. There was also an altar that stood just inside a large gap in the stones. The stones themselves obscured our vision of the room, and Shannon moved further forward trying to get a better look.

"I'd hate to be invited to the parties they had here," I said.

"Yeah, I don't think everyone made it home," she observed. "Should we go in?"

"I guess," I said, but for some reason, didn't really want to.

Shannon tried to get a bit closer, and I had to turn to the side to give her some room. As I glanced down, her foot hit a slick spot by the opening, and she fell down into the room, landing in a small puddle of mud. I made a feeble attempt to catch her but came up empty. Her flashlight hit the floor and spun, giving the chamber an odd, eerie, swirling light show and then went out.

"Are you okay?" I asked, jumping down into the chamber. It was at least three feet to the floor, and I feared that she was badly hurt. I shined the light into her face, making her squint.

"I'm okay, I think," she said, her face a bit red with embarrassment. She started up with my help, taking inventory of all her parts. "I may have a bruise or two," she said, trying to brush off some mud and finding a couple of sore spots on her backside and upper thigh. She brushed, again, at the mud but figured it was hopeless.

Shannon found her flashlight, and shook it, banging it against her hand. It came back on, flickering at first. She shined it forward and began to look around. There was a gap of maybe three feet between the walls and the stone circle, and we walked there together. The stone walls had an iridescent glow as the flashlights played against them. We peered into the holes, filled with the sightless heads of these ancient people. They ringed the entire room, spaced equidistantly.

As we continued, I touched the wall.

Shannon was watching me and asked, "What?"

"A couple of things," I said. "First, there isn't even a pebble on the floor. We had a pretty strong quake and a swarm of aftershocks and there doesn't seem to be even one rock dislodged from the walls or the ceiling. Second, is the odd way the walls reflect the light. When our flashlights shine out, we can light the whole room. It's dim, but it seems to be much more light than we're producing."

Shannon looked around and saw that the floor was free of debris and that her light seemed to reflect from the wall.

"Huh," she said.

We continued to walk the perimeter of the room, always watched by the sightless eyes of the skulls. We reached the stone altar, stopping there, and gazed upon the stone that sat at the opening of the circle. It looked, from this vantage point, like the stone pillars were the altar's audience. They were perfectly spaced in attendance, and the altar appeared to be ready to entertain them. When I glanced down at it at first, I thought the altar looked clean. It was one large piece of stone, smooth on top, but the sides were rough. Shannon looked closer though, touching it lightly, brushing her hand over an area close to the edge.

"Look at the stains," she said, pointing her flashlight to uneven color. She shined her light onto the side of the altar there. "Hmmm," she said grimly. "I think it's bloodstained."

I looked in the direction of her light and could see that something had streaked the sides of the altar, weaving rivulets down through the uneven path to the floor.

"Grizzly," I said.

We stepped into the center of the circle with the reverence of someone stepping into a church. Shannon shined her light around and then up to the ceiling.

"Look, Den," she said. Her words reverberated around the chamber, amplifying them.

I looked in the direction of her flashlight. The ceiling was somewhat smooth, except that it had drawings cut into it.

"Are those constellations, and a solar system?" I asked.

Shannon didn't speak at first. She studied the markings. "I think so," she said. "It looks like a starfield, and a sun orbited by eight planets. The orbit markings don't look exactly right, though."

"Our solar system?" I asked.

"Could be, or just a representation of a sun and planets," she said.

"Just a good guess?"

"Could be."

"I guess they don't respect Pluto either," I said.

"Guess not," she said, continuing to pan over the ceiling with her light. "Dennis, what do you think all those circles are, outside the star field?"

I looked at the exterior of the odd cave etchings. There were circles almost like bubbles, some overlapping, some appeared to be moving away, and some seemed to be engulfing some of the star field. These circles had the appearance of something important to the whole picture but didn't make sense to me.

"I don't have the faintest idea," I said truthfully.

"Huh," she said, panning her light away from the ceiling and onto the walls. There were the same glyphs that we saw on the floor when we first looked in the pit in the unearthed cave. They seemed to give me the same impression that some crop circles do. Perfect circles and absolutely straight lines.

The earth woke back up, shaking the chamber, but again nothing fell from the walls or ceiling. I was getting a real feeling of claustrophobia, and my imagination pictured the tunnel collapsing, trapping us underground.

"I think we need to leave," I said, hoping Shannon would agree.

She nodded and I could tell that even she was ready to go.

"I've seen enough for today," she replied.

We started back to the chamber opening, and Shannon turned to the glyphs on the wall.

"These are odd," she said. "It's the same circles by circles. They seem to interact, but some are far while others are close, and look at these two in the center. They actually overlap just a bit... Huh."

"Does that look familiar to you?"

"No. I just feel something from it like its speaking."

The earth rumbled again, and Shannon's flashlight blinked.

"Let's go," I said. I made a stirrup with my hands and Shannon stepped into it and pulled herself out of the chamber.

"Ouch," she said, rubbing her bottom. "That's going to be a nasty bruise."

She watched me push up on my hands and climb out. Wiping the mud from her hand on her shirt, she started forward, and I followed. We quickly walked through the bone hallway, and as we passed, I barely glanced at the poor contributors to the macabre scene.

We didn't waste time, and Shannon set a good pace towards the pit with the ladder. Shannon's light winked out on the way, and I took the lead, guiding us through the blackness. We passed the fork and trudged forward, being careful not to slip on the wet surface. My light flashed through the tunnel and I could see the very bottom of the ladder. There were more stones on the floor of the tunnel here, but considering all the shaking, it did well.

As we cleared the tunnel, I could see that the bottom of the pit had a lot more rocks in it than when we first came down.

"I don't think this part of the cave is very stable," I said guiding Shannon to the ladder.

She rapidly climbed, and I followed, pulling the ladder out. We walked from the cave into what had become the evening.

"We must have been down there longer than I thought," I said.

The sun had dipped below the hill to the west of the house, and it was going to get dark fast.

I drug the ladder as we walked off of the hill, and then I hefted it, carrying it towards the house.

Shannon turned to me and said, "I'm not sure you'll be able to build out here. As soon as people get wind of what we've found, everyone and their mothers are going to stop you in case this place is full of archeological artifacts."

"I think I've changed my mind about moving out here anyway. If I sell it, I'll have the money, and we could use it. George and Liz don't want me to move, and I'm happy there, and now this. It was probably the deciding straw."

"Want to guess at how old the bone room might be?" Shannon asked.

"I have no idea. You're the history nut. Do you remember reading anything about circle makers anywhere in Northern California?"

"Not off hand, I'm sure that there are some, but I'm a research nut also, and I'll find out as much as I can for you," she said then added, "Wait, I do remember something called the Medicine Wheel, somewhere. Let me think."

"Thanks," I said with a growing appreciation for Shannon, and something else, something very nice.

"I'll tell you one thing, Dennis, you sure know how to make a date exciting," she said with a smile as we reached the garage.

"Well, it takes a lot of planning, and pinpoint timing," I said with a straight face.

"And luck?"

"Maybe a bit of luck."

"Yeah, planning and luck," she said.

I opened the garage door and slid the ladder and rope in, closing it. We walked to the front door, and Shannon brushed at the mud on the back and side of her shorts, and down the side of her leg. I tried to help a bit, but it was pretty hopeless.

"You know, Den, there are a huge amount of myths and paranormal experiences attributed to stone circles. There are stories, fairy tales, you name it," she said.

My mind drifted first to Jonathan, and then back to the book we were listening to on the way in, where stone circles played an important role.

"Hmmm... Where do you think, the circular chamber is in relation to the house?"

"I don't know," she said looking back at the cleft in the hill and then around where we were. "If I was going to guess, I'd say around the back of your house to maybe the stone fence. We made some twists and turns, but..." she trailed off.

"I bet you're right," I said. "Let's go in. You're a mess," I said smiling.

"Charmer," she said.

I opened the front door, and the cat was sitting in the middle of the room. He blinked at us as if to say, "Oh, you again."

30

Sideways Chapter 20

"Shannon, I have stuff for dinner. Would you like to stay?"

"Dinner sounds good, but I'm such a mess," she said glancing down at her shorts and leg.

"You could give the car wash shower a test drive," I suggested teasingly.

"Well... Okay. Do you have towels and soap, and maybe some shampoo?" she asked, holding up a piece of mud caked hair.

"I do. I'll get them for you," I said turning.

She asked, "How about a robe?"

"I don't wear robes."

She nodded and we walked towards the bathroom being careful to avoid the cat.

Shannon looked at him, and the cat looked back as if to say, "What's it to you." I smiled and shrugged, and she shook her head.

We got to the bathroom with its stone colored tile on the floor. I'm always surprised by its size, and I looked at the shower which could easily fit two and my mind briefly drifted into a romantic fantasy. The bathroom, itself, had the usual things, including a rather large mirror above a vanity facing the shower.

I took a towel from a small linen closet in the short hallway, just outside the bathroom, and then pulled shampoo and body soap out from under the vanity.

"Here you go," I said, handing them to her.

She smiled, "I'll just be a minute, but I need to shake the mud and dirt from my clothes."

"Just shake it off in the shower, then you can wash it down the drain," I said.

"Okay."

"I'm going to get dinner started. It's going to take about an hour, so no rush," I said, not wanting her to feel like she needed to hurry.

I left the bathroom, closing the door behind me. As I walked to the kitchen, I thought that this date was going pretty well. Shannon and I seem to have a good rapport. We fall into a nice rhythm with our conversation, and even the silence between, always seems comfortable. I couldn't imagine anyone that I would rather be with. I hate to get my hopes up, though, and I feel like I need to be cautious, but this seems really nice.

I entered the kitchen, one I wasn't used to, but I knew my way around enough to cook a passable meal. I turned the oven on to 400 degrees, grabbed two baking potatoes, washed, and poked them with a fork, and then stuck them in to cook. I grabbed a pan to make a chicken sauté with a white wine sauce. I cut up some onion to sweat in the pan with olive oil. Once hot, I turned off the heat and covered them to sit for five minutes. "Hmmm, what veg might she like?" I said aloud, pulling open the refrigerator and gazing in. It was pretty bare, but I had a yellow squash and some carrots in the crisper with the potatoes. I chose the yellow squash which I would cut up and add to the dish just before I served it.

***

Shannon removed her shoes, socks, shorts, and top, and as she did, dried mud rained onto the floor.

***

I could hear Shannon open the bathroom door, and then the linen closet. "Do you need some help?" I called.

"No," she replied way too quickly. I'm guessing that she didn't have much on just then. I must admit that I found that image very appealing.

***

Shannon took another towel and spread it out on the floor. She began with her shoes, hitting them together in the shower, and knocking most of the dirt off the bottoms. She moved to her shorts, brushing them vigorously. As she worked, the lights dimmed way down. Shannon looked up and called, "Den?"

"That's odd," I said to myself. The lights didn't go all the way out, and then quickly returned to full strength.

"I think it's okay now," I called back. I grabbed the flashlight that still worked and brought it to the bathroom. "Shannon," I said through the door. "I'm leaving a flashlight by the door if you need it."

"Thanks, Den," she said.

It wasn't completely dark yet, but the bathroom only had one small window, and if the power went out, it would be hard to see.

As I left the hall, I got that strange sense of vertigo again. I stopped and put a hand on the wall to steady myself. It quickly passed, and I walked back to the kitchen. I saw the compass sitting on the table and glanced at it. To my surprise, and dismay, the needle was arching from north to south, back and forth. "What the hell?" I said aloud, and for a moment, I wished that we went out to dinner. The cat started pacing and quietly growled. He turned and walked out of the front room, heading back towards the bedrooms. My chicken needed my attention, but when Shannon came out, I was going to tell her about the compass.

***

Shannon continued to brush the dried mud from her clothes. She finished, removing as much as possible, and turned on the water in the shower, washing the mud down the drain. The water was getting warm, so she took off her bra and underpants, and looked at her backside. Where she had hit the cave floor on her upper thigh and bottom, she had two large bruises. "Ouch," she said aloud, poking them. She put her hand under the water to regulate the temperature, stepped out and grabbed the shampoo and body soap, and then stepped back in, setting them onto a small ledge in the shower.

***

I placed the chicken in the hot pan and seasoned it a bit while shaking the pan to flip the contents. The chicken was browning, and I could smell the herbs rise in the steam. I grabbed the bottle of white wine from the refrigerator and pulled the cork with a wine opener. I figured that we could drink this with our meal. The chicken was braised, so I poured in the wine, and it sizzled as it hit the hot pan, and then poured myself a small glass.

***

Shannon efficiently washed, enjoying the spray coming at her from different directions. Her leg and arm were crusted with mud, so she let the water run on them before she worked to scrub it off. She leaned her head back into the water, and soaked her short hair, brushing her fingers through the small mud caked area. Then turned her attention back to her leg and soaped it up watching the mud and bubbles run down. She was finally starting to feel clean and soaped the rest of her body enjoying the warm water gently pelt her skin.

As she leaned her head back into the water stream, she felt her ears pop. It was like driving into the mountains. She soaped her hair and began washing. It seemed like the atmosphere in the bathroom changed. The light seemed to dim and then brighten. Something was different. The air almost seemed heavy. The pressure increased in her ears, leaving her dizzy, and she rushed to get the soap out of her hair, suddenly feeling vulnerable, and not wanting to close her eyes for long to give up the advantage of sight.

She quickly opened her eyes finishing the rinse, and the light looked different in the room. She heard a low cracking sound and it startled her. She thought that maybe a light had burnt out around the mirror. The crackling reoccurred. It reminded her of static electricity when you pull two blankets apart that have just come from the dryer. She turned and looked in the direction of the mirror, and through the steam covered glass, saw colors that reminded her of Christmas lights.

It was nearly impossible to see outside of the stall, so she turned off the water, opened the glass door, and peered in the direction of the vanity. She then stepped out dripping, and saw an odd light show in the mirror, or maybe in front of it. Tiny pinpoints of colored light danced in the air along a pale blue, hair-thin, vertical line that seemed to split the mirror in two. Shannon stared at the sight in wonder and then felt a slight electrical charge gently touch her face. The thin blue line began to divide, as the electrical charge played against her body. It touched her face and seemed to move through it. She looked at her arms, holding them out, and the faint blue charge moved up both, caressing them, raising the short hairs, and slid to her shoulders, and then slowly moved across her chest. The charge then touched the rest of her body, pushing across her contours and out the back.

She felt like she had just been scanned. The tiny colors on the vertical line became agitated moving quicker, and the vertical line separated folding back on itself.

Shannon had looked up, staring at her nude body in the mirror, but it disappeared in the spreading blackness of the now opening vertical line. The air pushed against her, cool and insistent, as the space opened further in front of her eyes. Fear shot through her, and she began to back away, but the force from the mirror seemed to approach her like a freezing wind, forcing her back towards the wall. She began to lose her footing, because of wet feet, and she slipped against the stone wall, but the force became stronger, and held her tightly, pinned there. She was frozen in the forces embrace. She tried to move, and tried to scream, but had no control. A shadow appeared from the blackness, and then she felt her entire body invaded, like roots spreading from a tree, something moved between each pore, maybe each cell. She instantly became aware of every part of her body at the same time. She could feel her mind begin to short circuit, as blackness filled her vision. She began to lose consciousness. With a last breath, she whispered, "Help."

As Shannon wavered between consciousness and oblivion, the thought or quiet prayer seemed to have an effect. Whatever was happening abruptly stopped and receded like watching a movie in reverse. Shannon stared, uncomprehending with her mouth open, as the vertical line closed and the colored lights folded into it. Released, Shannon screamed!

***

I was adding chicken stock to my dish. "Shannon!?!" I dropped my spatula. It hit the side of the pan, bouncing off, and throwing some of my sauce onto the floor. The spatula landed on the tiles by the stove and I was on the run. I ran through the front room. The cat, who had returned, scattered. I turned to the bathroom and pushed the door wide. Shannon was standing there naked as the day she was born. I came up short, stopping, not expecting to see, well, so much of her. I looked at her face. She had an expression of pure horror.

"Shannon?" I said, not stepping forward.

She seemed frozen, except that she shook mildly as she dripped, still soaking wet.

"Shannon?!" I said again, this time more forcefully.

She just stood there staring into the mirror.

"Shannon!" I said again, increasing the volume, stepping forward, and looking into her eyes.

There wasn't much alive there. She just stood, dripping and staring into the mirror. I tried to hand her a towel, but she made no move to take it.

"Shannon," I said, again this time softly, and she turned her head slightly my way, but didn't take her eyes from the mirror. I tried to hand her the towel again.

She finally moved and crossed her arms under her breasts with her movements becoming jerky, and then she began to rock.

"What happened?" I asked.

She didn't answer. She then crossed her arms over her chest and continued the rocking motion.

I got in front of her face, trying to make eye contact, and I held her by her wet shoulders.

"Shannon," I said. "What's wrong? What happened? Are you sick?"

She glanced at me for a second, but her eyes became vacant again, and then she began to shake her head. The drops from her hair dripped onto my arms.

"Are you saying, no?" I asked, but I didn't think that's what she meant.

"Shhhhh," she said, trying to speak.

"What?" I asked as gently as I could.

I tried to hand her the towel again, but she wouldn't reach for it. She just stood there naked, now with her arms at her side staring through me into the mirror.

"I'm going to call an ambulance," I said, thinking that she was very sick or worse.

She shook her head emphatically no, and I tried to hand her the towel again. She obviously had no idea what was going on or that she had no clothes on.

"SHIT!" she finally said, in loud clipped speech, and it startled me. She began rubbing her hands and arms like they were crawling with bugs. I could see her cringe and goose flesh rise all over her body in waves.

I had gooseflesh on me now, also, as fear filled my mind. Her hands moved back to her sides, and her eyes became vacant again staring at something that I couldn't see, towards the mirror. Her eyes then filled with tears and began to overflow. Then I saw intelligence come back into them and she looked at me.

"Shit, shit, shit. What just happened to me?" she said in an angry, whispery voice.

Again, I tried to hand her the towel. She wouldn't take it, and she began to rub her arms again, down to her hands, where she stopped and looked at them as if seeing them for the first time.

She said, "I saw... I saw... What the hell did I see? It was in the mirror, or outside of it. I don't know... Pale colors... moving... Shit! Then it entered me!"

"Entered you? You mean sexually?" I asked, not being able to put that in any other context.

Shannon looked at me as if I was speaking Greek.

"What? ---No!" she said and looked at me like she wanted to say you fool. "Everywhere... Pushing through me... Probing maybe... Shit!"

She now had gooseflesh all over her, and I was afraid that she was going into shock. She wasn't making any sense, so I put the towel around her shoulders.

"Come with me into the bedroom, so I can help you get dressed," I said, pulling her from the bathroom.

She came with me, but walked like something was wrong with her, stiff-legged and stumbling, and she stared over her shoulder at the mirror. I had known Shannon for quite a while, by now, and I had never heard her utter an expletive, now they were flowing like she had Tourette syndrome.

As we entered the bedroom, she said, "What- the- hell- was- that?"

I shook my head, not that she was looking at me. She was somewhere else. I began to dry her off, getting a good look at her body. I know how most of her body looked, having seen her in swimming suits many times, over the past few months. She's very fair, but...

"Shannon, have you been nude sunbathing, or going to tanning booths lately?" I asked.

She looked at me, again, uncomprehending.

"Okay, listen to me. You are tan everywhere. I mean where the sun don't shine, everywhere, even under your hairline," I said pointing to the top of her shoulders, behind her neck. She already knew all the other places that I had looked, watching me dry her with the towel.

"That doesn't make sense," she said in clipped tones as her eyes filled with tears, again. "You need to get me out of this house, Dennis. Now!" she said and I could see panic setting in.

I draped the towel back over her shoulders, and kneeling in front of her, making eye contact, I said, "Shannon, I need to get your clothes. I'll be right back."

"NO!" she shouted, panicked, all the color draining from her face, and shaking her head no with her eyes wild.

"I can't take you out of here naked. I'll be right back," I said this time more forcefully.

She glanced down and saw that she was dressed in only skin, nodded spasmodically, and with a shaky voice said, "Okay."

I ran back to the bathroom, afraid of what might be in there, but nothing happened. I grabbed her clothes, piled on the floor, and ran back to her. She was sitting on the edge of the bed with the towel over her shoulders and her head in her hands with her elbows on her knees. She looked up at me with glazed eyes as I entered.

"You're going to be okay," I said, but not sounding reassuring. I straightened her up and removed the towel from over her shoulders. She seemed almost catatonic. I tried to put her underpants on, guiding each leg, but she wasn't helpful, and I couldn't get them up all the way. "You need to help me," I said.

She glanced at me like she just realized I was there, and she nodded. I picked up her bra and guided each arm in and then fastened it in the back. I slipped her shorts on and pulled her to standing, and then got her panties and shorts up and buttoned. She sat back down and looked at me.

"Thanks," she said and I could see some life come back into her. I put her shirt over her head and pulled it on guiding each arm through the holes.

"This is going to sound crazy, but you look tanned from the inside out, and I think you look more tan, now, than when I first brought you in here," I said.

"Help me finish dressing, Dennis," she whispered like she barely had enough energy to finish the last word. "I feel... I feel... like I want to run from this place."

It seemed like Shannon was stabilizing now, at least a bit. Her eyes had some intelligence back in them and when she made eye contact with me, I felt that she was there, but she looked weak. She kept getting chills on and off like she had the flu, and I worried that she may have caught some virus that would account for her symptoms and possible delirium. I knelt down and put on her socks and shoes, and then stood up and felt her forehead, but it was cool.

"I'm not sick," she whispered.

"Okay. Let's go."

I pulled her to standing and helped her walk, holding her around the waist. We didn't stop to turn off anything in the house. We were out of there. I know in horror movies and teenager slasher movies, people hang around far too long in strange situations. We didn't. We were gone. I guided her to my car, opened her door, slid her in, and buckled her seat belt. Then I remembered that I left everything on in the kitchen, including the burners and the stove.

"Shannon, I have to turn off the stove," I said knowing that it would catch fire.

"Let the place burn," she said and meant it.

"I'll be back," I said. "Five seconds."

She just stared forward.

I hustled back into the house and to the kitchen. I had no idea what happened to Shannon, but now, I was completely spooked. I continued to the stove, my dinner in the pan beyond recognition, and turned off the burner and the oven. I turned and looked at the compass on the table. It was arching back and forth, nearly making a full turn. I stared at it for a second and then was back on the run. Before I reached the door, the atmosphere in the room changed, like diving deep underwater. I could feel pressure. I had no interest in trying to figure out why. I was out of there, pulling the door closed behind me, and hoping to protect me from... What? Something.

When I reached the car, Shannon said, "You're late, that was seven seconds."

I smiled and was happy to see that she was approaching herself again. I drove from the house, leaving a cloud of dust from where I parked on the dirt. In the night sky, we could see the supernova, very visible to the south, and the aurora brighter than it had ever been, coloring the sky with curtains of red and green.

"I don't think your crazy uncle is so crazy now," Shannon said staring straight forward.

"You scared the crap out of me, Shannon. I thought you had a seizure or stroke or something."

"I wish," she said sarcastically.

"Are you okay?" I asked, feeling tears come to my eyes.

"Not really," she said.

"What happened?

"Something," she said. She leaned her seat back, stared out the window, and wouldn't speak for the rest of the ride home. Occasionally, she would shake as if she was having severe chills.

I drove into her complex, found a parking place, and helped her to her door.

"Den, don't leave me tonight," she pleaded with her eyes filled with tears.

I nodded and walked in, closing the door behind me. It was about 8:30.

"I need to call and see how Bryan is."

Shannon looked at me chastened. "I'm sorry. I forgot about Bryan."

"No worries, he's spending the night with his grandparents."

Shannon, who's strong, seemed like fine china to me right now, very breakable. I speed dialed and got Liz who sounded like she'd been laughing.

"Hello," she said.

"Hi, Liz. How was the day?"

"Dennis. We had great fun," she said and I could hear the joy in her voice.

"Can I talk to Bryan?"

"Sure," she said and held the phone away from her face. "George, bring Bryan to the phone."

Bryan loves to talk on the phone, even though he's nearly impossible to understand. He took the phone and held it up to his ear.

"Aahh," Bry said.

"Hi, sweetie boy. Did you have a fun day at the fair?"

"Uh huh," he said enthusiastically.

"I love you and I'll see you in the morning. Put Grandma Liz back on the phone. Good night."

Bryan handed the phone back to Liz and ran back to George.

"He really had a fun day," she said.

"I'm glad to hear it," I said, but she could hear something in my voice.

"Is everything all right, Dennis?"

"Let's just say that the day was somewhat unpredictable, to say the least."

"Oh, that sounds not so positive," Liz said back in the same cryptic language.

"I'll tell you tomorrow. Thanks again for watching Bryan, and his great day. See ya."

I put the phone back in my pocket, a bit lost in thought.

Shannon was recovering and she walked over to me and gave me a hug.

"Dennis, I know that this is going to sound strange, but I need to take a shower. I feel like I just ran a marathon. Why don't you pour us a couple glasses of wine and turn on the TV. I'll be fast," she said breathlessly, and she walked from me and went into her bedroom.

She walked back into the living room, carrying her nightgown and a change of underwear.

"Shannon?" I said.

She had turned to the bathroom, and she turned back.

"Ahh... I want to mention something else."

"What?" she said, looking at me quizzically and a little apprehensively.

"You know that small birthmark you had on the back of your knee?"

"Yes?"

"Well, the operative word there is *had*. It's gone," I said, referring to a quarter-sized brown mark that was just below her knee on the back of her calf.

She glanced down and behind her leg, not saying a word, and hastily turned back to the bathroom. As I heard the door close, I thought that there must be some serious inventory going on in there right now.

"Dennis, come in here," she said insistently.

I started for the bathroom, afraid of her tone. As I entered the room, I saw her in only her panties and sheer bra, both of which were pretty see through. I stopped, coloring a bit. Shannon looked at me as if I was crazy.

"Oh, you have got to be kidding. You're embarrassed. You've seen more of me tonight than most of my doctors." She shook her head, and I walked in the rest of the way, averting my eyes.

"In my defense, I was embarrassed then, too. Remember, I kept trying to give you a towel?"

Shannon gave me a puzzled look and a blank stare as if trying to remember.

"In your defense, the lights were on, but nobody was home. If you get my drift."

She abruptly changed the subject. "Look, you were right, but not just the birthmark. Every blemish, every scar, every mole, and those two bruises that I got in the cave, gone!"

"Damn," was all I could say.

"Look at me Den, I look like I just got back from Maui. I'm so tan, and my skin is perfect. This is just crazy."

"I'll tell you what I'm going to do," I said cryptically.

Shannon stared at me, blankly.

"I'm going to get Estee Lauder and bring her to the house. We could make a fortune!"

Shannon looked at me disgusted. "Oh really, jokes now," she said and I gave her a contrite look. "Dumb ass," she said, but I saw a smile leak into her eyes, as the corner of her mouth turned up. "Turn around," she ordered, forgetting the shower.

"I don't think you have anything I haven't seen," I teased turning around.

"I hope you poured the wine. I think some might be in order," she said as she removed her bra and underpants, dropping them to the ground. She slipped her short flannel nightgown over her head and pulled up her fresh panties.

We walked out of the bathroom, and I sat on the couch while Shannon got us both a glass of red wine. She sat down a couple of feet away from me and stared out, conjuring up an image.

"I'm having trouble remembering what happened, and what I saw. I'm so confused," she said, stopping and taking a large drink of her wine. "I think I was dying, Dennis."

When she said that, I could feel a cold chill run up my spine.

She said, "I don't know if the memory of what happened to me is going to come back, or if it's lost forever."

"You said something pushed through you or entered you. Do you remember that?" I asked, hoping to help.

"Well, yeah, sort of, but I'm not sure that's quite right," she said, pausing and taking another sip. "But it or they came in me, like through my skin, stopped like a kid whose hand is slapped in the cookie jar, and then rushed out. The odd thing is that, looking back, I don't think that it, or them, or something was trying to hurt me. It seemed like an accident. I don't know," she finished, and she looked despondent.

"Huh," I responded with nothing intelligent to add, and thinking that this just didn't make any sense. I looked back at Shannon who was sitting there staring at some unseen movie playing in her head, and she looked exhausted.

After a minute, she continued, "After it left me, I felt like my cells needed to reassemble, like everything was pulled apart, leaving space between." Shannon shook her head again and finished her wine. "I'm sorry, Den, I'm beat. I think I need to go to bed," she said and her words slowed and her speech slurred a bit.

I saw her eyelids droop, and I said, "If you have an extra pillow and a blanket, I can sleep on the couch."

She nodded and rose, then shuffled to a small closet next to her bedroom. She looked like she could barely walk, and I jumped up and walked close behind her in case I needed to catch her.

She opened the door to the closet, and handed me the pillow and blanket, and said, "See you in the morning." She forced a smile and I could tell that she had nothing left in the tank.

"Yeah, Shannon, I'll see you then."

She walked into the bedroom, not closing the door. I could hear her slide into bed with a squeak of the springs. I looked at the couch and figured that I would probably end up on the floor. The couch was small and my legs were going to hang over the side. This wouldn't be a comfortable night. I laid out the blanket, fluffed the pillow, kicked off my shoes, and turned out the lights. I pulled my knees up and stared out into her dark front room.

My mind began to race. What the hell happened at Jonathan's house tonight? What had she seen? And what happened to her. Poor Shannon, I thought... Great date, Den... Oh, really, jokes to yourself... Dumb ass.

Shannon wasn't making any noise now, so I figured that she was asleep. My clothes were bugging me, and making me uncomfortable, so I stripped down to just undershorts. I needed a shower, but I would never impose for that, so I curled back up figuring that I wasn't going to get much sleep. It's never easy to sleep in a strange place, and my mind wouldn't be still. I laid there staring for some time and finally got drowsy and drifted...

I woke up startled. Shannon was screaming! I flew off the couch, banging my shin on her coffee table, and headed into her room in only my underwear. In the two seconds, it took me to get to her door, I realized how inappropriately dressed I was, and I became embarrassed. When I entered, my adrenaline was flowing and she had ripped off her nightgown, kicked off her covers, and thrashed like she was being attacked.

"Shannon, Shannon," I whispered, shaking her shoulder gently.

Her skin was clammy, and she looked up at me like I was a complete stranger.

"Shannon, it's me, Dennis. You're having a bad dream."

I could see recognition enter her eyes. She took my hand and whimpered, pulling it to her cheek. I brushed the hair from her face with my other hand. It was stuck with sweat. She calmed, and I extracted the hand that she had taken ownership of and pulled her covers back up to her chin. I knew that she was too warm, and I figured that she would probably wake me again. I headed back to the couch, knowing that I wasn't going to go back to sleep tonight. I looked at the clock and it was only 11:45. There was still a lot of night left for nightmares.

I was wrong, I did fall back to sleep. Shannon woke me a couple of hours later, whimpering and softly talking in her sleep, but not in extreme distress, and I got up and looked in on her. She was lying on her side with the covers under her arm and over her chest, leaving her shoulder bare. She looked more comfortable and not so hot, and I went back to the couch.

I woke around 6:00. I thought that she had slept for the rest of the night. I peeked in on her, and she was breathing. That's good, I thought. I walked back to the couch and found my clothes, putting them on, and figured that I should go. I took a piece of printer paper from her desk and wrote a note:

Shannon,
Thanks for the date. I won't forget this one!!! Please call me when you wake up.
Den

I looked back in on her before I left. She was on her side in a fetal position with the covers pulled up to her chin. She looked calm and tan, and beautiful, and I sighed. I waited to see the rise and fall of her breathing. I could see her nightgown, balled up in the corner, and I looked back at her again with her hair in disarray, then turned, leaving her room.

I opened her front door, remembering that it was Sunday, and I didn't have any plans and hoping that she would call me soon. I stepped out running into two girls at the top of the stairs who gave me a funny look. I felt like I needed to defend Shannon's honor, but I knew the more I said, the worse it would be, so I nodded and bowed a bit, and walked down the stairs to my car.

It seemed like a lifetime since I had seen Bryan. So much had happened in one day that my head was spinning. I missed him and felt some guilt because I wasn't with him, even though it had only been one day and night. But then on the other hand, despite the weirdness of the last twenty-four hours, I couldn't wait to see Shannon again.

I drove home replaying the events of yesterday and found that I could barely keep my eyes open. I pulled in behind my house, parked and walked into the side door which led to the kitchen. I checked for phone messages. There were none, and I could feel all my remaining energy drain. Maybe I could grab a nap before Bry was delivered to me.

Everything then crossed my mind simultaneously. I wondered if Shannon might be awake yet, yesterday's weirdness, my chores and responsibilities, and my wife... Huh, Lauren, what do you think? I felt some guilt because of the growing feelings that I had for Shannon. Before it was maybe just attraction, but now it feels like more, a lot more. Something was happening between us, something very nice, before "IT" happened. Whatever "IT" was.

I dragged myself to the couch and turned on the TV. I surfed through the channels, not paying attention. Hey, it's the guy with the crazy hair on the History Channel. I stopped and turned up the volume. He was explaining how these aliens acted like gods to some tribe in South America, showing images of spaceman like creatures, with huge erect organs, carved into stone. I could barely keep my eyes opened, and I dozed off...

The next thing I knew, someone was pounding on the door. I looked up disoriented, rubbing my face and could see Liz through the window. I rose from the couch groggily and shuffled to the door. I must look like death, I thought and glanced at the clock. It was 12:05. I couldn't believe how late it was. I wished that I felt better and couldn't believe how long I slept. I pulled the door open.

"Hi, guys," I managed.

Liz looked at me with obvious concern. "Dennis? No offense, but you look like something that the cat drug in."

"Thanks," I said embarrassed. "Hey, buddy," I said, turning my attention to Bryan.

He leaped into my arms, hugging me and happy to be home.

"So, how was last night?" Liz asked, but really meant how much do you like this person? Did you sleep with her, and do you think we will like her? It's amazing how much can be conveyed in one simple question.

"Hey, Bryan, I think Sesame Street is on. Go change the channel," I said moving him from the conversation. I'm not sure what he might pick up, but I didn't want to take the chance. I looked over my shoulder as he scooped up the remote and deftly changed the channel to PBS.

When I heard Bert and Ernie, I continued, "Liz, Uncle Jonathan was right. There is something wrong with the house," I said, not quite knowing how to proceed here without Liz thinking that I'd lost my mind, and wanting to downplay what happened to Shannon, at least until I had a chance to think it through more thoroughly.

Liz looked at me with an expression that moved from concern to skepticism. "What happened, Dennis?" she asked.

"I took Shannon to the house to have lunch and maybe hike the land around it. We were having a nice day, and we sat to eat at Jonathan's table when the quake hit."

"Yeah, that was a bit of a shaker," Liz said.

"Did you guys have any damage?" I asked, changing the subject and feeling like I should have asked sooner.

"No," she said.

"Do you know how large it was?"

"I heard it was 6.0 located south of Sacramento," she said shortly but meant get on with it.

"The quake unearthed a cave in the hill on the west side of the house. We went inside the cave and found a tunnel that led to a large cavern with an ancient stone circle in it. It was amazing, and a real archeological find. Shannon slipped in the cavern and got covered with mud. It was getting late, and I asked if she would like to stay for dinner. She said that she would, but she was full of mud, so I asked her if she would like to use the shower while I cooked. She said okay, and I gave her a towel and soap and went to the kitchen to start dinner. She was only in there for about twenty minutes when she screamed."

"When she was in the shower?" Liz asked.

"Well, actually she had just stepped out. The rest is hard to explain, but something happened to her, like something unknown."

"Unknown?" Liz said questioningly with a great deal of skepticism.

I sighed knowing how this sounded. "Yeah," I said looking down. "I walked into the bathroom and she was nearly catatonic. She was staring, and I had trouble finding out what happened. I wanted to call an ambulance, but she said no. She said she wasn't sick, but I worried that she may have had some kind of seizure. She asked me to take her home, and as the minutes went by, she improved, and told me what she thought happened."

"I think you should have taken her to the hospital, Dennis," Liz said with the nurse in her coming out.

I sighed again. "I don't know. When I first saw her dripping there in the bathroom, I thought something was medically wrong with her, but as she began to tell me what she thought happened... I didn't think it was medical."

"Dripping?" Liz said, more statement than question, figuring out that she was dressed in only skin.

"Ah... Well," I stammered.

Liz let that go and said, "I think you need to get her to a doctor. Have you heard from her yet?"

"No. I checked on her before I left and asked her to call me when she woke."

Liz's eyes went up. "You stayed the night?" she asked.

"She didn't want to be alone. She was afraid, and I wanted to keep an eye on her," I said, but it sounded lame.

Liz looked at me sideways.

"Okaayy," she said, drawing out the word but meant that you don't have to explain yourself to me.

"No. It's not like that," I said but sounded defensive. "Something happened to her in Jonathan's house, just like he said it would. I'll tell you what, Liz, I don't think I'll ever go back out there, and I'm sure Shannon won't, ancient find or not."

"Let me go talk to George. You should try to call your friend," Liz said emphasizing the word *friend* and implying that we had become more familiar than that. I guess spending the night and seeing her naked does constitute more than friends, but it was all so innocent.

"Okay," I said, suddenly wondering if Shannon would ever want to see me again. She hasn't called either.

"That's a pretty wild story, Dennis."

"You're telling me. Most of it seems like a nightmare," I said shaking my head.

Liz turned and walked from my house. If someone had told me that story, I wouldn't believe it.

I went straight for the phone.

Bryan was giggling at The Count on Sesame Street.

I dialed and the phone just rang. "Come on, Shannon. Pick up," I said to no one. I got her voice mail. "Hey, Shannon give me a call. I'm worried about you," I said, sighed, and figured I would call again in about a half an hour.

I got lunch for Bryan. We had no plans for our Sunday. I worked around the house taking care of a few household chores as Bry finished lunch. I tried Shannon's cell again but got no answer. Bryan was getting antsy, so we drove to the library. When we got back, I tried to call Shannon again with no success. I puttered around the house, getting Bryan's clothes ready for school and watching a DVD with him. The time dragged and I looked at the clock every fifteen minutes with no call. I tried her again around 5:00 and began to worry more. Maybe she had to go somewhere? I wished she would have called. I fixed dinner for Bryan, and now I was feeling desperate. We ate and I tried to call Shannon again, with no success.

I called George and Liz and George answered.

"Hi, George. Do you think you could watch Bryan for me? Shannon still hasn't answered, and I'm really worried, and I want to drive over there."

"Sure, Dennis. Bring him by."

I picked up Bryan. "Hey buddy, Amma and Ampa want you to come and visit," I said, heading out the door and leaving dirty dishes in the sink.

I dropped him off and drove to Shannon's with my foot on the gas. I dialed her phone as I pulled into her lot and she finally answered.

"Hello?" she said in a raspy voice.

"Shannon, I've been trying to call you all day. I'm pulling into your lot now. I'll be right there." I hung up not waiting for her to say anything.

I raced into a parking space, jumped from the car and ran up the stairs. I knocked on the door and waited and waited... and waited. She finally opened the door.

"Did you slip me a roofie?" she asked.

"What?!" I said incredulously.

"Come in," she said, grabbing my arm sleeve and dragging me in like a three-year-old with a pull toy.

"Are you okay?" I asked, getting a good look at her.

"I don't know," she said, glancing up and catching the look on my face, "What?" she said.

Shannon looked like ten miles of bad road. She had bags under her barely opened eyes, her hair was sticking in all directions, and her nightgown was wrinkled to the point of being unsalvageable, with the edge being tucked into her underpants in the back, and the front unbuttoned to nearly her navel, showing most of her left breast, just hiding her nipple. I could tell that she was oblivious to her appearance because her underpants were rolled up and they barely covered her private parts. She looked asleep on her feet.

I walked up to her, straightened her nightgown and buttoned her up. She looked down at what I was doing and made no attempt to help.

She could see most of her own breast and some lower stomach and hip and she said, "You've sure seen a lot of *ME* lately."

I smiled and went down to one knee, pulling the nightie out of her underpants, and straightening them to more cover her private parts. I stood back up and smoothed the wrinkles on her shoulders.

"Well, for what it's worth, I didn't see all of your breast this time."

I'm not sure she had any idea how uncovered she was. She just stood there, eyes drooping, arms hanging limply and looking very much drugged and confused.

"Ummm," she said. "You don't do hair and makeup too, do you?"

"No, but why don't I see what you have to eat, and I'll fix something for you."

"You could talk me into that," she replied. She looked at me with a silly smile, "So how do I look?" she said, striking a pose and knowing that she was a fright, her sense of humor returning.

"You look... You look... You look tan," I finally said.

She smiled, again, and I could see that she was waking up a bit more.

"Give me a couple of minutes, and I'll try to improve this," she said holding out some crazy hair pieces. She turned and walked stiffly to her bedroom with her nightgown now covering her properly and came out with some sweats and underclothes. "I'm going to take a shower," she said almost mechanically.

"Okay, I'll see what's in the kitchen," I said.

She turned for the shower and I headed for the kitchen to see what I could find. I heard her close the door and I rummaged around her orderly refrigerator. It looked freshly scrubbed. I found eggs, a red potato for some home fries, and some bread for toast, perfect. I looked through her pots and pans and found a medium frying pan. I also dug up a bowl to scramble the eggs in and a spatula. I started to cut the potatoes into small chunks when Shannon yelled at me from the bathroom.

"Dennis! Come in here!"

I looked up. "Not this again. What's up with the shower?"

I stopped my cooking and headed hastily to the bathroom and opened the door. No shyness this time. Shannon was standing there in her underpants with a towel covering her bare breasts.

"Look," she said pointing to the back of her leg, where the birthmark was. "My birthmark is back, and some moles have returned and look here," she said lowering the towel about four inches below her collarbone. "A kid threw a steel toy car and hit me here when I was young. The only thing that's still gone is the two bruises that I got in the cave. They seem to be healed."

"Hmmm," I said. "I know what I'm going to do."

Shannon looked at me knowing something off-the-wall was coming.

"I'm canceling that call to Estee Lauder."

"Dumb ass. Get out of here," she said.

I smiled. "I'll have a good meal ready for you in about fifteen minutes."

I turned and walked from the bathroom closing the door behind me and got back to my cooking. Her apartment was quiet and I could hear the shower start and then water splashing as Shannon moved.

My attraction for her is different from anyone who I have ever known. She's pleasant to my eyes of course, but it's more the way she is. She has an easy way and there's this wonderful kindness in her. Her beauty comes, not only from what she is, it also comes from the things that she's not. She has me completely interested.

I heard the shower turn off, sending me from my thoughts back to my tasks. I uncovered the potatoes and browned them, flipping them in a very hot pan, and put down the toast. I then slowly poured the eggs in the side of the pan away from the finished potatoes and cooked them quickly in butter. I heard the bathroom door open, as the toast popped up. I finished cooking the eggs and buttered the toast as Shannon walked in the kitchen in heavy sweats and bare feet.

"Hey. Do you feel better?" I said with a great deal of affection.

She nodded. "It smells great in here, Den."

"Sit down. Breakfast is served. Do you want ketchup?"

"That would be good, thanks."

I plated the food and set it on the table. She ate slowly, and I watched, not speaking. She glanced up at me and recognized the look of concern on my face.

"Dennis, what's wrong?"

"I... I'm..." I stopped not sure of my words and then blurted out. "Shannon, I'm so sorry."

She smiled and then quietly laughed. "The food isn't that bad."

Then I laughed.

"Dennis, what happened to me wasn't your fault. You know..." she said shaking her head and taking another bite of food... "honestly, you are the most guilt-ridden person that I know. You must have gone to Catholic school."

"I did," I said smiling.

She giggled quietly.

"I guess I know but I feel responsible."

"I know you do, Dennis, and for some reason, it's kind of, the part of you that appeals to me so much. I don't think you would purposely hurt anyone. By the way, the food is very good." She took another bite. "I'm really all right, Dennis," she said continuing to use my full name the way my mother did when she was talking seriously. "We have some things to talk about, though, as I put this back together in my mind, but right now I'm all scattered."

She put her attention back to finishing her food. She cleaned her plate and looked up, "I know that this is going to sound weird, but I think I want to go back to bed."

"Would you like me to tuck you in?" I asked in a motherly way.

"Are you going to put me in my jammies, get my nummy, and read me a story?" she said picking up on my tone.

"All that," I said with a great deal of affection.

"Maybe next time."

"Let me clean up the mess," I said.

"No, just put some water in the pan and bowls. I'm beat."

"Shannon, I'm worried about you."

"I know but I'm fine. I'll call you tomorrow. Thanks for the food. I'm sorry I missed your dinner at the crazy house. I bet it was going to be good."

"Five star," I said.

"Shannon smiled. "Well, another time. Okay?"

"I would like that," I said.

She ushered me to the door and gave me a small hug. "Good night, Den."

"Call me in the morning, okay?" I said and knew I sounded pleading.

"I will," Shannon said, like a child talking to her mother.

I walked out and she closed the door behind me.

31

Sideways Chapter 21

I slept like a dead man until my alarm went off at 6:30 am. I got myself and Bryan up, fed, and ready for the day. As I finished packing Bryan's lunch for school, the phone rang. It was 7:30 and I hoped it would be Shannon. I hadn't stopped thinking about her for even a second. I hurriedly reached for the phone.

"Hello," I said.

"Hi, Den," Shannon said.

"How are you?" I asked, still very concerned.

"I'm much better. I can actually put two thoughts together."

"Should we cancel swimming?"

"No. I'll see you there."

"Okay. Good... that sounds good. I'm happy to hear your voice," I said and I knew that she could hear a lot of different emotions in that simple sentence.

"Den, I'm okay, really. I'll see you at swim. I need to go to the college today and thought I would talk to a professor of mine about stone circles. I have a suspicion about what happened. I don't know. I want to run something by him."

"Well, Okay?"

"I'll see you at 3:00. Bye, Den."

"Bye," I said as she hung up the phone.

I stood there for a second, wondering what she was thinking about the stones and thought admiringly, considering what happened, she didn't seem to have lost a step.

I took Bryan to school, telling his teacher that I would pick him up and then drove to the gym, and went through the motions of my workout, not seeing any friends, and lost in thought. What happened to Shannon, and me indirectly, has changed my whole perspective. Nothing that happened to her made any sense and all the skeptical arguments about hallucinations, hysteria, or delusions seemed null and void for this new reality. But what happened?

I drove home and walked into my house in a daze, puttered around, doing some chores and wondering what Shannon could have found out. Was there some connection with the stone circle in the cave under the house? My mind kept sticking on some kind of haunting, poltergeist, or heaven forbid, possession. It seemed that there had been many stories surrounding these circles and weird phenomena but they mostly seemed like a cartoon to me. What happened to Shannon was no cartoon.

32

Sideways Chapter 22

Shannon walked into her professor's office. He was a tall man with small shoulders, a bit of a pot belly, graying, and in his late fifties. He looked like he had never exercised much and spent most of his time in academia.

The office was small, almost closet like, with books and papers scattered on a small desk, and a full, wall-sized bookcase crammed with books. He was sitting at his desk pouring over something that had his full attention. As Shannon walked in, he looked up, over his glasses and smiled at her in a way that seemed suggestive. She had the idea that he was attracted to her. He had never made any advances but the way he looked at her sometimes left her feeling mentally undressed.

"Hi, Professor Wellington. Do you have a minute?"

"Shannon, come in. Sit down," he said, pointing her to the chair in front of his desk.

She sat down folding her hands in her lap.

"What can I do for you? Have you decided to take me up on that internship I told you about?"

"No. I'm still thinking about it," she said.

"It's a once in a lifetime opportunity. The lead archeologist on the site is a good friend of mine, a Doctor Arnold. He says that they think that this site will not only predate any known humans on the North American continent, he thinks it might predate all of human history. I'm going to take the year off to join him on this, and I'm happy you haven't ruled it out," he finished.

"That does sound exciting. I do have kind of an archeological question for you."

He smiled but showed some concern. "I hope you're not thinking about changing majors?"

"No," she said. "I have a friend who has stumbled onto a stone circle on some property that he owns. It looks old and he asked me to do a little research on these circles and some of the myths surrounding them. He's curious to know if circle makers were prevalent in North America."

Wellington's expression changed and Shannon had a hard time reading it. She got the feeling that he was hiding something. He looked down and then back at Shannon.

"Yes. I can send you out with some ideas. Most of the circles that I know about came here just before or after the revolutionary war with the Celtic immigrants but there are a few that are much older, possibly of Indian origin. It just so happens that I also have a friend who is giving a guest lecture here tonight and for the next three nights about stone circles, the ancient myths surrounding them and Celtic folklore. It's a very interesting topic. If you can get here around five, I can probably get you a minute or two with her before her lecture. She has been part of some rituals that take place in the circles. She says that she's a Caller because she calls down the sun or something like that. Your timing is excellent; she only comes here twice a year and the hall is usually packed. Would you like to meet her?"

"Thanks, that would be great," Shannon said.

"Good. I'll set it up. There are a lot of phenomena and superstition that surrounds these circles and other sites like them where stone was used or had been cut or moved in ways not easily explained. I have a good book on circles and other sites like Puma Puku. The stonework seems to be far above the technology of the age and the size of some of the stones that were moved is astounding. When it comes to stone circles, Gobekli Tepi is particularly interesting. It predates the oldest known cities in the world by around six thousand years. It's really quite amazing. There is so much that we don't know about ancient peoples. Here," Wellington said, handing Shannon the book. "bring it back to me when you've finished."

"Thanks," she said, opening the large coffee table sized book and thumbing through the pages.

"Come to my office at 5:00. I won't be here, but I'll let my friend know to meet you."

"Thanks, Professor. I'll be here."

"Shannon, this circle that your friend found... Well... it may be worth some money for him, especially if it predates the indigenous tribes. Doctor Arnold, the lead archeologist on the dig that I told you about, has a benefactor with a great deal of money at his disposal. They are looking for sites that may be similar to the one your friend found. Can you tell me more?"

"I'll tell you more, later, but I have something to do now and I have to go," she said not wanting to say more.

"Okay, let's talk later. If your friend needs someone to give him an idea of how old the site is, I'm sure Professor Arnold would be available."

"Thanks, I'll tell him," Shannon said but could see something in Wellington's eyes. She got up and walked towards the door with an odd feeling. "Thanks again, Professor," she said.

"No problem. My pleasure," he said and she walked out.

33

Sideways Chapter 23

I drove to Bryan's school, picked him up, and drove to the club for his swimming lessons with Shannon. It seemed odd to go through all the mundane things in life considering what had happened to her. But what else would you do?

We showered and walked into the pool area and could see Shannon sitting on a plastic lounge in her swimming suit with a large book on her lap, and we walked up unnoticed.

"Hi," I said, startling her a bit.

"Oh, Hi, Dennis. Hi, Bryan," she said, looking up.

"How are you feeling?" I asked.

"Much better," she said. "I'm learning a bit about stone circles." She raised the book off her lap, showing me the cover. "My professor gave this to me this afternoon."

"Let's get together tonight and talk about it," I said, wanting to not let her pull away from me because of what happened.

"Well, okay," she said, waiting for more.

"I was thinking, maybe, I could try cooking dinner for you again," I said.

She looked up at me, taking her attention from what she was reading and then looked back at her book and said, "I don't know, dinner with you is dangerous."

"Well, I thought that if I picked a place that didn't have strange phenomena, it might be safer."

"Hmmm. I'm not sure that strange phenomena doesn't follow you."

"True, but this time Bryan will be there to protect you," I said, glancing at Bryan.

"My hero," she said, closing the book, scooping up Bryan, and heading for the pool. "Okay. It's a date. I'll bring the wine."

Shannon and Bryan went through their usual routine, kickboard, superman float, and Bryan's favorite, underwater swim. Finishing, they walked from the pool. Bryan splashed up to me and I wrapped him in a towel.

"So, can I pick you up about 5:30," I asked.

"No, I have some running around to do, and then I'm meeting a lady, who is a friend of my professor's. He said that she's a Caller. That's someone who actually takes part in the stone circle rituals. She does lectures on Celtic folklore and she's at my college right now as a guest lecturer. He's arranged for me to meet her at 5:00. I'll come over after I talk to her."

"Okay. That should be interesting. So, do you think that the stone circle had something to do with what happened to you?" I asked.

"I don't know, Den. Maybe I'm reaching, but it feels like more than a coincidence, although it may be."

"Do you think you can be there by 6:30?" I asked wanting to plan the meal.

"6:30 it is. Oh, and try not to burn it this time," she said, and I laughed.

"I shouldn't if you keep your clothes on," I said.

Shannon gave me a funny look. I think it slipped her mind that she spent quite a bit of time that night in nothing but skin. She blushed bright red and then looked away. I laughed again, unable to contain it.

She looked back and said, "I promise."

I thought that I might have crossed the line a bit but Shannon can dish it out and can also take it.

Shaking her head, she said, "See you at 6:30."

I dried Bryan off and wrapped the towel back around him.

"Hey, Den, my professor said that there may be some money from the sale of your house to some guy who's the money behind that archeological dig that I told you about. I got the impression that stone circles are right up his alley. He also gave me the idea that the guy has a fat wallet. I know that this is premature but I thought I would tell you."

"Huh... Thanks," I said.

"He seemed odd about it though."

"Odd?" I asked.

"I don't know. Never mind. It may have just been my imagination."

"Where's your next lesson?" I asked about the cute little girl who usually followed Bryan.

"Her mom called and said that they would be fifteen minutes late."

I nodded, looked out towards the front desk and saw them come in. "There they are," I said. "I'll see you tonight."

"See you tonight," she repeated. "Bye, Bryan."

She smiled and we walked away. I looked back over my shoulder, wanting to see her again. She was looking at me and smiling. I do like that smile, I thought.

As I passed the mom and her little girl, I said, "Hi," and she said, hi, back, and we walked out to the car.

I buckled Bryan into his car seat and he said and signed, "Swim teacher come to dinner?"

"You don't miss a thing, do you? Let's go to the grocery store and buy something special for dinner."

"Chicken fingers?" he signed.

"Wow, you really do want to impress her, don't you? I was thinking more like steak with my special sauce, baked potatoes, and asparagus."

"Auughhh," Bryan said disgustedly.

"Well how about chicken fingers for you."

"Aaahh," he said enthusiastically.

"You got it, my sweet," I said and drove out of the lot.

We hurried through the grocery store, and as usual, I ran into some friends that I used to work with. A little small talk and we were off to the check stand. As we walked out of the store, we ran smack into Monica the lawyer.

"Well, if it isn't Dennis," she said in her way which sounded condescending but I think of as affectionate.

"Hi, Monica. How are you doing?" I said.

"Just fine. How about you?"

"Great," I said.

"I've heard that before," she said as a well-dressed guy in his late twenties, hustled towards her. She glanced his way and smiled, and he returned it. There was something in the way they smiled at each other that spoke of familiarity.

"Looks like you have a good night ahead of you. Catch you later," I said just before he arrived.

He reached Monica, and smiled at her, again, and then gave me a funny look.

"Hi," I said shaking his hand. "Monica did some pro bono work for me."

Monica laughed and shook her head. "See you, Den."

We turned for the car and could hear them laugh a bit as they entered the store. I put Bryan in his car seat and we drove away.

Pulling in behind my house, I couldn't see George or Liz outside and I couldn't help but feel happy about that. I didn't want to seem sneaky but I felt a bit like a teenager slipping into his girlfriend's window in the middle of the night. Silly.

Bryan and I carried the groceries into the house. I had the two bags and he had the chicken fingers. I checked phone messages, changed us out of our swimsuits and threw a load of wash in the machine. "Let's see what's on TV for you, sweetie boy." I turned on PBS to see if we were too late for Sesame Street and it was still on. We're in luck, just in time to hear the Count counting sneezes.

"Vun sneeze, two sneezes, three sneezes, I love to count sneezes, ha ha ha," he said.

"That Count is so silly," I said.

"Ahhh," Bry said back smiling.

I thought we should eat dinner around 7:00, so I'll get some cheese and crackers to go with the wine… Potatoes in the oven by 6:00… I think twenty to twenty-five minutes for the steaks… I wonder how she likes hers cooked?

I would need to wait until she got here to put the meat on. I continued to plan the meal in my mind, and bounced around the kitchen, trying to have everything under control, so I could give her my attention.

By 6:00 Bryan was tired of TV and wanted to play with his computer. He signed for me to set it up. We haven't had any trouble with it since that day that it wigged out at Jonathan's house. Humm. I hadn't thought about that for a while. That was odd, and I think I still have the paper where I wrote down the numbers that appeared in the balloons. I'll have to look for it. I must admit, that I now have a healthy respect for Jonathan. No more Crazy Jonny, now just crazy house. I have a friend who is deep into computers. I wonder if he might be able to give me some idea of what the numbers mean if they mean anything at all. I'll look for the paper, and if I can find it, I might drop it by his computer shop tomorrow.

***

At 6:25, Shannon pulled up to the address that Dennis had given her. She saw the big house in the front and could see the small house nestled in behind a nicely landscaped yard with a pool. She sat nervously in her car and looked at the large house. She wasn't sure how to get to Dennis', so she decided to knock on the big house's door, but first, she would gather her courage.

***

"George, did I just hear a car pull up in front of the house?" Liz asked.

George was reading, sitting in his favorite chair, and he leaned over and looked out of the window. He could see an SUV parked in front of their fence with a girl inside.

A girl in her early-twenties warily got out of the car, carrying wine, and walked towards the front door. She was slim, with her short hair combed neat, wearing jeans shorts, a yellow tee shirt, and sandals.

"Yeah. There's a car parked out front, and a very attractive girl has gotten out with a bottle of wine in her hand."

Liz walked to the window and smiled. "I think we're about to meet Shannon," she said.

The girl walked towards the door and before she could knock, it opened, and George stepped out with Liz behind him.

"You must be Shannon," he said warmly.

"You must be psychic," the girl said back, smiling and offering her hand to shake.

"No. I'm George, but I've heard a fair bit about you," he said shaking her hand.

"You must be Liz," Shannon said, reaching to shake Liz's hand. "I've heard a fair bit about you both also. It's nice to meet you."

"It's nice to meet you, too," Liz said unconsciously, sizing Shannon up. There are so many things that go into a first impression.

"Shannon, we also heard about what happened to you at Jonathan's house. We both hope you're all right," George said, and he got a look from Liz that he might have said too much.

Shannon picked up the look and said, "It's okay," to Liz. "I'm okay, but it was very strange. Both Dennis and I have been trying to figure out what happened. Whatever it was, it was intelligent and sorry at the same time. I'm still trying to connect all the dots, though. My memories of it seem to be spotty, with new insights happening, and then fading."

Shannon became embarrassed, knowing how that must have sounded, and also knowing how naked she was that night. Both thoughts left her disconcerted, not knowing how much Dennis had told them.

"Shannon, we believe you," George said, catching part of her worry.

"Thanks, I know how it sounds," she said, looking at the ground, and not knowing what else to say. "Your house is beautiful," she said, then, trying to change the direction of the conversation.

"Thank you," Liz said. "We'll walk you back to Dennis."

They led Shannon through a small white gate and passed the pool.

***

With the potatoes in the oven, I whipped up the sauce for the meat, a flavored butter, with fresh sweet basil. I got a head start on the wine with a small glass, and washed the asparagus, getting it ready to steam. I was about to start the grill when there was a knock at the door. I wiped my hands on the dish towel and walked there. When I answered it, I saw Shannon flanked by Liz and George.

"Ah... Hello," I said, looking from one person to the next.

Liz smiled, enjoying my discomfort. "Hi, Dennis," Liz said far too chipper.

"Liz, George, I would like to introduce you to Shannon," I said with some ceremony.

"We just met," Liz said.

"Come in guys," I said smiling. "Is it hot in here?" I asked, tugging at my collar.

"Hi, Dennis," Shannon said.

I opened the screen door and she walked in, wonderfully at ease. Then she saw Bryan, "Hi, Bryan."

Bryan's eyes lit up. "I," he said, unable to pronounce the h in hi.

Shannon went over and sat next to him, "What are you watching?" she asked and he pointed at the screen and smiled.

George said, "We would love to stay, but we have to go. Nice to meet you, Shannon."

She looked up and smiled.

"Yeah, we have to go," Liz said.

"It was nice to meet you both also," Shannon said.

"Bye, guys," I said, closing the door as they started away with Liz looking over her shoulder at me.

"Hi, again, Shannon," I said. "You found the place."

"Yep. Here's some wine," she said holding out the bottle.

"I'll open it," I said, taking it from her, and turning for the kitchen.

She got up and followed me in, "Nice place."

"Yeah, I really love it here. I think I'm pretty lucky."

"Nice in-laws, too, I must say," she added.

"They're great," I said, looking up and catching something in her voice.

"We had a bit of a talk," she said.

"Oh?"

"They seemed to know a lot about what happened to me."

"I told them, or at least I told Liz. I'm sure she told George... Are you mad?"

"No, but... Did you tell them that I was naked?" she said, blushing and looking up at me.

I burst out laughing. "Really, Shannon? Oh, that's pretty funny."

Shannon started laughing too. "Get me that wine," she said, and I poured her a healthy glass.

"Thanks," she said and sat down at the kitchen table looking away from me. I could see a growing blush on her cheeks and then travel to her neck and onto her chest. I smiled to myself thinking that she was absolutely beautiful. When she got here, I wasn't picturing her nude until she mentioned it, now I'm having trouble not thinking about it. I know that's what's in her mind right now, and there just isn't any way I can help. I know that I need to change the subject and try to put her at ease. I took a sip of the wine that she brought.

"This is good," I said.

"It is," she said with her discomfort rising. "So, is this too weird for you? I mean because of their daughter," she asked, referring to Liz and George. She looked at me with sympathy.

"Shannon, come here a minute," I said, walking back into the front room, where Bryan was watching TV. I led her to a picture of Bryan and Lauren. "This was Lauren, with Bryan," I said, lifting the picture. "I don't want you to feel uncomfortable, Shannon. The past is the past, and not me, or George, or Liz can do anything about it," I said, placing the picture back down.

Shannon smiled at me, but her eyes were sad. "It didn't seem so real to me, I guess until I came here tonight," she said.

"George and Liz had a talk with me a couple of months ago and said that people shouldn't be alone. They could tell that I was lonely. They said that if I decided to date again, that they would be okay with it, and then they proceeded to set me up on the date from hell."

Shannon laughed, and we walked outside to start up the grill.

"So, how do you like your steak?" I asked.

"Medium rare."

"Perfect, me too," I said. "Oh, how did your meeting go with the Caller lady?"

"That was very weird," Shannon said, and she gave me a disturbed look.

"What?"

"Well, first I started talking to her about your circle, and it seemed like she was giving me this rehearsed speech. Scripted you know."

"She's probably tired of telling everyone the same thing," I said, taking a sip of wine.

"That's what I thought. She seemed to be spitting out a generic lecture, and she looked at me like why don't you just come tonight and save me the trouble of telling you this now, but she forged on and told me about how Scottish and Irish people came over before the Revolutionary War, bringing their old religion and superstitions that predate Christianity. I told her that your circle was in a cave, and she was surprised that it was underground. She said that it didn't make sense because the sun and stars are important parts of the circle ceremonies. She said, though, that these circles are supposed to mark points of power in the earth, and maybe that had something to do with its location. Some shadow crossed her face then, and I thought that she might be hiding something."

"Well, isn't most of that stuff supposed to be secret?"

"That crossed my mind also, but there seemed to be more. She said that she had no more time to chat and that she needed to go, so I followed her out the door. She started to walk away kind of fast, obviously finished with me. I told her, as she was starting to get some distance from me, that something strange happened to me near the circle, and, Dennis, you wouldn't believe it. She stopped in mid-stride and turned back to me slowly. I could see the blood drain from her already pale face, and she became noticeably frightened. She walked back to me, took my arm, and pulled me close whispering in my ear, 'I need to talk to you, but not here.' I said, 'What?' Not able to keep up with this change in attitude. Then she said, 'Can you meet me back here on Wednesday?' I said, 'Okay,' and then she says, 'Same time same place, but in the parking lot,' and then she turned on her heels and strode away for her lecture, I guess, but as she walked away she kept looking over her shoulders, left and right like she was being followed. It left me with goosebumps," Shannon finished.

"Damn," I said.

"I know. It was bizarre!"

"So, I guess you're going to meet her?"

"Oh yeah. She knows something."

We walked back inside and I refilled our wine. I put Bryan's chicken fingers in the oven and got the steaks for the grill.

"Come back outside with me?" I asked.

She nodded and followed me back to the grill. We could see Bryan through the screen door, watching one of his favorite DVDs, and bouncing to music with a look of pure delight on his face. I put the steaks on with the sizzle of the meat hitting the hot grill. The evening was warm, without a breeze, and we sipped our wine, as the smoke from the meat drifted around us in clouds of aroma.

"Are you sure that meeting this lady again is going to be worth the effort?" I asked.

"I think so, but I'm not sure. It couldn't hurt, though, because we're no closer to knowing what happened to me."

"I guess," I said, not fully convinced.

I flipped the steaks and walked back into the house, asking Shannon to follow. She sat at the table while I started the asparagus. I took the basil butter from the refrigerator so that it would be close to room temperature when I smothered the steak with it, and then I refreshed our wine, set the table and checked on the chicken fingers and potatoes. As I worked pulling dinner together, I noticed Shannon watching me, and giving me a funny look.

"What?" I said.

"You would make someone a good wife someday," she said teasing.

"I've gotten better at this. It's called on the job training."

She smiled and took a sip of wine. I knew she was giving me a bad time, but I could also tell that she was somewhat impressed. She got up and walked over to Bryan to give him some attention. He had moved to his computer and he was showing Shannon one of his favorite games. I walked over and topped off her wine again.

"Not too much," she said. "I promised to keep my clothes on, you know."

She smiled, and I smiled back. "Feeling a little uninhibited, are you?" I asked.

"Yep. I think skinny dipping out there in that pool would be fun," she said giggling.

"That would get Liz and George's attention," I said, and we both started laughing a little too much with the wine having some effect.

I went back to the kitchen, hearing the water boil for the asparagus, and the timer go off for the chicken fingers, and potatoes.

"Dinner time," I said.

Bryan ran to the table and Shannon followed. I got the steaks from the grill, and let them set for about five minutes, and then scooped out some baked potato for Bryan, making sure it wasn't too hot. I put him in his booster seat and gave him some asparagus with mayo first, then gave him his chicken fingers with some ketchup and his baked potatoes in a bowl. Shannon sat to Bryan's right, and I arranged her food as artistically as I could and set it in front of her.

"Would you like some mayo with your asparagus?" I asked.

"Yes, thanks," she said.

She stared at the food for a minute and then cut her steak. I watched to make sure it was medium rare as ordered. I had already cut mine and was pretty sure hers would be. She took a bite.

"This steak is wonderful," she said.

"Thanks," I said, and was sure I beamed.

The conversation became a little surreal with all that had happened to us. We talked about the club, and people that we both knew. I asked her about school and her classes. No change there. Bryan was finished and I got him down and cleaned him up, and also the floor under him which was always littered with remnants of his meal. I began rinsing the dishes, and Shannon sat at the table, finishing her wine.

"What do you have planned tomorrow?" I asked.

"I'm going to visit my mom. I don't work."

"Oh. How is she doing since your grandma passed away?"

"Not good. It's been hard for her."

"I'm sorry."

"Yeah, so, I'm going to spend some time with her. I bring my laundry and a book, and just hang out. She seems happy after a day like that with me."

"Is she lonely?"

"Some, I think, but she has friends and other relatives, kind of close. I think losing Grandma hit her harder than she imagined it would."

"Tomorrow, I'm going to bring that weird code that was on Bryan's computer to a friend of mine. The guy is way deep into computers and I want him to see it," I said, finishing the dishes, and I sat at the table with Shannon and finished my wine. "Would you like a little more wine?" I asked.

"No thanks, but I would like some water." I got up and got her a bottle and she asked, "Why do you want to show him the code?"

"I don't know. I don't even know if it is a code. I didn't think a lot about it until after you had your experience in the house, and, now, I have a feeling about it."

"Dennis," she said seriously. "There was something intelligent behind what happened to me. I know it. I do feel much better, but there are gaps in my memory, and a nagging feeling that I'm missing something."

We had an awkward moment. "Walk outside with me?" I asked.

She nodded and we passed Bryan poking at his computer. We walked out the screen door and I showed her to a couple of wicker chairs on my small porch. We could see Bry through the window, giggling.

The yard felt like a vacation spot with dim lamps casting shadowy light around the pool area, and the night air warm.

"It really is beautiful out here," she said, looking around.

The moonless sky was clear and the stars were countless above, with the aurora visible to the south.

"I do love it here," I said wistfully. "George and Liz both constantly primp this yard."

"It looks like it."

"You know, Shannon, we have found ourselves in a mystery."

"Yeah, a spooky one," she said.

"I wonder if we'll ever know what happened."

"Maybe," she said. "Maybe not."

Shannon glanced at Bryan playing on his computer, through the window. "So, the computer is working okay now?"

"Yeah, that's the weird thing about it. It's been perfect. The code never returned, and Bryan has played the balloon game several times since."

"Huh," she said and I could see her mind working.

"What?" I asked.

"I don't know. Something just struck me... It was nothing."

"What?" I asked again, a little more persistent.

"I'm not sure. Never mind," she said, but I knew she thought of something.

"Come on, don't leave me hanging."

"Well, it's something in my memory. Was Bryan on his computer, at the table at the Crazy House, when it wigged out?" she asked.

"Yes," I said.

"Did he say something while he was there?" she asked, looking far off as if watching something.

"Yes," I said wondering where she was going.

"Huh," she said, and I could see her turn more inward, but her face seemed to pale.

"What?" I said feeling the goose flesh begin to creep.

"I'm not sure. Let me think about it."

"Okay?" I said.

Abruptly she said, "Dennis, I have to go. I'll see you on Wednesday."

"Okay," I said. "I'll walk you to your truck."

I walked back inside and picked up Bryan while Shannon waited. It seemed like she was in a hurry all of a sudden. I carried Bryan out to her car, and Shannon walked quietly with us. It was an odd change of mood. She seemed happy before but then turned inward. I didn't want to press her, but I could feel the gooseflesh rise.

"Thanks for dinner, Dennis. It was great. I'll see you at swimming lessons," she said, and she wrapped her arms around Bryan and me in a big group hug. She walked around to the driver's side and looked back over her shoulder. "You were right, the dinner was five star," she said. She got into the car, and I waved both happy and sad at the same time.

She drove off and I turned back to the house. "Let's get you ready for bed," I said to Bryan, throwing him onto my shoulders and bouncing him back to the house. I stopped to check the barbeque to make sure that I had turned off the gas, and then went inside, closed the shades, and got us ready for bed.

When I tucked Bryan in he said and signed, "Had fun with swim teacher."

"Me too, buddy. Me too."

As I slipped into my bed, I wondered what Shannon saw in her mind. I know that something entered there, but she wouldn't share it. I don't think that I ever told her any details about that day. I just mentioned what happened to Bryan's computer. Maybe I told her a little, I just didn't remember. On another track, I hoped that she had a good time tonight, and I began to consider all those things that don't make me the catch of the year. I hoped that I would fall asleep quickly because my thoughts were disturbing me. My eyes got heavy and I drifted...

I woke with my bed shaking. There was a woman there, and I looked closer at the long brown familiar hair.

"Lauren?" I said questioningly. I turned on the light to get a better look. There was a lean, nude woman sitting on the side of my bed, facing away from me with long brown hair flowing down her back.

"Lauren," I said again recognizing her familiar lines and muscles. "Where's your nightgown?" I asked.

She turned and looked over her shoulder.

"I was hot," she said.

"Oh... Wait. How can you be here?" I asked admiring those long muscles that lined her back. She was a runner, and I loved the way it looked with each tiny muscle defined.

"I'm always here for you, Dennis," she said smiling, and I thought she was lovely. I slid over to touch her, my body full of need, but she shook her head no.

"But it's been so long, and I miss you," I said, not understanding why she wouldn't touch me.

"Soon," she said again looking over her shoulder, but this time slightly turning, and her hair flowed over her shoulder covering her chest. "But you are in danger, and first must resolve a problem."

"What?" I asked not understanding. She turned to face me, her breasts now visible, and I wanted her more than I could stand. As I moved to touch her, again, she got up and walked towards the bathroom with her hair swaying down the middle of her back.

"Wait," I said desperately.

She turned back to me, and everything went into slow motion, her hair moved like she was under still water. Her body was beautiful, lean, fit, and athletic. My eyes traveled up her nude form, gazing over the familiar contours.

"Lauren?" I said recognizing her body, but those weren't her eyes. They were black, with no white in them and it made her sockets appear to be empty. Fear shot through me as she turned to me and knowing that she had my full attention she began to speak.

"There's a storm coming, Dennis, and you need to be ready," she said in a haunting voice that I barely recognized as hers. She turned and walked away into the bathroom of the house that we shared before I lost her.

"Stop! Wait!" I yelled, but she didn't answer. "Please don't go," I begged, desperate for her to stay.

She turned the corner into the bathroom, and I jumped from the bed and rushed trying to catch her, but she was gone.

"No," I said in despair and I began to weep...

My bed shook again, and I sat straight up and woke to a dark, empty room. As my mind began to clear, I felt, maybe, irrationally, that my wife was here. The dream was so vivid. Was this some kind of visitation from the grave? Something that I didn't believe in. I'm shaken by the dream, lonely for my wife, and afraid of the dream message that may have been nothing more than my brain's synapses misfiring in my sleep. Desolate, I turned to the wall and wept alone with no arms to hold me, and no soft words to comfort me.

34

Sideways Chapter 24

I woke up exhausted from my unsettled night with the dream springing forward in my mind. I could see it complete, my wife first beautiful, then ghostly. I just laid there, trying to figure out what the dream really meant. Was it a warning, or some message from beyond? I have always hated my dreams, but this one left me devastated. Lauren, from time to time, would show up in my dreams, but usually, it was just something frustrating. This was both frightening, and destructive, and I felt crushed.

Arriving at no conclusion about the meaning of the dream, I glanced at the clock. It was 5:30, and I scraped myself from bed and walked in to check on Bryan. I felt like I needed to see him. He was snoozing, breathing softly with the angelic look on his face that he has when he sleeps. I started the coffee and turned on the business station.

I knew that this dream was going to haunt me all day, and I watched TV trying to rid myself of its lingering effects. My mind drifted to Shannon, and the evening with her. I enjoyed it very much, and it seemed to end too soon. I wondered if she felt the same. It was hard to tell, though, because she seemed to leave abruptly. My mind wandered to the Caller lady that she met. That was definitely odd. I became disturbed by my mind jumping all over the place, and then the coffee maker beeped and sputtered, and I got up for my first cup. I didn't seem to be able to concentrate on anything, and nothing seemed to make any sense.

I walked to the couch, cup in hand, and stared at the TV, unseeing. My alarm went off in the bedroom, and I walked in and turned it off. I took off my underclothes and grabbed a change, and then headed to the shower, hoping to restore some coherent thought to my troubled mind.

Finishing, I peeked in on Bryan. "Time to get up, sweetie boy. I know, don't tell me, five more minutes."

"Ahh," he said, not opening his eyes, but reaching for Pooh.

I left his room and started breakfast, grabbed some more coffee, and got his lunch ready. I walked back in and he was asleep. I shook him gently and he turned and smiled at me.

"How's the sweetest boy that there could ever be?" I said.

Smiling, he hugged Pooh again.

I noticed that the stuffed animal population had grown in his bed from the night before. There were at least ten sharing his bunk. I picked up a stuffed robin and danced up his arm with it. "I want some birdie food," I said in a cartoon voice.

Bryan smiled knowing that I was going to be silly.

"Do you have some birdie food for me?" I continued. "Maybe some bugs, or berries, or seeds, or some juicy worms? Yeah, some juicy worms. I like those."

"Ahh," Bry said giggling.

"I just learned a new birdie dance that I want to show you, but first I need to check your ears for worms. Do you have worms in your ears?" I said.

"Noooo," he giggled.

"Oh. Okay, I'll dance."

Bryan, now fully awake, watched as I danced up and down his arm with the stuffed bird.

"Hey, can you fly like me?" I said, making the bird spring from his arm and fly crazy.

Bryan smiled and said, "Noooo."

"Come on, my sweet, time for you and your birdie friend to get up. He has birdie school today."

As a parent, I've learned that there is nothing quite like the sound of your children laughing, and I've also found that I will go to great lengths, including making myself look and sound like a complete idiot, just to hear it.

I sat him up and slipped him into his sweatshirt. He jumped out of bed and headed to the bathroom, and I finished getting his breakfast ready. Thankfully, our daily routine broke the spell of my disturbing dream. We finished and drove to school. I pulled up, and everyone was at the buses, getting the kids off.

"Hi, Miss Kathy," I said, walking Bryan over.

"Hi," she said.

"There you go, Bryan, have a great day, and be safe in everything you do," I said, giving him a hug and turning him over to Miss Kathy. "I'll pick him up today," I said.

Miss Kathy smiled and nodded, and I turned to my car, thinking about stopping by the computer store on my way home from exercise.

I drove to the club, skipping the coffee shop, and not remembering much about the drive. When I checked in at the front desk, I could see Jason in the weight room. As I entered, he looked my way and I could see his eyes widen.

"Hi, Dennis," he said. "Ah, don't take this wrong, but have you gotten any sleep in the last week?"

"Not much, to tell you the truth," I said, opening the locker, and putting my bag in. "Jason, do you believe in ghosts?"

"Yes, but I also believe in the Tooth Fairy and Santa Clause, so I'm probably not the person to ask."

I smiled.

"Why?" he asked.

I debated what to say next. "I have had a … different from normal week, and I'm confused. I'm looking for the rational, but this time it's nowhere to be found."

"You're being very cryptic. Purposely I'm guessing," he said looking at me and I nodded my head slowly.

"It's just weird, Jason," I said, wishing that I hadn't started the conversation.

He said, "I think that there are many things in the world that go unexplained. Too many to be coincidence or swamp gas. The trouble is that there are too few people who have experienced those kinds of things. I personally haven't had any firsthand experience."

I got to my workout and let the conversation drop. Jason didn't pry but would look at me funny from time to time. I found myself weak and having trouble getting my whole workout in, so I quit and didn't push myself. I got my bag from the locker, and said, "I'll catch you later, Jason. I need to go see a friend about a computer problem."

"Okay, Den. You take it easy."

I drove downtown to First Street Computer. An old friend of mine from high school owns the store. He does networking for local businesses, and some small jobs for people having trouble with their personal computers, including replacing broken hardware and retrieving data from crashed hard drives.

Brandon was something of a legend in our high school. Two years younger than me, he got kicked out his junior year for hacking the school's computers to change a grade. They caught him, but a couple of months later all the school's computers crashed. No one was ever caught for that little caper, but the suspicion was revenge. He changed schools and kept hacking as a fun hobby, and then he made computers his livelihood. He now says, raising his right hand, that he would never hack again. Yeah, right.

I walked through the front door, and a low-tech device, a bell hanging on the handle, announced my arrival.

"Hi, Brandon. I was hoping you would be here," I said walking up to his counter.

"Dennis, good to see ya. How long has it been," he said poking at a keyboard and then turning his attention to me.

"I think at least a couple of years."

"Finally messed up your computer so bad that you need professional help?"

"Well, to be honest, I have a bit of a mystery on my hands, and I was hoping you might be able to shed a little light on it."

"I'll give it a shot. Is this a Windows-based computer?"

"Yes."

"You know, they are full of mysteries."

"You're telling me," I said smiling.

"What's the problem?"

"My son Bryan was doing a simple learning program. It's a game where balloons rise up and you pop them by clicking on them with your mouse for the appropriate words, colors, whatever. You get the picture. It started to wig out. I've watched Bryan and worked with him on this program many times, so I know it well. The balloons began to rise so fast that it was impossible to read."

"Sounds like a software problem to me," Brandon said.

"Yeah, that's what I thought at first, until..." I paused, pulling a small piece of paper out of my pocket.

"Until what?" Brandon asked.

"Well, the balloons began to slow down. At first, they still seemed random, but they continued to slow, and soon they became ordered, rising up in rows, always repeating the same number and letter sequence. Each balloon had two digits in them," I said, handing the paper to Brandon. "Here," I said pointing. "I thought it may be some kind of self-diagnostic, giving me a code to explain why the program was no longer working the way it was supposed to. I read through the tiny pamphlet that came with the game, finding nothing. I was wondering if this looks familiar to you."

Brandon listened patiently to my description, and then he said, "It looks like hexadecimal to me. It's a programming code."

"Any idea what it means?" I asked.

He shrugged and walked to his keyboard. "It can't be much. It's pretty short." He started typing rapidly on the keys and wrote a short note on the piece of paper that I gave him. "Does this mean anything to you?" he asked. The note read, "WHO ARE YOU," with no punctuation.

I looked at it and felt a chill. "No," I lied.

"Was the computer online at the time?" he asked.

"No. I wasn't home, and the place I was at isn't set up for that."

"Huh... Beats me, Den. You do have a mystery on your hands."

"Thanks, Brandon. I'll catch you later."

"Good to see you, Den. Don't be a stranger."

"Take care and thanks again," I said turning for the door. The phone rang and Brandon answered as I was walking out.

Brandon said into the phone, "Hi, Mara. Are you in town tonight?" Then I heard him say. "Great."

I let the door close thinking that Brandon had a date, and I went to my car. I climbed in scratching my head. Was this some kind of message? Oh, come on, from who to who. That doesn't make any sense.

As I drove home, it seemed that there were a lot of ends coming together, but everything, except Shannon's encounter, could be written off to something else. Even her encounter could have been some kind of mental thing or seizure or mini-stroke.

So, we have the stone circle with all the legends, the computer message, Shannon's notion that she encountered intelligent beings that communicated to her, the compass going crazy and Jonathan's letter. It seemed like a lot to be a coincidence. Still, it doesn't prove anything, but I have a strong sense that Shannon wasn't sick and that her understanding of what happened to her carries the most weight. Something happened. Something that for now can't be explained. Shannon's meeting with the Caller lady tomorrow should be interesting.

I drove home lost in thought. I showered, ate, changed and picked up Bryan from school for his speech therapy in Sacramento.

Debbie, the therapist, noticed that I was distant, but I couldn't help being a little mentally preoccupied with the mystery.

35

Sideways Chapter 25

The next day, I picked up Bryan from school for his swimming lesson. I wondered what Shannon would think about the message on the computer. I'm sure it will validate her impression, that what happened to her at the "Crazy House" had something intelligent behind it.

Bryan and I showered and walked out of the locker room. As we entered the pool area, Shannon walked out of the girl's locker room, dripping. She turned to us and smiled, with the outline of her body visible through her wet suit.

"Hi," she said.

"Hi, Shannon. How was your day with your mom?"

"It was fine, but my attention was elsewhere all day."

"And where was your mind traveling?"

"A couple of places."

We walked to the pool steps. "Care to expand?" I asked.

"Well first there is this bizarre mystery that I hope to have a little light shed on today, and then I had a wonderful evening with a great guy and his son, and that kept interrupting my thoughts."

"My mind was moving in the same direction if you happen to be talking about me, and not some other great guy you had dinner with."

"I was thinking about you, Dennis," she said directly. She smiled at me with a very vulnerable smile, and I thought that she may be starting to fear her feelings for me. I looked into her eyes and thought that I would never feel this way again. It was a moment charged with so many possibilities.

I said, "I stopped by and talked to my friend that knows computers and got some information about that odd code that appeared on Bryan's computer. I think you'll find it interesting."

She gave me a look that said that's okay, Dennis, I'm not going to press you about your feelings for me.

"What did he say?" she asked.

"He said it was a programming language, and that the code was a question."

"Really?" she said not being able to imagine what it could possibly be.

"Yeah. The question is 'Who are you,' with no punctuation." I could see the blood drain from her face as she processed the message.

"They are trying to communicate," she said and her eyes filled with tears, remembering what had happened to her.

I had a sudden case of denial. "I don't know, and who the hell are they?"

"Something is all I know... Something," she said in a low voice, sounding ghostly.

We became lost in our conversation, and twenty minutes flew by, taking most of Bryan's lesson. We tried to make sense of all the things that we knew, and all the available information, but there was too much of the puzzle missing. We also discussed the fact, that what happened to Shannon might not have any explanation that we could ever understand, any more than an ant could understand an airplane flying overhead. We sat quietly on the steps up to our waist in the water, while Bryan splashed around in the pool.

"Shannon, I'm hungry for pizza," I said. "How about you meet us tonight after you see the Caller lady? I'm buying."

I glanced at the front desk and could see Shannon's next lesson walk through the door, and into the lobby of the club.

"Let me think about it," she said.

"Okay. Come on, Bryan, I'm your swim teacher today," I said walking into the water and picking him up.

Shannon walked out of the pool to greet the little girl and her mom. She started her lesson and turned to me with Bryan.

"No charge for today's lesson," she said smiling.

I laughed and watched her with the young girl. She's so great with the kids that she teaches.

Bryan and I swam and played, catching all the imaginary Pooh Bear characters in the pool and sending them back to the Hundred Acre Woods with magic words.

Shannon was nearly finished with her lesson, and I asked her, "So, does pizza sound good to you?"

"Yeah, Den. Pizza sounds great."

"Good. Okay then. Bryan likes Round Table because it has a big TV. Is that okay with you?"

Bryan's eyes lit up as he heard the word pizza, and he signed it to me by squiggling two fingers against his palm.

"That's fine. I should be done by six," she said.

"Perfect," I said carrying Bryan from the pool.

36

Sideways Chapter 26

Shannon continued the lesson with the little girl, but her mind wandered and kept flying to the place where she would meet the Caller lady. She thought back to their first meeting, and the Caller's strange reaction to Shannon mentioning that she had an unexplainable experience at Dennis' circle.

Finishing the lesson, Shannon walked to the woman's locker room. It was an open shower with four heads and two ladies in their sixties, showering there. Shannon took off her suit, smiling at the two ladies who had been talking animatedly but stopped as she entered. Shannon wrung out and rinsed her suit and showered.

She dressed quickly, and then jogged to her car, remembering that she needed gas. The traffic could be brutal this time of day, but she felt that she should have no trouble getting to the college on time to meet the caller.

She gassed up and got on the highway driving into a jam, so she exited onto the side streets avoiding the worst of the traffic. Shannon began to feel stressed, both because she was starting to run late, but also not sure of what this odd lady was going to tell her. The Caller lady didn't seem unbalanced, but she seemed eccentric, and that may be contributing to Shannon's unease.

Shannon got back on the freeway, as she could see that the pace had picked up, and she soon exited off at the college. As she drove into the lot, Shannon could only see an ocean of cars, and she realized that she had no idea where the lady could be, not having given explicit instruction as to where to meet.

"Boy, would I make a good spy," she said aloud.

She decided to drive towards the entrance of the building where Professor Wellington's office was. As she approached, she saw the telltale red hair of the lady, lurking under a tree to the right of the entrance.

The Caller had the look of a time long past. In her early to mid-forties, she appeared to be a cross between the eighteenth century and the Hippie movement of the sixties. Her hair was long and curly and fanned out to nearly the width of her shoulders and she was wearing an earthy brown dress with geometric, loud designs of intersecting squares and rectangles.

The Caller saw Shannon and waved her over, and Shannon took a deep breath wondering what the lady could possibly tell her. The lady seemed impatient as she walked towards Shannon, again looking over her shoulder, seeming to be afraid of being followed.

Shannon drove to the curb, and the lady jumped into the passenger side of Shannon's car. "Drive," the lady said imitating a bad spy movie.

"Ah, hello?" Shannon said, a little taken aback.

"What happened to you in the circle?" the lady said abruptly.

"Wait, why are you so spooked? Are you afraid of being followed?" Shannon asked, wondering if there was some danger.

"No," the lady said. "Just of being overheard."

"Oh, well there isn't anyone else here, now. Can you tell me your first name, again?" Shannon asked forgetting what she said from the day before.

The Caller took a deep breath, and relaxed. "It's Murron (pronounced MUHR-IN). My mother was from Scotland, and loved the ancient names," Murron finished, and Shannon could hear her Scottish brogue, as she softly rolled her r's. "I need to talk to you about things."

"I'm Shannon. Okay, let's talk," she said, finding a parking place away from most of the other cars.

The Caller began, "There are things happening around standing stones that have, at least to our knowledge, never happened before," Murron said getting to the point. "We, the people who are the keepers of the rituals and secrets, have knowledge that goes back at least three thousand years, before the birth of Christ. The things that are happening are not in any of our legends, and there are some pretty scary things in them."

"So, how is this different, and why?" Shannon asked.

Murron paused. This wasn't the way she thought the discussion was going to play out. She debated going further and knew that Shannon wasn't going to give any information without some in return.

"We do have legends of shades or spirits in the stones, or using them to travel maybe, it's sketchy."

"Sketchy, or you don't want to tell me?" Shannon pressed.

"I can't tell you everything. I've sworn an oath, but I can tell you what has been happening in the last five or six months. Will you tell me what happened to you?"

"I will," Shannon said.

"As to why this is happening, I have no idea. Something changed. There is an order to the universe that may have been disrupted. We truly don't know."

"So, what's happening?"

Murron paused, and relaxed, gathering her thoughts. "Around five or six months ago, strange things began happening in and around the standing stones. It didn't happen everywhere, and it didn't happen every time, but people began disappearing. We would gather in our groups and we would choose which circles we would meet at. We had a large group of people who were interested in the ceremonies, so we would divide up and go to different circles. We were mostly in England, Scotland, and Ireland. There are many circles in those regions, and it was an exciting time because our numbers were growing. Then it happened. A small group of enthusiasts went to a small circle, north of England. I instructed the person leading the group, myself, on the rituals. I went with a separate group, and the plan was to meet back at my home afterword to talk about the day. They never showed up. We went to the circle to try to find them, but they were all gone. It was a dozen women, some of whom were my friends," Murron said and tears came to her eyes.

"Maybe they decided to leave and not be part of your group anymore," Shannon said.

"No, they were really gone. Their families filed missing person's reports, and there were articles in the papers. No, they were gone," Murron finished emphasizing the word gone. "This was only the first occurrence. There have been at least sixteen that I'm aware of. We have had some survivors. Not all the occurrences end in death, but most do. The witnesses said that the air crackled and electricity touched everyone, and then something happened like the people disintegrated, just blown away, like leaves blowing in a stiff wind. Scattered... Gone. We know that something has changed. We just don't have any idea what or why. We are losing Callers like me at an alarming rate. Some of what I do is very secret. I can't give the knowledge to just anyone. Now a kind of hysteria is breaking out amongst our ranks. People won't attend the ceremonies. They're afraid, and so am I. There are rumors of demons, aliens, UFO's, and every other strange superstitious creature that has ever been imagined being involved, but this is different. This is something new. We fear that our religion will be swept away. We have no protection. We have spells and incantations, but nothing has worked."

"Have you told the authorities?"

"No, we're afraid of being blamed, but we had nothing to do with this. It feels like some kind of dark magic," Murron said.

"Dark magic?"

"People always think that something that they can't explain is dark magic. It's probably why most of the world's superstitions have come about, to begin with, but yes, it feels like we pushed open a door that was meant to remain closed. That's the only way I can describe it," Murron finished, looking expectantly at Shannon.

Shannon began, "I don't know what happened to me, but I'll tell you all I know. First of all, I wasn't in a stone circle. I was above one. The circle is located underground and my friend's house sits above it. Some of what you described did happen to me like the air crackling and being touched by electricity. In my case, the air parted and a hole opened and then I was invaded."

Shannon recounted everything that she had told Dennis. She explained small details to Murron who listened patiently asking few questions.

Then Shannon said, "The difference between what you have told me, and what happened to me is this, the creatures that I encountered did not mean to harm me, it was an accident. They were surprised that they were in me, but it wasn't like they were trying to possess me like they were spirits, it was more like they were in between my cells, maybe even inside my atoms, but they left me fearing that they were going to kill me... Sounds crazy, huh?"

"It sounds different, but maybe it's not so different. You could have ended up just as dead."

"Yeah."

"I didn't mention the air parting," Murron said, "but that also was described. The people who survived in our group felt that something was malevolent in the circle."

"That could just be fear," Shannon speculated.

Murron sat back and nodded. "What do you think you encountered?"

"I don't know, yet."

"Yet?"

"Yeah... Well...This is going to sound even more strange. As time passes from when this happened, I remember new things. I felt like I was pulled apart, and maybe I was, but there is this odd reassembling happening, and I have new memories from the experience."

"When did this happen to you?"

"Last Saturday night."

"That's only five days ago," Murron said.

"Yes."

"Oh, my. I'm sorry. I was being insensitive."

"It's okay. I'm surviving, but I'm not whole. I'm damaged, and that's why I wanted to meet you. I want to know what happened to me," Shannon said.

Murron looked down, shaking her head and said, "And now it's happening here, and I've heard rumors of odd occurrences in other places like Turkey, Peru, India, China, the Middle East, and Australia. I don't know what happened to you, child. If I did, I would tell you," Murron added with sympathy. "Thank you, Shannon, for telling me your story. I'll tell you this. You aren't crazy, and you're not alone, but what is going on is a mystery to me."

"There seems to be some similarities, but my encounter seems different from what is going on in your circles," Shannon said again.

"I don't know. If you learn anything else, please call me," Murron said handing her a card with her name and phone number. "I have a book. It's called a Grimoire and it has ancient knowledge. I'll pour back over it. Call me, Shannon."

"Thanks, I will," Shannon said, taking the number.

Murron smiled and stepped out of Shannon's car, walking back towards the college. Shannon pulled out, and got on the freeway, driving towards the pizza place where she would meet Dennis and Bryan. As she drove, she considered that something was going on in the world, something different, something unearthly. She didn't, however, see how the information that the Caller gave her was the same as what happened to her. It didn't really fit, at least not completely. It would be good to talk it out with Dennis.

37

Sideways Chapter 27

"Okay, buddy boy, pizza time," I said to Bryan, who jumped up from the floor where he was watching TV. I picked him up and we were off to Round Table. Our drive was about fifteen minutes, but the freeway was packed, so I used some side streets to get us there by six.

We drove into the lot, which was full of cars, looking for a spot close to the restaurant. The Round Table was by a Safeway and other stores, all of which seemed busy. I got lucky and saw a car pulling out of a spot close, so I pulled in. We hopped out of the car and could see Shannon standing outside, waiting for us. She looked our way and smiled, and I was again taken aback by my attraction to her.

"Hi, guys," she said as we walked up.

"Hi, Shannon. Have you been here long?" I asked.

"Just got here about five minutes ago."

We walked into the restaurant, together, looking for a booth where Bryan could see the TV, and we could talk without being overheard.

"Over here," I said, leading us to a booth in the corner. Most of the tables were empty, with families filling the rest, and we slid into the booth on red vinyl benches.

"What kind of pizza do you like?" I asked Shannon.

"Usually pepperoni," she said.

"That sounds good. Will you sit with Bryan for a minute while I order?"

"Sure," she said and she began having a conversation with Bryan and making him giggle. I ordered three salad bars, the pizza, milk for Bry and two glasses of red wine.

I carried the drinks and the salad plates back and said, "I hope you like salad."

"Salad sounds good," she said, taking one of the plates from me.

"Go ahead and get yours and I'll go when you get back," I said.

She got her salad, and I got ours, and we began sipping our wine.

"So, did the lady show up?" I asked.

"Oh yeah. I'm not the only one who has had strange experiences."

"Really. So, she was interesting?" I asked.

"More than that, she was terrifying," Shannon said, looking up and making eye contact with me, and giving me the impression that I needed to listen closely.

"Huh," I said.

"I think I may be very lucky. Not everyone got to walk away from their experience," she said, and I could see that Bryan and I were eating, but Shannon was just pushing lettuce around on her plate. My mind flashed back to the bone cave. I don't think they walked away either.

"Shannon, are you okay?" I asked.

"Yeah, I'm all right, but her stories were scary. I still don't think that, whatever I encountered, wanted to hurt me, though."

"So, what did she tell you?" I asked.

"Well, to start with, this..." Shannon stopped as a teenage girl brought our pizza to the table.

As the girl walked away, I pulled some pizza, and set it on Bryan's plate.

Shannon continued, "This lady is very afraid. That much was clear. She said people are dying around these circles and it seems to be intensifying."

"Do you think this lady is okay, mentally I mean?"

"Well, at first I thought she was a lunatic, but the more I talked to her, the more I started to believe her. I will admit, though, that I'm not one hundred percent sure. I'll tell you what, she completely believed me. She knew roughly what to expect from my story."

"What else did she tell you?" I asked.

"At first she almost demanded that I tell her what happened to me. She was very aggressive. I got her to settle down, and she took a deep breath and slowly began to tell me what was happening in the circles that she knew about. I guess she figured that bullying me wasn't a good way to get information, and her attitude changed. People are disappearing, Dennis. She said that a dozen people, some of which were her friends, went to circle ceremonies, and never came back. This religion that they believe in is steeped in superstition, so they began to try incantations to stop the evil, but nothing worked, at least not so far. She said that she was going to go back and check her Grimoire again to see if she had missed something, but she didn't think so."

"What's a Grimoire?" I asked.

"It's a book of magic, you know, spells, curses, and that kind of stuff. I'm not even positive that the book is Celtic. I'm not sure," Shannon said.

Shannon took a bite of pizza and sipped some wine.

"Do you think you found out anything that helped you?" I asked cautiously, not wanting to imply that she had wasted her time.

"I don't think so. I mean, it was kind of comforting to know that I'm not the only person that this has happened to, but most of what she told me didn't exactly sound like what happened to me. The people were touched by electricity and the air parted, but the sense was that whatever they encountered was malevolent. I didn't get that from my experience."

"I don't know. I'm skeptical," I said.

"Well, what do I know," Shannon said defensively. "I didn't see the dead people, but I'll tell you this, the lady is scared. I mean real, no bull, real fear. If she was acting, she deserved an Oscar."

We paused and ate a bit. Bryan enjoyed the big TV, even though there was a baseball game on, and he isn't even remotely interested in sports.

I broke the silence. "Did she say anything else?" I probed.

"She said that there is wild speculation starting in her religion. People are saying it's U.F.O.'s, demons and maybe aliens. She has all but ruled these types of things out, though. She thinks it's something different. Something that has never happened before. She said that their knowledge goes back five thousand years, and nothing that she knows of, like this, has ever happened before. She's afraid that her religion is going to be wiped out. These stone circle people are taking precautions to survive. With Samhain, I mean Halloween coming, they are thinking about not having the rituals that they usually have, and to these people, it's important."

We began to eat again, and I finished my wine. Shannon's was also getting low.

"Would you like another glass?" I asked.

"Yes, thanks."

I got up and ordered two more glasses of wine while Bryan slowly ate his pizza, with a look of delight on his face as he watched the big TV. Shannon managed to finish her salad and one piece of pizza. I came back and couldn't help wondering why I hadn't heard about these things in the news. As I sat down, I handed her the wine.

"Thanks," she said.

"Shannon, why haven't we heard about this in the news? It seems like it should be a big story."

"I wondered the same thing. I think it's mostly a local story, and the Caller lady said that what happened to me was the first time she knew of it happening here. She named a bunch of countries where the anomaly had happened, but there aren't any bodies, just witnesses that won't talk and missing persons. These people are Druids, so they mostly only know about the Celtic places, like Scotland, Ireland, and England. I wonder if we hooked up with other groups if we might get similar stories. I don't know."

I said, "I'm not sure what to think. On the one hand, I know what happened to you was real, but on the other, some of what she said sounds like crap. The only reason I believe her somewhat, is because I think you probably have a decent bullshit meter."

"But?" Shannon said.

"I don't think I have a 'but'. Just a we'll see."

Shannon left the pizza and moved strictly to her wine. She sat back and held her wine looking at me.

"What?" I said.

"I think we should go back to the house," she said, looking into my eyes, and I froze in her gaze.

"I don't know," I said.

"Think about it."

"I don't just think about it, I dream about it and wake up in a cold sweat."

"There is a difference between what was happening to the Caller lady and me. Whatever I encountered wasn't trying to hurt me. It sounded more like what she was talking about was evil."

"Yeah, but you don't know that for sure," I said.

"I know something. I'm remembering little things. Something tried to help me," she said.

"Huh," I said and got the impression that Shannon hadn't told me everything.

"Think about it," she said again.

"Umm, I really don't know," I choked out.

We were finishing our wine and pizza, and the conversation stalled. Shannon became quiet, and I could tell that she wanted to hammer me more about going back to the house. I couldn't possibly see what we would discover there that could help. Shannon has something internal going on that I don't think she even understands. I have something internal going on, also, but it's my growing affection for her, and I'm finding it difficult to say no, even though it scares me to death.

We finished and got up, walking towards the door. As we walked outside Shannon turned to me and thanked me for dinner. Then she said, "Dennis, I want you to think about going back to the house. I work tomorrow. Are you going to the club?"

"Yeah," I said.

"Good. I'll see you there." She hugged Bryan and said goodbye to him bowing down to eye level, and then she turned to me again. "Think about it, Den," she said and I nodded.

She gave me a small hug and turned towards her car. I put Bryan in his car seat and drove home. I'll think about it, I guess. I'm not sure I could think of anything else.

38

Sideways Chapter 28

The next day I dropped Bryan off at school and drove to the health club. I could see Shannon's car as I pulled in. She said she had some early lessons. As I walked in, I could see Shannon at the front desk, engrossed in a conversation with the manager. She saw me and smiled.

"Good morning," I said.

"Good morning," the manager said, taking charge and moving to the front.

"I got ya," the Manager said.

I left their odd conversation and walking into the weight room.

I saw Jason, on the bench press finishing a set, and straining to get the last rep in.

"Hi, Jay," I said, walking to the locker to put my bag in.

"Hey, Dennis," he said expelling some air with the effort of putting the weights on the bench rack. "What's up with you?" he said.

"Not much," I said. "How about with you?"

"Sadly, nothing new."

"Well, let's get in shape. That would be new," I said laughing.

I glanced at the front desk to see if the manager was finished with Shannon. He wasn't.

Jason watched me as I watched Shannon. He smiled. Len walked into the weight room and waved.

I glanced back over my shoulder and saw as the manager turned away from Shannon, and she was looking at me, smiling. "Be right back," I said walking from the weight room. I walked up to her. "I thought he would never leave," I said quietly.

"He was going over my schedule. No big deal."

"Good. I was hoping you weren't in trouble," I said teasing.

"No, I've been a good girl, *here,* lately."

"Do you have a break coming? I feel like coffee and a bagel," I asked.

"A bagel?"

"Okay, a donut, but you get the picture."

"I have a half hour break between my next lessons."

"Would you like to go to the coffee shop with me? I'm buying," I said.

"Well... I don't know. Let me check my very full social calendar," she said smiling.

"I'm pretty sure that you're all booked up, but I was hoping that you could squeeze me in."

"Oh yeah, booked up," she said self-deprecating. I looked at her, and all of a sudden understood that she really had no idea how desirable she was.

"I'll tell you what. If all the guys around here had any idea you were available, the line would start at the door and go for miles."

I could see her smile and then blush. "That's a gross exaggeration, but thanks."

"Just a half hour now," I said, looking at the clock and walking away.

"Hey, I just made space for you on my calendar," she said.

I looked over my shoulder and smiled. "I thought you might."

"Dumb ass," she said laughing.

I walked back into the weight room, and Jason looked up and said, "All I heard was 'dumb ass'. Way to go, Den."

"That's just Shannon's way of saying yes to coffee."

"Well, at least she has you pegged," Len said deadpanned.

"Thanks, it's nice to know I have friends that support me," I said.

We worked out for a bit then I said, "Got to go."

Walking from the weight room, I could see Donna arrive and Shannon get her coat. I walked out.

"Let me throw this in my car, Den," she said as we walked to the door. I let her walk out first and I followed.

"How about I drive?" she said.

"Sounds good," I said, walking to her car. I threw my bag into the back, and we started for the coffee shop. "So, have you read any good books lately," I asked. She looked at me puzzled. "I mean about stone circles. Did you learn anything new?"

"Not really," she said as she pulled out of the parking lot. "The Caller lady gave me more information regarding our situation, but what I did learn from the book is that there are a lot of these circles around the world. Some very ancient like Gobekli Tepi. It dates back around twelve thousand years. That's six thousand years older than the oldest known city, and it's full of stone circles."

"Where's that?" I asked.

"Turkey."

"Huh."

"There are lots of other ways that ancient people worshiped the sun, gods, and spirits. It may be that these types of phenomena have always been happening."

"Maybe you're right, but it seems like something has changed, but what?" I said and Shannon shrugged.

"I don't know," she said.

We continued to the coffee shop and found a parking place close to the door. Entering, we approached the counter and saw Lenny toweling off the nozzle that he uses to heat the milk for his mochas and lattes.

"Hi, Lenny," I said.

"Hi, Mister Den. What can I get for you today?" he asked.

"What do you want, Shannon?" I asked.

"I'll have a medium coffee and a cheese bagel."

"Would you like that toasted," Lenny asked.

"Yeah, that sounds great," she said.

"And for you Mister Den," Lenny said while cutting the bagel in two, and putting it in the toaster.

"I'll have a nonfat mocha, and that big, messy looking apple fritter," I said.

Shannon looked at me. "Bulking up?" she asked.

"I'm getting mas-q-lear," I said making a muscle with my arm and sounding like our former governor. "Let's sit ova deare," I said continuing the impression, as Lenny brought our food to the counter. I said thanks and led Shannon to a table in the corner.

We sat and Shannon picked up the stone circle discussion. "I keep reading points of power like the circles mark something."

"Like maybe access points?" I asked.

"Yeah, but from where to where?"

"Into my shower for one," I said with a wry smile.

"Dennis, I'm really trying to forget how naked I was that night," Shannon said, emphasizing my name.

"I know," I replied with a wide grin.

"Back to the subject please," she said.

"Shannon, have you ever tried an apple fritter?" I asked, holding up a warm, butter dripping bite.

"No," she said, and I fed it to her. The act of feeding her that bite was somehow so innocently intimate, that I couldn't take my eyes from her as she ate it, and I could feel something stir in me.

She said, "That was really good. Too good."

That very nice moment passed, and we finished our coffee talking in circles about circles.

"We keep going over the same things," I said. "I don't think there is an answer to what happened to you, and I don't think anyone can help us."

"You're probably right. The Caller lady's a dead end," Shannon said resigned.

We finished and threw our trash away and walked out to her car. Climbing in, Shannon asked, "Have you thought any more about going back to the house?"

"You aren't going to let that go, are you?" I stated.

"No, because the answers are there, at least I think it's a chance to get some answers."

"How, Shannon? I mean you can't be serious about wanting to be invaded again, and I don't own a Ouija board."

"Look, I think something fixed me when I was all messed up, but there's an incomplete part of this, like hearing a sentence that ends in the middle. I can't fully explain this, but something's there."

"Huh," I said, listening closely to Shannon trying to explain.

"I have some other things to tell you, but not here or now," she said driving back into the health club's lot. "I have to go back to work. I need to cancel Bryan's lesson tomorrow. Can you come to my place for dinner?"

"Okay."

"Tell that sweet little Bryan boy that I'm sorry, and we will have a lesson next week."

"Okay. What time would you want me to come?"

"Around 6:00."

"Are you going to cook, or do you want me to bring something?"

"I'm cooking. Are you feeling brave?"

I smiled. "Can I bring anything?" I asked.

"A bottle of red wine."

"Okay. I need to ask Liz and George to watch Bryan for me."

"If they can't, just bring him," she said.

"Okay. See you at 6:00," I said, getting out of the car. Shannon got out and locked up.

"See you tomorrow night, Den."

"Sounds good. See you then," I said, and Shannon looked at me for a long moment.

She turned then and walked towards the club. After a couple of steps, she turned back and said, "Thanks for breakfast."

"Let's do it again," I said.

"Sounds good to me," she said as she reached the door. She pulled it open and walked in.

As I drove home, my mind raced. What's going on here? What's going on is that someone has breached this fortress that I had built around myself. I didn't think that I would ever find someone who I would let beyond those ramparts. They were high and thick and Shannon slipped in.

But the house... That house... I know that I would never let Bryan go there, and now I'm feeling very protective of Shannon, not wanting to put her in harm's way. I also know that she won't easily take no for an answer. She's a very brave girl and probably stronger than I could ever hope to be. I just don't know. I can't see any answers there. I don't think there's anything there but dust... Oh and the cat... My new cat. I forgot about the cat.

39

Sideways Chapter 29

Friday night arrived, and I guiltily dropped Bryan off with Liz and George. I've been relying on them too much lately. I carried Bryan and knocked on the door. They answered with giddy snickering.

"Having fun?" I asked.

"Just being silly," George said.

"At my expense?"

"Nooo," George said dragging out the "oooo."

"Have fun tonight," Liz said.

"I won't be late," I said, and I kissed Bryan goodbye. "Thanks for watching him for me."

"Anytime," George said, in an upbeat voice. He reached for Bryan. "Let's go, big boy. Daddy's got a date."

Why do they make me feel like a teenager going to the prom? I do think that there has been an interesting metamorphosis take place. They want me to be happy, and they have definitely adopted me as their little boy.

I drove to Shannon's apartment arriving right on time. I bounced up the stairs and knocked on the door. She answered smiling, in basic Sacramento dress, shorts, a tee shirt, and barefoot.

"Hey, Den," she said swinging the door wide.

"Hi," I said handing her the bottle of wine.

She walked back to the kitchen, bustling around, finishing her dinner, and straightening her mess.

"Sit down, Dennis, and I'll open the wine."

"Would you like me to do it?" I asked, trying to be of some help.

"Yeah, thanks. That would be great," she said, handing me the wine opener. She went to the cupboard, pulled two wine glasses and handed them also to me. I poured two glasses of wine and she said, "Dinner is just about ready, so why don't you sit down." I nodded and she brought two nice salads to the table.

We sat across from each other, sipping the wine and enjoying the salads. Shannon seemed nervous. I don't know if it was because she was worried if I would like the food, or if she had some other reason, but the conversation was sparse, and a bit clunky like walking into a pitch-black room and bumping into the furniture.

"Great salad, Shannon. I really like salad. I could eat it every night."

"Me, too," she agreed. I topped off her wine as we finished the salads and she said, "I'll get dinner."

She stood up and went to the oven and pulled out lasagna. It looked perfect, with golden, bubbling cheese, dripping over the edge a bit. She cut two pieces, set mine down and waited as I took a bite.

"This is really good," I said, and meant it, but I would have said the same thing even if I didn't.

"Thanks. It's the only thing I can make," she said looking down, and we both laughed. She took a big sip of wine.

"I'm sure you could make cup-o-noodles, also."

"Well, maybe."

We finished the dinner, and I helped her wash and dry the dishes. She covered the left-over lasagna with foil and slid it into the refrigerator. I topped off her wine, again, and we moved to the couch.

"Dennis, I really enjoy being with you. I'm very comfortable with you," she said shyly.

I smiled, "I feel the same way." I could tell that Shannon wanted to expand, but I could feel her pull back. "Are you okay?" I asked thinking that there was something else that she wanted to say, and I was hoping that there wasn't a big "but" in there somewhere.

"Well," she said hesitating, "I just hope you do feel the same. I do really like you. Sometimes I'm not sure because you're a little hard to read. It's like you're interested, and then you're not."

"Here's the thing," I said, hoping that my size eleven didn't end up in my mouth.

"There's a thing?" she said.

"Yeah," I said pausing. "I like you very much, and I'm very attracted to you, and I think that things happen in their own time. I've been married and in love, and right now I'm enjoying our friendship. I don't want to mess that up. I think I really need your friendship. I'm kind of afraid of losing that."

"I'm not trying to rush you into anything," she said. "Sometimes, after seeing some guys for a week, I can't keep their hands out of my shirt, and I don't like that. I just want you to know that I think I understand you, and I like what I see," she said and we moved to a comfortable silence.

"Shannon, I want you to know something. If I took everything that I was looking for in someone, put it in a mixing bowl, and mixed it up, when I poured it out, it would be you. I would hate to put a you're perfect for me on anyone, but you're as close as I could ever imagine."

"Is there a "but" in that mixing bowl, Dennis?"

"The only thing is that I think I'm kind of damaged. I feel myself pull back even when I don't want to, and I have some depression following me around. It's not there and then, surprise, its back. I think you may need to be a little patient with me."

"I don't mind," she said understandingly. "I watch you sometimes. You seem like the kind of person who's naturally happy, and you seem kind and good. Sometimes you're laughing or smiling, and then a shadow will cross your face, and instant sadness shows up in your eyes. It's like your mind leaves."

"I can't believe that showed. You're observant, and on the button," I said.

"It's subtle, but it's there," she said.

"Damn."

"Is it your wife?"

"Sometimes. Sometimes it's Bryan."

"I thought that," she said and I smiled a half smile. She reached for the remote. "Let's see what's on TV." She turned it on, began surfing through the channels, and stopped on *Sleepless in Seattle.* "I love this movie," she said.

"I do too, but it's a little close to home," I said.

"Yeah, I guess you're right."

I said, "With one big difference. Tom Hanks is such a great guy in the movie, and I'm no Tom Hanks. As a matter of fact, I'd probably marry him."

Shannon gave me that, you're stupid, but I like you look. It's a very nice look.

We sat quietly for a couple of minutes watching Tom miss his chance with Meg, and then Shannon changed the direction of the discussion.

"Dennis, I want to talk to you about going back to Jonathan's house. I'm not quite sure how to say this, but I almost feel compelled. I don't want to say that I'm being called, but it's almost like that."

"Maybe I should go back first. Besides, I think I'm going to need to get the cat," I said.

"The cat. I forgot about the cat," she said.

"Yeah, well, I've kind of become attached to him and when we left, he was in the house. I'm sure he's fine for now. I had a big bowl of water there and a lot of dry food, not to mention all the furry delights he can snag, but he's used to being outdoors and that litter box isn't going to be a picnic. I'm going to bring him home."

"Dennis, I don't think you need to protect me there. I have impressions in my mind that tell me we would be safe. Remember that I said, that I needed to reassemble after "It" happened?"

"Yeah?"

"Well, as I'm reassembling, I'm getting thoughts, messages, I don't know, whiffs of impressions about what really happened. Whatever it was, it was as surprised it was in me, as I was surprised it was there. Once it recognized I was real and conscious, it left me in horror. Like walking in on someone naked."

"Well, I know how that feels at least," I said smirking. Shannon colored a bit on her cheeks, and I continued, "You know that whatever was there is probably long gone by now, and I can't help but hope so."

"I know, but I don't think so... I'm not sure, but if we don't go soon, I think we will miss them," she said and I blanched.

"I want to miss them. You don't?"

"I don't know, Dennis. Maybe I do, but..." She trailed off.

"What?"

"Let's go back," she said and her eyes were pleading.

"I know I'm going to regret this, maybe we can go back tomorrow. I'll have to ask Liz and George to watch Bryan. I'm not bringing him there."

"Good," she said.

She seemed sufficed for the moment, but I felt the icy touch of fear.

"Dennis, there's something else. I've been constantly having dreams since this happened. I think they left messages in my mind, but I can't access them. There's something deep in the cracks. I just don't know what it is, and I think my dreams are trying to tell me... And there is this urge to go back to the house that I don't fully understand. I dream all night, different dreams, remembering all of them, and they always start or end in that house, or it's in the background."

"Huh... an urge?"

"I don't know. Kind of," she said shaking her head in a whispery voice. "I don't quite have the words for it. Also, remember when we were talking about Bryan's computer, and I asked you if he was at the table?"

"Yeah, I remember that."

"Well, this is going to sound crazy, but I could see him there, from above. Maybe it was a dream. I don't know, but he said someone was in his computer."

"Damn, Shannon! He did say that."

"You know, there is no way that I could know what he said unless you told me. Did you tell me?"

"I don't think so. I'm not sure I said that because it hasn't crossed my mind."

We both sat quietly for a couple of minutes as the gooseflesh crawled slowly up my spine.

Shannon broke the silence. "I've been having wild dreams," she said looking away in a low whisper.

"Wild? Like what?"

"I can't describe most of them, but I think they are trying to get my attention using extreme symbolism."

"How extreme?" I asked.

"Very," she said coloring.

"Like what?"

"Well... scary or violent, and some are different," she said.

"Different? How?"

"Well... some are hypersexual," she said turning crimson.

"Really, like what?"

"No. There is no way that I could tell you."

"Maybe I could help with the symbolism. What was the last one that you remember?"

"I don't know, Dennis. I would really have to clean it up, or I would be too embarrassed."

"I think you could sanitize it if you want because I don't think the importance would be in all the graphic detail."

"I don't think..." She trailed off.

"Give it a shot. I'll listen in a clinical manner."

"Oh sure, you haven't heard it yet."

"Try me."

She paused contemplating then told me about a dream where she was by Jonathan's house. It was graphic, very sexually charged, and involved being intimately touched by the wind of all things, but to me, the symbols were clear enough. She was being compelled to go back to the house and she didn't feel that what she encountered there meant her any harm. When the dream concluded, she had an intense, happy ending and woke to a voice which said, "The Gift."

Shannon had begun the story slow, but by the time she finished, she was blushing brightly and speaking so rapidly that I could barely keep up. I looked at her and could see a blush deepening and traveling down her neck.

After listening, I said, "This doesn't seem that bad to me. It just sounds like your basic sex dream, only minus another human. But the words, 'the gift', you don't think it had anything to do with your happy ending?"

Shannon looked at me sideways, controlling her embarrassment and said, "No."

"Well, it still just seems like a sex dream."

"Dennis, I'm giving you the PG 13 version. The dream was triple X in every way."

"Oh," I said.

"I believe it lasted all night."

"Oh?" I said again, this time questioningly, trying to get Shannon to expand.

She paused, not finished, but was silent. I don't think she knew how to continue.

"Is there more about the dream that you want to tell me?" I asked.

Shannon looked at me very disconcerted. I could see her draw back. There was something in the detail that was bothering her. I could see her debate with herself, not sure if she should continue. "Shannon, what is it?"

"In a way, the dream left me feeling guilty, and disturbed, and kind of frightened."

"Guilty, why? It was just a dream," I said.

"No, it wasn't just a dream," she said.

She paused again and turned inward watching some images play in her head. "I'm going to have to tell you a lot more detail for you to understand, and I don't know... This dream was different, more real, more personal."

"I don't think it's going to change my opinion of the dream." Then I suggested. "Are you so bothered by it, that you want to confide in me, just to get it off your chest, maybe?"

She nodded slowly making eye contact and then turned away. She began, "I told you that I was being pleasured, but it was more. The wind started gentle and slow like a full, intimate body massage, but became intense, surprising me by entering me. It was almost desperate, clutching me, holding me in place and moving inside me. At first, when this started, I became a little afraid, but that soon faded. I could feel everything, even the motion inside me, but now it wasn't like wind anymore, it was solid. It felt like lips, and hands, and... well, you know... It would slow down or stop the motion, and then it would make me beg to have more, and I would... I would beg. I climaxed over and over in different positions as it moved me, and I was desperate to please this wind. I wanted to give it everything it wanted so it wouldn't stop, but it just wanted to have me."

I nodded sympathetically.

She continued, "When I began to wake, I was naked and sweating profusely. I could still feel everything, where and how I was touched and kissed, and I was unhappy to be waking up. I wanted more. I had all those orgasms and I wasn't satisfied. I wanted the wind to return, but it was gone. I felt out of control. My covers were gone, and I woke further, feeling for the wind on my body, but it wasn't there. The wind was like a drug, and I was desperate for more. I started to come to my senses. I looked around, confused. My covers were ripped from the bed, and my bedclothes were on the other side of the room like they were blown there. My sheets were soaked and needed to be changed. The thing is that I'm not sure that I was fully asleep the whole time, and I'm not sure I was alone," she finished and I could feel her despair.

"Shannon, do you remember if you were by Jonathan's house the whole time that this was going on, or were you home?"

"Let me think... Towards the end, I remember, facing the water, and I didn't even care if someone could see me. I was completely exposed and engaged, and I didn't even care... I didn't see anyone, but I would have continued even if there was a crowd there."

I was surprised by how frank and graphic Shannon had become in her description of the dream, and I felt very close to her.

Shannon sat quietly.

I'm thinking that, right now, she probably feels like she's said too much.

"Shannon," I said and she turned to me. "Dreams really mess with perception sometimes. I remember having a dream just recently that only lasted twenty minutes, but it was about me needing to get to work. No matter how hard I tried, I couldn't get there, and by the time I reached work, my shift was over. I lived nine hours in the dream, in twenty minutes. I think that your dream probably started early in the morning when it was still dark. You may have woken, went back to sleep, and went right back into the dream. I understand why you're upset by it, though, but it doesn't change my opinion of it," I finished.

"Okay?" she said, listening and waiting for more.

"First, I'm going to assume your point of view, and let's say that this is a planted message from whoever they were at Jonathan's house, and not just your subconscious' way of working out your fears. I'm positive that they didn't visit you last night. It is interesting to me, though, that you didn't feel violated. You never tried to resist this wind, allowing it to pleasure you sooooo... thoroughly."

Shannon didn't say anything, and she punched me in the arm.

"Ouch," I laughed, rubbing it. "Okay, just kidding."

"You said you were going to be clinical," she said, disgusted and not looking at me.

"Okay, this is my impression. I don't think anything in the dream mattered as much as the voice at the end. For the most part, I think dreams are just our subconscious' way of telling us what's bothering us. The more disturbing the dream, the more disturbed we are by the underlying reason. But in this case, I'm going to go out on a limb, and you can tell me how it feels to you. The wind might represent the whoever they are, but I think it represents some message left by them. The happy endings, lucky girl," I said glancing at

Shannon, who gave me another disgusted look, "means that 'the gift' that is being referred to is something very positive, or they think so. It may be some knowledge that they have planted that may come out when you need it, or want it. The rest of the dream was just attention-getting," I finished.

Shannon nodded and said, "Huh," then began thinking, again, trying to make it fit, and showing some recognition.

"Maybe," she said, nodding but then she shook her head. "Something's there. I just can't retrieve it. It's just out of reach. It's frustrating."

"Another thing to think about," I said. "This just struck me. The wind is such a natural thing, maybe it's because you don't think that, the whatever they are, pose a danger, and shouldn't be feared like some ghost, or alien, or something like that. I really don't think you were visited by some amorous creature."

"Okay?" she said expecting more.

"For humans, sex is attention-getting, but when it happens in the movies or on TV, usually it's some stylized version of it. The sex begins and they fade to black, and everyone wakes up happy, but in real life, when sex happens, it's very real with all the X's, all the body parts clearly visible, all the sounds and... well, gasping. No censoring. It wouldn't surprise me that the dream was so graphic. It was like real life, not some stylized unreal version of it."

"So, you think the dream seemed so real because my subconscious didn't censor it."

"Well, yeah. Why should it? It's you talking to you."

"Okay?"

"Think about sex. It's such a weird thing for humans with all the social, moral, and psychological aspects of it, but think of how common it is. Everyone at some point in their lives will probably do it. We all came here as a result of it, and it's no big secret what happens in the course of it, but if you were walking down the street and someone was engaged in it on the street, well gross. It's kind of a unique thing in the world. It's very intimate and personal. It's perfect for your subconscious to use as an attention-getting symbol. I really don't think that the whoever they are, knows squat about sex. I think it's all your symbolism based on your life experiences. What's being used in the dream is something to get your maximum attention, but not from them, from you. I don't think they made a special trip here for a roll in the hay."

"Huh," she said turning back to me. "You know, I feel better."

I smiled, happy to know that I may have been some help. We both took a couple of minutes to think.

Shannon didn't seem embarrassed anymore, and I felt like she trusted me with something very personal. She also seemed relieved that she could tell someone about the disturbing dream.

After a minute, I said, "It's hard to tell though, if it's your subconscious or if, like you think, it's some message. If they buried something, it's buried deep, but I really think that the symbols are all yours. You had a very strange experience."

"That it was, Den," she said. "Now you have me thinking about the symbols in the rest of my dreams. Most of them make me just want to run for a cold shower."

"It will be interesting to see if you dream tonight. Do you notice any similarities in the dreams? Maybe not the subject matter, but in the outcomes?" I asked.

"I will think about it," she said.

"I would also be interested in your violent dreams. What are they like?"

"They're different. In them, I'm in impossible situations, hopelessly trapped or surrounded by enemies, you get the picture. I usually escape, or brutally kill all the bad guys."

"Do you have help?"

"Not that I can remember, I'm usually an army of one, but I'll find a weapon that has been left or overlooked, and then I get to vanquishing."

"Huh. That's interesting... I don't think we will be able to figure out beforehand what the dreams mean, but I'll bet there won't be any question after."

"Do you think so?" she wondered.

"I do. If your dreams are some message from your, whatever they are."

I stopped for a minute, and Shannon paused with me, both of us with our own thoughts.

"The vision about Bryan in the house is different though," I said. "That needs more thought. It's like you were watching him through them. That's strange. That may be a more important part of the message than we think."

"Why do you say that?" she asked.

"I'm not sure, but it feels like it has something to do with their message."

"Huh," she said and she looked up at the ceiling. "I think they touched him. In the vision, he reacted to a shock, but it wasn't like me. It was through the computer. He froze for a minute with his fingers on the keyboard, and then pulled his hand back. The air didn't part though, at least not that I could see, but that shadow thing, the one I saw, was there."

"Oh," I said.

Shannon looked to be in a trance. Her eyes stared off into space, and then she seemed to lose all her strength.

"Dennis, I'm tired. Can we pick this up tomorrow?"

"Yeah. It's getting a bit late. I don't want to impose on Liz and George too much, and if I'm going to ask them to watch Bryan tomorrow, well, I should go."

"I had a good time with you, tonight, Den. Thanks for listening. I'll see you tomorrow?"

"Yeah, I'll call you early to make plans," I said and could see her fade before my eyes. "Thanks for dinner, and for trusting me with your dreams. I... well, I'm sorry if I had some fun at your expense. I really tried to help."

"You did, Den. I think a lot," she said, approaching me and giving me a hug. I turned and she patted my back and said, "I think tomorrow will be good."

I nodded and walked out the door saying goodbye, but suddenly very preoccupied.

As I walked down the stairs my mind began to whirl. What did I just agree to? I'm not sure we should approach that house without something to protect us, but what could shield us from what might be there? Maybe we could wear little foil hats. "Crap!"

Driving home, I still wasn't sure I wanted to go back to that house. I know what I said to Shannon, but I think I need to sleep on it. I know that I need to go back, but I think I should go alone.

I pulled into the small parking place behind my house and jogged to Liz's back door. I knocked and Liz answered.

"Come in," she said quietly.

I looked at the couch, and there was Bryan, sleeping like an angel.

"Maybe you should leave him here tonight," she suggested. George walked in smiling.

"No, thanks anyway. I'll just carry him home. Did you have a good night?" I asked.

"We did, Dennis," Liz said.

I walked to the couch and slid my arms under Bryan, lifting him, and laying his head on my shoulder. He didn't even move.

"Thanks for watching him for me. I can't tell you how good it feels to leave him someplace where I know he's safe."

I turned to the door, and George opened it saying good night. I carefully stepped down the back stairs and carried Bryan to the house where I took off his orthotics and slid him under his covers. Suddenly I was exhausted and could barely keep my eyes open. I cleaned up, slipped out of my clothes, and crashed into bed.

40

Sideways Chapter 30

I woke early from another unsettled night, groggy, and in need of coffee. These nights have become more the rule than the exception. As I came to, my mind raced, thinking about my evening with Shannon. Maybe she was right, and there was nothing to fear from Jonathan's house, but maybe she's wrong. I got up and checked on Bryan, who was still fast asleep. I slipped on some sweats, and as I walked into the front room, I could hear Liz gardening out by the pool. I looked out the window and could see her on her hands and knees scraping weeds that had sprouted between some of the flags. I started the coffee, and as it brewed, I brushed my teeth. The pot beeped as the coffee finished, and without any enthusiasm, I shuffled into the kitchen for a tall cup.

I peeked back in on Bry who was softly breathing as he slept, and I put on a tee shirt and slipped out of the door to talk to Liz.

"Hi," I said startling her. She didn't hear me coming.

"Oh, Dennis, you scared me," she said reflexively putting a hand on her chest.

"Sorry," I said. She could tell that I wanted something.

"What, Dennis?"

"I think I need to get the cat. I left him in the house and I think I'm going to need to bring him here. I was wondering if you might watch Bryan while I go out to the house and get him. I don't want to bring Bryan out there."

"Sure. What time?"

"Well, Shannon said that she wanted to go with me. I'm thinking sometime this afternoon, but I need to call her first to see what she has planned."

I could see the look of concern on Liz's face, but she was skeptical about what had happened to Shannon, thinking that there must be some other explanation.

"I want to tell you to be careful, Dennis, but how do I tell you to be careful from whatever happened out there?"

"I know. The funny thing is that if it wasn't me, I wouldn't believe it." I heard the phone ring in my house. "I'm going to get that. I'll let you know what time," I said, turning, and jogging for the house. I got the phone on the sixth ring. "Hello," I said.

"Hey, Den," Shannon said. "What time were you thinking about going to Jonathan's house today?"

"I don't think you should come," I said bluntly.

"If you don't bring me, I'll drive out there myself. I'm not letting you go alone."

If you were in a bar fight, you would want Shannon backing you up.

"Listen, Dennis, whatever happened to me was an accident. They left messages between my synapses. What happened to me was a mistake. I'm sure of that, and I want to be there just in case."

"Just in case what?" I asked.

"In case they are still there," she said.

I couldn't speak. For some seconds, there was silence.

"Dennis?"

"I'm still here," I said.

"So, what time do we go?" she said insistently.

"Give me at least a couple of hours," I said.

"I have to run out to my moms, today. I promised to go shopping with her. Is there any chance that you could wait until around 4:00?"

"Okay, 4:00," I said. I heard a knock at my door and looked up. "Shannon, George is at my door. I'll see you at four."

I opened the door and saw George there with a grim expression. "Hi, George. Come in."

"Dennis, I was thinking that maybe I should go out to the house with you," he said.

"Thanks, but I really don't think that anything is going to happen. The more I think about it, the more I think that whatever happened to Shannon was one of those things that never happens again and is never explained. Also, Shannon needs to heal. If we go and nothing happens, it may do her good."

"Papa," Bryan yelled from his bedroom.

"There's Bryan. Thanks anyway, George. Can I bring him by at 3:30? Shannon has some running around to do first."

"Sure, that's fine," he said.

"George, if anything odd happens, we are out of that house. I'm not hanging around for trouble."

"Okay," he said relenting. He looked at me for a beat too long and then turned and walked out.

I walked into Bryan's room. "There is my sweetie, good boy," I said sitting on his bed.

"Papa, home today?" he said and signed.

"I will be home most of the day, and then I have something to do with your friend Shannon, but I won't be late."

Bryan made his irritated noise, "Me too," he said clearly.

"Not this time, buddy boy but I promise, next time." I got the feeling that he wanted to be with Shannon. "Amma and Ampa are really happy that you are going to be with them. I'll be back in a couple of minutes to get you up."

Bryan turned his attention to three Beanie Baby puppies. I started his breakfast and got out his clothes. I refreshed my coffee, and then set up a chair in front of the TV, so Bry could watch it while he was eating. I walked back into his room, picked up one of his stuffed puppies and wrapped the paws around Bryan's arm and said in a silly voice, "I'm hungry for some Kibbles and Bits."

Bryan giggled.

"We better get your puppy friend some food," I said lifting Bryan and the puppy and carrying them into the living room. Bryan wanted me to get the other two puppies, also, so I did and settled them to eat while Elmo sang a song on Sesame Street.

We ate and dressed, and the time dragged. I kept looking at the clock, which barely seemed to move, and played with Bryan, without much enthusiasm. I usually loved this time with him, but today, I couldn't keep my mind here.

We had lunch and I poked around the house doing some busy work as Bryan entertained himself. Finally, the clock seemed to move normally, and 3:30 arrived. I carried Bryan to Liz and George's back door, then knocked and they answered not speaking.

"Hi," I said.

"Hi, Dennis," they said together.

I kissed Bryan and handed him over.

"Call us when you get there," Liz said.

"I will. I'll call before we go in the house."

Liz seemed to relax a bit when I said that.

"Thanks for watching Bryan for me," I said, having some trouble making eye contact.

"Be careful," Liz said.

I smiled and nodded, but thought, I'll be careful. Be careful about what? How can you be careful from what happened? Bring a gun? Maybe holy water.

I feel like I need to prepare, but I can't think of anything that would make a difference. My pulse began to race as my apprehension increased.

I walked back to my place, waving goodbye, and grabbed my coffee for the road. It had been reheated too many times and it tasted like mud. As I drove from the driveway, I called Shannon on my cell. She answered on the first ring.

"Hey, Shannon, I'm on my way."

"See you in a few minutes, Den."

The next thing I knew, I was pulling into a parking place by Shannon's SUV. I didn't remember anything about the drive and my heart continued to race. I left the car, ran up the stairs, and was about to knock when Shannon opened the door.

"Oh, so now you're psychic?" I said.

"No, I just opened the door because I thought I heard some buffalo running up the stairs."

"Oh," I said, standing there stupidly.

"Come in," she said, grabbing my sleeve and pulling me in. She turned and gave me a brief hug. "Do you think we should bring anything?" she asked.

"Do you have a spare exorcist?"

"I know I'm going to sound redundant, but I don't think we are in any danger there."

"So, you don't think that there is some evil there," I asked, posing the thought that had been lurking in the back of my mind.

"Evil?" she said pausing. "Evil is a matter of perspective. To a rabbit a mountain lion is evil, but the big cat's just hungry. If they meant to do me harm, I would have been in the oven with an apple in my mouth. There was nothing stopping them. If they were some kind of aliens and were collecting specimens, I would have been in a Petri dish or suspended in a fluid for the viewing pleasure of their children. So, evil, no."

"Okay, but what then?" I asked.

"This was something else. If we go into space, we're prepared. We're all suited up, and as ready as we can be. These guys were just there. They didn't get it either."

"So, you don't think they were waiting for an opportunity to do whatever they did to you."

"No, but here's the odd part. I think they learned from me. By the time they left me, they knew me intimately. This stuff is still coming to me, but I remember lists of words being sucked out of my consciousness. Random words leaving at the speed of light, like watching a computer screen as words fly over it. I could see and hear the words. They were processing them, and some didn't seem to make any sense so they discarded them," Shannon said, finishing and as she did, she stared off, mentally leaving.

I looked down at her arms, and they were full of goosebumps, and I could feel them rise and crawl up my spine also.

Shannon started again, but this time seemed to speak dreamily, "The words appeared like a fever dream, and I could see them leave, and as the creatures vacated me, the words trailed off, incomplete. It was very weird."

I stared at her as she came back.

"Let's go," she said.

I looked at her with growing dread. Shannon looked at me, realizing my fear. I was obviously spooked by the situation, but now even Shannon was giving me the willies. She smiled, probably reading my mind and took my hand, smiling broadly again.

"Come on, Dennis," she said and I nodded.

We walked down the stairs, hand in hand, and headed to my car. After we climbed in, she turned to me and said, "It's going to be all right, you know."

"I hope you're right, but if anything seems threatening, we're out of there. *If* we get the chance to leave," I said, remembering Shannon's inability to move and some of the Caller's stories.

I started out of Shannon's complex, and the next thing I knew, I was winding up the road to Jonathan's house. As I approached, it loomed malevolently behind the rock wall like it should have been framed by black clouds, driving rain and bolts of lightning. But it just sat there like I first time I saw it, serene and peaceful and I remember thinking how much I loved the setting. Now it reminds me of a nightmare that you can't wake up from.

We had been nearly silent for the entire drive. No jokes now. I pulled in and turned the car heading out for as fast a get-a-way as possible. We both just sat there, not making any attempt to leave the safety of the car. I looked over my shoulder at the house, and it seemed quiet, and then I looked at Shannon.

"I don't want to stay here very long," I said.

"Let's play it by ear, Den."

"Let's roll," I said with mock courage.

"You first," she said and we both laughed nervously.

We climbed out of the car and walked towards the trunk. Stopping there, I pulled out my cell phone and checked the time. It was later than I thought, and the sun was dipping towards the hill where we found the cave with the stone circle just a week ago. It seemed longer than that. We both just stared at the house. I called Liz and George to tell them that we were at Jonathan's.

"Hello," Liz said.

"Hi, Liz. We're here and it looks quiet," I said.

"Be careful, Den," she said, but I'm not sure that she thought that there was anything to be careful about, but I could feel her unease.

"See you in a bit," I said, putting the phone back in my pocket.

I got my cat carrier from the trunk, then started for the house, not looking at Shannon. I walked up the two steps, stopped and listened. I couldn't hear anything, so I peeked into the window by the door. The place was dark, and I couldn't see the cat. I glanced back at Shannon again, and then to the heavens in silent prayer.

I reached for the doorknob, turning it carefully. We left in a hurry the last time we were here, so the door wasn't locked. As I slowly pushed the door open, the cat bolted from the house like his tail was on fire, and Shannon and I both jumped.

"Damn!" I said feeling my heart pound in my chest.

Shannon giggled, "Well, at least he's still with us."

I stuck my head in the door, looking first left, and then right. Shannon was right on my backside peeking in over my shoulder but content to let me go first. The house smelled acrid, like burnt wiring. "Smells like week old burnt dinner, and litter box," I said.

"And a little singed me," she said trying to joke but I could see that she was worried.

We cautiously continued further inside. The back drapes were drawn, and the front room was dark, not having many windows. The first thing I saw, was my brand new, forty-inch, flat screened TV, which wasn't even completely set up yet, cooked with a streak that appeared to have flashed through the middle of it like a lightning bolt. It had a scorched mark that traveled from the TV, onto the wall, and up to the ceiling.

"Damn!" I said. "That thing cost me six hundred bucks. Oh, it's on now!"

Shannon looked at me as if to say dumb ass but refrained.

As I lamented my TV, Shannon glanced towards the dining room table, and nudged me, turning my attention towards the laptop sitting there. The screen glowed but was facing the kitchen, so we couldn't see it. As we approached, I could see the pan of burnt chicken still sitting on top of the oven.

I pointed and said, "You don't know what you missed."

"That's okay, I lost my appetite that night," she said.

My attention was on the chicken, but Shannon turned to the laptop.

"Hey, Den," she said motioning in that direction.

I moved enough to get a look at the screen. It was on, and one lone question mark sat on the top, with the cursor blinking next to it. My eyes widened, but Shannon shrugged.

"Shall we check the bathroom?" I asked, sensitive to Shannon's experience there.

Her expression was one of palpable fear, but she turned and walked towards it, and I fell in behind, admiring her courage. I saw her that night. She wasn't just afraid. That was bone chilling, pants wetting, heart-stopping terror, but she pushed on, and we turned the corner to see the flashlight sitting on the floor. The bathroom door was opened, and we peered in. The towel was on the floor where she had left it, and the lights were still on. We stepped further in and could see the mirror where the force seemed to emanate from. It was intact, but the whole area was discolored. The wall and sink that were formerly brown, were now a dirty gray. Shannon's attention went to the opposite wall. She reached out and touched a burnt image of her outline that appeared to have been photographed in negative on the wall. She turned to me, and I saw her eyes fill with tears.

"Huh," I said, reaching out myself and touching the strange image.

Shannon became agitated and turned towards the door.

"Shannon, are you okay?" I asked.

She nodded yes but walked quickly out. I caught up with her and caught her arm.

"Hey," I said, turning her. Her eyes were full of tears, and I pulled her to me. "Shannon. It's okay."

She buried her head in my shoulder, and I held her there.

"I'm okay now," she said.

"Let's go. I'll try to get the cat. I don't know what I expected," I said.

"Well, your dinner probably scared them out of here," she said both laughing and crying at the same time.

The cat wandered back in the front door. "Hey, good, he's back," I said. "I'll put him in the carrier."

He began to hiss.

"It's okay. I'm going to take you to a new home," I said, trying to calm him.

He arched his back and walked sideways towards the hall looking at the laptop.

"What's up, buddy?" I said, but he continued to hiss and lay his ears back.

Shannon took two steps towards me, and the cat's gaze stayed fixed in the direction of the laptop. Then there was a crackling sound, like an animal gnawing on dried bones. The sound seemed to come from the direction of the dining room table. By the hallway, the cat howled, and hissed, turning in circles, disappearing into the hall, and then peering around the corner with his ears back.

"What the hell?" I said and looked back at Shannon who stood stark still with all the color drained from her face, staring at the dining room. "What?"

Shannon didn't speak. She just pointed to the dining room. When I looked, the wall that was burnt behind the laptop, became distorted and rippled like heat waves in the desert.

"Oh shit," I said. "Does this look familiar?"

Again, Shannon didn't speak. She just stood transfixed, staring at the unbelievable scene. The wall was deformed, moving in every direction, like someone had thrown a rock into a pond, and then a thin vertical line split the air. It was pale blue and the width of a human hair, but it was still visible. Colored lights, the size of pinheads danced around the line and began to vibrate.

"Let's get out of here," I said.

"It's like they were waiting for me," Shannon said dreamily.

"Shannon, we need to go, now," I said forcefully.

"Wait," she said, mesmerized by the scene.

The colored dots seemed to fold into the vertical line but would then reemerge. They were yellow, blue, green and red, and they pulsated as their movement quickened. The vertical line then began to fold out, opening like a ripe peach, and it seemed that the lights were pulling it apart. As it opened, the center showed black, like space, deep and translucent. The colors then bled back into the opening like drops of paint into black water.

We watched with open mouths as it continued to open further.

"If we don't leave now, I don't think we're going to get out of here," I said.

Shannon was frozen, her eyes locked on the scene.

I reached out to shake her, but just then, tendrils leaped out of the black opening. Shannon and I both took a couple of steps back. They expanded in all directions, slowly covering the walls like fog rolling over the hills of Northern California. The air around this strange fog became distorted the same as what we first saw just minutes before and as the fog expanded, nearly all the air in the room took on this same distortion. It was like being in the middle of a fishbowl surrounded by water that didn't touch us.

We stared, first in wonder, and then with fear as the fog and the distortion barred the doors and windows. We were trapped and not going anywhere.

The tendrils then reached for Shannon. Several of them undulated towards her, becoming one, stopping in front of her, not touching her, suspended, and pulsing. Around each tendril, the air had been noticeably distorted. The tendril which had now become one appeared to be moving in a kind of clear liquid. This tendril hovered in front of Shannon's face and seemed to be staring at her. It moved slightly left then right as if identifying her. It then moved closer to her face and came within a hairs width from touching her cheek. She reflexively closed her eyes but didn't back away. The tendril then, like a snake recoiling from a strike, suddenly pulled back and surrounded the laptop. For just a moment, I thought that they were going to invade Shannon, again, and my legs felt like jelly.

"What the hell is going on?" I said in a whisper.

"They know me," Shannon said.

The tendril which had reached out to the laptop, divided again, then surrounded the laptop like an octopus, caressing it the way a lover might caress another, gently covering the keyboard and surrounding the screen. The cursor on the laptop backspaced, erasing the question mark and the screen went black.

"What's going on?" I asked, again, and we stared.

The screen came back on, turning white and the cursor moved to the center of the screen, with first periods, and then a word appeared in all caps:

...........................WAIT.........................

"Wait? Wait for what?" I said.

Shannon shrugged. "I think we're going to find out."

Shannon was pale white and looked like someone who had just seen a ghost. Her face was drained of color, and her eyes were fixed and staring.

"I wonder if they can hear us?" she asked.

The computer started again:

.............ERROR...........MISTAKE........

.................ERROR.........................

"What is this?" I asked.

"They're trying to communicate," she said.

"Communicate? Are they saying that they made a mistake or that they're sorry?" I asked with a flash of insight.

Shannon shrugged not taking her eyes off the computer.

"I wonder if they're sorry for nearly killing you, or for seeing you naked?" I nervously joked.

Shannon punched my arm and grabbed a chair setting it a few feet from the computer. She pulled it back further, at least four feet away, and then turned it backward and straddled it, resting her arms on the low back.

"Shannon, wait," I said alarmed.

"They don't want us to go, Dennis," Shannon said, looking around. "Get a chair." She spoke dreamily, and not sounding like herself.

I looked around and the walls seemed to faintly pulse as the translucent, grainy fog, ebbed and flowed. We weren't going anywhere. I very reluctantly took a chair and sat next to her facing the possessed laptop.

The response from the computer was slow, and we watched as each period would click off and then each letter of each word in an almost rhythmic, deliberate cadence.

.......WAIT...........LEARNING.....

.................LINKING...............

"Who the hell are you?" I said astonished.

...........DO NOT UNDERSTAND....

.................SIMPLIFY....................

"What? Simplify? Simplify what?" I said.

"Maybe they don't get the words *'the hell,'* in that context," Shannon said in a giddy voice.

I looked at her. "You're enjoying this," I said.

She giggled nervously like a child not supposed to laugh in church. "I'm telling you, Dennis, they don't mean us any harm," she said. "Okay. Who are you?" she asked.

...........................WAIT...........................

.............WE ARE WAVES...................

.......LINKED CHAINS....................

...................BUT…..YOU…….ARE…

.MOSTLY….EMPTY….SPACE.............

....

"We are?" Shannon said. "So, you can see us?"

...........................WAIT........................

…………..WE PERCEIVE YOU.........

…YOU ARE BITS OF SOMETHING....

.......ABOVE..AND BELOW…………

…......THAT IS WHY WE DID NOT KNOW

YOU WERE..

…WE SEE EVERYTHING AS IT IS.....

WE COULD NOT UNDERSTAND HOW

YOU COULD BE…………………………

…..YOU ARE CLOUDS OF SOMETHING

WITH ALMOST NOTHING BETWEEN..

…………………….WE……………………….

…………….MOVE BETWEEN……………..

"Between?" I said. "It sounds like they are describing atoms."
The computer came back to life:

…........ATOMS....................................

....WE DID NOT KNOW YOU WERE..

…..CONSCIOUS...............SENTIENT..

…….……...WHEN WE ENTERED THE

BEING WE WERE SHOCKED TO

HEAR AND UNDERSTAND…………

……………….WHEN WE ENTERED

WE KNEW AND COULD FEEL YOUR

FEAR...

…..YOU ARE MORE CLEAR TO US

NOW..........WE SEE HOW YOU ARE

BOUND..

"How can you understand us?" Shannon asked, glancing my way and shrugging.

..................................WAIT..........

......WE ENTERED BETWEEN YOU

AND THE OTHER WITH THE

FADING LIFE FORCE.....................

"Jonathan?" I said questioningly.
Shannon nodded.
"Do you think they killed him?" I asked.
"Not intentionally, but maybe," she said.

......WE....CONNECTED....LINKED..

..YOUR LIFE FORCE BEGAN TO FAIL...

.....I ABSORBED BUT NEEDED TO LINK

 WITH YOU TO UNDERSTAND....

...I TOOK FROM YOU....THEN LINKED

TO COMMUNICATE.....................WE

INTERLOCK TO GAIN KNOWLEDGE..

.......WE TRIED TO JOIN YOU BUT YOUR

LIFEFORCE WAS FAILING..........YOU

BEGAN TO DISORGANIZE...............

……..WE NEEDED TO RECEDE……….

"Disorganize?" I said.
"They don't have to tell me that. I was living it," Shannon said.
"Why were you here?" I asked.

…..............WE WERE NOT.....................

THEN WE WERE.................................

……WE WERE PULLED........................

...SURPRISED TO CROSS THE VOID.....

……SURPRISED...........TO BREACH THE

MEMBRANE………………………

….BUT ONCE THERE.....WE..

EXPLORED THIS NEW WORLD....

"I still don't see how you can understand me," Shannon said.

…..........LANGUAGE IS CODE....

…..NOTHING MORE...........EASY TO

LEARN..

…..........................WE JOINED YOU

FOR A SHORT TIME........YOU TAUGHT

US......SOME..

"Were you waiting for me to come back?" Shannon asked.

..........YES.........................ANOTHER

COMMUNICATION.......IF POSSIBLE..

.....THE RIFT IS TENTATIVE...............

..MAY CLOSE FOREVER...........IT IS

SMALL BETWEEN HERE AND THERE...

....

....

It seemed that they waited for a question and as they waited the periods clicked off, one by one, slowly.

"So, you came through some kind of rift?" I asked.

.......YES.....HERE THEN THERE..

........IT IS OPEN THEN CLOSED....

...THEN OPEN AGAIN....................

..............WAIT................................

......YOU ARE FADINGGG....

..........WAITTTT...............

In that instant, all the tendrils faded, becoming pale but they didn't recede back into the rift. It seemed that they were struggling to remain here though. The air remained distorted.

"Where are you from?!" Shannon shouted.

It seemed too late, and they continued to fade. The fog that blocked our escape then pulled back into the rift and the air returned to normal. The one tendril that had reached for Shannon pulled almost into the blackness, leaving the laptop, but stopped, and turned more opaque. It slowly poked back out of the darkness and traveled out like a blind person reaching forward as to not run into something or trip. I thought it was looking for Shannon again. It slinked forward, back towards Shannon, passing me, and almost caressing her face. It moved around her, taking her in, observing her contours. She stayed motionless as it seemed to examine her, and then it stopped and slowly went back to the laptop. The periods began again.

…..……WAIT………………………….

…………………………………FROM……

…..…..SIDEWAYS……………………….

..WE ARE BESIDE YOU ALWAYS

MAYBE BUT YOU ARE UNKNOWN..

…………………………WAIT………………

……………………………………………………

………….WE ARE PUSHED AWAYYY…..

The lone tendril started to fade a bit but came back. "Sideways? Do you understand sideways?" I asked.

……..BUBBLES…..ON…LIQUID…..

……….MOVING…….DRIFTING……

………………MOVE……..CLOSE...

………..MOVE…… AWAY………..

...CHANGING………..SOMETIMES

.....OVERLAPPING..........

"Are there other beings sideways?" Shannon asked.

.......YES................MANY.....................

...............THERE ARE LEGENDS AND

WE HAVE BEEN BREACHED................

......TO DESTROY..............LONG AGO....

.............SO SAY OUR LEGENDS...............

...........WE ARE FINITE........BEFORE WE

WERE......THE LEGENDS WERE.............

"What happened?" I asked.

…....................WAR...................IN.

….THE HEAVENS......................

"There are legends and in ancient writings that speak of war in the heavens.
The Bible and also Hindu texts both mention it," I said.
Shannon agreed having spent some time on ancient history.
"So, what happened? What was the outcome?" I asked.

...........WE WERE SPARED.................

....................…......PROTECTED BY THE

GUARDIANS WHO ANSWER TO ONE

...........................WAIT.....................
…..

The periods seemed to mark time as the tendrils faded.

"I think we're really losing them this time," I said and felt an overwhelming sadness. I was so afraid before, and now I desperately wanted them to stay. I had an inspiration. "When you say wait, are you linking with others of your kind?"

Shannon gave me an odd look. That hadn't occurred to her, and she looked at the computer for the answer.

…..

….......................................

The periods clicked off and I saw the tendrils nearly disappear, then come back.

…..

..YES WE MUST JOIN TO LEARN

THEN SEPARATE.............................

…….........ATTEMPTED TO LINK WITH

YOU...........COULD NOT CONTINUE......

…..

"That explains it," Shannon said. "They were trying to gain knowledge from me the way they know. So, how do you use the computer?" she asked.

The tendrils were back to full strength now, and the laptop screen glowed brightly, but the tendril covered small parts of it, sometimes obscuring the view.

….............CONTAINS LANGUAGE..........

........WE THOUGHT SENTIENT................

..........................INCORRECT...................

...........WITH YOUR CONTACT........WE

UNDERSTOOD...

...............SIMILAR LANGUAGE TO US....

......THE LANGUAGE OF KNOWLEDGE....

…...SIMILAR.................................WE

ABSORB..

.....................WE TOOK FROM YOU.....

...COULD NOT LINK AGAIN................

....ALTERNATIVE COMMUNICATION...

......................................IF POSSIBLE....

....

"So, you took knowledge from my mind?" Shannon asked.

…......YES................TOOK...............

..................AND........GAVE...............

.............SOMETHING........................

"I knew it. I told you, Dennis." She paused. "What did you give me?" she asked with that dawning on her.

................SOMETHING........................

...........................YOU......WILL....

KNOW...

"I will know?" Shannon repeated confused.

.....YOU WILL KNOW....THE WAY...

ALL THINGS ARE............. YOU..............

.... WILL KNOW........HOW ALL....

.......THINGS ARE.......................

"What the hell does that mean?" I asked.
"Don't know," Shannon said feeling blank.
The periods clicked off.

…...

........YOU ARE MOSTLY EMPTY SPACE......

...........BUT CONNECTED.............................

....................YOU WILL KNOW..............

…..............NO.......TIME........................

…..

"You said 'no time'. Why?" she asked.

…...........TEAR CLOSING................DOOR

TO SIDEWAYS CLOSING.........................

DOOR.................TO............YOU

CLOSING..............................WAIT.....

........BEWARE......THERE ARE OTHERS

WITH YOU FROM..............

SIDEWAYS............WE SAW THEM....

...............THEY ARE THERE BUT

NOT THERE.....................................

....YOU............

ARE......................BEING......

OBSERVED....................................

"Are we in danger?" I asked.

.....POSSIBLE........................WAIT.........

.....................UNKNOWN......................

"Do you know who or what they are?" I asked more insistent.

.........NO........SOME LEGENDS SAY....

................TAKERS.......OF.............

...............UNKNOWN.........................

....BEWARE.

"Maybe this is the caller's problem," I offered.

"Maybe," Shannon said.

"Do you think that they are watching us now?" I asked suddenly full of fear and I looked in all directions like I would see them.

"I don't know," she said.

"Well, don't you think that might be important?" I asked, getting upset.

…..............NOT HERE NOW............

.............BUT BEFORE.....................

…..THERE BUT NOT THERE..........

"Damn," I said.

"How much time before the rift closes?" Shannon asked.

........WAIT...........................

...............................UNKNOWN.....

..IT IS FADING...........................

...THERE THEN NOT THERE.........

...FADINGGGGGG.................

"Why is the doorway open now?" I asked.

……SOMETHING HAPPENED…

………………FROM YOUR SIDE........

....YOU BECAME SHADOW FROM

NOTHING......................LIKE VAPOR.....

....YOU WERE NOT.....THEN YOU WERE

......IT WAS ALL CHANCE........................

.............YOU ARE FADING................

…...............................REGRETFUL….

…..

We waited again as the tendrils faded. Some minutes passed and not even a period flashed up on the screen. I began to get up. Shannon touched my arm as the periods started again.

…...

CANNNNN…NOOOOOOOOOT..............

..........REMAINNNNNNNN.......

..CCCCCLLLLOOOOOSSSSSIIIINNG...

..........TTHEE VVVVOIDDD...............

CLOSINGGGGGGGGG.....................

The tendrils pulled away from the laptop and receded into the black opening. That was that.

Then just for the space of about three seconds, the blackness widened, and we looked deep into the space. Something was just inside the vast blackness and it brightened. It was a small waving, pale, linked chain, of moving energy that looked as though it was suspended in liquid. This flat rope contained every color in the rainbow and it twisted and turned like a flag blown in a mild breeze. One of the chains disengaged from the other, and they vibrated like they were electric. We both gawked into this void which was like looking out a window. It looked vast, like its own universe. There were small pale colored smudges further out and they spread into an infinite depth. It was open and huge. Then the colored pinpricks of light appeared around the edges, and like a movie in reverse, the rift closed to first the pale blue vertical line, and then disappeared, taking our breath with it. We felt an odd suction pull us towards the rift, but then we were gently freed.

We both just sat there and stared.

"What just happened here, Dennis?"

"I'm not sure," I responded dumbly.

"Did we just talk to some alien or ghost... or something?"

"Maybe both, or maybe there was never a difference," I said.

"Huh," she said.

We continued to stare at the computer screen, thinking that it may come back to life, but it just sat there with the cursor blinking after their last stammered words.

"Huh," I said.

"So, what they were describing as '*sideways*' wasn't the name of their world. They were saying that they live right beside us," Shannon stated.

"That's what I thought they meant, and all the stuff that I thought was crap might be true, but we're not talking different planets here. I think we're talking different dimensions. That would explain a lot, UFO's, ghosts, some superstitions, and even God and angels all wrapped up into dimensional realms of some kind."

"Huh," Shannon said and then grinned. "What about Bigfoot?"

"That's still crap," I said smiling.

Neither of us had moved from our chairs, yet. There was an odd feeling of shock.

I said, "Some things like UFO's might not be from some planet thousands of light years from here, maybe they're not even mechanical. This may have been going on for centuries."

Shannon speculated, "The Caller said that the circles marked points of power, but maybe they just marked weakness in the fabric of space allowing an occasional breach. So, now I'm thinking that these weaknesses come and go."

"So, some circles wouldn't have anything happening in them, while others would have some kind of anomaly," I said.

"And I'm sure that anomalies could happen anywhere there was a weakness. If there happened to be a shaman around he would probably plop a circle of stones there," she said.

"So, this is probably the Caller's problem. Something happened that allowed multiple breaches at the same time, and they were just caught in the storm," I said. "Nothing evil, just the wrong place at the wrong time."

"Who do you think the 'guardians of the one' are?" Shannon asked. "Do you think the 'one' is God?"

"Don't know. Their legend says that they were rescued by something. The only thing that comes to my mind is Arc Angels. If you hear that they're coming your way, you're having a bad day. It's my own bias, though. Some things that they said are hard for me not to put in some religious context."

"So, you think that the 'one' that they mentioned is God?" she asked, again.

"Maybe their version of Him. Maybe He rules all the dimensions. I'll tell you what. The universe is far stranger than I ever thought or could have ever imagined. Now I wonder if where we are, is reality or if it exists somewhere outside of us, somewhere sideways."

We got up and left the chairs where they sat. The rooms that we could see looked normal now, except for a couple of prominent burnt marks and one fried TV.

"I feel like I want to ask them a lot more questions, Dennis. I didn't get the feeling, though, that they were any more intelligent than us. They seemed pretty normal, except that they could invade my body and pull me apart."

"So, what do you think that they meant by, 'you will know the way all things are'?" I asked.

"I have no idea, but they put something in me," she said. "I know they did. I can almost feel it. It helped me survive, but it's more. I just don't know."

"Maybe someday you'll know," I said.

Shannon shook her head, and then a shudder of fear passed through her that I could see.

"What's wrong?" I asked with some fear of my own.

"I don't know, Dennis. I don't think we can tell anyone about this," she said, and I could see her mind churning.

"Why? What about the scientific community, or the authorities, or someone?"

"I think they might just stick us in a padded room, or worse," she said.

"Worse?"

"Yeah, like take me, and turn me into a lab rat."

"Oh," I said. "You're right. Any person who ever came forward with this type of thing is always discredited," I observed.

"We need to keep this quiet. Now I'm a little sorry I told the Caller lady."

"Why?" I asked.

"I don't know. I guess we're in the same boat. I'm just feeling paranoid."

"I was thinking," I said, trying to break Shannon away from her own thoughts. "All those people who saw strange lights in the sky, and everyone who saw a ghost in the night, may have really been seeing something."

"Maybe," she said with a shrug.

"Let's get out of here and think. My head is spinning. Different beings in different dimensions? It's just crazy," I said and started for the door.

"Maybe we can pick up some information in the media, or online about this happening to other people, besides the Caller. Not everyone would shut up about it," she said.

"We can keep our eyes open, and our heads down," I said, and Shannon smiled knowing that I was fully on board with keeping our secret.

"I wonder if governments already know that this is happening?" she asked.

"And they're covering it up?"

"Yeah," she said.

I shrugged.

"Too many questions without answers," she commented then said. "Let's get out of here."

We continued to the door. Shannon was behind me and said, "There's just one more thing."

I turned to face her, wondering what she meant. She took hold of my sleeve and pulled me towards her and kissed me. She put her other arm over my shoulder and I felt her hand in my hair. My arms instinctively moved of their own volition, pulling her closer so that I could feel the front of her body fully pressed against mine. We separated for a second, looked into each other's eyes, and moved back to a full embrace, our lips tightly together.

Shannon pulled back smiling. "I can't tell you how long that I've wanted to do that," she said, not taking her eyes from mine.

I was speechless, but I didn't want this to end.

"It's been a very long time since I've been kissed like that," I said, and I pulled her back to me, kissing her again. We separated slowly.

"Well, I thought that if I was ever going to kiss you, I was going to have to be the one to do it, or it might not happen," she said teasing me.

"Oh, I think I would have gotten up the courage, eventually," I said, but there wasn't any question which of us was the bravest. It was Shannon. She pulled back, looking at the ground.

We started out the door, and Shannon stopped abruptly. "What about the cat?" she said.

We both started laughing.

"I'll get him," I said.

We turned and walked back in. I looked at the cat carrier still lying in the middle of the living room floor, and then I looked at the cat. He was sitting by the fireplace with a defiant expression. "I don't suppose that you want to go to a new home do you?"

He turned to me and yawned.

"Humm." I picked up the carrier and sat it down by him and turned to Shannon. "Do you believe in miracles?" I asked.

"Tonight, I would believe almost anything," she said.

The cat watched us talk, and then padded into the carrier, and laid down.

"Damn," I said.

"No more denying the existence of God," she said.

"Huh."

"Den, do you think that some of these beings can come through when they want?"

"Maybe, but it seems not. It seems more like a crime of opportunity, with conditions and circumstances being just right."

"I wonder if God did have something to do with this. Maybe there is some hierarchy controlling or ruling," she said.

"People think that God is so unnatural, but maybe He arose from this multiverse first, and became self-aware."

"Or maybe this is his creation," she said.

"I hope we're not some god child's ant farm!" I said.

"What an awful thought," Shannon responded.

I grabbed the litter box and Shannon grabbed the cat carrier, after closing the small door. "Come on Patches," She said using his new name.

We walked out of Jonathan's crazy house.

"So, what do we do now?" she asked.

I popped the trunk and set the litter box inside.

"I don't know... I think I'm going to learn to play tennis," I said.

Shannon stared at me with her mouth agape.

"You may have just learned one of the deepest mysteries of the universe and you want to learn to play tennis," she said, more a statement than a question.

"Yeah. Do you want to learn with me?"

"NO... Well, maybe, but-"

I interrupted her, "Your right, it may spoil some vast eternal plan, but yes, it looks fun," I said nonchalantly.

"Huh?" she said mystified.

"And one more thing?" I said, stepping towards her.

"Okaayyy. And what's that?" she asked, wondering what I was going to say next.

"I was hoping you would kiss me again."

"I don't know, Dennis. There may be some vast eternal plan disturbed if I do."

"I was hoping we could take our chances," I said, moving closer. Shannon set the cat down.

"You are stupid," she said shaking her head.

"But you like me," I said finishing her sentence.

"Yeah, Den, I like you a lot," she said, reaching for me and looking into my eyes.

I reached out and took the outsides of her arms and pulled her gently to me, needing only to bend slightly, I just brushed her lips with mine. I felt her hands reach around to my back and pull me against her, gently bringing our lips closer. I will never forget that kiss, and I knew that I had found someone special, not just a lover, but a friend that I could always trust.

We separated, and Shannon put her hand on my shoulder, as I glanced back at the house. I then turned towards the car and looked again at her with a sense of good fortune. We both turned our attention to the sky, the auroras, barely visible now, and the supernova fading some. Shannon, still resting her hand on my shoulder gave it a slight squeeze and then released it, dropping her hand. For just an instant, from the corner of her eye, she could see faint strands of color connect her hand to my shoulder. She turned back rapidly, looking closer, but could no longer see anything.

"Dennis, did you see that?" she asked with her eyes wide.

"What?"

"I thought I saw... No, never mind. It was just a trick of the light," she said shaking her head. "It was nothing."

THE END

"The end?" Stephen thought aloud.

41

Stephen, in a frenzy, finished typing... THE END... He sat back and stared at the final page. I think it's done.

He thought that it felt done, but was it?

"Mary!" he called loudly.

She came in thinking that something was wrong.

"What, Stephen? Are you okay?"

"Yes, I think I'm finished."

"Finished? You mean the first draft?"

"No, I mean the book."

"You've only been on this book for a short time. It usually takes you longer for your rewrites."

"I know. I'm going to print it. Will you read it? I think I'm going to send it in like it is, and I want your opinion."

"Okay?" she said skeptically.

Mary had always been Stephens' ideal reader. Every time he would finish a book, she was his first proofreader. He completely respected and valued her opinion and instincts. She had caught some glaring screw-ups in the past, and nothing that was wrong with a storyline ever slipped by her.

Three hours later, Stephen printed his pages. Mary was reading in the living room, and he hand-delivered his manuscript to her. She gave him a funny look.

"What?" he said.

"Well, and don't take this wrong, but it usually takes you at least six months to finish a book. I mean really, Stephen?"

"Mary, you are the person I trust most in the world. If you say it's not finished, or think something is missing, well, okay. Just read it with an open mind."

"Okay?" she said with a shrug, and looked at the cover page:

SIDEWAYS

Stephen Fremont

Stephen stood looking over her shoulder as she finished the first short chapter, and she shrugged again. She started the second chapter, and Stephen noticed a change in her attitude.

"Go away, Stephen," she said feeling his gaze.

"Okay, ah..."

"It's already better than I thought. GO AWAY."

He knew that he was being distracting, so he decided to take a walk. He grabbed his coat and walked back into the room.

Mary was smiling.

"I'm going for a walk," he said.

Mary waved but kept her nose in the book.

If Mary likes it, I'll drive it over to the publisher, personally, he thought.

Finishing his walk, he entered the living room and looked expectantly at his wife. Mary didn't look up.

"Well, what do you think so far?" he asked.

"I don't get it."

"Don't get what?"

"I don't get how you were able to write this so fast, and while I'm really enjoying the characters, I'm curious. You've never raised a special needs child, and some of this info seems, well, personal."

"To tell you the truth, some of the story just came to me. I've told you before how I see scenes in my head and hear dialog, well, I heard and saw most of this and just wrote it down. It was like being a fly on the wall in other people's lives. Finish it before you tell me more."

"Okay, Stephen. Order a pizza tonight. I'm not leaving this book."

Mary is a very fast reader, and it wasn't unusual for her to knock out a novel in two or three days, so she had put everything aside to finish Stephens' book. By the end of the third day, she called him in. "I've finished," she said, resting her hands on the manuscript, sitting in her lap.

Stephen sat down. "Well?"

"I loved the book and the characters. The book feels a little short, but the story is complete enough, and I'm left with questions. Were you thinking about writing a sequel?"

"Right now, I don't know. It feels like there is more to the story, but nothing has come to me since I finished. It's like my characters are continuing their lives without me."

"Huh... Okay. This is my honest opinion. This is not your best work, but it's good. I think your publisher will be happy enough. I think she will think that you are planning a sequel, and it's part of the plan. The story itself is complete enough inside the framework of the story, but I want to know what happens to Dennis, Shannon, and Bryan, and what did Shannon see at the very end when she touched Dennis' shoulder? It seems written to a point of time with the future to come, and that's fun. I don't like long-winded books, and I hate flat characters, and I was happy with both things in "*Sideways*" but I wish that there was more to the story. I want Shannon and Dennis to live happily ever after. I want Bryan to be okay. I hope you write the sequel."

"Thanks, Mary. You know, your opinion means more to me than anyone else's. I'm going to leave the story as it is and drive it into San Francisco tomorrow or the next day. Do you feel like a day trip? We can get lunch on the wharf."

"Sounds good. Let's go tomorrow," Mary said.

After a good night sleep, Stephen and Mary drove the roughly two hours from Roseville to San Francisco to see Stephen's new publisher. She was expecting him at 10:30, but he got hung up in traffic and arrived there at 10:45. Stephen said hello to the receptionist, and she buzzed him in, while Mary remained in the small waiting room.

The door opened into Joanne Cohen's office. Stephen walked in, happier than he had been in months, and relieved to have finally gotten over the terrible case of writer's block that had plagued him. Joanne greeted him, rising from behind her desk. She wasn't tall, but projected authority, dressed in a black skirt, white shirt, and black coat. She was blond and looked close to forty, with her hair pulled into a tight bun, and wearing black-rimmed glasses. She reached for Stephen's hand and shook it warmly.

"Hi, Stephen. I'm so glad you could come."

"Sorry, I'm a little late. I always forget how bad the traffic can get."

"No problem. When I heard, you were coming, I blocked off the whole afternoon. So, do you have the manuscript?"

"Right here," he said, handing over a manila envelope.

"Please sit down, Stephen. Do you want some coffee?"

"No thanks."

"I'm going to read and edit this myself. I'll contact you with any revisions, and the art. If it's where we want it, I'm going to put a rush on printing it. I'm hoping to get it out before the holidays."

"That sounds good to me, Joanne. Let me know," Stephen said with a half-smile. His mind traveled to the story, and to an odd uneasiness that had continued to niggle at him since he finished the book.

Joanne caught his expression and asked, "Is everything alright?"

"Yes, everything's fine," he said, standing up and reaching for her hand.

"Thanks again, Stephen. I think we can pull this off," she said, smiling confidently.

Stephen smiled and walked from the office. He could see Mary, sitting and reading a magazine. As he closed Joanne's door, he had a fleeting sense about the story. Something about the book and the images that consumed his mind while he was writing it disturbed him in a way that he couldn't put his finger on. He shook it off as Mary looked up. They walked from Backstreet Publishing and had a nice day by the San Francisco Bay.

Four days later, Joanne called. "Hi, Stephen. I just finished the book, and really enjoyed it. I would like to send a few revisions to you via email and then I think we can proceed. Also, send me any ideas for the art, if you want. If not, our art department will handle it. I would like to get this going. I have everything halted so I can ramrod it through."

"Okay, thanks, Joanne. I'll get right on it when I receive your email. Talk to you soon," Stephen said hanging up.

42

Cliff Evan's poked and punched the keyboard, and as he did so, the images in his mind seemed to fade. Dennis and Shannon left the house and looked into the sky. "I think that's it," he said aloud. He felt so close to finishing that he had called in sick for the last couple of days, just to wrap up this obsession of a story. For the past few weeks, he hadn't been able to think about anything else, and now he typed:

THE END

The end! he thought. Damn... Is it finished? I think it is. The last few paragraphs gave him trouble and were the hardest as the story seemed to fade, and nothing popped back into his mind. He considered the story and felt that it could end there, but something might be missing. He thought that maybe he should write a final chapter, but he felt like a dry well, unable to conjure any more images. The story was gone.

He pushed back away from the computer and felt a sense of pride. Even if no one ever read the thing, at least he finished it and liked the way it turned out. He began to reread the last chapter, and found a few misspellings, but couldn't find any other problems that he wanted to change. He knew he was an amateur, and there had to be things that he didn't know was wrong with the novel.

He decided to stay home for the next few days and read the book from the beginning to the end, and then after correcting the things that he could fix, send it out to see if he could sell it. He would try sending it to a couple of local literary agents, he thought, and maybe a publisher or two. They can only say no. Maybe a movie director would pick it up as a screenplay.

"Ha, fat chance," he laughed.

He knew that he was having delusions of grandeur, and he laughed at himself, again. Oh, well, nothing ventured, nothing gained, he thought.

He worked on the novel for the next week, feeling that he could never get it just right, so he picked a major publishing house, two local agents, a movie director, and a sci-fi television station to send the manuscript. He also sent out several query letters via email. He put five hard copies in manila envelopes and went to the post office and mailed them to addresses that he had picked up online. Now I wait, he thought. He got several no's right away in response to his emails then waited…

Four weeks went by, and nothing had been returned. He woke around three in the afternoon from working all night, and one of his envelopes was in the mailbox. He grabbed it, and ran up to his apartment, and pulled it open. There was a form letter saying thanks, but no thanks from one of the local agents, impersonal, and without feeling. The next day he received the manuscript back from the major publishing house saying that they don't handle new writers, without some known track record. He knew that this could happen but couldn't hide his disappointment.

Early the next week he had all but given up when he received the third manuscript back. As he tore it open, he saw a hand-written letter from the second agent:

Dear Clifford,
Thank you for submitting your manuscript. We thought it was good but needed editing. We are busy with other projects right now, but maybe in the future, if you don't sell it to someone else, we can do business. Keep writing. You have talent.
Sincerely, Angela Harding

Cliff folded the letter. I guess I shouldn't have gotten my hopes up, he thought with a sigh. I'm sure the others aren't interested either. He waited for another two weeks but got no response from the director, or the TV station, and he figured that his manuscript just lined their trash cans.

He took his last week of vacation, and despite the waterfall of rejection, he still felt that he had accomplished something that he had always wanted to do, write a novel. He thought about his characters, Dennis, Bryan, and Shannon. In the time it took him to write the book, he had become close to them in an odd way. They weren't completely real, but there was something about how vivid their images were in his mind. Something that made him sorry that the book was finished. Maybe I should try a sequel, he thought, and the possibility gave him joy. Then he remembered that tonight he was due back to work, and that thought depressed him. He knew that he was barely replaced and that his department was trashed. I'm going to need a good book to get me through the first few brutal nights back. I'd better run to the library.

43

Stephen heard the phone ring. "I'll get it," he called to Mary. "Hello."

"Hi, Stephen. I have some news," Joanne Cohen said.

"Hi, Joanne. What's up?"

"We have pulled this together, and the book is going to be published, and on the shelves in one month. I have two hundred advanced copies of the hard-backed edition being delivered next week, and one being sent to you at the end of this week. Look it over, I think it turned out great. I have arranged for a book signing event at an exclusive bookstore in San Francisco. I'll have a couple of dates to run by you in a couple of days," she finished.

"Sounds great, Joanne. You really did pull this together," he said.

"Okay, I'll get back to you," she said, and Stephen could hear in her voice that she loved this kind of pressure.

"Talk to you later," he said, hanging up and smiling to himself.

Mary walked into the study. "What was that?" she asked.

"That was Joanne," he said. "She has pulled off the impossible and said that the book will be on the shelves in one month. She's also arranging several book signings with advanced copies. She's trying to schedule the first one for two weeks from now."

"Wow, Stephen, a girl of action," Mary said.

"No kidding," Stephen said shaking his head.

A week later, Joanne called back. "Hi, Stephen, can I run a couple of dates by you?"

"Sure."

"I would like to schedule the signing in San Francisco for next Friday at 3:00. If that doesn't work, we can try a different day," she said.

"No, Friday will work," he said.

"Great. I will work on the two signings in Sacramento, and get back to you."

"Sounds good, let me know."

"Great," Joanne said, hanging up with bubbling enthusiasm.

Stephen walked from the study, and into the living room. Mary was standing by the door. "Was that Joanne again?" she asked.

"It was. She wants me to do the book signing in San Francisco next Friday. I told her that would be fine. Will you come?"

"Of course," Mary said.

"Joanne wants to do two signings in the Sacramento area also."

"That will be fun, and close to home," Mary said.

"Yeah, it will," he said.

The day of the San Francisco book signing arrived. Stephen and Mary drove south on interstate eighty towards the city. The drive was long, and they arrived and parked in a lot a block from the bookstore. As they entered the store, they could see that the place was buzzing. There was a line that started at a table and wound out the door. Stephen saw Joanne waiting there, and copies of *Sideways* stacked in boxes beside the table. There were two of his books in holders, standing upright, with the red and white cover facing forward, and the title on the top. Stephen could see the grayed-out silhouettes of a man holding the hand of a child on the cover and he felt a slight shiver as the image brought to mind the visions that had inspired the book.

Stephen said hello to Joanne and sat down at the table. Fans gushed as he signed copies of "*Sideways,*" and Mary stood next to Joanne who was positively exuberant. The signing ended only after the two hundred books sold. Joanne thanked some of the store personnel and walked over to Stephen.

"That went well," she said beaming.

"It did, Joanne. Thanks for the great job," Stephen said.

"Stephen? May I ask you a question?" Joanne asked.

Mary walked over and stood next to Stephen.

"Of course, Joanne. What's on your mind?"

"I was wondering if you planned to write a sequel to this book. It ended like the story needs to continue."

Mary smiled knowing that she had made the same comment.

"Mary said the same thing," Stephen said, smiling at his wife. "She also thought there was more to the story."

"I thought it ended a little abruptly," Mary said.

"I'm not trying to be critical, I was just wondering," Joanne added.

"I have outlined a sequel, but this story was peculiar. The way it came to me and some of the detail. I've had the same feeling for small parts of different books, but this entire book felt that way. I feel that my outline for the next book isn't the truth. I need to have the same images and feelings that I had in the first book to write a sequel. I know this probably sounds odd to you, but it's even more odd to me." Stephen shrugged. "So, I honestly don't know," he finished.

Joanne took everything in that he said but didn't quite get the difference between his inspirations for other books and "*Sideways.*" Then she said, "I hope you don't take my criticism wrong, I'm a big fan of your work, and I enjoyed reading '*Sideways*'."

Stephen could see some genuine shyness peek through her tough exterior.

"No no, don't worry. I don't have thin skin. I actually agree with you and so does Mary. Good night, Joanne. I'll see you in Sacramento."

The next week, Stephen met Joanne for the first Sacramento book signing, and the reviews started to trickle in from critics who had received advanced copies of the book. "*Sideways*" was getting a mixed reaction at best. Some critics liked the book, but most were lukewarm to it, not thinking it was his best work, and pointing to books that he had written twenty years ago, as the golden age of Stephen Fremont.

"I guess you were right, Mary," he said to his wife as they sat together watching TV. "I'm getting panned by most of the critics, and I don't think any of them loved it."

"Oh well, Stephen, Barry Bonds didn't hit a home run every time he came to bat either. For what it's worth to you, I loved the characters in this book more than in any other book you've ever written, and to me, they seemed more real."

"Thanks, Mary," Stephen said and he put his arm around her.

"Have you thought any more about the sequel," she asked.

"I've thought about it, but I keep waiting for the story to burst into my mind the way "*Sideways*" did, and that just hasn't happened. I've been trying to put my finger on the images that I saw in this book, and the way the images looked in my mind in other books. Most of the time, I don't see the characters so vividly, they appear kind of fuzzy at the edges. The other books seemed like imagination, this book... I don't know... It was similar but different," he trailed off and went to that place in his mind where Shannon, Dennis, and Bryan lived. He shook his head.

"Huh," Mary said, not able to understand the distinction. "Let's go to bed, Stephen." She took his hand, and they turned out the lights and went upstairs.

44

Angela Harding was at her desk, looking over several new manuscripts that had just arrived. She was in her fifties, with short gray hair, and had been a literary agent for the best part of her working career after graduating from Brown University. Her father had owned the Harding Agency before she took over and gave her the love of fiction. He had lived to eighty-nine and worked until his health failed. Angela took over just two years ago, and the business continued to flourish.

Her phone rang, and she picked it up with the usual, "Harding Agency."

"Hi, Angela. It's Stacy."

"Hi, Stacy. I'm glad you called. I just got a new manuscript that I would love for you to read. Are you in town?"

"That's not why I'm calling. Have you read the new Stephen Fremont book?"

"No. I heard that he had a new book out, but I don't know anything about it. Why?"

"He just had a book signing in Sacramento, a couple of days ago, and I happened to be there."

"Okay?" Angela said.

"I picked up his book, and started reading, and it was very familiar," Stacy said, slowing her words.

"Familiar?"

"Yeah. Do you remember that book that you gave me to read by Cliff something or other? I told you that it was a good story, but that the writing was rough and it needed too much editing."

"Yeah, Cliff Evans?"

"Fremont's book had the same title, *"Sideways."* I had just finished that Cliff guy's book, so I started thumbing through Fremont's, and it's almost the exact same story, not word for word, but close."

"Same characters?"

"Yep."

"Huh, how could this Cliff get access to Fremont's book?" Angela asked rhetorically.

"Do you think he copied it and was trying to sell it before Fremont did?"

"I don't know how. This just doesn't make sense," Angela remarked. "Thanks, Stacy, I'll try to figure it out from here. I'll call you back," Angela said hanging up. "What the hell?" she said aloud.

Angela's mind went into overdrive trying to reconcile this oddity. "What to do?" she asked herself aloud. Lots of mines in this minefield, she thought. I don't even have a copy of Cliff's book anymore.

She tried to consider all the possibilities. This guy, Cliff, is going to see Fremont's book eventually. Humm... We're a small agency, Fremont's publisher is large and I'm sure lawyered up... I need to sleep on this one.

The next morning, Angela drifted into work. She sat at her desk and decided to see what Cliff had to say. She pulled up his phone number and dialed.

"Hello," Cliff said in a sleepy voice.

"Hi, Cliff. It's Angela Harding. I'm the literary agent that you sent your manuscript to, and I sent you back the letter."

"Oh yeah, hi," Cliff said, trying to clear his head. He had just dozed off on the couch.

"Can you send me back a copy of your book?"

"Sure. Why?" Cliff asked. "Are you thinking about trying to get it published?"

"No, to be honest with you, your book is very similar to Stephen Fremont's new book, and I want to compare them."

"I didn't know he had a new book out. I usually try to get his books. I'm a fan of his stuff."

"It's not on the shelves yet. One of my readers happened to be at a book signing of Fremont's and picked up an advanced copy."

"So, how did you find out?" Cliff asked.

"She read your manuscript also and called me. Fremont's book is named *"Sideways".*"

"No shit," Cliff said. "So, do you think this guy ripped me off?"

"I don't know what happened, but if he plagiarized you, and we can prove it, you'll be able to sue him."

"So, what now?" Cliff asked.

"I have the date I received the copy from you. We would need to prove that you wrote it first, so anything with dates will be helpful," Angela suggested.

"Why would someone like Fremont rip off my story?"

"To be honest, Cliff, people are going to think the opposite."

There was silence on the line as Cliff pondered those words. Then he forcefully responded, "What? ME! I wrote my book. Something's wrong here, and it ain't me."

"Okay, okay. Give me a couple of days, and I'll get back to you after I've had a look at both books."

"I'm mailing it right now, FedEx. You should have it by tomorrow," Cliff said.

"Thanks, Cliff, talk to you soon," Angela said hanging up. She then called Stacy. "Hi, Stacy. Did you buy a copy of Fremont's book?"

"Yep."

"What are the chances that I could get a look at it tomorrow?"

"I'll drive it to you, and you can give me the new book to read," Stacy said.

"Thanks, that would be great."

Angela hung up and stared at her wall. She began to think, this just doesn't add up. Unable to focus on anything but the *"Sideways"* mystery, she wondered if there could be any other possibilities. Cliff doesn't seem like the type to copy Fremont's work, but who knows, I just talked to him on the phone. Fremont doesn't seem like he would do that either. Hum…

Unable to concentrate, Angela decided to leave early. She passed her secretary. "I'm gone for the rest of the day. See you tomorrow," she said, waving and heading out of the door.

The next day, Cliff's book arrived at 10:30. Angela opened the FedEx package, removing a manila envelope, and then slid the manuscript out laying it on her desk. She began the story with the death of Jonathan Bartoli and then moved to Dennis and Bryan. She disappeared into the pages, and despite the rough writing, began to wonder about the story and the characters. Her secretary interrupted her, "Angela, Stacy's here."

"Thanks. Send her in," she said, still looking at Cliff's novel.

Stacy walked in with a red and white, hard-backed book in her hand, and she passed it to Angela.

"Here you go," Stacy said.

Angela looked up and said, "Hi, Stacy. Thanks. This should be interesting."

"Not just interesting, creepy," Stacy said.

"I don't know. There's usually a good explanation for things like this," Angela said. "Here's the new book, and I think it looks promising," she said, handing the manuscript to Stacy.

"Thanks," Stacy said, turning for the door. "I should be done by early next week."

Stacy walked out, and Angela began skimming both books, side by side. It only took an hour for her to reach the same conclusion that Stacy did.

"Holy Christopher Columbus," she said aloud. "This is the same story. Huh."

She sat back in her chair staring at the doppelganger books. "What to do?"

She picked up Fremont's book and looked at the publisher and knew Backstreet Publishing by reputation. This is going to be sticky, she thought. She paused again and then said aloud, "What happened here?" I guess I'll contact Backstreet. Maybe I can arrange a meeting with them… I guess... What to do?

45

"Sideways" officially hit the bookshelves, today. With the first two book signings being successful, tonight's should go well, Stephen thought. He peered into the mirror, finished shaving, and rubbed his chin. Mary peeked in and coughed.

"Stephen, I don't think I'm going to go with you tonight. I'm feeling a bit under the weather."

"I heard you coughing. Are you okay?"

"Yeah, just a cold I think, but I don't feel like going out."

"Okay. I should be home around 7:00."

"I know it's early, but I've warmed up some of last night's dinner. Come and eat before you go," she said.

"I don't have much of an appetite," he said.

"You seem nervous. You've done hundreds of these signings. What's wrong?"

"I don't know? I've felt this way since I published *"Sideways."* There seems to be a constant, low level, adrenaline rush pushing through my veins."

"Are you going to do more signings?"

"I don't think so," Stephen said as he sat down and began to eat. "Joanne wants me to go to some of the main cities in the U.S. but I haven't agreed yet, and I'm not under contract to do so."

He finished the dinner and got up from the table, then walked his dishes to the sink. "Thanks, Mary. I'll see you tonight," he said, then leaned over and kissed her goodbye.

The drive to the bookstore took about forty minutes. He parked and walked to the door. The place was busy, just like the other two signings, and as he walked in, he could see the table with the book *"Sideways"* filling a shelf to the right. Stephen looked for Joanne, who didn't seem to be there yet. A loose line was beginning to form close to the table, and a few people noticed him. Joanne walked in the door and strode up to Stephen.

"Hi, Joanne, I was hoping you were here."

"I just stepped out for a smoke," she said. "I'm trying to quit, but when I get nervous-"

"I understand," Stephen said.

"Are you ready?" she asked.

"Sure."

As he sat down, the line became more organized, with maybe twenty people columned down the middle of the store. He began signing and happily answered a few questions from some of the people in line as they reached him. Most wanted him to write sequels to their favorite Stephen Fremont books, but some just wanted to thank him for continuing to write entertaining novels. Stephen was not a big fan of the spotlight, and while flattered, he also felt a little embarrassed to hear the constant accolades.

One by one, the people filed by. He glanced at Joanne and smiled, and she smiled back with a look of pure satisfaction. He finished with a lady who bought two books and had him sign one to her daughter, and then a man with a child walked up with his copy, laying it down in front of Fremont.

"Hi, Mister Fremont," the man said.

"Hello," Stephen said, just glancing up and lifting his pen.

"Could you sign this book to Dennis, Bryan, with a y, and our friend Shannon?"

Stephen glanced up and smiled. "You're kidding, right?" he said getting a better look. Fremont's face then drained of all color, as his eyes fixed on the man with the child in shocked disbelief.

"No, not at all," the man with the child said. "This is my son Bryan."

Stephen seemed to stammer, and Joanne thinking that the guy must be a crackpot stepped forward.

"This isn't funny," she said, taking charge.

"No, I don't think its funny either," the man said.

Joanne continued to protest, and the people standing behind the man were becoming impatient.

"What is this?" Joanne said but Stephen stopped her.

"Can I talk to you over here?" Stephen said to the man and child. He got up and motioned for Joanne to join them. When they got out of earshot of the other customers Stephen said, "Dennis and Bryan?"

The man nodded yes, and Joanne said, "What?!"

Stephen turned to Joanne, and she could see that he was visibly shaken.

"What, Stephen?"

"I... I'm... This is too weird," Stephen said stammering and shaking his head.

Joanne pointed at the man with the child, and said, "This guy thinks he's from your book?"

Stephen continued to look pale and nodded. "Yes," he said and turned back to look at the man with the child. Stephen studied the man's face and the child's. "Can you come to my house tonight? It's not far from here?"

"Are you kidding?" Joanne protested.

Stephen turned to the man and handed him a business card. "This is my home address. I should be there by 7:00."

The man nodded and walked from the store, carrying the child, while Stephen and Joanne stared after him. The child peered over the man's shoulder and smiled.

"Will you come, too, Joanne?"

"I don't think I would miss it," she said. "Stephen, what is going on?"

"I know him and his child."

"I don't understand."

"You will," Stephen said.

As Stephen began walking back to the table, Joanne whispered more to herself than to Stephen, "What the hell was that?"

He turned back, hearing her. "Something... Something that I can't explain."

The rest of the signing went on without any more interruptions. As scheduled, it ended at 6:00, with nearly every book sold. The shock of the man with the child faded from Joanne's mind but haunted Stephen. The bookstore employees scurried around straightening the area, pulling down the table, and the manager thanked Stephen for doing the signing.

He and Joanne stepped out of the store, and Stephen pulled his cell phone from his pocket. "Mary, I have some guests coming at 7:00. I wanted to let you know... I know. This couldn't be helped... I'm on my way home and should be there in forty minutes. I'll explain it then." He put his phone away and glanced at Joanne. "You can follow me. It's not far."

"Stephen..." she said but he interrupted her.

"I need to collect my thoughts. I'd rather explain it to you and Mary together."

She nodded. "Okay," and walked to her car.

They pulled out together. He was glad for the time it took to get home. It gave him time to process what had happened at the store. He had an odd picture beginning to form in his mind but couldn't quite understand it. This guy, Dennis, was the person in the images that he saw as he wrote "*Sideways.*" And the child, damn, he wasn't just similar, he was exact... And what happened to Shannon? Stephen continued to roll thoughts around in his mind, having flashbacks to scenes in the different chapters. The first encounter with the beings in the bathroom, and the second encounter when they purposely communicated with Dennis, and Shannon. So, how had he slipped into these private moments in these people's lives? He had eavesdropped on their conversations, their thoughts, their dreams... and even had seen them undressed for God's sake. Extremely embarrassed he blushed red, happy he was alone. "Welcome to the Twilight Zone."

Stephen pulled into his driveway with Joanne close behind. It was about 6:45, and they both got out of their cars.

Joanne walked up to him. "Stephen, what is going on?" she said quietly, not accusingly.

"I've been trying to figure that out. I don't have any real answers. Let's go in and talk to Mary. I'll explain more there."

They walked up the brick steps together. Stephen opened the door, and Mary greeted them. She could tell by the look on Stephen's face that something was wrong.

"Stephen?"

"Hi, Mary," he said hugging her.

"Hi, Joanne," Mary said.

"Hi, Mary," Joanne said with the same look as Stephen.

Mary looked at them both. "Okay, what's up?" she asked.

"Mary, do you remember how I told you that the story and images were somehow different in *"Sideways"* than from other books?"

"Yes?"

Stephen sighed, "Well tonight you are going to meet Dennis and Bryan from my book."

"What?" Mary said skeptically and turned to Joanne.

"Stephen thinks that a guy who came to the book signing was Dennis Olsen from the book," Joanne said.

"I don't just think it. I've asked him here. I want to talk to him and find out what he has to say. I'm not sure if he will bring Bryan, but he'll be here at 7:00."

Mary looked again at Joanne, who still looked skeptical, but unsure.

"How, Stephen?" Mary asked.

"I don't know, but I think we're about to find out," he said, hearing a car door close outside.

Mary peeked out of the window and saw a gray Honda Civic pull in behind Joanne's Mercedes. She saw a man step out and gaze up at the house. He seemed to take a deep breath, and steel himself before his first step towards the door.

***

Before I could knock, Stephen Fremont opened the door. I could feel the nerves throw butterflies into my chest and wetness under my arms.

"Hi, Dennis, welcome," Fremont said smiling warmly and obviously recognizing me. At the bookstore, I wasn't quite sure if he did. He ushered me into the skeptical gazes of two women who looked like they had both just seen a ghost, and maybe they had. They stood like twins with the same posture. Both had their mouths slightly open, and their arms crossed. I smiled self-consciously at them, having trouble making eye contact.

"Hello," I said.

"Hello?" they both said flatly, sounding more like a question, and perfectly synchronized.

I looked at them and smiled.

"Dennis, please come and sit down," Stephen said, showing me to a chair. "This is my wife Mary, and this is Joanne Cohen, my publisher." I nodded and they both stood still and unblinking. "I'm curious, Dennis, how did you hear about the book so fast?" Stephen asked.

"When you did the book signing at the Embarcadero, in San Francisco, my in-laws, George and Liz were there for the weekend. George is a fan and purchased it there. It didn't take him long to figure out that the characters in the book were familiar, so he showed it to me."

"Oh," Fremont said nodding.

"Mister Fremont," I started. "How did you find out all that stuff about Shannon and me? We didn't tell anyone except George and Liz. Shannon was completely paranoid but it isn't only that. You seemed to have peered into over three months of my life, my thoughts, and my dreams. How?"

"Oh please," Joanne interrupted with some venom. "You believe this guy?" she said to Stephen.

"I know how this sounds," I said.

"I think this guy's looking for a payday," Joanne said.

"No. I don't want money. This has nothing to do with money. I'm just trying to understand."

Fremont took charge and said, "Joanne, please wait. Let me start from the beginning."

"You wrote things that no one could know," I said interrupting. "I told Liz and George some things, but I didn't tell them about Shannon's dream, and I didn't tell them that the creatures communicated with us when we went back to the house. Shannon is going to kill me when she sees this book. She's going to think I told you all that stuff."

Both Mary and Joanne became silent. They knew that this wasn't just some con job and Stephen's reaction confirmed that.

Stephen began again, "I was having a terrible time writing my next book. Each time I would start, I would quickly reach a dead end. I've had this happen before, but I have a good idea when I can finish a book, and when it's going nowhere. I was becoming very depressed and thought that I would never write again. Then something happened. It was when we were having those severe solar storms that an inspiration came to me. It started as an idea but exploded into a flood of ideas that blossomed into your story."

"Really, Stephen, are you sure about this guy?" Joanne protested mildly, starting to give in.

"Forgive me, Dennis. I need to get a bit graphic here. Joanne, this *IS* the person in my mind when I wrote "*Sideways*," not just someone who looks like the person, and when I saw Bryan there was no doubt. I've seen all these people most intimately, both metaphorically and literally. I could pick Shannon out of a crowd of thousands, including every mole and birthmark. I've seen their dreams, been in their showers, and heard their most intimate thoughts. I don't care if you don't believe him," Stephen said pointing at Dennis. "I'm telling you, he isn't lying."

"Okay," Joanne said backing off.

"Dennis, what do you want? How can I help?" Stephen asked.

"I'm just trying to understand."

Stephen started again trying to explain. "Something came over me that I thought were ideas for this book, but it wasn't just imagination, it was visions. I know that now. The only way I can describe it is that it was like smoke at first smooth and almost orderly. Then it began to roil, like from a volcano, about the time of the supernova. I couldn't stop writing. It was odd, and I kept telling Mary how weird it was. The smoke of the story began to fold and twist. I could see threads of your life appear, and then Shannon's life, and then yours would reappear. I chose to write some things and not others based on the flow of the story, and what I thought would be interesting to the reader."

I asked, "Other things had happened since the book's end; why didn't you write about those things?"

"The visions abruptly stopped where I ended the book, and they haven't returned... Why? Obviously, I get that Shannon hasn't seen the book..." Stephen said looking a bit confused. "What happened to Shannon?"

"Well, she kind of left me," I said and my heart sank. It felt like losing her all over again. I looked at Mary and thought I saw a tear come to her eye.

"Oh. I'm sorry," Mary said seeing my grief.

"Did she go with her professor and his archeologist friend?" Stephen asked.

I nodded and fought back a tear of my own. Everyone there knew the story because they had all read or written "*Sideways*."

I began again, "Shannon became paranoid, and there was something else going on inside her that she would never tell me. I could barely get anything out of her. She stopped calling me and wouldn't return my calls. At first, besides being afraid, she said that she felt funny since she was invaded, but she couldn't explain it. Then out of the blue, she told me that she was dropping out of college and going on the dig. She said that she was going to leave in two days and that she was sorry to spring it on me. We talked about a few personal things and she kissed me goodbye, then turned and walked away not looking back."

"I'm sorry, Dennis. I don't know what to say," Stephen said.

There was an awkward silence then, which lasted a couple of minutes.

Stephen looked up and said, "Dennis, do you understand 'sideways', or do you have any theories about these dimensions?"

"To me, it seemed like they were describing a multilayered reality. I think of it being like a computer's operating system, designed, or maybe just exists to allow some interaction, but in the same way that computers can be hacked, or get viruses. It's like the walls can become sometimes vulnerable. In this case, the creatures were pulled towards us, and sort of found themselves here, so whatever separates us from other worlds isn't perfect. It's good and mostly reliable, but not perfect. I'm just a carpenter, and I think Einstein would lose a lot of sleep trying to figure this one out. You know, though, your guess is as good as mine. You saw and wrote everything that the beings told us. You've pretty much seen everything," I finished with a bit of a blush.

There was another awkward silence, and I knew that there was nothing more to accomplish here. I just wanted to try to understand how he knew all those things that were in the book.

"I think I should go," I said, standing and reaching for Stephens' hand.

"If I need to reach you, can I have your number?" Stephen asked.

"I guess." I wrote down the number and handed it to him.

"Thanks, Dennis. If there's anything I can do," Stephen said.

"I'm not sure anyone can do anything," I said. "Maybe the book will just go away after the initial buzz."

"If it would help, I'll stop personally promoting it, but it's already out there, and impossible to retrieve. The truly startling thing is that the things that happened in the book were real," Stephen finished.

Joanne and Mary both paled with that reality sinking in.

"Oh, and I would love to meet Shannon someday," he said.

"Maybe someday. It was a pleasure to meet you," I said shaking the two ladies' hands, and walking towards the door. They all smiled at me but stood in stunned silence as I walked out and closed the door behind me.

46

The next day, Joanne, still stunned from the strange night with Fremont and the mysterious Dennis, sat in her office. She was hoping to talk Fremont into a book tour, nationwide, but this Dennis has thrown a monkey wrench into that.

As she stared into space, the phone rang.

"Backstreet publishing, Joanne Cohen speaking."

"Hi, Ms. Cohen, my name is Angela Harding, and I have a bit of a mystery on my hands that I need to talk to you about."

"There's a lot of that going around these days. What's up?"

"Well, a client of mine wrote a book recently, and it's very similar to the one your client, Stephen Fremont, wrote."

There was nothing but silence in response.

"Ms. Cohen? Are you still there?"

"Ah, yeah. I'm still here. How close are the two books?"

"They're nearly identical. My client submitted the manuscript on September 2nd. When did you get the Fremont manuscript?"

"Let me look." There was a pause. "September 2nd."

"Wow," Angela said almost speechless.

"Angela, I need to see you. This book, well... I think we all need to meet."

"Do I need lawyers?"

"No. Let's do this informally with you, your client, Mister Fremont and myself. I think you will find it enlightening."

"Okay."

"Can you send me a copy of his book?" Joanne asked.

"Sure."

"Thanks. Give me a day. I'll call you tomorrow."

"Sounds good."

"Talk to you tomorrow."

***

"Thanks," Angela said hanging up the phone. Ms. Cohen sounded conciliatory. Strange. She sat back stunned. "That was bizarre... I expected hardball... What was that?"

She got right on the phone to Cliff, waking him.

"Hello," he said in a raspy, groggy voice.

"Cliff, this is Angela. I just spoke to Fremont's publisher, and they want to meet with us. I expected them to come off aggressive, but they just seemed perplexed, and I don't think completely surprised."

"They weren't aggressive because they know that they ripped me off," Cliff said.

"I don't know? I'll call you back with the day and time for the meeting."

"Okay."

Angela hung up and stared into space. Why weren't they more aggressive? "Humm..."

47

Joanne sat at her desk and stared out the window. She could see parts of the Embarcadero between the buildings, and just a sliver of the San Francisco Bay with the Bay Bridge that stretched over to Oakland. She reluctantly reached for her phone. When she dialed, she knew that the world had changed. First, this Dennis guy and now this. She dialed Fremont's number.

"Hello," Stephen said jogging to the phone.

"Hi, Stephen, I hope you're sitting down," Joanne said.

Stephen was hit with a sudden adrenaline rush and sat down. "What now?" he asked.

"It seems someone else wrote your book. It was submitted on the same day that I received yours, and the word is, that it's nearly a carbon copy. I think that the agent that contacted me, probably rejected it, but now she's involved with her client's welfare."

"Damn. Do you know what this means?"

"No, Stephen, but please tell me because I feel like I just fell down the rabbit hole."

"It means that however the story came to me, it went elsewhere. How curious."

"They want a meeting?"

"I'm sure they do."

"Their client thinks you stole his book."

"I'm sure he does... Set up the meeting. I'll call Dennis. If he comes and brings Bryan, this guy will reach the same conclusion that I did."

"You've reached a conclusion?"

"Well, only that something strange happened over that short period of time that no one can explain."

"Okay," Joanne said, resigned to not having any real answers.

"I'll call you back after I talk to Dennis," Stephen said, hanging up the phone.

***

Mary walked in and could tell by the look on his face that something was wrong, and something else had happened. She looked at him, silently asking what the call was about.

"Well, Mary, after writing stories for all these years about weird occurrences, I've become part of my own story. How strange."

"Who was on the phone?"

"That was Joanne. It seems that another author has written the exact same book about Dennis and Shannon."

"I don't get it?" Mary said.

"It was those images... The visions... He had the same visions, and I'm sure other people did too."

"How strange," Mary said, echoing Stephen, and feeling the goose flesh slowly creep up her spine. She walked over and put her arms around him, suddenly needing to be hugged.

48

Angela agreed to meet Joanne and Fremont at Joanne's office in San Francisco. She knew that it was Backstreet's home turf and that this was probably designed to be a power play, but the tradeoff was that maybe they would offer an easy settlement. Time to call Cliff back. She dialed, and got his machine, asking to leave a number.

"Hello, Cliff. It's Angela. I have some news. Call me back."

She hung up and sat back in her chair mulling over the possibilities, and ramifications. Everything about this didn't make enough sense. She picked up a new manuscript and started to read it but couldn't concentrate. The phone rang and she lurched for it.

"Hello," she said.

"Hi, Angela," Cliff said in a sleepy voice.

"Hi, Cliff. Fremont and Backstreet publishing want an informal meeting. I think they want to deal, but they weren't specific."

"Do you think they want to buy me off?"

"I don't know. It could be a power play to scare you away."

"I really don't have anything to lose, and I don't scare easy. What are they going to do, take my small apartment from me?"

"Okay. I'll take the meeting, and we'll play it by ear. I'll call you back."

"Thanks, Angela. See ya."

Angela called Joanne Cohen back, setting up a meeting for three days later.

When the day for the meeting arrived, Cliff nervously bumped around his bathroom getting ready. He stressed about what Fremont might say. He knew that he had written his book, and couldn't imagine what other claim Fremont might make against the truth. Angela wanted them to drive to the meeting together but Cliff wanted to drive alone.

The phone rang. Cliff walked over and answered, "Hello."

"Hi, Cliff," Angela said.

"Hi."

"Would you mind riding together? I think we should discuss the meeting," Angela suggested again.

"Okay. I'll meet you at your office," Cliff relented.

He drove to her office, and not having been there before, wasn't sure where it was, but the complex was small with few businesses and a small parking lot.

He parked, found the office and walked in. Angela was standing by her receptionist as he entered and turned when she heard the door. The office was small with a couple of chairs and a table which had a few magazines stacked neatly on top.

"Hi, Angela? I'm Cliff," he said as he approached her, extending his hand. They had only talked on the phone, and this was the first time that they had met face to face.

"Hi, Cliff. I'm happy to meet you. Are you ready to go?"

"I guess," he said.

Angela turned back to her receptionist, "I'll be gone for the rest of the day." The receptionist smiled and nodded, and Cliff and Angela walked out of the office.

Angela walked Cliff to her silver Mercedes and unlocked his door. Cliff could feel the butterflies swarming in his stomach as he slid into the car. She looked at him and smiled.

"Are you okay?" she asked.

"I guess. I'm not sure what to expect or what to think?"

"Honestly, Cliff, me either. This is the strangest thing that I've ever heard of."

"Well, I guess we'll find out together," Cliff said.

They drove to San Francisco in relative silence, not talking much about the book. Cliff had begun to relax, but as they crossed the Bay Bridge, his butterflies took flight again. They exited off the freeway and turned onto Market Street looking for parking. It was a foggy morning, and the mist drifted low to the ground, pushed by a mild breeze.

They parked in a lot and walked half a block to the building that housed Backstreet Publishing. It looked weathered, with stains covering the tan exterior, but when Cliff and Angela walked through the large double doors, they opened into a crisp, clean interior.

They walked to the elevator and rode to the third floor. As the doors opened, they could see that the entire floor was Backstreet Publishing. Its open floor space screamed success, as employees scurried around, busy with projects.

"Wooh," Cliff said looking at the plush open space. "This doesn't look good for us."

"They're a very successful firm. There's the office," Angela said pointing.

Cliff could feel his nerves rise as they approached the door. Angela glanced over at him and smiled reassuringly. They opened the door to Joanne's office and walked up to a receptionist who smiled pleasantly.

"Hi. Are you Angela?" she asked.

"Yes."

"Joanne is expecting you. I'll tell her you're here." She picked up the phone and announced to Joanne that they had arrived. "Go right in," she said.

Angela opened the door and walked in followed by Cliff. The office was spacious, with a small meeting table to the left, and Joanne's desk to the right. Angela noticed that there were five people in the room when she only expected two. They all turned to face her, and she smiled warily.

"Hello," Joanne said as they entered.

"Hello," Angela said, trying to gauge the tone of the meeting, but the mix of people was odd. She watched Cliff follow her in, looking down, and appearing uncomfortable. As he looked up, he froze in his tracks.

"What? How?" Cliff said and then stood with his mouth agape.

Angela looked at Cliff, then at Joanne, and then back at Cliff. She was unable to figure out what he was thinking by the strange expression on his face. It wasn't fear, or guilt, it was wonder. She glanced back at Fremont and Joanne standing together, and then again back at Cliff who was looking at a man standing by a child. The child was sitting at the meeting table, playing on a computer. There was another woman there, standing by the window. The child looked like he may have some problems. It was subtle but apparent.

"Hi, Cliff," Fremont said warmly. "It was a shock to me also."

Angela sidestepped further into the room, sliding against the wall, trying to see everyone simultaneously.

***

"Hi, Cliff. I'm Dennis, and this is Bryan," I said.

"I know," Cliff said quietly, his eyes wide. Angela started to speak, but Cliff cut her off. "Angela, I would like to introduce you to Dennis and Bryan from my book."

"What?" Angela said sharply.

"Where's Shannon?" Cliff asked.

"She's not here, Cliff, and we'll get to that," Fremont said.

"Please sit down," Joanne said, pointing them to a couple of chairs.

Angela was having trouble following, so she remained silent. Fremont took the lead in the meeting as everyone sat down around the meeting table.

"First, I want to introduce you to my wife, Mary," Fremont said.

Mary smiled.

"You already know Dennis and Bryan, and this is Joanne Cohen, my publisher."

"Papa!" Bryan said with some agitation. Cliff looked at the child with wide eyes, having trouble reconciling these people that he knew from the visions in his mind with the reality of them being in front of him in the flesh.

"It's uncanny, isn't it?" Fremont said.

I said, "Let me help Bryan with the computer. I knew he would be bored."

Cliff turned to Angela. She looked back at him, and said sharply, "What-is-going-on?"

"We're getting to that," Joanne said. "Just sit back and enjoy the ride."

Fremont started again, while everyone took their seats. "Let me tell you what we know, and what we think we know. Your account of how the book came to you will probably be helpful also. It may help us piece together this mystery, but I don't know. First, before we get started on what's really important in this... thing that's happened, I want you to know that half of any money that is made from this book will go to you and Angela's firm. I'm completely giving up my share to help defray the costs to my publisher."

"That's generous," Angela said suspiciously, but Cliff didn't even seem to react to the offer of money.

"The story that I... we wrote was real?" Cliff asked astonished.

"Yes," I said as I sat next to Bryan, and helped him with his game.

"But how?" Cliff asked.

Angela was still silent, not believing her ears.

"We don't know, Cliff," Fremont said. "You, I, and who knows how many other people, somehow became voyeurs in these people's lives in ways that seem... well, inappropriate."

"I'm sorry," Cliff said, looking at me.

I said, "Believe me, Cliff, as weird as this is for you, it's been an acid trip for me. The trouble is what's next? Every time I think things are going to calm down, something springs back up like cancer."

Mary said, "We're trying to help Dennis if we can."

Angela finally found her voice, "Wait. You're saying that everything that happened in the book was real?"

"Yes," I said without blinking.

"Huh," she said with it starting to sink in.

Cliff shook his head, and then looked up. "The house, what happened to the house?"

"I sold it," I said.

"But the stone circle? And who would buy it?"

"Well, to make a long story short," I said. "Shannon introduced me to her professor, who introduced me to his archeologist friend, who introduced me to this guy from a Ko Lynn Corporation. He inspected the cave and cut me a check for one point five."

"One million five hundred thousand dollars!" Cliff exclaimed, his eyes wide.

"Yeah. It was a pretty nice premium over the assessed value," I said.

"That's some serious cash, but..." Cliff said.

"I really didn't want anything to do with the house," I said cutting him off. "I just wanted to forget about it. The more Shannon and I talked about it, the more withdrawn she became. I think it's the main reason why we... well, she left," I finished.

Bryan started laughing at the computer, "Funny bugs," he said and signed.

"Damn," Angela said feeling the reality set in. She looked at Joanne who shrugged.

Fremont wanted to get back to the mystery. "Cliff, did you see anything else after you finished the book?" he asked.

"No, I barely saw the end. It became murky after the beings from sideways couldn't return. The rest was disappearing as I wrote it. I'm not sure that I even got it right. I was kind of winging it. It was passing quickly, and I was having trouble seeing it. I read your book, Mister Fremont, and the ending did seem a little different from what I wrote."

"When I think back to the visions that inspired the book," Stephen said. "It seemed that they were so close to normal imagination that it was hard to discern, but I knew that there was something different. I just couldn't figure it out. It was as if it came through the same part of my brain."

"You're exactly right. That was my experience also," Cliff said. "Now I don't know if I wrote the book at all. I knew something was weird when I was writing, but I just didn't understand what. I'm not a writer, but I've wanted to be, and I've started and stopped several books lately, and I thought that this was the one. I'm a fan of yours, Mister Fremont, and have read or listened to most of your books. The idea came to me when I was driving to work and continued that night when I was listening to one of your books. I work nights at Safeway and listen to audiobooks to keep me company while I'm there. Do you think that connected us, while you were connected to Dennis and Shannon? Did I somehow become connected to you?"

"Not completely, Cliff, but maybe partially. You knew Dennis and Bryan instantly. You were there, and I don't think just through me. I also knew something was wrong with the visions that I was receiving about Dennis and Shannon, and I've been a writer for a long time. The images came to me like imagination, but it was more, and I kept telling Mary about it, but I could never fully explain the difference. I'll tell you this, though, the visions were relentless."

"Huh," Cliff said, trying to shake off the reoccurring chills that had plagued him since he arrived at Joanne's office.

Everyone else just listened as Fremont and Cliff tried to work out the details of their visions.

Fremont continued, "There's something else. It seems that we were both able to look forward in time. When I made my first outline, Shannon and Dennis hadn't even been to the house yet."

"That's true. I actually saw the whole story at once in a flash, and then it disappeared and returned, but I remembered parts of it from the first vision. Somehow my mind processed the entire story in the brief seconds as I was driving to work," Cliff said, remembering the first night that the vision came to him.

"I have a theory," Fremont said. "I've been giving this a lot of thought. Has anyone heard of the Einstein-Rosen Bridge? It's a theory where space and time are each considered things and subject to disruption. Einstein's thought was that space could be ripped and torn, and wormholes could appear allowing some movement or interaction to occur between vast distances, or maybe dimensions, and that this could have an effect on time. The very first thing that I saw was Shannon frozen by the beings right as she left the shower," Fremont said.

"Oh, she'll be glad to hear that," I said with a chuckle.

Stephen smiled, "I'm sorry about that. I do think, though, that's when it happened."

"That was the first thing I saw also," Cliff said. "I thought that the girl in the vision was in terrible trouble. The story seemed to mushroom in all time directions from there."

"That's right," Stephen said remembering. "So, whatever made this occur probably happened at that moment, forcing the visions forward in time. It's probably how the creatures came through, also, some rip in space-time. I'm sure that I'm explaining this theory too simply, but something happened to all of us, and nothing in the natural world can explain it. The interesting thing about Einstein was that he thought things that no one had ever considered before. I'm not sure if he had everything right, but he was very intuitive. One thing, though, was that he thought that nothing could exceed the speed of light. It turns out that at least a couple of things that I know of, seem to be able to do so. Neutrinos, which are subatomic particles, as I understand it, have been measured to exceed it, and also the knowledge in two matched subatomic particles can also exceed it."

"What?" Cliff said.

"These particles have spin. If one particle is separated from the other, and the spin is reversed, then the other particle instantly reverses no matter how far apart they are. It's an odd anomaly. Einstein knew of this and called it spooky. Maybe more of these types of anomalies exist than we're aware of, and they allow for the kind of random clairvoyance that we experienced with Dennis and Shannon."

The group sat quietly for a time digesting Stephen's attempted explanation.

"So, now what?" Cliff asked.

"Indeed," Fremont said. "What do you think, Dennis?"

"I'm not sure what to do," I said. "I can envision this story really getting out of control. There are a lot of people who know that parts of this story are true. I just don't know... And then there's Shannon. I haven't heard from her since she left, and I can't contact her."

"She left just like in the story?" Cliff asked.

"Yes," I said. "With the group going on that archeological dig."

"So, they aren't allowing them to call out?" Cliff asked.

"No. She just left a short time ago, and the story she gave me was that the dig was secret. No one was allowed to bring cell phones, and no one was allowed to contact anyone until they got the okay from the main archeologist. They said that the site that they were working on was special and that they didn't want word of it to leak out. I don't think that Shannon was lying, but I do think that she wanted to be as far away from everything, including me, as she could get. She told me that they were going to be put on a bus and that all the windows were going to be blacked out so that no one could see where they were going. I thought that this was crazy, so I went to the college, and watched as the bus left, and sure enough, all the windows were black. I was suspicious, but Shannon's professor and a small group of students from the college were all going and she said that they were all jazzed."

"Any idea where they were going?" Fremont asked.

"She thought Wyoming or Montana but there's a huge amount of country out there, and that may have been misdirection."

"So, Shannon hasn't seen the book?" Cliff asked, and as he did, his words slowed.

"No, Cliff, she left before I even knew about the book, and when she sees it she's going to flip out. She changed shortly after everything happened. She became so quiet," I said speaking slowly and turning into my last memories of her. "I could see the wheels turning in her head, all the time. She would stare away, constantly, sometimes mentally leaving in the middle of a sentence. She hinted that she was different since she was invaded by the beings from sideways. They didn't mean to hurt her, but something inside her was different, and she couldn't put her finger on it. I started thinking that they purposely did something to her, but she said no. It had something to do with the way they put her back together. She became obsessed with what they told her, that she 'will know the way all things are', but then she just became quiet. I tried to get her to talk about it. I tried to find out exactly what was bothering her, but she started to avoid me, and then she said that she was leaving. I was devastated, and at first, I thought that she was just trying to forget, but it was more, there was something else, and I never got it out of her."

The room grew quiet, and everyone could feel my rekindled sorrow. I looked away and then began to quietly speak. "She told me not to wait for her. She said that if I found someone else, that I should feel free. I just stared at her.

I couldn't believe it. After all that we went through together, and she just left me," I finished and stared out the window.

"Thank you, Dennis," Stephen said. "I'm sorry for your loss."

I said, "I didn't want to be a big part of this meeting. I just wanted to help Mister Fremont convince you that the book was real. Come on, sweetie boy, time to go." I said, stood up and collected Bryan and his laptop. "It was a pleasure to meet all of you. I can't tell you what to do. I don't even know myself. I just hope you think of Shannon in your decisions." I shook everyone's hand and carried Bryan out of the door.

***

The group had gotten up from the table and milled around in stunned silence. Stephen said, "Thanks, Cliff. I'm not sure that there is anything else to say right now. I hope the settlement is adequate for you."

"Thanks, Mister Fremont, its fine. Do you think there is anything else that we can do?"

"I think that the best thing that we can do is shut up about it, and hope that the story and the novel just fade like other books do. People aren't flocking to it, but I've started getting fan mail from people who are approaching the book kind of cult-like. That often happens, and I usually don't pay much attention to it, but this situation is different."

The meeting ended then, with handshakes and good-byes.

***

Bryan and I walked out to our car. "Well, buddy boy, are you hungry?"

"Ahh," Bryan said meaning, yeah, but it sounded like, 'what do you think?' and I chuckled.

"You are the best boy that there could ever be. Do you know that?" I said.

"Ahhh," Bry said again, but this time sounding like he was saying of course.

I laughed again. I slipped him into his car seat and thought that the world doesn't always give you what you want, but it usually gives you what you need. I thought about Shannon out there somewhere in the world and felt like I would never see her again. I sighed and said, "Let's go eat, and then go home, buddy boy."

"Ahhh."

THE END

THE GIFT BEGINS

... Shannon finds herself on a bus to, who knows where. At that moment, she regrets the rash decision to leave school and Dennis, but something is disturbing her from inside, something that doesn't feel right and it emanates from a deep place. She knows that she has changed, not just psychologically and emotionally, but also physically in a way that is barely detectable... Barely.

She thinks that its roots lie in the message that the creatures from sideways told her, that she "will know the way all things are." What could that mean? She stares forward, but every window in the bus is black with a partition that prevents her from looking out the front, and as the bus bumps along, a nagging fear grows as her unknown destination draws close.

In the second book from the Sideways Series, *The Gift*, Shannon finds out exactly what the creatures from sideways were talking about when they told her that she "will know the way all things are," and the meaning changes her forever...

Made in the USA
Middletown, DE
19 November 2018